Out of
HOURS

February 2014 **March 2014** **April 2014**

May 2014 **June 2014** **July 2014**

Out of
HOURS

Enticing the Nanny

REBECCA WINTERS
BARBARA McMAHON
CHRISTIE RIDGWAY

Published in Great Britain 2014
by Mills & Boon, an imprint of Harlequin (UK) Limited,
Eton House, 18-24 Paradise Road, Richmond, Surrey, TW9 1SR

OUT OF HOURS…ENTICING THE NANNY
© 2014 Harlequin Books S.A.

The Nanny and the CEO © 2011 Rebecca Winters
Nanny to the Billionaire's Son © 2008 Barbara McMahon
Not Just the Nanny © 2010 Christie Ridgway

ISBN: 978 0 263 24595 0

027-0414

Harlequin (UK) Limited's policy is to use papers that are natural, renewable and recyclable products and made from wood grown in sustainable forests The logging and manufacturing processes conform to the legalenvironmental regulations of the country of origin.

Printed and bound in Spain
by Blackprint CPI, Barcelona

The Nanny
and
the CEO

REBECCA WINTERS

Rebecca Winters, whose family of four children has now swelled to include three beautiful grandchildren, lives in Salt Lake City, Utah, in the land of the Rocky Mountains. With canyons and high alpine meadows full of wild flowers, she never runs out of places to explore. They, plus her favourite vacation spots in Europe, often end up as backgrounds for her Mills & Boon® romance novels, because writing is her passion, along with her family and church. Rebecca loves to hear from her readers. If you wish to e-mail her, please visit her website at:www.rebeccawinters-author.com.

To my wonderful parents,
who made life wonderful all the time and gave
me every opportunity to find my life, just as the
Mother Superior at the convent helped
Maria to find hers

CHAPTER ONE

"Ms. CHAMBERLAIN? You're next. Second door on the left."

"Thank you."

Reese got up from the chair and walked past the woman at the front desk to reach the hall. At ten o'clock in the morning, the East 59th Street Employment Agency in New York's east side was already packed with people needing a job. She'd asked around and had learned it was one of the most reputable agencies in the city. The place reminded her of her dentist's office filled with patients back home in Nebraska.

She had no idea what one wore for an interview to be a nanny. After changing outfits several times she'd opted for a yellow tailored, short-sleeved blouse and skirt, the kind she'd worn to the initial interview on Wednesday. This was her only callback in three days. If she didn't get hired today, she would have to fly home tomorrow, the last thing she wanted to do.

Her father owned a lumberyard and could always give her a job if she couldn't find anything that suited her, but it wouldn't pay her the kind of money she needed. Worse, she didn't relish the idea of seeing Jeremy again, but it would be inevitable because her ex-fiancé happened to work as a loan officer at the bank where her dad did business. Word would get around she was back.

"Come in, Ms. Chamberlain."

"Hello, again, Mr. Lloyd." He was the man who'd taken her initial application.

"Let me introduce you to Mrs. Tribe. She's the private secretary to a Mr. Nicholas Wainwright here in New York and has been looking for the right nanny for her employer. I'll leave you two alone for a few minutes."

The smart-looking brunette woman wearing a professional business suit was probably in her early fifties. "Please sit down. Reese, is it?"

"Yes."

The other woman cocked her head. "You have excellent references. From your application it's apparent you're a student and a scholar. Since you're single and have no experience taking care of other people's children, why did you apply to be a nanny?"

Reese could lie, but she had a feeling this woman would see right through her. "I need to earn as much money as possible this summer so I can stay in school until graduation. My academic scholarship doesn't cover housing and food. Even those of us born in fly-over-country have heard a nanny's job in New York can pay very well, so I thought I'd try for a position." Hopefully that explanation was frank enough for her.

"Taking care of children is exceptionally hard work. I know because I raised two of my own."

Reese smiled. "I've never been married, but I'm the oldest in the family of six children and did a lot of babysitting over the years. I was fourteen when my youngest sister was born. My mother had to stay in bed, so I helped with the baby. It was like playing house. My sister was adorable and I loved it. But," she said as she sighed, "that was twelve years ago. Still, taking care of children is like learning to tie your shoes, don't you think? Once you've figured it out, you never forget."

The other woman eyed her shrewdly while she nodded. "I agree."

"How many children do they have?" *Please don't let the number be more than three.* Although Reese wouldn't turn it down if the money was good enough.

"Mr. Wainwright is a widower with a ten-week-old baby boy named Jamie."

The news concerning the circumstances came as a sobering revelation to Reese. She'd assumed she might end up working for a couple with several children, that is if she were ever offered a job. "Then he's still grieving for his wife." She shook her head. "How sad for him and his little boy, who'll never know his mother."

Reese got a swelling in her throat just thinking of her own wonderful mom still remarkably young and vital, probably the same age as Mrs. Tribe.

"It's a tragic loss for both of them. Mr. Wainwright has arranged for a nanny who's been with another family to start working for him, but she can't come until September. Because you only wanted summer work, that's one of the reasons I was interested in your application."

One of the reasons? She'd aroused Reese's curiosity. "What were the others?"

"You didn't name an unrealistic salary. Finally, one of your professors at Wharton told me you've been on full academic scholarship there. Good for you. An opportunity like that only comes to a very elite group of graduate students. It means you're going to have a brilliant career in business one day."

To run her own brokerage firm was Reese's goal for the future. "That's my dream."

The dream that had torn her and Jeremy apart.

Jeremy had been fine about her finishing up her undergraduate work at the University of Nebraska, but the scholarship to Wharton had meant a big move to Pennsylvania. The insinuation that she was too ambitious led to the core of the problem eating at him. Jeremy hadn't wanted a future-executive for a wife. In return Reese realized she'd had a lucky escape from a future-controlling-husband. Their breakup had been painful at the time, but the hurt was going away. She didn't want him back. Therein lay the proof.

Mrs. Tribe sat back in her chair and studied Reese. "It was my dream, too, but I didn't get the kind of grades I saw on your transcripts. Another of your professors told me he sees a touch of genius in you. I liked hearing that about you."

Reese couldn't imagine which professor that was. "You've made my day."

"Likewise," she murmured, sounding surprised by her own thoughts. "Provided you feel good about the situation after seeing the baby and discussing Mr. Wainwright's expectations of you in that regard, I think you'll do fine for the position. Of course the final decision will be up to him."

Reese could hardly believe she'd gotten this far in the interview. "I don't know how to thank you, Mrs. Tribe. I promise I won't let him, or you, down. Do you have a picture of the baby?"

A frown marred her brow. "I don't, but you'll be

meeting him and his father this afternoon. Where have you been staying since you left Philadelphia?"

"At the Chelsea Star Hotel on West 30th."

"You did say you were available immediately?"

"Yes!" The dormitory bed cost her fifty dollars a night. She couldn't afford to stay in New York after today.

"That's good. If he decides to go with my recommendation and names a fee that's satisfactory to you, then he'll want you to start today."

"What should I wear to the interview? Do I need some kind of uniform? This is completely new to me."

"To both of us," came her honest response. "Wear what you have on. If he has other suggestions, he'll tell you."

"Does he have a pet?"

"As far as I know he's never mentioned one. Are you allergic?"

"No. I just thought if he did, I could pick up some cat or doggie treats at the store. You know. To make friends right off?"

The woman smiled. "I like the way you think, Ms. Chamberlain."

"Of course the baby's going to be another story," Reese murmured. "After having his daddy's exclusive attention, it will take time to win him around."

Mrs. Tribe paused before speaking. "Actually, since his birth, he's been looked after by his maternal grandparents."

"Are they still living with Mr. Wainwright?"

"No. The Hirsts live in White Plains. An hour away in heavy traffic."

So did that mean he hadn't been with his son for the

last couple of months? No…that couldn't be right. Now that he was getting a nanny, they'd probably just left to go back home.

"I see. Does Jamie have paternal grandparents, too?"

"Yes. At the moment they're away on a trip," came the vague response.

Reese came from a large family. Both sets of grandparents were still alive and always around. She had seven aunts and uncles. Last count there were twenty-eight cousins. With her siblings, including the next oldest, Carrie, who was married and had two children under three, that brought the number to thirty-four. She wondered if her employer had any brothers and sisters or other family.

"You've been with Mr. Wainwright a long time. Is there anything of importance I should know ahead of time?"

"He's punctual."

"I'll remember that." Reese got to her feet. "I won't take any more of your time. Thank you for this opportunity, Mrs. Tribe."

"It's been my pleasure. A limo will be sent for you at one o'clock."

"I'll be waiting outside in front. Oh—one more question. What does Mr. Wainwright do for a living?"

The other woman's eyebrows lifted. "Since you're at Wharton, I thought you might have already made the connection or I would have told you. He's the CEO at Sherborne-Wainwright & Co. on Broadway. Good luck."

"Thank you," Reese murmured in shock.

He was *that* Wainwright?

It was one of the most prestigious brokerage firms in

New York, if not *the* top one with roots that went back a couple of hundred years. The revelation stunned her on many levels. Somehow she'd imagined the man who ran the whole thing to be in his late forties or early fifties. It usually took that long to rise to those heights.

Of course it wasn't impossible for him to have a new baby, but she was still surprised. Maybe it had been his second wife he'd lost and she'd been a young mother. No one was exempt from pain in this life.

Nick Wainwright stood at the side of the grave. *In loving memory of Erica Woodward Hirst Wainwright.*

Thirty-two years old was too young to die.

"I'm sorry I neglected you so much it led to our divorce, Erica. Before we separated, I never thought for one moment you might be pregnant with our child, or that you'd lose your life during the delivery. My heart grieves for our little boy who needs his mother. It was your dying wish I raise him, but I feared I wouldn't know how to be a good father to him. That's why I let your parents take care of him this long, but now I'm ready. I swear I'll do everything in my power to be a better father to him than I was a husband to you. If you're listening, I just wanted you to know I vow to keep that promise."

After putting fresh flowers against the headstone, Nick walked swiftly to the limo waiting for him in the distance. He hadn't been here since the funeral. The visit filled him with sorrow for what had gone wrong, but with the decision made to take Jamie home, it felt right to have come to her grave first.

This early in the morning there was only his chauffeur, Paul, to see his tall, dark lone figure get in the back wearing a pale blue summer suit and tie. As he closed the rear door his eyes flicked to the newest state-of-the-art infant car seat he'd had delivered. Before the morning was out, he'd be taking his ten-week-old boy back to the city with him.

"Let's head over to my in-laws."

His middle-aged driver nodded and started the car. Paul had worked for Nick's dad, back when Nick had been in his early teens. Now that his father was semi-retired and Nick had been put in as head of the firm, he'd inherited Paul. Over the years the two of them had become good friends.

Once they left the White Plains cemetery where members of the prominent Hirst family had been buried for the past one hundred and fifty years, he sat back rubbing his hand over his face. In a few minutes there was going to be a scene, but he'd been preparing himself for it.

Prior to the baby's birth, Nick hadn't lived with Erica over the nine months of her pregnancy. Her death had come as a tremendous shock to him. Though he'd allowed her parents to take the baby home from the hospital, he hadn't intended on it lasting for more than several weeks. In that amount of time he'd planned to find live-in help for the baby. Because of his guilt over the way their marriage had fallen apart, he'd let the situation go on too long.

When Nick had phoned the pediatrician in White Plains who'd been called in at the time of delivery, he'd informed Nick that if he hoped to bond with his son, he shouldn't wait any longer to parent him on a full-time basis.

The doctor gave Nick the name of Dr. Hebert Wells, a highly recommended pediatrician who had a clinic on

New York's upper west side and could take over Jamie's care. Then he wished him luck.

Following that conversation, Nick had phoned his attorney and explained what he wanted to do. The other man had contacted the Hirsts' attorney to let them know Nick was ready to take over his responsibilities as a father and would be coming for Jamie to take him home.

Erica's parents had wanted Nick to wait until the nanny they'd lined up would be available. They wanted control over the way their only grandchild—a future Hirst who would carry on the family tradition—would be raised. That meant having equal input over everything, the kind of children he associated with and where he would attend school from the beginning through college.

But Nick wasn't willing to wait any longer. Through their attorneys he promised to consult them on certain matters and bring Jamie to White Plains for visits, but deep down he knew nothing he said would reassure them. Time would have to take care of the problem.

Nick's family, who lived on Long Island, wanted control of *their* only grandchild, too. But they were at the family villa in Cannes with friends at the moment, confident Nick would do what had to be done to keep his in-laws pacified.

"Erica's parents seem willing to keep him for now," his mother exclaimed. "It would be better if you let Jamie stay with them for the next year anyway. You can go on visiting him when you have the time. It's the best arrangement under the circumstances."

Nick knew the script by heart. His own parents had already found another suitable woman for Nick to meet when he was ready. They saw nothing wrong in letting Erica's parents oversee Jamie's care, a sort of consolation prize to remove their guilt by association with the son who'd divorced "the catch of the season."

Their attitude came as no surprise to Nick. He'd been an only child, raised in virtual luxury by a whole staff of people other than his own parents. What they never understood was that it had been a lonely life, one that had caused him great pain. He didn't want that for Jamie. But deep down he felt nervous as hell.

Though Nick might have been the whiz kid who'd risen to the top of Sherborne-Wainwright, a two-hundred-year-old family investment brokerage, he didn't quite know what to do with Jamie. The world of a two-and-half-month-old baby was anathema to him.

He'd visited him every Saturday, but was an unwelcome visitor as far as Erica's family was concerned. They had a well-trained, well-vetted staff, plus a private nurse to see to Jamie's every need.

Weather permitting, he would carry the baby outside to the English garden where he could get away from the officious woman in her white uniform. Otherwise Nick remained in the nursery, but he was superfluous in the help department. The staff had everything covered ahead of time. That in itself made it impossible for him to get close to his son.

As the old Georgian colonial estate came into sight and they passed through the outer gate, Nick determined everything was going to change, starting now. He alighted from the back of the limo. "I won't be long, Paul."

The slightly balding family man smiled. "I'm looking forward to seeing him. He's bigger every time we come."

That was the problem. Jamie was changing and growing with each passing day and Nick wasn't here to see it happen. The commuting had to stop so the fathering could begin.

Before he reached the gleaming white front door, Erica's father opened it. Walter had a full head of frosted brown hair and a golfer's physique. Erica's parents were handsome people, but his father-in-law's glowering expression brought out Nick's temper, which he did his best to keep under control.

"Walter?"

"Before I let you in, I want you to know Anne's in a highly emotional state."

"You think I'm not aware of that?"

The older man grimaced. "She asked me to tell yo—"

"I know it by heart, Walter," he broke in. "Though I can't go back and change the past, I intend to do the right thing for our son. I told that to Erica when I stopped at the cemetery a little while ago."

Walter's eyes flickered as if he were surprised by the admission. After a slight hesitation he said, "Come in the dayroom. The nurse has Jamie ready for you."

"Thank you."

After three years of marriage—the last year spent in separation while the divorce was being finalized—his in-law's home was full of ghosts from the past. In the beginning his wedding to Erica had been happy enough. Everyone claimed the lovely Hirst daughter was the catch of the season, but time proved they weren't meant for each other, and she'd spent a lot of her time here rather than the city.

There'd been unmet expectations and disappointments on both sides. The sameness of their existence had become so severe, they'd drifted apart. The last time they'd been intimate, it had been a halfhearted attempt on his part to rekindle what they'd lost, but the spark was gone.

He followed his father-in-law through the house until they came to the dayroom, a contemporary addition that had been constructed after Erica had moved back with them. No doubt to keep her busy with something to do while she waited for the baby to come.

Anne's series of decorators had filled it with pots of flowers and rattan couches covered in bright prints of pink and orange. The floor-to-ceiling windows overlooked several acres of garden and manicured lawns that were green and smooth as velvet.

His mother-in-law sat in one of the chairs, stiff as a piece of petrified wood. Nick's gaze flew to his son, who was lying in the fancy baby carriage. He'd been dressed for travel and was wide-awake.

Nick had no complaints about Jamie's care, but couldn't wait to take him away because he'd be damned if he would allow history to repeat itself for one more day. Nick had been emotionally neglected by his parents. Erica had suffered the same fate though she could never admit it and preferred living in denial.

There'd been a lot of damage done. He wasn't about to commit the same crime where Jamie was concerned.

"Hello, Anne."

She couldn't bring herself to look at him.

Nick walked over to the carriage, still awed by the

fact that he was a father, that he and Erica were responsible for Jamie's existence.

The baby had inherited Nick's long, lean body and black hair, but Nick saw hints of Erica's nose and bone structure in his face. She'd been an attractive, slim brunette of medium height like Anne.

"Hi, sport. Remember me?" Nick leaned over and grasped Jamie's tiny hand. One look at Nick and the baby breathed a little faster with excitement. He wrapped his fingers around Nick's index finger. The next thing he knew it went to his mouth, always to the mouth, causing Nick to chuckle.

So far his eyes were a muddy color and would probably go brown like his and Erica's. No doubt they would fill with tears when he took Jamie away and the baby discovered himself in strange surroundings. Better get this over quick.

Seizing the moment, he lifted the baby and propped him against his shoulder. "Come on, son. We're going to take a little ride in the car with Paul. Would you like that?"

Walter handed him the quilt and a diaper bag. His eyes sent a message to Nick that he'd better live up to his promises. "The nurse printed out Jamie's routine and the things you'll need after you get to your apartment."

"I can't thank you enough for watching over Jamie until now. I promise I'll bring him back next Saturday for a visit."

"We'll expect you." But Walter couldn't get Anne to lift her head.

"Anytime either of you wants to see him, just come by the apartment. If I'm at work, the nanny will let you in."

Anne's head flew back, revealing a face devoid of

animation. "Barbara Cosgriff can't let their nanny come to you until September. There's no reason to take our grandson yet." The reproach in her voice was palpable.

"There's every reason, Anne. I miss my son and am engaging someone else until then."

"Who?" she demanded.

"I'm not sure yet. My secretary has been interviewing applicants all week. By tomorrow I expect she'll have found several for me to talk to personally. She'll do a thorough vetting. That woman is worth her weight in gold and has never let me down yet."

"What does she know about being a nanny?"

"Though I realize you can't comprehend it, she's been an exceptional working mother for me and that has never changed since she came to work eight years ago. It tells me she'll know what to look for. Keep in mind that the nanny she finds will only be with me three months until the Cosgriffs' nanny becomes free."

That was what he was saying now, yet in fact he had no idea if he would hire the Cosgriffs' nanny at all! But that revelation could keep for another day. "I plan to work shorter hours this summer, so it won't be as if Jamie's alone with her twelve hours a day."

"If you'd taken more time off to travel with Erica, you could have saved your marriage."

No. Nothing could have saved it, Anne. But to get into a postmortem with her at this stage would be futile.

"Your penthouse isn't suited to having a baby there, but somehow you insisted on Erica living there with you so you could be close to your work. She needed a real home where she could entertain."

His temper flared again, but he managed to keep it

contained. "She made it into a place where she could invite her friends after the opera and the ballet. I offered to buy Sedgewick Manor in the Hamptons for her, but she preferred to stay with you because she said it suited her better. Jamie and I will manage."

Nick didn't know how yet, but he'd figure it out. He kissed the baby's silky head. "Thank the nurse for the notes. I'm sure I'll need to refer to them until I get used to the routine."

She kept her hands tightly clasped in her lap. "The nurse said he'll be ready for another bottle when he goes down for his nap at noon."

"That's good to know. We'll be back at the apartment by then." Hopefully at that point Nick would have heard from Leah Tribe about the new nanny.

"See you next Saturday. Remember you can call anytime."

Nick turned and walked through the house with his son, still disbelieving this day had come and he was leaving the whole dreadful past behind. It was like tearing off a straitjacket.

When Paul saw him, he got out of the limo. Together they put Jamie in his new car seat. Nick could have done it without Paul's help, but he was grateful for it because it would probably have taken Nick half a dozen tries to get the confounded thing right.

The older man studied his tiny features for a minute. "I see a lot of you in him, Nick. He's a fine-looking boy."

"Blame that on his mother."

Paul patted his shoulder. "I'll drive carefully."

"I'm not worried."

He put the diaper bag on the opposite seat, then sat

next to Jamie and fastened his own seat belt. As they started down the driveway, he looked around but only saw the closed front door of Hirst Hollow. It symbolized a closed life because both sets of parents had been emotionally unavailable.

You should have done this sooner, Wainwright.

But it was too late for more regrets. He needed to let the past go and concentrate on Jamie. When he looked down, he caught the baby staring at him.

Nick smiled and put out his hand so he'd grab it. His little fingers took hold with surprising strength. No tears yet. They hadn't been gone long enough for Jamie to miss the familiar faces of his nurse and grandparents.

He fought down the anger generated by his own lack of action up to now. Mired in guilt, he'd been slow to pull himself out of a depression that had its inception long before Erica's death. His estrangement from her had been one thing, but to realize his son barely knew him twisted his gut.

A chance remark by a client last week had wakened him out of his morose stupor. "With your wife gone, that new baby of yours must be a real joy to you. There's nothing like a child to make the pain go away." The comment made him realize he could be a good father.

Once his client had left the office, Nick had got on the phone to his attorney and let him know he planned to bring Jamie home where he belonged. After setting things in motion, he'd called in Leah to help him start looking for a nanny.

Nick studied the little scrap of humanity strapped in the infant seat next to him. Jamie was *his son*. Flesh of his flesh. It pained him he'd waited this long to go get him. Emotion grabbed him by the throat.

"I know this is a brand-new experience for you, sport. It is for me, too. You have no idea. I'm more the baby than you are right now and frankly, I'm terrified. You're going to help me out, aren't you?"

For answer, Jamie gave him a big yawn. A laugh escaped Nick's throat. He'd never been responsible for anyone before. Except that wasn't exactly true. When he'd taken on a wife, he'd promised to love her in sickness and in health, for richer or poorer, until death do us part.

He sucked in his breath. He'd only done the for-richer part right. But now that he had Jamie, he realized he'd been given a second chance and planned to do all of it right.

Nick had come along late in life, his parents' only child. No siblings to play with. They hadn't allowed him a pet because both his parents didn't want to deal with one. It was too hard, they said, when they went on vacation.

He had two cousins, Hannah and Greg, the children of his father's oldest brother. They rarely played together. It wasn't until after he and Greg were taken into the firm that he got to know him better. In Nick's loneliness growing up, he could see why he'd turned to books. Over time he'd found solace in his studies and work.

Erica had been a socialite wife like her mother, like Nick's. One eternal round of beautiful people enjoying their financially comfortable, beautiful lives. Not until Nick was part of the firm did his own father take an interest in him because he had a head for finances. But by then the damage had been done. They didn't have that emotional connection he'd hungered for from childhood.

He caught Jamie's busy feet with one hand and squeezed gently before letting them go again. Nick would be damned if he let the same thing happen to him and his son. Unfortunately two and a half months had already slipped by. Precious time that couldn't be recovered.

While they drove on, he opened the diaper bag and pulled out the instructions. Besides sending along some supplies, the nurse had left exact notes on her routine with Jamie, how much formula he needed, how often, nap times, that kind of thing.

He'd already arranged for the department store to deliver a crib and a new infant car seat that had come yesterday. As he thought over the list of things still to be done, his cell phone rang. Glad to see it was his secretary, he answered.

"Leah? Any success yet?"

"I've found someone I believe will suit you and the baby."

A Mary Poppins type only existed on film. "As long as she likes children and is a real motherly type and not some cardboard creation, I bow to your wisdom."

"I'll let you be the judge. She knows she hasn't been hired yet. I told her a limo would be by to pick her up at one o'clock so you could meet her and make a final decision."

"She can start today?"

"Yes. She needs a job badly."

Excellent. "What's her name?"

"Reese Chamberlain."

"Tell me more about her."

"If you don't mind, Nick, I've decided to take a leaf out of your book. You once told me you prefer to attack a new project without listening to any other voices first while you formed your own opinion. I think that's a good philosophy, especially in this case. She'll be standing in front of the Chelsea Star Hotel on West 30th."

Ms. Chamberlain really was in financial difficulty if she'd had to stay there.

"Tell Paul to look for the woman in yellow," Leah added.

"You're being very mysterious, if not cryptic. Give me something to go on."

"I'll wager she's not like anyone you ever met."

"That sounds promising."

"I hoped it would."

He made a sound in his throat. "Are you still accusing me of being a cynic?"

"I wouldn't do that. If I've made a mistake, call me later and let me know so I can keep looking for the right person."

"Do me a favor and phone Ms. Chamberlain. If she can be ready in forty-five minutes, we'll pick her up on the way to the apartment."

"She might not be available before time, but I'll see what I can do and get back to you." She clicked off.

Nick pocketed his phone, wanting to approve of Leah's assessment of the woman because there was no time to lose. Establishing a routine for the baby with the new nanny ASAP meant he'd sleep better nights. Any more weeks spent with his grandparents and Jamie would think the nurse in the starched uniform was his mother. Heaven forbid.

CHAPTER TWO

REESE had barely reached the hotel when her phone rang. She checked the caller ID and her stomach clenched. She might have known this job was too good to be true. Better to brave the bad news now and get it over with before she left for the airport. She couldn't afford to pay for another night here.

"Mrs. Tribe?"

"Ms. Chamberlain? I'm glad you answered. I've spoken with Mr. Wainwright. He's on a tight schedule and would like you to be out in front of the hotel in approximately forty minutes. Is that possible?"

She breathed a huge sigh of relief. "No problem at all."

"That's fine then. I'll let him know. Good luck to you."

"Thank you again."

After hanging up, she hurried to the dorm she'd shared with three other women. The one with Gothic piercings and purple streaks in her hair was still there stuffing everything on the bed into her backpack. She flicked Reese a glance. "How'd that interview go, honey?" Her Southern drawl was unmistakable.

"I think I got the job, but there's one more test to pass."

"I'd rather blow my brains out than be a nanny. They couldn't pay me enough."

Reese decided a response wasn't necessary. She only had a few items to pack in her suitcase and got busy.

The woman finished packing her things and turned to Reese. "It's been nice meeting you, honey. Y'all be careful now."

"You, too. Good luck finding your boyfriend."

"I'm going to need it." The door closed. Peace at last.

Reese went to the restroom to freshen up. One look in the mirror and she decided to put her hair back in a ponytail. Babies loved to tug on loose strands. Hers would be better confined. With the heat already building outside, messy limp hair and a flushed face wouldn't make the best impression. She had the kind of skin that splotched when the temperature soared.

After applying a fresh coat of lipstick, she left the bathroom, anxious to get this final interview over. With her purse and briefcase in one hand, and her suitcase in the other, she went downstairs to the lobby to check out. Unfortunately other guests anxious to get out sightseeing had the same idea. She had to wait in line.

There was a small crisis behind the desk. The computers were down. If the problem didn't get resolved fast, Reese was going to be late. Five minutes went by. She made the decision to go outside. Of course it meant losing her place in line. If her ride had come, she would ask the driver to wait while she settled her account.

Sure enough a black limo with smoked glass had

pulled up in front. As she hurried toward it, a uniformed chauffeur of middle age got out. "Ms. Chamberlain?"

"Yes. I'm sorry if you've been waiting. I'm still in line to pay my bill. Could I leave my suitcase with you? I'll run back inside. I shouldn't be much longer."

"Take your time."

"Thank you."

Ten minutes later she rushed back outside. The driver opened the rear door of the limo for her so she could get in.

"Oh—"

"Oh" was right, Nick thought to himself as the long-legged, ash-blonde female took the seat opposite him and Jamie. She brought a flowery fragrance into the limo with her. What was she? Twenty-five, twenty-six?

Her modest blouse and skirt couldn't hide the curves of a body well put together. She had to be five-eight in her bone-colored sandals and was so different from the image he had in mind of a plump, fortyish maternal type, he couldn't imagine what Leah had been thinking.

Maybe the wrong person had gotten in the limo, but she was wearing yellow.

"You're Reese Chamberlain?"

"Yes."

"I'm Nicholas Wainwright."

Her light blue eyes flared as if in surprise. "How do you do," she said in a slightly husky voice that for no particular reason appealed to him. When she saw the baby who'd fallen asleep, her eyes sparkled with life. She leaned toward Jamie, seemingly oblivious to Nick. "Oh—look how darling! All that black hair and those long, silky lashes against his cheeks."

Her gaze finally darted to Nick's. "I'm sorry to have kept you. Mrs. Tribe warned me you were a punctual man, and now I've already committed my first sin. But the computers were down at the hotel and I had to wait in line until they could check me out."

No New Yorker here or anything close. Midwest maybe? "So my driver explained. We're not in a hurry. Jamie's being very cooperative."

"He's a wonderful boy." When her eyes lifted, he could see they'd darkened with emotion. "I'm so sorry about your loss. If you decide to hire me, I promise to do everything I can to make your son as secure and happy as possible until your permanent nanny comes to live with you."

Either she was the greatest actress alive, or this was her true self. Leah was a shrewd judge of character. Something had to have appealed to his secretary for her to pick a woman whose age and looks were totally wrong for the position. She appeared too healthy to be a model, yet had the right bones and height. All Walter and Anne had to do—or anyone else for that matter— was get a glimpse of her and...

The limo was already working its way through traffic. Paul would have them deposited at the front of the apartment before long. Nick needed more information so he could decide if he would send her back to the hotel before they ever got out of the car.

"Room and board aside, what kind of salary were you expecting, Ms. Chamberlain?"

She named a figure below what he'd anticipated she would ask for. "Does that sound all right to you?"

"It's fine," he muttered, bemused by everything that

came out of her mouth. "Tell me what happens when you leave me in September?"

"I'll move back to Philadelphia."

His dark brows lifted. "Another nanny position?"

She studied him with a puzzled expression. "No. I'll be in school again. I guess Mrs. Tribe failed to mention that to you."

Something had been going on with Leah he didn't understand. Without all the facts, he was at a loss. "She probably did, but I'm afraid I've been preoccupied with the arrangements for my son."

"Of course. She said your in-laws have been helping out. There's nothing like family coming to the rescue in a crisis. The baby will probably have a hard time with me at first, always looking for you or his grandparents. Were you thinking of giving me a trial run? I'll do whatever. And please don't worry. If you decide to look for someone else, I have a backup plan."

He blinked in surprise. "I thought you needed a job."

"I do, but if all else fails, I'll fly home and my father will let me work for him this summer. It isn't what I want to do," she added, sounding far away, "but as I told you, there's nothing like family in an emergency. Dad's a sweetheart."

What had Leah said? *I'll wager she's not like anyone you ever met.*

"Where is home?"

"Lincoln, Nebraska."

So Nick was right. "What does your father do for a living?"

"He owns a lumberyard. I've helped in the office before."

"You're a long way from home. I presume college brought you to the East Coast."

"That's right. I'm a business major."

Nick's black brows furrowed. "Have you ever been a nanny?"

"No," she said forthrightly, "but I come from a large family and have done my share of tending children."

"Your mother worked, too?"

A gentle laugh escaped. "Oh, she worked—but not outside the home. Being the mother of six children is like running a major corporation. She's been on call 24/7 since I was born." Her eyes wandered to Jamie. "There's nothing sweeter than a new baby. All they really need is lots of love between eating and sleeping."

Suddenly the door opened. Paul stood there, reminding Nick they'd arrived. He'd been so engrossed in the conversation he hadn't noticed the limo had stopped. Unless he could come up with a compelling reason not to hire her right now, taking her upstairs would be as good as a fait accompli.

While he hesitated, a piercing siren filled the air, the kind that sent an alarm through your body. It was so loud it woke Jamie, who came awake startled and crying. Before Nick could turn to get the baby's straps undone, Ms. Chamberlain had already accomplished it and plucked him out of the car seat.

In an instant she had him cuddled against her shoulder. She'd moved too fast for it to be anything more than her natural instinct to comfort. "Did that mean old siren scare you?" Her hand shaped the back of his head. "It scared me, too, but it's all right." She rocked him, giving him kisses until his frightened cries turned into whimpers.

"Sorry," she said, flicking her gaze to Nick. "I didn't mean to grab him, but that siren made *me* jump and it was easier for me to dive for him than you. His heart is pounding like a jackhammer." She started to hand the baby to Nick, but he shook his head.

"He seems perfectly happy where he is for the moment."

With those words it appeared he'd sealed his own fate. Still bemused by what had happened, he turned to an oddly silent Paul who'd already pulled the diaper bag and her suitcase out of the limo.

The baby was gorgeous. He had the overall look and coloring of his dark, striking father, but it was apparent his mother had been a beauty in her own right. No wonder Mr. Wainwright seemed to brood even as he spoke to Reese. She hadn't the slightest idea how long he and his wife had been married. What mattered was that she'd only been dead ten weeks.

Reese had undergone her own crushing pain when Jeremy had broken their engagement, but at least they hadn't been married or had a child. She didn't even want to think about the white-hot pain Jamie's father must still be in. Reese couldn't figure out how he was coping.

There was nothing she could do to alleviate his anguish. But if given the chance, she would love his little boy and make him feel secure during the hours his father was at work. By the time fall came and the new nanny took over, his daddy would have put more of his grief behind him.

Last Christmas Reese had been in agony over her split with Jeremy, but six months had gone by and she was still alive and functioning better these days. Though it would take Mr. Wainwright longer to heal, she was living proof that you didn't die of a broken heart. But he wouldn't want to hear those words right now so she wouldn't say them.

"Shall we go up?"

His deep voice broke into her reverie. She turned her head, surprised he'd already gotten out of the limo. Reese took a quick second breath because it appeared he wasn't about to send her away yet. Feeling the baby cling to her had made the whole situation real for the first time. She discovered she wanted this job very much.

"Jamie seems to have quieted down," she commented.

"Thanks to you." The comment warmed her before he reached for his son. Though he was tiny compared to his father, they looked so right together in their matching colored suits. She surmised Mr. Wainwright was in his early to mid-thirties although age was hard to tell and could add years when one was grieving.

Realizing she would become morose if she kept thinking about it, she stepped out of the limo with her purse, determined to put on a bright face for Jamie. That was her job after all. She followed his father inside a prewar brick-and-limestone building. Evidently there'd been massive renovations because the interior exuded luxury. They entered the elevator and rode to the fourteenth floor.

When the doors opened, she glimpsed a penthouse the public only got to see from inside the pages of *Architecture Digest*. The apartment itself was a piece of modern sculpture with its tall curving walls and a sweeping loft where she glimpsed a library of books and statuary. At every turn she was surprised by a bronze étagère of Mesoamerican artifacts here or a cubist painting there.

Impressions of Old World antiques, objets d'art and moiré silk period pieces flew at her like colors through a prism. There was a grand piano and a set of gorgeous Japanese screens in one section. Everywhere she looked, her gaze fastened on some treasure. A grouping of eighteenth-century furniture faced the fireplace. She wouldn't know where to begin describing the layout or furnishings of this Park Avenue address.

Months ago she'd seen an article with pictures in the *Times* of a condo something like this one that had just sold for thirty million dollars. She supposed his wealth could have come through his business endeavors.

But his breeding gave her the sense that he'd been born into the kind of family whose wealth had been one of the mainstays of Wall Street for generations. Mrs. Tribe hadn't let on. If Reese had been in her place, she wouldn't have, either.

"Since you're from Nebraska and the wide-open spaces, you'll probably find the area out here more to your liking."

She followed him across the living room's velvety Oriental rugs to the span of rounded arched windows reminiscent of the Italian masters. He opened some sliding doors. When she stepped out on the terrace, she felt as if she'd entered a park complete with trees, hedges, a pool,and tubs of flowering plants placed around with an artistic flare.

As she walked to the edge, she had an unimpeded view of Park Avenue down to the Helmsley building. The whole thing was incredible. "I would imagine after a hard day at the office, this is your favorite room, too." She saw a telescope set up at one end beyond the patio furniture. When Jamie was old enough, he'd be enthralled by everything he could see through it from this angle.

"It can be pleasant if it's not too hot. I can't say I've spent that much time out here lately, but I do use the gym every morning. It's on the upper deck of my terrace. You'll see the stairs. You're welcome to work out if you want."

"Thank you."

She sensed he was in a dark mood. Lines bracketed his mouth. "Let's go back inside. I'll let you pick the bedroom you'd like, but perhaps you'd like to freshen up first. The guest bathroom is through that door."

"Thank you. I'm pretty sure Jamie's diaper needs to be changed. Could we go to the nursery first?"

He shot her an intense glance. "For now there's only a crib in my bedroom that was delivered yesterday. I haven't decided where he should sleep yet."

So Jamie *had* been at his grandparents' from the start. Why? "I see. Well, let me wash my hands first." She slipped inside the bathroom that looked more like an arboretum with plants and flowers. After washing and drying her hands, Reese joined him just inside the sliding doors and trailed her employer through the fabulous apartment to the master bedroom with a decidedly all-male look.

It had been decorated along straight lines and contemporary furniture with accents of greens and blues. Some graphics on the walls. No frills, no sense of femininity. Above all, no family pictures. Too painful a reminder? Maybe he kept them in the living room and she hadn't noticed.

The walnut crib stood at the end of the king-size bed. It had a crib sheet but no padding. The diaper bag had been put in the room along with her suitcase. Without hesitation she reached inside the bag for a diaper. Along with a dozen of them it contained a twelve-hour supply of small, individual bottles of formula, another stretchy outfit, a shirt and a receiving blanket. She pulled it out and spread it over the top of the bed.

"If you'll lay him on this, we'll change him."

He walked over and put Jamie down. "Okay, sport. This is going to be a new experience for all of us."

Mr. Wainwright wouldn't be the first man who'd never changed a diaper. "The baby's so happy with you, why don't you undo his outfit. We'll work on this together."

Reese smiled to herself to see the good-looking, well-dressed executive bending over his son to perform something he'd never done before. He seemed more human suddenly and even more attractive.

It took him a minute to undo all the snaps and free his legs. Reese undid the tabs on the diaper. "Lift his legs." When he did, she drew the old one away and slid in the new one. "Okay. Lower him and put up the front, then fasten it with these side tabs."

The baby's body was in perpetual motion. You could hear him breathing fast with animation. "He likes all this attention, don't you." She couldn't resist kissing his tummy after his father had finished. In truth her physical awareness of Mr. Wainwright had caught her off guard.

"Great job, Daddy. You did it so fast, he didn't have a chance to get you wet." His quiet chuckle pleased and surprised her. She'd like to hear that sound more often, then chastised herself for having any thoughts of a personal nature about him.

"While you finish dressing him, I'll get rid of this." She took the soiled diaper and headed for a door she could see across the room, thinking it was the bathroom, but it led to an office where he could work at home. "Oops. Wrong room."

"The bathroom's behind me. I didn't realize it was your destination." By now he was holding Jamie against his shoulder again. They really did look gorgeous together.

Reese averted her eyes and moved past him before opening the door to the elegant bathroom. She put the diaper on the marble counter, madly compiling a mental list of all the things they would need to make his apartment baby friendly.

After washing her hands, she came out again and said, "Do you know my whole family could fit in there comfortably?" His lips twitched. When they did that, he didn't look as stressed and was too attractive by far. "How many bedrooms are there besides this one?"

"There's one across the hall from my room, and one at the other end of the apartment."

"I've been thinking… Would it be possible to move your office to that other bedroom, or to somewhere else in the apartment entirely?"

He cocked his dark head. "Anything's possible."

"It's just that your office is the perfect size for a nursery because it has a door leading into your room as well as the hall. If you put Jamie in there, he'd be close to you. I assume that's what you want. As for me, I could stay across the hall where I could hear him, too. I don't know about you, but when I was growing up, I didn't like being isolated from my parents."

He stared at her so hard, she couldn't imagine what was going through his mind, but it made her worry she might have overstepped her bounds. "What do you think?" she prodded quietly.

"It's a brilliant idea, one I would never have thought of."

"Oh, good." Reese was amazed he would admit something like that. Most men had too much pride. She liked that quality about him very much. To her alarm, she realized, there wasn't anything about this man she didn't like.

Why hadn't his wife fixed up a nursery before the baby was born? Had they lived somewhere else? Maybe he'd only recently moved in here, but why hadn't he brought everything for the baby with him?

Whatever the answer, you would have thought his wife would have taken on the job of getting prepared for a baby, but she was gone now. All he had was Reese.

"I tell you what. If you want to stay here with Jamie, maybe you could ask your driver to take me to a store where I can get all the things we need in one stop? It'll take a limo to bring back everything we require in a single trip."

When he didn't respond she said, "Or else I'll make a list for you and you buy everything while I tend the baby? Later we can move furniture and get everything set up. It's kind of fun to do together. Jamie can watch us. He's very bright and alert. By tonight we'll have this place transformed and he'll know he's home with his daddy."

She watched him reach in his pocket for his cell

phone. "I'll call Paul and tell him to meet you out in front. He'll take you to a place where I have an account. Buy whatever we need. When you get back, the concierge will arrange to get everything upstairs."

To not have to worry about money would be a first in her life. Since it was for Jamie, she would take his father at his word and enjoy her shopping spree.

"After you've returned I'll ask the chef to send up a meal for us. Are you allergic to anything?"

Chefs, a doorman, a concierge, no ceiling on expenditures— One could get used to this instantly.

"No, but thank you for asking. Are there certain foods you can't tolerate, Mr. Wainwright?"

"No."

"What about the baby?"

"So far no problems that I know of."

"Thank goodness. Excuse me for a minute while I freshen up in my bedroom."

She reached for the suitcase and briefcase and carried them across the hall to the other bedroom done in an opulent Mediterranean decor. It had its own ornate en suite bathroom with two sinks. She would use one of them to bathe Jamie. Afterward she couldn't wait to wrap him up in the plush lavender towels hanging from a row of gilded hooks.

Reese looked around, incredulous that this was happening. Her thoughts darted to her employer. How was is it possible she'd be sleeping across the hall from the most fabulous man she'd ever met in her life?

After Ms. Chamberlain left the apartment, Nick fed the baby another bottle. He'd watched the nurse burp Jamie and had gotten that part down right. Once Jamie fell asleep, Nick laid him in the center of the bed and put the quilt over him. In the process he noticed the time on his watch. It was after three. The day had gotten away from him completely.

He reached for his cell phone and called the office. "Uncle Stan?"

"Where have you been? I need to discuss the Grayson merger with you. I've run into a snag and want your help."

"I'm aware of that, but it won't be possible today or tomorrow. Can't you talk to Uncle Phil?"

"He's at the dentist getting a new crown this afternoon."

"Then ask Greg."

"He doesn't know all the ins and outs. It's too tricky for him."

"Nevertheless I can't come in the office until Monday."

"That might be too late, Nicky." His father's younger brother had always been an alarmist.

"Sorry, but it can't be helped."

"Since when? I don't understand."

No. He wouldn't. His uncle and aunt had been childless. "Today I brought Jamie home for good."

There was a deafening silence. "I thought he—"

"He's been with his grandparents too long as it is," he broke in.

"But how will you manage?"

So far…better than Nick had thought possible. "I've hired a nanny." A totally feminine, beautiful, unexpected young woman. The image of her clutching Jamie to her while they were still in the limo—as if she was the mother—refused to leave his mind.

"I had no idea you'd even been looking for one. Your father never said a word."

"He and Mother were already in Cannes when I made the decision."

"I hear a decent one is almost impossible to come by. Is she over forty?"

His patience was running out. "Why do you ask?"

"Because anyone younger who still has their eyesight will do whatever it takes to get set up with you."

If Nick had inherited a cynical gene, it had to have come from his uncle. But in this case he wasn't worried. Leah would have done a thorough check of Ms. Chamberlain's background. He paid his secretary a salary that ensured mistakes like the one his uncle was talking about didn't happen.

"See you on Monday, Uncle Stan," Nick muttered before clicking off. Now to get busy dismantling his office. But before he did that, he changed out of his suit into something more comfortable.

To his relief, Jamie slept through the next two hours. By the time the concierge rang him at five and told him he was on his way up with Ms. Chamberlain, Nick had just wheeled the baby crib into the empty room.

He walked through the apartment to the entry and opened the door. Soon his nanny emerged from the elevator carrying bags in both hands. As she passed by him she said, "Merry Christmas." She was intriguing and amusing at the same time.

Behind her came the concierge pushing a dolly loaded with cartons. Paul brought up the rear with more bags. He winked at Nick, who was still reacting to her comment. "This bag goes in the kitchen. Then we have one more load," he whispered before heading for the other room.

"You've done the work of a thousand—" she exclaimed to Nick after the men had filed back out of the new nursery. "Jamie's going to *love* this room once we've whipped it into shape. How's he doing so far?"

She had such a vivacious personality, Nick was mesmerized. No wonder Leah had picked her. Ms. Chamberlain had to have stood out a hundred miles from any of the other nanny candidates.

"He's still asleep on my bed."

"I'll just wash my hands and peek in on him."

"While you do that I'll ask the kitchen to send up our dinner." He made the call, then started looking through the bags, curious to see what she'd purchased for one tiny baby. In a minute the concierge came through with even more cartons.

"Have fun putting all this together, Mr. Wainwright. Leave the empty boxes outside in the hall and I'll pick them up."

Nick thanked him and walked him out in time to ask the waiter to set up their dinner in the dining room. Halfway back to his bedroom he met her in the hall carrying Jamie in her arms. "This little guy was awake. I guess he could hear the noise and started to fuss. He needed a diaper change and let me handle it, but I think he wanted you to do the honors."

"Well, now that the deed is done, our food is ready in the dining room."

"That sounds good. If you'll open the carton that says *baby swing,* we can set it up in there and he can watch you while we eat. It will be perfect for him when we go out on the terrace during the day."

He hadn't seen one of those at the Hirsts'. "You want to swing?" Nick gave him a kiss on the cheek before heading into the nursery. Reese followed him and waited while he opened the carton.

"There should be some batteries taped to the inside of the lid."

"Batteries?"

"They make it swing and play music at the same time."

Though he moved millions of dollars around on paper every day, the world of a baby and all its attendant necessities had passed him by completely. Whether his boy needed a swing or not, he had one now. Thankfully it wasn't as difficult to put together as installing the base of the infant car seat in the limo. It had taken him several attempts before he'd managed to do it right.

"Let's go try this out."

"Your daddy's a genius to assemble it so fast, Jamie."

"Don't speak too soon in case it goes crashing down, taking my son with it."

"We're not worried."

He stared into her shimmering blue eyes, dumbfounded over Leah's find. "Then you should be."

CHAPTER THREE

WHEN Nick looked at her like that, Reese's heart began thudding for reasons she didn't dare explore right now.

She followed him back to the living room. The floor-to-ceiling French doors at the end had been opened to reveal a dining room that took her breath. First came the chandelier of Czechoslovakian glass. One of this kind and size was a museum piece. She thought the same thing of the massive Italian provincial hutch that lined the far wall.

Its shelving held handblown Venetian glass and stunning pieces of china no longer made. On the opposite wall was a long European hunt board with its distinctive stylized pheasants and peacocks. A still-life oil painting of fruits hung above it.

The window featured tapestries with tassels pulled halfway down depicting various pastoral scenes. When she could tear her gaze away, it fell on the rectangular table of dark oak dominating the room. She counted sixteen chairs around. The exquisite woodwork was complemented by the upholstery fabric, a blend of rich green and cream striping on velvet.

Two candelabras with lighted tapers flanked a breath-taking centerpiece of fresh flowers including creamy lilies and roses interspersed with greenery. The top of the beautifully carved table had such a highly polished surface, everything gleamed. Two places nearest the doors had been set where their dinner awaited them.

She finally looked at her employer. "I'm afraid whoever dreamed up this masterpiece of a room didn't have that swing in mind." He'd set it on a gorgeous Persian rug at the corner of the table.

"I have to give my wife credit for much of the apartment's decor."

So they *had* lived here together. How painful this must be for him. "She had incomparable taste."

He took the baby from her and fastened him in the seat. "Let's see if he likes this." When he pressed the button, it started to swing and played "Here We Go Round the Mulberry Bush." Jamie looked at his father. The baby acted happy and it brought a ghost of a smile to his father's lips.

Mr. Wainwright's eyes unexpectedly narrowed on her features. "Your contribution to the room keeps it from feeling like a museum. Shall we eat?"

Reese could imagine the apartment felt that way to him with his other half gone out of his life. But he had his adorable son staring up at him in wonder, as if his father was the whole world to him. That had to compensate for his loss.

Leaving him to sit at the head of the table, she took her place at the side just as the song changed to another nursery rhyme. It played a medley of ten tunes.

He removed the covers from their plates, sending a mouthwatering aroma through the room. "Help yourself to coffee or tea."

"Thank you, but I'll just have water." She poured

herself a glass from the pitcher and drank a little before starting in on her food. "This roast chicken is delicious."

"I'll tell the chef. He was plucked from a five-star hotel in Paris."

"The chicken or the chef?"

His deep laugh disarmed her. "Touché."

She laughed with him. "It explains the buttery taste I love. I'm afraid I'm as bad as Julia Child. We think alike. Butter is the building block for good food."

His dark eyes flicked to hers. The candlelight reflecting in them made the irises look more brown than black. Until now she hadn't been able to decide their exact shade. "You eat a lot of it out in Nebraska, do you?"

"We Cornhuskers never heard of cholesterol," she teased, laying it on a little thick. "In truth, all of us healthy farm girls thrive on it."

One dark brow shot up. "If I offended you, I didn't mean to."

She smiled. "I know you didn't. I was just having fun."

"That's a refreshing quality of yours, Reese. Mind if I call you that?"

His genuine warmth came as a surprise. She hadn't expected a truly successful, wealthy CEO like him to be so well-rounded. It was probably that quality as much as his brilliant mind that drew people to him and made him such a paragon.

"To be honest, I hate being called Ms. Chamberlain, *Mr.* Wainwright."

He smiled. "If that was more funning on your part, I still get the hint. Call me Nick."

"Thank you. I was afraid it wouldn't happen for a while."

Another chuckle ensued. "Am I that impossible?"

Reese was already too addicted to his potent charisma. "Not at all, but I'd like Jamie to know I have a first name. Ms. Chamberlain is kind of heavy for a ten-week-old." She put her fork down. "Speaking of the baby, I know it looks like I bought out the store, but everything I purchased was for a reason. Of course I'll take anything back you don't like or find necessary."

"I'll reserve judgment until tomorrow. We've worked hard enough today and need an early night."

"The only thing we ought to do before turning in is to fix up Jamie's crib."

"What's wrong with it?"

"Nothing, but it needs a mattress cover under the fitted sheet and a bumper pad to go around the edges so he won't hurt his head against the bars. And I bought a cute little mobile with farm animals that plays tunes. Anything with bright colors and he'll reach for it."

He glanced down at Jamie. "You know what, sport? I have a feeling Reese is going to spoil you rotten."

"That's the plan," she interjected. "You can't spoil babies enough because they're too cute." She leaned over to cup his cheek.

"Would you like dessert?" he murmured.

She felt his dark gaze on her, making her so aware of him, it sent heat to her face. "I don't think I have room for any, thank you. The dinner was wonderful."

Reese started to get up from the table, ready to take the dishes into the kitchen. She assumed it lay beyond the door at the other end of the dining room. But he said,

"Leave everything for the waiter. He lets himself in and out. So do the maids."

"I didn't realize." She remained in place.

"When you need a wash done for you or the baby, just put it in a laundry bag on the counter in your bathroom. You'll find them in the cupboard beneath the sinks. If you need pressing or tailoring done, phone them to indicate what you want."

She left her napkin next to her plate. "Do you always have your meals brought up?"

"No. Most of the time I eat out. Occasionally I fix something in the kitchen and sit at the island. While you're here, feel free to order whatever you want from downstairs. All you have to do is pick up the house phone and dial one for the chef's office, or two for maid service. They come in every morning. Your job is to take care of Jamie, nothing else."

"Understood."

"You're welcome to fix your own meals whether I'm home or not. Tomorrow there'll be time for you to look around the pantry and compile a list of groceries you'd like to have on hand. Dial three for the concierge. Give him the list and he'll see they're delivered."

He pushed himself away from the table and stood up to take the baby out of the swing. "Come on, Jamie. Let's see how long it takes your old man to put that mobile together."

"You've been given a reprieve on that one," Reese said, bringing up the rear. "The only thing you have to do is fasten it to the end of the crib and turn on the music. There's a small sack of batteries somewhere, but give me a minute to make up the crib first."

He moved fast on those long, powerful legs. She had

to hurry to keep up with him. When they reached the nursery, she found the item for him, then quickly got busy. After she'd tied the last part of the bumper pad, she reached for Jamie.

"I'll feed him while you set up the mobile."

She darted into Nick's bedroom and got a bottle of formula out of the diaper bag, sat down on the end of his bed and fed Jamie.

"You're a hungry boy." He drank noisily. His burps were noisy, too, making her laugh. When he'd drained his bottle, she wandered back into the nursery where she found Nick watching the mobile turn while it played a song.

He glanced at her as she walked in. "I know I didn't have one of these when I was growing up."

She nuzzled Jamie's neck. "I think you're going to like what your daddy just put up." When she lowered him to the mattress, the tune drew his attention, as did the plush animals going around and around.

"Look, Nick—his cute little body is squiggling with excitement. He loves it!"

"I think you're right." When she looked up, their eyes caught and held. The intensity of his gaze made it difficult to breathe. "If you want to call it an early night, go ahead. I'll get up with him during the night. Tomorrow will be soon enough to take care of everything else and set up a schedule."

Then he looked back at Jamie with so much love, Reese was spellbound. She got the hint. He wanted time alone with his son. Nothing could be more natural or more reassuring to Jamie who, would be spending tonight in brand-new surroundings.

"I'll say good-night then and see both of you in the

morning." As she reached the door, she turned around. "Thank you for giving me this opportunity. I'm very grateful. He's a precious boy."

Without waiting for a response, Reese slipped out of the nursery to the bedroom across the hall. After taking a shower and getting ready for bed, she climbed under the covers and reached for her cell phone to call her parents. It was an hour earlier in Lincoln.

"Reese? I've been hoping you'd call, honey."

"Sorry about that, Mom, but I've been so busy today, this has been my first chance to call. I've gotten myself a nanny job."

"Of course I'm happy for you, but everyone misses you."

"I miss them, but with the salary I'll be making here, I can concentrate my time on studying for the Series 7 and the Series 65. I have to take the test at the end of July before classes start again at the end of August. It shouldn't be a problem putting in the hours I need and still work around the baby's schedule." But she needed to get busy right away, which didn't give her much breathing room.

"You only have one child to look after?"

"Yes. He's ten weeks old. Oh, Mom, Jamie's the most beautiful child you ever saw." That was because his father was the most arresting male Reese had ever laid eyes on in her life. The byplay of muscles beneath his T-shirt revealed a fit masculine body. Working out in his gym on the roof every day was the reason he was so buff.

"What are his parents like? I hope they're nice. Do you think you'll all get along?"

Reese bit her lip. "There's just the father. His wife died during the birth."

"Oh, no—"

"It's very sad."

"What's his name?"

"Nick Wainwright. He's the CEO at Sherborne-Wainwright. It's the kind of brokerage company every student at Wharton would kill for in order to be able to work there. Would you believe I've been installed in his penthouse on Park Avenue? If Jackie Onassis were alive today, she would gobble it up in a second."

Her mom chuckled. "Be serious."

"I am. Who ever dreamed I'd be an honest-to-goodness nanny in a household like his?"

"How old is he?"

"It's hard to tell. Thirty-three, thirty-four maybe."

"Well...you've got a terrific head on those shoulders and broke off with Jeremy for a reason. I don't have to worry about you losing sight of your career plans just yet, do I?"

"Nothing could make me do that."

"I believe you. Destiny has already singled out my brilliant daughter for something special. Tell me more about this financial prince of Park Avenue."

"Mom—" Reese laughed. "Financial prince...what a thing to say."

"Tell me the truth. Is he as gorgeous as Jackie's son was?"

Her mother would keel over if she ever got a look at Jamie's father. "There are no words."

"Well. Coming from you, that says it all."

Reese was afraid it did.

"Still, if I know my daughter, you won't let anything

get in the way of your goal. I happen to know you're going to be a big name to contend with in the business world one day."

Reese's eyelids prickled. "Thanks for believing in me, Mom."

"Oh, I do! Just don't let those mothering instincts make you too attached to the baby. It can happen."

Reese knew it was one of the hazards of the job, but she'd deal with it. Jamie was an adorable little boy and it would be so easy to get attached to him, but Reese reminded herself that she would only be here for three months. "I love you. Give Dad and everyone else my love. I'll call you soon."

Once she'd hung up, she checked her phone messages. One was from her roommate, Pam, who'd gone home to Florida for the summer. Reese would call her sometime tomorrow.

The other call came from her study partner, Rich Bonner. He'd asked her to phone him back as soon as she could. He'd flown home to California for a break before returning to Philadelphia. Like her, he was preparing for his exams. They'd done a lot of studying together. Reese knew that Rich wanted more than just a platonic friendship with her, but she wasn't interested, not that way.

If she didn't return his call for a while, he'd hopefully get the hint. One of the problems with Rich was that he was highly competitive. As long as they remained friends, he had to be nice to her when she got higher grades than he did.

But Reese wagered that if she were ever to become his girlfriend, he'd start telling her how to live her life. Heaven forbid if she landed a better job than he did after graduation. Worse, what if she were married to him and he expected her to stay at home? Another control freak like Jeremy. Help. No more of that, please.

With a sigh, she turned off the lamp at the bedside and pulled the covers over her. Having taken Nick at his word that he would be getting up with the baby, she'd closed the bedroom door. Starting tomorrow night she'd put the new baby monitor in her room so she could hear him cry.

The day had been long and she felt physically exhausted, but exhilarated, too, because she'd found the kind of job she'd been hoping for, never dreaming it really existed. Now she didn't have to go home. Instead she could make the kind of money her father wouldn't be able to pay her by her staying right here in New York.

All she had to do was look after one little baby in surroundings only an exclusive group of people would ever know about or see. When Reese had mentioned Jackie Kennedy to her mom, she'd also been thinking of her son John Jr.'s Tribeca apartment.

It must have been over ten years ago she'd seen a few pictures of the interior following his death when she'd been a teenager. From what she remembered, it wasn't nearly on the same scale of splendor as Mr. Wainwright's fantastic residence. The architectural design for making the most of the light was nothing short of breathtaking.

Like the man himself. *Breathtaking.*

"Good morning, Reese." Nick put his newspaper down on the glass-top patio table. He'd seen her ponytail swinging as she'd stepped out on the terrace and closed the sliding door. In a modest pale orange top and jeans that still managed to cling to her womanly figure, he was going to have difficulty keeping his eyes off her.

"So *this* is where you are." She walked right over and hunkered down in front of Jamie, who was strapped in the swing wide-awake. He liked the motion, but Nick hadn't turned on the music yet. "I've been looking for you." She kissed his cheek and neck. "Hey—you're wearing a nightgown. Do you have any idea how cute you look?"

Jamie transferred his attention to her while he took little breaths as if he recognized her. Naturally he did. Nick could have been blindfolded but would still know her by her scent. It reminded him of wildflowers. This time she kissed his son's tummy, causing him to smile. "Did you sleep through the night like a good boy?"

"He had a bottle at two-thirty and only woke up again at seven-thirty."

"Well, good for you." She tickled his chin and got him to laugh out loud. "Five hours is terrific. The sixty-four-thousand-dollar questions is, how's Dad?" She shot Nick a direct glance. The iridescent blue of her eyes was an extraordinary color.

"Dad's all right for an old man. What about you?"

"I got a wonderful sleep and now I'm ready to help put that nursery together."

"Not before you eat breakfast or you'll hurt Cesar's feelings."

"Chef Cesar?" she teased.

"That's right. He made a crab omelet in your honor with plenty of butter."

"Did you hear that, Jamie? I guess I'd better eat it while it's still hot." She sat down opposite Nick and removed the cover on her plate. "Croissants, too?" Her gaze darted to the baby, who followed her movements while she ate. "We're going to have to go for a long walk in the stroller to work off the pounds I can already feel going on. But that's okay because this food is too good to resist."

Nick couldn't imagine her ever having that kind of a problem. "Coffee?"

"Please."

To his dismay he discovered Reese had another quality he liked besides her ability to have fun. She enjoyed everything and ate her meal with real pleasure. No female of his acquaintance did that, certainly not Erica, who was constantly watching her figure.

He found Reese a woman devoid of self-consciousness. For some men, it might be off-putting, but for Nick it had the opposite effect…a fact that troubled him more than a little bit. She was his nanny for heaven's sake!

After finishing her coffee, she looked across at him with a definite smile in her eyes. "Before we put our shoulders to the wheel—is there anything I should be worried about in the *Wall Street Journal* this morning?"

He chuckled. "Not unless you've been following news on the euro."

"Is it good or bad?"

Her question surprised him for the simple reason he couldn't imagine it being of interest to her, but she was being polite so he would return the compliment. "Overnight it staged a late surge in U.S. trading, rebounding sharply against the dollar. As a result it unwound the 'carry' trades and sent the Australian dollar and Brazilian real plunging."

Her well-shaped brows knit together. "Is that a critical situation in your eyes?"

"No, but it has some global economists rattled."

"Well, if you're not upset, then I'm certainly not going to be." She got to her feet. "If you don't mind, I'll carry him back to my bedroom and give him a quick bath. Then we're all yours."

Nick had no idea what to make of her. But as he watched her disappear with Jamie, he decided it didn't matter because his son appeared to be in the best of hands. Yesterday morning he couldn't have foreseen the changes that had already taken place since he'd picked her up in front of the hotel.

He gathered up the swing and headed for the nursery. After putting it in the corner, some impulse had him walking across the hall to her room. She'd left all the doors open, so he continued on through. When he reached the bathroom, the sight that greeted him brought a lump to his throat.

Reese had filled one of the sinks with water. While she cradled the back of Jamie's head in the water, she washed his scalp and talked to him in soothing tones. His son was mesmerized. Slowly she rinsed off the baby shampoo, then took a bar of baby soap and washed his limbs. With the greatest tenderness she turned him over and washed his back. He made little cooing sounds Nick felt resonate in his body.

Without conscious thought he reached for one of the towels and held it up for her. Their eyes met for an instant. She said, "While you dry him off, I'll find him a new outfit to put on."

Nick cuddled his boy to him, uncaring that he was still wet. He smelled so sweet. As he felt Jamie burrow into his neck, a feeling of love flowed through him so intense, he was staggered by it.

"What do you think?" she asked when he appeared in the doorway to the nursery, holding up three outfits. "The white with the tiger, the green with the fish or the navy with the Snoopy?"

"Maybe we should let Jamie decide." He turned him around in his arms and walked over to her. "I wonder which one he'll go for."

She laughed in anticipation, watching him closely. "His eyes keep looking at the dog."

"Every boy should have one," Nick declared. "Snoopy it is."

"Did you have a dog?"

"No. What about you?"

"We went through three before I left home."

Reese had the diaper ready. Nick lowered his son in the crib and put it on with no hesitation this time. She handed him the one-piece fitted suit with no legs. After he'd snapped it, he picked him up again.

"Let me brush his hair and then he's ready for the day." As she lifted her arm, it brushed against Nick's. An unconscious thing to be sure, the lightest of touches. But he'd felt her warmth against his skin and the next thing he knew it had swamped his sensitized body.

He hadn't been intimate with a woman since the last time he'd slept with Erica. That was the reason for this total physical reaction. *It had to be.*

"First things first," she declared. "There's a diaper pail around here somewhere with a scented deodorizer. Ah—" She opened one of the cartons. "Just what we need." After lining it, in went the diaper. Then she lifted her head, causing her ponytail to swish like quicksilver. "Where do you want the crib to go?"

He struggled to concentrate. "How about the far wall. The sun won't reach him there when the shutters are open, and it will leave both doorways free."

"Perfect." She moved things out of the way so she could roll it into position across the hardwood floor.

Nick settled Jamie back in his swing and they got to work opening all the boxes. While he put the stroller together, she stacked diapers, baby wipes, powder, baby cream, lotion and ear swabs in the changing-table compartments. After watching her bathe the baby with nonallergenic products, he realized there was a reason for everything she'd bought.

"I'm glad you took the Oriental rug away. I can't wait for you to see the baby furniture," she said as he reached for one of the bigger cartons.

Curious himself, Nick opened the box and discovered a child's antique white dresser with olive-green trim and a Winnie the Pooh hand-painted over the drawers. The next box held a child's chair in the shape of Piglet. A big Eyeore dominated the oval hook rug. In another carton he found a lamp whose base was shaped like a honey pot. The last carton was the biggest. When he opened it, he found an adult rocking chair with Owl as the motif.

"That's so you can sit in here and feed him while you rock him to sleep." She'd thought of everything. The set charmed him. *She* charmed him.

He took all the boxes out of the apartment and piled them in the hall. When he came back, Reese had placed the furniture around and had put a soft, furry Winnie the Pooh in one corner of his crib.

"You've turned this room into the Hundred Acre Wood. I like it."

She whirled around with an anxious look on her face. "Honestly?"

"I doubt there's another nursery more inviting. Jamie will grow up loving to be in here. Thank you for helping me." She was an amazing person who had the knack of making everything exciting.

"I haven't had so much fun in years."

Neither had he. The ramifications of that admission were beginning to haunt him. "It's noon. We need a break."

Reese nodded. "I think your son is ready for another bottle." She finished putting the outfits she'd bought into the dresser drawers.

"As soon as I wash my hands, I'll be right back to try out the rocker with him."

When Nick returned a few minutes later he found her putting more things on top of the dresser. Besides a large, colorfully illustrated edition of Winnie the Pooh, plus a leather-bound book that said *Baby's Memories,* she'd added a pacifier, a couple of rattles, some infant painkiller, a baby thermometer, his little brush and a box of tissues.

In an incredibly short period of time she'd written Jamie's signature on the face of his apartment. Now it was *their* home, father and son.

At the thought of what would have happened if he hadn't hired her, he experienced real terror because it had opened up an old window of time. For a moment he'd glimpsed the painful gray emptiness of yesterday. He wanted that window closed forever so he wouldn't have to know those emotions again.

Needing to feel his son's wiggly body, he drew him out of the swing and they sat down in the rocker. Reese had put the bottle of formula next to it. While Nick fed him, she placed a burp cloth over his shoulder. He felt her gaze and could tell something was on that fascinating mind of hers. "I'll be right back."

Before long she returned with her phone and started snapping pictures of him and Jamie, of the room itself. "I'll get these photos made into prints and start his scrapbook. My mom kept one for each of us and I still look at mine. When you get time, give me any photos you'd like to add."

"I'll do that." When he'd separated from Erica, he'd instructed the maids to put the wedding album and photos in the dresser drawer of the bedroom at the other end of the hall.

"While you're at it, if you have his birth certificate and the picture they took of him at the hospital, I could add it," Reese suggested. "There's a family tree in his book where I can put in pictures of you and his mother, and his grandparents. After he's older, he'll pore over them for hours."

Nick smiled as the ideas rolled from her. She seemed to really care about Jamie and his future. She was remarkable.

"Later on I'll see what I can dig up."

"Good." She took one more picture of the stuffed animal in the bed. "We'll call his baby book *The Penthouse at Pooh Corner*."

Nick broke into laughter. He couldn't help it, even though it startled Jamie, who fussed for a minute before settling down again. Her way of putting things was a never-ending source of delight.

In the doorway to the hall she said, "You two deserve some quality time together so I'm going to leave you alone. While you're feeding him, would you mind if I took a tour of your apartment?"

"This is your home for the next three months. I want you to treat it as such."

"Thank you."

Actually Reese's request was an excuse to go back to her room. She'd have all summer to admire the treasures in Nick's home and much preferred to do it when she had the apartment to herself.

The important thing here was to give him time alone with Jamie. Tomorrow he'd have to go back to work. Today was a gift he could enjoy with that adorable little boy who was an absolute dream to take care of.

For the moment she needed to acquaint herself with his kitchen. The disposable bottles of formula the nurse had sent in the diaper bag would be gone in another couple of feedings. Reese had bought the same brand of powdered formula and a set of bottles yesterday. She needed to run them through the dishwasher.

When she reached the fantasy kitchen, she wished Julia Child had been with her so she could hear her go into ecstasy. Now *there* was a chopping block befitting a piece of veal she could slap down and pound the life out of before she turned it into mouthwatering *escalope de veau*.

While Reese was still in a bemused state, the house phone rang. It sounded so loud, she jumped in surprise and hurried to pick it up for fear it would wake Jamie, who was probably asleep by now.

"Hello?"

"Ms. Chamberlain? This is Albert, the concierge."

"Oh, yes. Thank you for your help yesterday, Albert."

"That was quite a collection of things you bought. How's the nursery coming along?"

"We've got it all put together."

"That sounds like Mr. Wainwright. Does the work of ten without thinking about it. I'm calling because his in-laws have arrived and want to come up. Is he available to talk to?"

Reese was pretty sure Nick wasn't expecting anyone, but that wasn't for her to decide. "Just a moment and I'll tell him to pick up the phone." She put the receiver down and hurried through the apartment to the nursery.

The baby had finished his bottle and lay against Nick's shoulder with his little eyelids fluttering. Reese hated to disturb them, but she had no choice. She walked around in front of him. He raised those dark eyes to her face in question.

"Albert is on the phone. He says your in-laws are downstairs and want to come up," she mouthed the words.

Nick brushed his lips against the baby's head before getting to his feet in one lithe male move. "I'll talk to him from the phone in my bedroom."

After he left with Jamie, she walked back to the kitchen. The second she heard Nick's deep voice, she hung up the phone.

The bottles were still waiting. She removed the packaging before loading them in the dishwasher. The lids and nipples fit inside the little basket.

Beneath the kitchen sink she found a box of dishwasher detergent that hadn't been used yet. She undid the seal and poured some in the dispenser. Pretty soon she had the machine going on the wash/dry cycle.

While she waited, she opened the canister of powdered formula and read the directions. Once the items were dry and sterilized, she measured enough instant formula into each, before adding the required amount of water.

Nick chose that moment to bring an attractive, well-dressed older couple into the kitchen. "Sorry. I was just making up Jamie's formula." She wiped her hands with a clean cloth.

Nick's eyes glimmered with some emotion she couldn't put a name to. "No problem. Reese Chamberlain? I'd like you to meet Jamie's grandparents, Anne and Walter Hirst. They wanted to be introduced."

"Of course." She walked over to shake their hands. "It's a pleasure to meet you."

CHAPTER FOUR

REESE had once seen the original oil painting of Grant Wood's *American Gothic* in Chicago. It depicted a farmer and a woman with stern faces standing in front of a white farmhouse. In the man's hand was an upturned pitchfork.

Though Nick's in-laws were good-looking people, they could have been the models for the painting. Mr. Hirst wore an expression of dislike in his eyes as he said hello. She could imagine him coming to life to poke her with his farm implement. His wife remained stiff and mute. Reese felt for the brunette woman who'd lost her daughter so recently. Lines of grief were still visible on both their faces. Pain, pain, pain.

This had to be brutal on Nick, who was still trying to deal with the loss of his wife, too. He shifted Jamie to his other shoulder. Looking at Reese he said, "I explained that the three of us are still getting acquainted. Leave what you're doing and come with us while I show them the nursery."

There was enough authority underlining his words for Reese to know he expected her to join them. Why, she didn't know, but she did his bidding without question.

When they reached the nursery she heard a sudden gasp from Jamie's grandmother.

"What a surprise!" his grandfather said. "Where did your office go?"

"It's dismantled in another bedroom. As you can see, we're coming along thanks to Ms. Chamberlain, so you don't need to be concerned about the baby's welfare. Sit down in the rocking chair and hold Jamie. He just had his bath and a bottle. I doubt he'll be hungry for another couple of hours."

Nick handed her the baby. Reese held her breath, hoping he wouldn't start to cry having to leave Nick's arms. To her relief he just looked up quietly at his grandmother. It was a sweet moment. Jamie had a wonderful nature.

"I'll get a chair from my room for you, Walter." Nick was back in a second. "Now you can enjoy him together." With wooden movements, he sat down next to his wife.

By tacit agreement Reese left the nursery with Nick and they headed for the kitchen. "What can I do to help?"

Aware of his body close to hers, she was all thumbs. "I just need to finish off making up these bottles." Nick found the lids and tops and before long the task was done and eight fresh bottles had been put in the fridge.

"I had a feeling they'd make a surprise visit," he murmured, "but not before tomorrow."

What he meant was, he knew they'd show up when Reese was alone to see how she was handling their grandson. But by their appearance today, it was clear they hadn't been able to wait that long.

"They're missing Jamie," she said. "Who wouldn't? He's as good as gold. Not one tear yet."

Nick nodded. "I know. I've been waiting."

"Not all babies have his wonderful disposition. It should ease your mother-in-law's mind that he's adapting so well to the change in surroundings."

He trapped her gaze. "That's because you haven't given him a chance to get upset. When I put in for a nanny, I never thought Mary Poppins would actually pop inside the limo."

Reese's mouth curved upward. His comment took the chill off the remembered moment when his in-laws had first looked at her as if she was an alien. "I'm afraid there's only one of those."

Better that Nick saw Reese as a fictional character.

Unfortunately she couldn't say the same thing about him. Meeting him had caused her to view him as someone very real and charismatic in spite of his deep sorrow, or maybe even because of it. Not for a second could she afford to forget this was a man who'd just lost his wife. It hadn't even been three months. Reese needed to focus on Jamie and nothing else.

"To be honest, I was afraid I'd pop in that limo and find Captain Von Trapp surrounded by seven precocious children all needing individual attention at the same time."

His low laughter rang in the spacious confines of the modern kitchen. No matter how hard she fought against it, the pleasing masculine sound connected to every atom in her body. She caught Nick's gaze and something intense passed between them, stealing Reese's breath.

"Nick?" Both of them turned in the direction of his mother-in-law's voice. The interruption had spoiled a conversation she'd been enjoying, and something else had passed between them, too, that Reese wasn't prepared to think about just yet. "We'd like to talk to you for a minute please."

Her brittle words expressed in that demanding tone meant she'd heard them laughing together. Reese feared it had been like an affront to her sensibilities. This was awful. Nick shouldn't have come into the kitchen with her.

"Of course, Anne." He glanced back at Reese. "Excuse me. Why don't you call down and order sandwiches and salad for us. Have them set up our lunch on the terrace. Cesar knows what I like."

"All right." Reaching for the phone, she gave Nick's order to the kitchen and asked them to add a pot of coffee. The waiter was to bring their lunch up to the patio table.

Relieved to be alone at last, Reese tidied away the things she'd used in the kitchen until it was once again spotless, then she walked out to the terrace, the only safe place in the apartment at the moment. While she waited for the food to come, she looked through the telescope. Once she'd made some adjustments, she had a bird's-eye view of one part of the Big Apple. Starting tomorrow she'd take Jamie out exploring in the stroller. Central Park was only two blocks away.

Last year she and Pam had come to New York for a few days on the train, but they'd been short on time and money. They'd ended up seeing one Broadway show and spent two days visiting the Metropolitan Museum of Art. That was it. The equivalent of a grain of sand in the middle of the Sahara.

"Ms. Chamberlain?" She lifted her head from the

eyepiece and discovered a uniformed waiter with dark hair transferring plates from a cart to the table. His black eyes played over her with obvious male interest. He was probably in his early twenties. "I know I haven't seen you before. I'm Toni."

"Hello."

"I understand you're the new nanny."

"That's right."

"I work here Thursdays through the weekend."

"Do you like it?"

He grinned. "I do now. If you want anything, call down to the kitchen when I'm on duty and ask for me."

"I believe we have everything we need," a deep, masculine voice answered for her. Nick had come out on the terrace, surprising both of them. He had an aura that could be intimidating. Just now he sounded vaguely dismissive.

"Good afternoon, Mr. Wainwright." Toni took hold of the cart and left the terrace without delay.

"Was he bothering you, Reese?"

She shook her head. "He was being friendly. That's all." She walked over to the table with its large white umbrella and sat down beneath it. "Are your in-laws still here?"

He took a seat opposite her. "No. After Jamie went to sleep, they left to meet friends for lunch. Otherwise I would have invited them to have a meal with us."

"Do you think this visit has helped them?"

Nick took the covers off their dishes. She hadn't had a club sandwich in years. "I'm sure it didn't, but there wasn't anything they could voice a complaint about.

It's apparent that with you here, everything's under control."

But Reese knew they *had* made scathing remarks about her. If the looks Mrs. Hirst had given Reese in the kitchen could inflict damage, she would have been vaporized in an instant.

"Earlier Walter told me Anne was…fragile," Nick added, as if he were choosing his words carefully. "After the way they both behaved today, I can see they're still not happy with the idea of my bringing Jamie home. I should have made the break sooner."

Reese sensed he was in a brooding mood. "It's hard to make decisions when you're grieving."

"You have some knowledge of it?" He'd posed the mild question while devouring his sandwich.

"My fiancé and I broke up at Christmas. It hit me very hard, but I couldn't compare it to your loss. When you have a child born into the world, you don't expect to have to carry on without your wife."

A bleak look entered his eyes. "Erica was in good health until she went into the hospital. Her labor wasn't normal. By the time she got there, the placenta had torn and she'd lost too much blood faster than they could replenish it. The doctor performed a Cesarian before Jamie got into trouble."

"Thank heaven for that," she whispered. "He's a little angel."

He studied her through a veiled gaze. "Does that mean you're not ready to back out of our contract yet?"

"If you knew me better, you'd realize I'd never do that, but I'm assuming your in-laws don't have much faith in me. From their perspective I suppose it's understandable."

"I'm very pleased you're here to help with Jamie, so let's not worry about them. As you said, when a person is in mourning, their emotions are in turmoil. Nothing would help them but to have Erica back."

Nick was talking about himself, too, obviously. Reese didn't know how he was functioning. The best thing to do was change the subject.

"I've been thinking. How do you feel about my taking Jamie out and about in the stroller tomorrow? Just short little forays at first. Depending on how he does, maybe longer ones."

"That's fine. Later today we'll program your cell phone so you can call me or Paul at any time. When you want to take Jamie farther afield, arrange it with him. He'll drive you to spots where you can explore to your heart's content. I'll give you a remote to the penthouse to keep all the time. All I ask is that you check in with Albert coming and going. It's for your safety."

In other words, with Nick's kind of money he would be a natural target if someone decided to arrange a kidnapping. Only now was she beginning to realize what an enormous responsibility she'd taken on. "I'll be extremely careful with him, Nick."

"I have no doubt of it." He finished his salad. "I'll open a bank account for you first thing in the morning so you'll have funds to draw on."

"Thank you."

"We haven't discussed your hours yet. If I can depend on you Monday through Friday until five every day, then you can be free to do as you wish the rest of the time. How does that sound?"

Incredibly generous. "I couldn't ask for a more perfect arrangement. But please feel free to depend on me if something comes up in the evening or on a weekend and you need my help."

"If that should happen, I'll pay you overtime."

"That won't be necessary. Being allowed to live here in such luxury with all my meals paid for is like another salary in itself. I wouldn't dream of taking more money than we agreed on." She helped herself to the salad.

An amused gleam entered those dark eyes. To her chagrin her pulse sped up. The phenomenon kept happening the more she was around him. "Since we have that settled, are there any questions you want to ask me?"

"There's only one I can think of right now. Do you know when Jamie's supposed to go in for his next checkup?"

"The nurse indicated he saw the doctor three weeks ago. I'm going to be taking him to a new pediatrician here in the city named Dr. Wells. I'll give him a ring tomorrow and find out when he wants to see him. They'll send for his records right away."

"I think that's wise in case he needs another immunization soon."

He sat back in the chair to drink his coffee. One of the first things she'd noticed in the limo yesterday was that he didn't wear a wedding ring. In one way she thought it odd because his wife's death had been so recent. On the other hand, maybe he'd never worn one, or possibly he didn't like rings of any kind. *And maybe you're thinking about him way too much for your own good.*

"If there's anything you want to do for the rest of the afternoon, take advantage of the time, Reese. I plan to get a little work done around here and do a few laps in the pool."

"How can you do any work when your office is in shambles?"

A chuckle escaped his throat. "I'll worry about it later."

"The mess will still be there later. Why don't we tackle the other bedroom while Jamie's out for the count? I'll feel much better if we set it up for you. Don't forget I'm the one who managed to get everything knocked out of whack. Kind of like the little kid who comes along and destroys the puzzle you just put together."

His haunting smile turned her heart over. "Okay, let's get busy." He rose to his tall, imposing height. "But when we're through, I'll take care of Jamie until I leave for work in the morning."

"He'll be thrilled with all your attention."

Hurrying ahead of him, she walked through the apartment to peek on the baby, who was fast asleep. He looked so precious with his arms and legs spread out, his little hands formed into fists.

"Not a care in the world," Nick murmured near her ear, surprising her. She could feel the warmth from his hard body. For a moment she had the urge to lean into him and cling. Almost dizzy from unbidden longings, she turned away. But in the next instant she spied a glint of pain in those dark orbs and despised herself for being so aware of him when his thoughts had absolutely nothing to do with her.

Leaving them alone, she rushed out of the nursery and down the hall to the other bedroom. The room was a vision of white and café-au-lait with an exquisite white lace throw over the down-filled duvet.

White lace curtains hung at the huge window that gave out on a fabulous view of the city. There was a love seat with a jacquard design in the same colors and a white rug with a deep pile in a geometric design of coffee and beige.

When Nick came in she said, "This is a beautiful room. Luckily it's big enough to accommodate everything if we move the love seat against that other wall. What would you think if we put your desk in front of the window where you can look out? If it gets too bright you can always draw the sheers.

"And on the left here we'll set up your computer system. Keep in mind that if you get tired, you only have to take a few steps to the bed."

His hands went to his hips in a purely male stance. He glanced around at all his state-of-the-art equipment without saying anything. She wandered over to the window and looked out while she waited for him to make a decision.

"I've got a better idea." Reese turned to him, curious to hear what he had to say. She felt his penetrating glance. "I'm going to give up having an office altogether and work from a laptop in my bedroom when I'm forced to."

"I don't understand." She was incredulous.

"There are only so many hours in the day. If I can't accomplish what I need to do at the office, then I'll turn it over to someone else. I have my son to think about now." His explanation sounded more like a declaration, as if his mind had been somewhere else. "Please feel free to enjoy the rest of your day. I'm going out to the pool."

Reese had been dismissed. Now that their business was concluded, naturally he had other plans that didn't include her. Silly how bereft she felt.

Needing to shake the feeling, Reese went to her bedroom to start studying. But an hour later she realized she'd been going over the same section of work a dozen times and nothing was sinking in. All she could think of was a pair of dark eyes that set her heart rate fluttering.

What she needed was a good walk in the park to clear her head.

"Albert?" Nick approached the front desk at three in the afternoon. "Has Ms. Chamberlain gone out with Jamie yet?" It was Friday. He'd turned over some work for one of the office staffers to finish up so he could come home early and spend it with Jamie.

"She left maybe a half hour ago."

"Thank you."

Disappointment crept through him because it wasn't only his son he'd been longing to see. All week he'd found himself watching the clock. When it was a quarter to five, he'd called Paul to be out in front of the building to drive him home. Today he couldn't take it any longer and knew he had raised eyebrows when he'd taken off from work two hours before time.

He realized that their constant togetherness over those first two days had spoiled him. Now, Nick missed talking to Reese. She was the most alive woman he'd ever met. Intelligent. Her conversation stimulated him and there was no question Jamie adored her.

Since he had no legitimate reason to prevent her from doing what she wanted with her spare time, he usually took his son up on the roof to the gym and worked out in front of him.

Throughout the week she hadn't called down to the

kitchen for dinner once. That gave him no opening to join her. Apparently she liked fixing her own food and ate before he arrived, frustrating him no end.

Not able to take it any longer, he broke his own rule and phoned her. She answered on the fourth ring. "Hello, Nick? Are you phoning from your office?"

Her voice sounded tentative, if not a trifle anxious. He brushed aside the thought that he knew her voice so well already, knew how she was feeling simply from the tone of it. He had to remind himself that as much as he enjoyed Reese's company, she was only temporary in his and Jamie's life.

"No. Where are you and Jamie?"

"At the park. Is anything wrong?"

He sucked in his breath because it seemed there had to be some kind of emergency in order for him to be with her at a different time than the schedule dictated. The schedule *you* established, Wainwright!

"I was able to tie up work early and decided to spend the rest of the day with my son."

"I'll come right home then."

"That won't be necessary. Tell me where to find you."

Nick heard her hesitation. He didn't know if it was because she wasn't sure of her exact location, or if she didn't want his company. If it was the latter, was it because she was afraid to be alone with him? In his gut he knew she wasn't indifferent to him, but maybe she didn't want the relationship between them to move to a more personal level. He knew it would be a mistake to blur the lines between them, but Nick was becoming more and more enchanted with Reese.

He grimaced when he thought she might be in contact

with her ex-fiancé. Was it possible she still had feelings for him? Nick had too many questions for which there were no answers yet.

"We're in front of the Sweet Café watching the sailboats."

"Don't leave. I'll see you shortly."

Once he'd hung up, he shrugged out of his suit and changed into more casual clothes. To save time, he had Paul drop him off near the east rim of the pond.

A mild breeze kept the sun from being too hot. Tourists and locals came here in any kind of weather, but there were more people than usual milling about this afternoon. Quite a few of them were pushing children in prams and strollers. Nick scanned the area looking for Reese's ponytail. She didn't appear to be around.

One knockout blonde with hair attractively tangled caught his eye over by the water where she was examining one of the sailboats. She wore a filmy layered top in blues and greens over a pair of jeans defining womanly hips. Her slender yet rounded body reminded him of someone. He moved closer and suddenly his heart pounded with ferocity because he saw Jamie in the stroller in front of her.

"Reese?"

She whipped around, causing her wavy ash-blond hair to swish against the top of her shoulders. The change of hairstyle had thrown him. He couldn't decide which one he liked better. Her hair had the kind of texture he'd love to work his fingers into.

At first glance her eyes flickered, causing them to reflect the blue off the water. They seemed to search his for a long moment before she averted them and leaned over to pull Jamie out of his seat.

"Look who's here." The second Jamie saw Nick, he grew more animated and squirmed to reach him. "You know your daddy all right." Reese gave a gentle laugh as she handed him over.

Nick kissed his son, rocking him for a minute while he enjoyed the smell of her flowery scent on the baby's cheeks and neck. "Have you missed me today? I know I've missed you." He pressed a kiss to Jamie's tummy, provoking more smiles and laughter.

Today she'd put him in the green suit with the grouper fish on the front. In his tiny white socks and white high-tops, the picture he made tugged at Nick's heart. He was proud to claim him and grateful for the meticulous care Reese took of him.

He flicked his gaze to her. "Have you walked to the north end to see the Alice in Wonderland statue?"

She nodded. "It's wonderful. I particularly loved the Mad Hatter. I can't wait until Jamie's old enough t—" She stopped midsentence. He found it fascinating how an unexpected flush spilled into her cheeks.

"To *what*?" he prodded, already knowing the answer.

"I have a tendency to run on sometimes. Obviously I won't be around when he's older…it's just sometimes difficult to think about not seeing this little one grow up." Nick was gratified to find her this attached to Jamie already. In truth, for the past week he'd been imagining a future that included the three of them. Since the moment he'd brought her to the penthouse, he'd been happier than he'd ever been in his life.

He couldn't pin it down to any one thing or moment. All he knew was that she was on his mind to the point it was interfering with his concentration at the office. "Let's grab a bite while we're here. Have you eaten?"

"I hadn't planned to until we got back to the penthouse."

"Are you hungry?"

"I have to admit a salad and lemonade would hit the spot." No doubt she kept her expenses down by not spending money on food.

"I'm hungrier than that." Since the advent of Reese in his life, his appetite had grown. Food tasted better. The sky looked bluer. When he woke up in the morning, the world seemed filled with new possibilities. He looked down at his son. "What about you, sport?"

Reese answered for him. "I'm sure he wouldn't turn down a bottle. It's warm out here."

With Jamie against his shoulder, Nick pushed the stroller. Together they made their way to an empty table and sat down beneath the umbrella, welcoming the shade. As he looked around, it dawned on him he hadn't been here in years. He'd been so busy making money for the brokerage, this part of life had passed him by completely.

"Here's a bottle for him." Reese handed him a burp cloth, too.

"Thank you." His breath caught when their eyes met. "The waiter's coming over. Will you order me a steak sandwich and coffee while I feed Jamie?"

The baby nestled in his arm, eager for his formula. He was hungry and virtually inhaled it, then let out several burps loud enough to bring some other diners' heads around with a smile.

Laughter bubbled out of Reese. He loved hearing it.

"Your son would be welcome in some parts of the world where it's polite to burp after a good meal."

He continued to rub Jamie's back in order to get out all the air. By the time his eyes fluttered closed, their food had arrived. Nick lowered him into the stroller and put the canopy down to shield him from the sun.

While Reese ate her salad, he attacked his sandwich. "Did I tell you I'm taking him to his grandparents in the morning?"

She nodded. "I bet they can't wait to see him."

"Next time I'll take you with us."

A shadow crossed over her lovely face. "Why would you do that?"

"For one reason, you'll be ready for a change of scenery. For another, Jamie is already attached to you. Another week of enjoying your exclusive attention and he'll have a hard time being separated for a whole day. With you along to reassure him, things will go better." He could tell by the shadows in her eyes she was worried about it.

"Don't be concerned. You'll be free to walk around certain parts of the grounds. Hirst Hollow is open to the public on Saturdays. You'll be enchanted with the flower gardens."

Reese finished her lemonade. He could practically see her mind taking it all in, working up a protest. After she put her glass down, she didn't disappoint him. "No matter what, your mother-in-law won't be enchanted to see the nanny along for the ride, especially this nanny!"

"Anne's going to have to get used to it. You're an integral part of my household."

"But Jamie doesn't come from a normal household."

"Go on," Nick urged, drinking the rest of his coffee. He was curious to hear the words she was getting ready to spout from lips he suddenly realized he'd love to taste.

"You don't really want me to spell it out."

"You're wrong," he fired back. "I'm fascinated by everything you have to say on the subject."

"If I told you, it could be taken as an insult, and that's the last thing I would want to do when I've been given a dream job."

"At least do me the courtesy of telling me how my son's home is *not* normal. I have to work, and I need someone to look after Jamie—what's wrong with that?"

He was prepared to hear that he made the kind of money that separated him from the masses, but she said something else instead—something that touched on that painful area of his soul no one else knew about or understood.

"In the short time I've worked for you, I've learned that Jamie is a Hirst and a Wainwright, two blue-blooded American families."

"You mean we only breathe the rarified atmosphere of the elite upper class from England going back several hundred years? You're right, Ms. Chamberlain. Someone put it much better than I could. 'In our world men were better than women, horses better than dogs, and Harvard better than anything.'"

Her cheeks turned to flame, but she held his gaze. "I should never have brought this up."

"Why not? It's the truth. Did you know the

Wainwrights have had horses on Long Island going back at least two hundred years? Nothing's more important than pedigree and belonging to the right clubs. Not even marriages have as much significance as long as the principles belong to that exclusive world where the women provide the decoration.

"Everyone has rank, some higher than others. One is aware of his social placement at all times. That's only the outer shell we're talking about. Unlike the soft meat of the crab, their inner stuffing is even harder. It blinds them to the loving and understanding of their own children."

As he spoke, emotion darkened her eyes.

"Erica's and my family share an ancestry that has been in love with itself for generations. They've continued to hone the 'right' way to do things to a fine art while at the same time distancing their offspring by their criticism and lack of affection."

He heard Reese's sharp intake of breath before she said, "For that very reason certain things aren't done, like hiring an unsuitable nanny, someone like me."

"Correct. The way you hug and kiss Jamie all the time, you're probably the most unsuitable nanny in existence, which makes you perfect for the job."

Her delicately arched brows knit together. "That sounded like a declaration of war."

"War…divorce… Ultimately they're the same thing. It's time the cycle of neglect ended, starting with Jamie."

"So you're using me for a guinea pig?"

Nick nodded without shame.

"Mrs. Tribe mentioned that you'd be hiring another nanny in the fall. What about her?"

"Since my mother-in-law was the one who arranged for her in the first place, I'll let her fix the mistake. Barbara Cosgriff's another blue blood. She and Anne make up part of a very elite circle. The Cosgriffs won't be in need of their nanny by September, therefore, they're delighted to do this favor for my mother-in-law, who spoke for me without my permission, something she's good at doing."

"So whom do you plan to hire?"

"I'm not sure of anything yet, but it goes without saying that whoever she is, she'll be entirely unsuitable."

A small sad smile broke the corner of Reese's wide mouth. "You're a clever man gaining my sympathy so I'll be a willing accomplice."

"Let's just say that for Jamie's sake, I'd like your help. Are you with me on this?"

Her gaze darted to the baby, who was just starting to wake up. She let out a troubled sigh. "You're my employer. I need this job and I love Jamie, so I'll do my best for you."

Nick ignored the little dart he felt when she referred to him as her employer. He hoped she might be inclined to do it for him. Shaking this off, he pulled out his wallet and put some bills on the table. "You have another full week before I force you to face the dragon. Put the thought away until you have to deal with her."

"That's not so easy to do."

"But possible. Remember I've had longer practice at this than you." He stood up. "If you'll push the stroller, I'll carry Jamie back to the car. He loves his bath so much, I think I'll take him for a little swim and see how he does. Have you been swimming yet?"

She hurried to keep up with him. "I don't have a suit."

"But you *can* swim?"

"Yes."

"In my teens I did a lot of sailing. It's a sport I'd like to do with my son. If he's going to share that love with me, then he needs to start getting used to the water. Already he feels safe with you. The next time you go out with Jamie, buy yourself one. Consider it your uniform and put it on my account."

If she wanted to squirm her way out of that, *too bad.*

CHAPTER FIVE

On Saturday, Reese tried to study, but finally gave up. With Nick and Jamie gone from the penthouse, she was at a totally loose end. After fixing herself a sandwich for lunch, she took off for Macy's at Herald Square.

The crowded ten-story department store contained everything including the unimaginable. One would have to be here days to see it all. She ended up spending hours walking around. Eventually she found some swimsuits on sale for her and Jamie.

With Father's Day coming up, she shipped her dad a small framed picture of New York showing Park Avenue. She slipped in a note telling him to hang it in his office.

While she was looking at the toys, she discovered a wooden hand-painted toy sailboat in sky-blue with a white canvas sail Jamie could give his father. It was the perfect size to fit on a desk or a dresser. The artist on hand personalized it on the keel for her with quick-drying black paint. *The Flying NJ.* When it was finished, she asked the salesgirl to gift wrap it.

Since she was in the right place, she purchased some doughnut toys and a colorful octopus that played classical music when you touched the tentacles. By the time she got back to the apartment, it was after seven.

As she turned down the hall to her bedroom, she almost bumped into Nick. "Oh—I didn't realize you were home." Her pulse raced out of control to see him standing there in tan trousers and a midnight-blue silk shirt. He looked and smelled marvelous.

His dark eyes took swift inventory of her in her jeans and layered top. "Looks like you've been having fun. Is there a bikini inside one of those bags?"

Her cheeks grew warm for no reason. "Yes, among other things."

"I hope you put everything on my account."

Reese shook her head. "Not today. Excuse me while I put them away."

He rubbed his hard jaw. "I don't know about you, but I haven't had dinner yet. Paul is going to drive us to Nolia's in Greenwich Village. The salmon and sea bass are to die for."

She bit her lip. He obviously needed to unwind after being with his in-laws. "Won't it make too long a day for Jamie?"

"He's staying in tonight. Rita, one of the maids who's been working here a long time, is going to take care of him while we're gone. I'm expecting her any minute."

Reese took a shaky breath. Going out to dinner with Nick alone wasn't part of her nanny job, but as the thought of turning down his offer entered her mind, she realized that she wanted to be with him so badly, she felt an ache to the palms of her hands.

"What should I wear?"

"Anything you feel like."

In other words, formal dress wasn't required. She was hot and sticky and needed a shower first.

"Don't take too long. I'm starving," he said in a husky tone.

She'd been hungry when she'd walked in the door, but with those words her stomach had too many butterflies to know what she was feeling. "I'll hurry."

Ten minutes later she joined him in the foyer wearing a sleeveless dress with a rounded neck in an all-over black-on-white print. The summery outfit could be dressed up or down depending on her accessories. After brushing out her ponytail, she'd caught her hair back at the nape with a black chiffon scarf and slipped on low black heels.

When Nick saw her, the unmistakable glimmer in his eyes set a tone for the rest of the evening, making her feel feverish throughout their delicious dinner. A live jazz band prompted Nick to dance with her. He drew the eyes of every woman, young or old.

She thought of Cinderella, who got her chance to be spun around the castle ballroom with her prince. But in that childhood fairy tale, the author never described the feelings running riot inside the scullery maid who for one night had been transformed into a princess. The adult thoughts and desires of a woman weren't meant to be read by dreamy-eyed little girls.

Nick had told Reese he wanted her to experience some nightlife while she was in his employ. In her naïveté she'd given in to that temptation and thought she could handle it, but if he pulled her against his hard-muscled body one more time he'd feel her trembling.

"You're a wonderful dancer, Reese."

"Thank you. So are you."

"I could do this all night," he murmured near her ear.

Don't say another word, Nick. "If I hadn't walked around Macy's all afternoon, there's nothing I'd like more."

"I forgot about that. You should have said something sooner. We'll go."

Ever the consummate host who went out of his way to make her comfortable, they left the restaurant and rode back to the apartment in the limo. The maid was there to meet them.

"Jamie never made a peep."

"Thank you, Rita."

"Anytime." Her brown eyes flicked to Reese with interest before she left the penthouse.

When the door closed, Reese looked up at her incredibly handsome escort. "Thank you for a lovely evening, Nick. I must be the luckiest nanny in New York with the nicest employer and the sweetest little boy."

His eyes were veiled as he smiled at her. "We'll have to do it again."

No, no.

"Lest you've forgotten, Cinderella only had one night at the ball. It wouldn't do for the hired help to expect a repeat with the prince. Good night, Nick."

Reese left for her bedroom having meant what she'd said. To lose her head over this man when she was being paid to do a job for him would bring heartache—the kind she instinctively knew she would never recover from.

For the rest of the week she made certain she and Jamie were there to greet him when he walked through the door of the penthouse, but that was all. Once she'd told him about Jamie's day and answered any questions he had, she disappeared to get going on her studies.

On the following Friday she was studying on her laptop when she heard Jamie's distinct cry through the baby monitor. He hadn't built up to it. One minute it was quiet in the room. In the next, he'd let go as if he'd awakened with a nightmare, or was in pain.

He'd only been down for an hour since his one-o'clock bottle. She slid off the bed and rushed across the hall to the nursery. Alarmed to see him in so much distress, she picked him up to comfort him.

"Uh-oh—you're hot." She walked over to the dresser with him to get the thermometer. To date his health had been so perfect, she'd almost taken it for granted.

"Hmm…101.4. That's not good. Let's check to see what's going on." When she undid his stretchy outfit and diaper, she discovered he'd had diarrhea. "Oh—you've got a stomachache." She got him all clean again and put him in a fresh diaper and a shirt.

For the next hour she walked him around the apartment on her shoulder, singing every song she could remember to comfort him. He remained restless and whimpered, then let out another heartrending cry before she felt him have another loose movement.

Back she went to the nursery and cleaned him up once more. This time she applied some rash cream so he wouldn't get sore. When she picked him up again, he burrowed into her neck, still feeling hot.

Without hesitation she carried him to her bedroom and phoned Nick on her cell. This was the first time she'd called him at his office since coming to work for him. Though she hated disturbing him, she knew he'd want to be told.

"Reese?" He picked up on the third ring. "Is there a problem?"

"I'm glad you answered. Jamie's come down with diarrhea and is running a temperature of 101. He's going to need fluids to lower it, but I'm not sure what the doctor would prescribe."

"I'll phone Dr. Wells right now. How long has Jamie been sick? When I left him this morning, he seemed fine."

"I know. He woke up crying in the middle of his afternoon nap. My sister Carrie uses Pedialyte when her baby gets dehydrated, so ask the doctor about that. Since we don't have any on hand, I'll give him some water for now."

"I'm on my way out the door," he declared in a decisive tone. "I'd planned to come home early anyway." Secretly she was relieved. Normally Nick hid his emotions well, but this was his little boy who was ill. He must be as nervous as she was, if not more so. "While you try to get more liquid down him, I'll call the doctor then stop by the drugstore."

"Good."

"I'll be home soon."

After she hung up, she went to the kitchen for a bottle and filled it with cool water. Jamie seemed eager enough to drink, but by the time she reached the nursery and fed him a little, he threw up.

She put him in the crib and changed his clothes for a second time. His temp had climbed another tenth of a degree. She wet a cloth and sponged his forehead and cheeks.

Before long Nick entered the penthouse. "Reese?"

"In the nursery."

As he came through the door, Jamie threw up once more. It frightened him so much he started crying harder. After she'd wiped off his mouth, Nick pulled him out of her arms and cuddled him against his chest. "Hey, sport—what happened to you?"

Her gaze fused with Nick's. "Did you reach the doctor?"

"His nurse said he'd call me back. In the meantime we're to try and get liquids down him in small increments."

"I've been doing that, but after a minute, up it comes. It must be some kind of flu."

"Maybe the Pedialyte will stay down." Nick kissed his forehead. "The nurse said it was good to use. I got him cherry. He's a lucky little guy you're here for him."

Nick was always ready to praise her. It made her want to do everything right in his eyes. "I'll take it to the kitchen and put some in a sterile bottle." When she returned to the nursery Nick told her the doctor had called. "We're to keep a close eye on him. If we can't get anything to stay down, we're to take him to emergency. The hospital will keep him informed."

She nodded. By evening he'd thrown up enough times to convince her this was serious. His temperature never dropped. "He seems too lethargic."

Lines marred Nick's face. "Let's take him to the hospital. I'll tell Paul to bring the car around."

"While you hold him, I'll put some things in the diaper bag for him."

In a short time they left the penthouse. Paul drove them to the E.R. entrance and they hurried inside with Jamie lying limp against his daddy's shoulder.

One of the emergency-room staff showed them to a

cubicle. Right after that another person came inside the curtain. His tag said he was Dr. Marsh. He got to work checking the baby's vital signs. "How long has he been sick?"

Jamie didn't like being examined. His cries wrenched Reese's heart. "Since about two o'clock. It came on so fast I couldn't believe it. We've tried to get liquids down him, but he just spits it up and hasn't urinated for several hours."

"We'll have to culture him to find out if this infection is bacterial, but I'd say he's picked up Rotavirus."

"What is it exactly?" Nick's features had darkened in anxiety.

"A disease of the bowel that causes diarrhea and vomiting. Most children have had several incidences of it by the time they're five."

"How would he have gotten it?"

"It's transmitted several ways, but I would imagine your son picked it up through the air. Someone's cough could have spread it. It's highly contagious."

"I've heard it's serious—" Reese blurted.

"It can be when left untreated. If I'm right, we'll put him in isolation and hydrate him with an IV to bring back his body's salt and fluid levels to normal. He should get through this just fine."

Should? She and Nick shared a panicked glance.

"Who's your pediatrician?"

"Dr. Hebert Wells."

"In a minute a team will come in to take a blood sample. When we know for sure what we're dealing with, we'll call him. If it's bacterial, your doctor will treat him with an antibiotic."

Reese hugged her arms to her waist in agitation.

"What more could we have done to have prevented this?"

The doctor eyed her with compassion. "As long as you're constantly washing your hands before and after you attend to your baby, that's pretty much all you can do." Jamie wasn't *her* baby, but she loved the sound of it.

"Reese has been very careful about that," Nick interjected. "I need to do it more often."

"Washing hands can prevent all kinds of illnesses."

Nick's lips tightened. "If an IV is called for, where will you insert it—he's so small?" He'd taken the question right out of her mouth.

"The IV team will decide, but probably in his foot. It hurts for a minute, but then it's over." Reese shared another worried glance with Nick.

"Go ahead and hold your baby until one of the staff shows you to the isolation area."

As the doctor left the cubicle, Nick reached for Jamie. Once he was back in his father's strong arms, he quieted down a little bit, but clearly he was miserable. Reese smoothed her hand over the back of his head. "You're all wiped out, aren't you, sweetheart."

"We're both here—" Nick talked to his son in a low, comforting tone "—and you're going to get feeling better soon."

Reese wanted to believe it, too, but she'd heard the underlying concern in his voice and was scared to death herself because the illness had robbed Jamie of his vitality.

In a minute someone came and took them through double doors to a restricted area where they were set up in a private room. Jamie cried some more. "I think he wants you, Reese." Nick handed the baby to her.

She hugged Jamie close and sang to him. The music kept him somewhat calm. When she lifted her eyes to Nick, she caught a look of such pain in his, it shattered her.

Something in his expression told Reese that Nick was thinking about his wife and how he'd lost her so quickly after they'd reached the hospital. In the two weeks she'd known Nick, he'd never talked about her except to explain how she'd died. Reese refused to consider the possibility that he was worrying his son would be taken from him, too, in so short a time.

"Nothing's going to happen to Jamie," she assured him with her heart in her throat. "You heard the doctor. Everyone's had Rotavirus in their lives. Even the two of us, and we're alive and healthy, right?" She flashed him a coaxing smile.

Reese wasn't destined to hear what he would have said back because two technicians came into the cubicle wearing masks. Jamie didn't like that and turned his head into her neck.

The taller one said, "If Mom and Dad will step outside the curtain, we'll get this over with quick." He reached for the baby Reese had to give up, but it killed her because Jamie cried out in protest.

"It's okay, sport," Nick assured him. "We'll be right outside." He reached for Reese's hand and led her beyond the curtain. She knew he wasn't thinking as he drew her along with him, but a sensation of warmth traveled up her arm into her body. He didn't let go the whole time Jamie cried. With both their emotions raw, the feel of his hand gripping hers gave her the strength to deal with this crisis.

The technician had called them Mom and Dad. Right now she couldn't imagine feeling any different if Jamie were her son. She loved that baby with every fiber of her being.

All these years she'd planned for a career, not realizing what it meant to love a child like she loved Jamie. The bond with him was so strong, it tore her apart to think of leaving him right now. When the day came that she had children of her own, how would she be able to leave them?

What if she *were* his mother and had to get back to her job of running a company? She couldn't see it, not when Jamie needed her and Nick so desperately.

Together they stood having to endure his frightened cries. "For the last two weeks he's only been with the two of *us,*" she whispered. "He's not used to anyone else."

In a minute the team left and another masked team showed up with their cart. "Stay where you are. This won't take us long."

Nick squeezed her hand gently before letting it go. She presumed their arrival made him realize he'd been holding on to hers all that time. Reese wished he wouldn't have relinquished it. Without that physical connection, she was snatched back from her fantasy about being Jamie's mother. Nick had been part of that fantasy, too. The three of them, a family. How was she ever going to say goodbye to them when the time came?

Deep in turmoil, she heard the baby let out a yelping cry like the one she'd heard through the monitor. They'd just jabbed him, she was sure of it, the poor darling. In reaction she smoothed her hands nervously over jean-clad hips.

It had been hours since she'd looked in a mirror. At least her hair was back in a ponytail and not messy. When they'd left for the hospital, she'd been in too alarmed a state to think about changing out of the jade-colored T-shirt she'd put on to study. But none of that mattered with Jamie lying there feverish and sick.

"They're taking a hell of a long time in there," Nick muttered.

Reese bit her lip. "It seems that way to me, too."

"At this rate he's going to think he's been abandoned."

"But he won't remember once it's over."

"I'm not so sure of that." Something in his tone told her that wasn't idle talk. She wanted to ask him what he meant, but one of the team came outside the curtain with the cart, preventing further conversation.

"You can go back in now. We've attached his foot to a pad for protection. You can hold him all you want, just be mindful of the tubing."

She and Nick hurried back inside to rescue his howling child, but were met by the other technician. "Wash your hands first, then put on the sterile gloves from the container on the wall. After you've done that, wear the masks we've left on the counter. Do this every time you leave the cubicle for any reason until the doctor tells you if your baby has Rotavirus or not. Dispose of everything in the bin inside the bathroom here. Leave through the other door that leads into the hallway."

"Thank you," they both said at the same time.

Once they were alone, Reese urged Nick to wash first. "Jamie needs you." Though everything in her screamed to pick up the baby, he wasn't her son and it wasn't her place.

The warning Reese's mother had given her about not getting too attached to the baby had gone by the wayside the first time she'd laid eyes on Jamie. The beautiful boy had caught at her heartstrings. After meeting his father, Reese knew why. Now—after loving and playing with him over the past two weeks—there were so many heartstrings being pulled by both Wainwrights, she realized she was in terrible trouble.

Once they were washed, gloved and masked, they spent the next hour taking turns holding him while they tried everything to settle him down. Finally he fell asleep and Nick lowered him to the crib.

"He's not in pain right now, Nick."

"We can be thankful for that small mercy at least."

"You look exhausted. This is going to be an all-night vigil. Why don't you slip out and grab a bite to eat in the cafeteria first. When you come back, I'll go get something. I'd rather it was you he woke up to later."

Nick's eyes looked fierce above the mask. "He wants you just as much." Her heart pounded dangerously, but it wasn't from hunger or fatigue. "I don't know what we'd do without you."

She knew the waiting was getting to him, but the more he kept telling her that, the more she wanted to believe it. "Hurry, before he wakes up looking for you."

"All right, but I won't be long." He disappeared into the bathroom and shut the door. Reese walked over to the crib and looked down at the dear little boy she'd been privileged to take care of so far.

When Reese had helped her mom with her baby sister, she'd only been fourteen. Though she'd loved Emma, she couldn't compare the feelings and emotions that filled Reese now. Jeremy had riddled her with accusations about being a cold woman who put a career above the feelings a *normal* woman possessed.

If he could see into her heart and soul right now, he would discover Reese was more than normal, and Jamie wasn't even her son!

After consuming a sandwich and a piece of pie in record time, Nick left the cafeteria and walked outside the hospital doors. He had a phone call to make, but cell phones weren't permitted inside. His father-in-law answered.

"Nick?"

"Sorry to call you this late, Walter, but I thought you should know I won't be able to bring Jamie to White Plains tomorrow."

There was a long silence. "Anne predicted right about you."

He took a fortifying breath. "Jamie's in the hospital with a bad flu bug of some kind. They'll be keeping him overnight. Depending on what's wrong after the tests come back, he might be here tomorrow night, as well. I'll keep you posted and we'll plan to bring him to White Plains next weekend instead."

"What kind of flu?" Anne demanded. She'd picked up on another house phone the minute Walter had told her who was calling.

"We don't know yet."

"This never happened when he was with us."

Nick was sorry she'd come on the line. This was exactly what he'd hoped to avoid. "Every child gets it, Anne. The point is, he's receiving excellent care. I have to go back to him now. Tomorrow I'll let you know how he's doing. Good night."

He hung up. It was automatic for him to check his voice messages. To his surprise there was one from his father. While his parents were traveling, they never called him. Out of curiosity more than filial duty, he clicked on.

"Nicholas? This is your father." Nick shook his head because that was the way he always started out any phone call to him. The distance between them continued to widen. "Your mother and I are back on Long Island. I came in the office and discovered you'd already gone home. Stan tells me you've got the boy with you at the penthouse. Why you would do that baffles me and could prove to be very unwise. We ran into the Ridgeways while we were vacationing in Cannes. They'll be back next week with their daughter Jennifer who's been staying with friends in England. She's a lovely young woman we want you to meet. Better not spring Jamie on her at first. You know what I mean. I expect a call from you before you go to bed."

Before I go to bed?

His father could say that when he never phoned for months at a time?

Nick clicked off. The pain he'd carried since he could first remember life kindled into white-hot anger. His parents could wait. Reese couldn't and neither could Jamie. He'd been gone too long as it was and hurried back to the E.R.

To his relief Jamie was still asleep. Reese's blue eyes, those mirrors of the soul, fastened on him with intensity. "The doctor still hasn't come back with the results."

"It's a busy night here. Why don't you go get something to eat now?"

"I will."

After she left through the bathroom, he washed his hands, then slipped on new gloves and a mask. Thankful his son was getting the rest he needed, Nick pulled up one of the chairs next to the crib to watch him.

He'd grown over the past couple of weeks. His father's question about why he would bring Jamie home to live could be answered by the baby lying right in front of him with an IV in his tiny foot.

This was why! There were changes going on every day of his son's life. Nick wanted to be in on all of them. No more chunks of time missing he could never get back.

Had his father or mother ever actually heard Nick say his first word or seen him take his first step? When Nick had gotten the flu as a baby, someone on the staff would have taken care of him. Nick's mother wouldn't have been able to tolerate being thrown up on. She would have left that to a nurse.

Reese on the other hand loved and kissed Jamie to death. That was her nature. Because of so much one-on-one attention, his son was blossoming. *You can't spoil a baby enough.* Those were her words. Nick believed in her philosophy. Every baby should be so showered.

Nick's parents didn't have a clue. They'd been raised by nannies and their parents before them. His father's mention of the Ridgeway's daughter, another woman who had to be made in the express image of the other women in Nick's life, sickened him.

"Mr. Wainright?" Dr. Marsh had come in.

Nick got to his feet. "What's the verdict?"

"Your son has Rotavirus. I've talked to your pediatrician. He'll be by in the morning on rounds unless the baby's temp spikes. In the meantime we'll continue to do what we're doing and will come in at intervals to check his vitals. Do you have any questions for me?"

"Not that I can think of right now."

"If you and your wife need a cot, they're in the closet behind you."

"I appreciate you telling me that."

"This part of the hospital has been redone for the comfort of the parents."

"Whoever planned it must have had a baby here at one time."

"No doubt."

"For your information, my wife has passed away. Reese is the nanny."

Nick had to give Dr. Marsh credit for not reacting the way he probably would have under other circumstances. "You're lucky to have found someone who has a strong mothering instinct. That's going to help your son."

"I agree."

Reese returned soon after the doctor had left and washed her hands. "Do you know anything yet?"

He told her what he'd learned. She finished tying the mask and walked over to the crib. "I should think sleep is the very best thing for him."

"We're going to need it, too. It's after eleven." He went to the closet and pulled out the made-up cots, placing them end to end. There was enough room for the staff to move back and forth changing the IV while they did vitals and programmed their notes into the computer.

He heard a sigh. "Bed sounds good. Thank you for setting them up." She removed her sandals and slipped under the covers with her head at the far end. Maybe she'd done it on purpose so their heads couldn't possibly be close to each other. He was sorry about that, but at least they'd be spending the night in the same room with Jamie.

Nick shut off the overhead light. After studying his son for another few minutes, he took off his shoes and lay down on top of the cot, putting his hand behind his head. From his vantage point he could see her lying there on her side toward Jamie.

"Reese? Are you asleep yet?"

He watched her shift in the cot. "No. I know you're worried about Jamie, but he's getting the best care possible."

"I believe that, too. I just wanted to say that the reason I was so long was that I had to let Jamie's grandparents know he wouldn't be coming to White Plains in the morning."

"I'm sure they were upset."

Reese didn't know the half of it.

"Don't be surprised if they show up tomorrow."

"That would only be normal. In my family if anyone were in the hospital, a whole crowd would descend." Nick couldn't imagine what that would be like. "Too bad your parents are away and don't know he's ill."

"Actually they got back from Cannes today. I listened to my father's message on my voice mail."

"Are they coming over here tonight?"

"No. I didn't call him back."

A long silence ensued. "I see."

"You don't see at all, but you're so polite, you would never pry."

"Your personal life is none of my business."

"That's an excellent response."

"What do you mean?" She shot straight up in the cot. "I don't understand."

Just then one of the staff came in to check on Jamie. "How's he doing?" Nick asked as the nurse finished on the computer.

"His temp is up a little from before, but these things take time. Try to get some sleep while he's quiet."

Nick's stomach clenched. There was no way he could do that right now. He got up from the cot and walked over to the crib. At this point Reese joined him.

"He's *got* to be all right, Nick!" He heard tears in her voice.

Without conscious thought he put his arm around her shoulders and pulled her to his side. After dancing with her last week, he needed her warm, curvaceous body next to his. Though she'd told him no more repeats, the fact that she didn't fight him right now revealed her deep need for comfort, too.

"What you said earlier," she whispered. "If I—"

"Forget it," he broke in. "I'm afraid I'm not myself tonight. We may be employer and nanny, but sometimes the lines get blurred. We've lived under the same roof for two weeks now. I find myself wanting to ask you questions I have no right to ask."

"I know what you mean." The tremor in her voice made its way through to his insides.

"So you admit you're a little curious about me."

"Of course." He noticed her hands cling to the edge of the crib. "I wouldn't be human otherwise."

"Go ahead and ask me why I haven't told my parents about Jamie being sick."

She bowed her head. "Not if you don't want to talk about it."

"Actually I do. You recall our conversation about my family being blue bloods? Well, I made a vow that Jamie's life is going to be different. Yes, he's a Hirst and a Wainwright, but I won't let him grow up under a system where appearances count for everything. That kind of life might be desirable at first, but it ends up destroying you."

"You feel like that's what happened to you?" she asked quietly.

"Our whole families have been destroying themselves for generations to the point that they don't have that human quality of giving and receiving affection. They don't feel it."

She looked up at him with eyes that were suspiciously bright. "But you're nothing like that!"

The impulse to crush her in his arms was so strong, he forced himself to let go of her altogether. "I was on my way to being exactly like that until a client made a chance remark three weeks ago that opened my eyes."

"What did he say?"

"He'd been offering his condolences and said there was nothing like a child to help you get over your loss. He obviously assumed I was the typical new father having to get up with him in the night for his feedings. But he didn't realize he was talking to a Wainwright who'd come from a cloistered, upper-class aristocracy.

"You can't imagine how I felt at that moment knowing Jamie was at my in-laws' being taken care of by their staff and I'd let it happen. Worse, my own parents saw nothing wrong with it. But the real crime was the one I'd committed by letting him go home with them in the first place. By turning over my son's life to the hired help, I'd virtually abandoned him."

"But if you hated what your parents had done to you, then—"

"I know." He raked a hand through his hair. "It's complicated. At the time of Erica's death, everything was murky. But standing here now next to my son, I see things so clearly it terrifies me that I was once that other man.

"The truth is, I could have called my father back tonight and told my parents about Jamie, but they wouldn't have cared, and it wouldn't have occurred to them to come to the hospital. They've been emotionally absent from my life for thirty-four years. That's never going to change. My uncles, my cousins, they'll never change, either."

"Oh, Nick…I'm so sorry. I had no idea."

"How could you possibly know? You come from another world. A *real* world."

"At least Erica's parents have been there to support you."

"That's where you're wrong. They despise me."

"Because you hired me?"

"No, Reese. My problems with them stem back to a year ago when Erica agreed to a divorce."

"You divorced her?" She sounded shocked.

"Yes. We'd made one more stab at trying to patch up our two-year-old marriage, but it didn't work. It wasn't until after we separated that she told me she was pregnant. She moved back with her parents. I didn't see her again until I got a phone call that she was on her way to the hospital. You know the rest."

"So that's why there was no nursery at the penthouse."

"I let her have carte blanche decorating the apartment so she could entertain in style, but more often than not she stayed at White Plains. We lived apart much of the time, a situation that suited both of us. I know you can't comprehend that."

She kept her eyes averted. "It's just so sad."

"At the time it was simply the norm. When she died, I was devastated, but it was my guilt over our failed marriage that put me in a dark morass. I let them take the baby home. The problem is, Erica's parents believe that Jamie—and all the money that comes with him as my heir—belongs more to them than to me after I'd damaged the family pride. It was a case of 'it's just not done.'"

He heard a little moan come out of Reese.

"You sound horrified. A normal person would be. But in my world, I'd broken the code of our social mores by divorcing her and was viewed as a revolutionary. Letting her parents keep our son for a time would look good on the surface. My parents would prefer it if things stayed that way. Anything to preserve the image."

She shook her head. "How awful."

"I debated telling you all this. It's so messy and complicated and I'll understand if you don't want to involve yourself with it all. If you want to leave my employ, I'll give you a check for the full amount we agreed upon. But I would ask you not to leave until Jamie's on the mend."

Leave him and the baby?

If only Nick knew what Reese was really thinking.

Though the day would come when she would have to go, she would never be ready to give up him or the baby.

She sucked in her breath. "Don't be ridiculous. The arrangement we made was that I wouldn't go until the end of the summer. If you're still in agreement, then let's not talk about it again."

Relief flooded her system when she heard him say, "Then we won't."

"Good. Right now your son needs us focusing on him and nothing else."

No sooner had she delivered her words than Jamie woke up crying. Nick hurried around to the other side of the crib to pick him up.

"Does he still feel as hot to you?"

His dark eyes flew to hers. "Yes."

That one word filled Reese with fresh alarm. Jamie's temperature had been elevated for close to eighteen hours now. The IV was supposed to be doing its job.

They took turns holding him. The minutes passed. Another nurse came in to check on him. She left without saying anything to them. That really frightened her. This went on for another half hour. Then Dr. Wells walked in the room already masked and gloved.

He gave them a quick glance. "Sorry to hear your son's been sick, Mr. Wainwright. Let me take a look at him."

While Nick handed the baby over, Reese stood back to watch the pediatrician, thankful he'd come. In a minute he lifted his head.

"I'm going to have you start feeding him some formula. The nurse will bring it to you. Just an ounce at a time. He might throw it up at first, but you persevere and we'll see if it finally stays down. I'll be back later."

The next hour was nightmarish with Jamie spitting up ten minutes after every ounce. She didn't know how Nick was holding up. He'd taken over because of love for his child. That was the way it should be.

She folded the cots back up and put them away so there was room for the chairs. When she sat down next to him and the baby, the sun had come up. Though the blinds were closed, light illuminated the room.

Reese checked her watch. "Nick—do you realize he hasn't thrown up for twenty minutes?"

His head lifted. "That's definite progress." He sounded elated.

"It *is!*" she cried.

The nurse came in a little while later. "How's he doing?"

"It's been a half hour since he last threw up."

"Terrific." She took the baby's temperature. "It's down four-tenths. I'll call Dr. Wells and tell him. Let him sleep now." She hurried out of the room.

Nick stood up and lay the baby back down in the crib.

Reese followed him over. "The worst must be over."

They both heard the door open and Dr. Wells came back in to examine the baby. "He's going to be fine. For the rest of the day give him formula when he seems ready for it. We'll keep the IV going. This evening I'll come by on rounds. If all is well, he'll be able to sleep in his own crib tonight."

"That's wonderful!" Reese cried as he left the room. Luckily her mask muffled its full intensity.

Nick turned to her. His hands shot out to grasp her arms. "*You're* wonderful. I don't know what I would have done without you." Between his husky voice that sounded an octave deeper and those dark fringed eyes that were looking at her with such gratitude, she was overwhelmed by the feelings he engendered. But growing alongside her great happiness was a new fear clutching at her.

Last night he'd talked about the lines between nanny and employer getting blurred after living beneath the same roof. Try spending the whole night together in the same hospital room with the little baby they both adored.

This morning she couldn't find the lines anywhere.

CHAPTER SIX

"Is THE diaper bag packed?"

"All done."

"Don't forget your new bathing suit."

Reese blinked. "We're going swimming?"

"We might."

"In your in-laws' pool?"

"Maybe. They have several."

She'd been swimming in the pool on the terrace every afternoon while Jamie was napping. He'd had a slight cold since they'd brought him home from the hospital last Saturday night, but Dr. Wells said it was to be expected. A week later Jamie was well and beaming. Next week she'd be able to move him around on top of the water and see how he fared.

"Ready?" he called out.

"Just about."

While he was moving around in the apartment, she hurried back to her bedroom and stashed the new suit inside her purse. After breakfast she'd gotten dressed for the drive to White Plains. She'd chosen to wear a rose-colored sundress with a white, short-sleeved bolero jacket. It was a step up from jeans, more presentable for a nanny who was about to face the Hirsts again. A white ribbon for her ponytail to match her sandals, and she left the bedroom.

"Let's go!"

After putting the freeze pack with the milk into the diaper bag, Reese met him in the foyer. Nick had dressed in cargo pants and a tan crew neck shirt. Even though he'd shaved, there was that hint of dark shadow that gave him a slightly disreputable look, adding to his sensuality. The sight of him looking beyond handsome with his wavy black hair and the relaxed look on his face took her breath.

She quickly switched her gaze to his son strapped in his carryall. Nick had put him in his white outfit with the tiger on the front. The baby was three months and a week old now. He was bigger and looked so healthy you would never have guessed he'd been ill a week ago. Unable to resist, she kissed his cheek several times. His little mouth curved into a smile that reminded her of Nick. It turned her heart right over.

She tickled his tummy. "We're going on a trip in our favorite rocket ship." She sang the song one of her friend's four-year-old loved. Jamie loved it, too.

He laughed out loud, provoking a grin from Nick. His gaze found hers. "You sound happy."

"Who wouldn't be? When I think of last week…"

"Don't remind me."

They left the apartment. Soon they'd climbed in the limo and were headed out of the city under a semicloudy sky, but nothing could dim her elation at being able to spend the whole day with Nick and Jamie.

Since that night in the hospital when he'd told her about his background and failed marriage, she wasn't as nervous to meet Erica's parents. Forewarned helped her to be forearmed.

Nick's decision to break from tradition and bring on the condemnation of two families had been made because of his love and need of Jamie. It took an incredibly strong man of amazing character to do what he did. It couldn't have been easy and she didn't envy him having to deal with his in-laws today. For that reason Reese intended to be his support.

In some way things had been easier since the hospital. The bonding that had taken place with Jamie made everything they did seem more natural when the three of them were together. Nick had come home around four every afternoon. She understood his need to spend as much time as possible with his son.

Reese felt as if the penthouse had become a happy place for Nick. Nothing could mean more to her when she realized how much of his past had been marred by the weight of a painful childhood as well as a difficult marriage. Nick still hadn't told her all that had gone on between him and Erica to drive them apart, but then Reese was only the nanny. Every once in a while she had to remember that, but it was getting harder and harder.

On this trip she sat next to Jamie, who loved his pacifier and blue rattle. With Nick sitting straight across from the baby, he could talk to him and keep him entertained, but it was Jamie who entertained them. Every time he laughed, his pacifier fell out and Nick put it back in. Jamie thought it was a game and kept doing it. Maybe he was too little to realize what was going on, but it was hilarious and they laughed all the way to White Plains.

When they came in sight of the Hirst estate, Reese

understood even more the dividing line that separated people with lifestyles like Nick's and his former wife's from the rest of the world. They drove past a sign indicating public parking around the west side of the two-story mansion. Paul took the tree-lined driveway to the front entrance and helped Reese out with the diaper bag. Nick followed with Jamie and the three of them started up the steps. By the time they reached the front door, Walter Hirst had opened it. The older man couldn't hide his surprise at seeing Reese.

"We're in the dayroom."

If it had been Reese's father who'd opened the door, the first thing he would have said was something like, "There's my grandson! Come here and say hello to your old granddad." He would have reached for the baby and walked him through their house to show Grandma.

Reese had thought she was prepared for this, but even with the explanations Nick had given her, to see and feel the continued lack of personal warmth and affection coming from Erica's father disturbed her.

The interior of the mansion might be an architectural triumph of nineteenth-century elegance, but the only life Reese could see came from Jamie, whose head kept turning as they followed Mr. Hirst to a room with a surprising contemporary decor. His grandmother, wearing a stylish two-piece suit in lime-green, was just walking through the doors leading in from a beautiful flower garden Reese could see beyond her.

"We didn't expect you this early. I take it Jamie's better now."

"He's fine," Nick stated. "In fact you're perfect, aren't you, sport." He kissed his cheeks while he undid the straps and lifted him out. "You'll notice he's grown."

"Put him down in the carriage."

With no playpen or swing, Nick had little choice unless he wanted to plop Jamie in his grandmother's arms. But she gave no indication that she wanted to hold him. Reese knew there were many people in the world who couldn't show affection, no matter their social class. Still, this was Jamie's family and it just didn't seem natural.

Now that she thought about it, a hint of Nick's rebellion had come out when he'd shown them the nursery and deposited Jamie in her arms. Today he held back and abided Anne's wishes.

The trouble with a carriage was that it blocked part of the view for the baby, who started crying as soon as Nick moved out of his line of vision. Reese's first instinct was to take him right out. Like Nick, she, too, had to hold back from grabbing him.

"I brought this." Reese set the diaper bag down on one of the chairs. "It has enough bottles and diapers for today."

"We have everything he'll need. Walter? Will you tell the nurse they're here." Jamie was not happy and his cries were getting louder.

"I'll be back for him at six." Nick flicked Reese a glance. "Let's leave them alone, Ms. Chamberlain."

They walked out the mansion through the front door with Jamie's cries still following them. She assumed he meant they were going to explore the estate and go swimming later on. To her shock Nick headed for the limo and helped her inside.

She stared at him in puzzlement. "I thought our plan was to stay close by. What if Jamie needs you?"

"Then he'll cry his heart out until he falls asleep."

"Nick..."

His grim expression was too much. The past week had been so carefree, Reese could hardly bear to see his brooding expression come back. "I didn't have a choice, Reese, because I made them a promise. But after today, all promises are off."

He flicked on the intercom. "Paul? Drive us to the heliport."

"Where are we going?" she asked when he'd finished.

"Out on my sailboat."

Her heart thudded with sickening speed. "If we need a helicopter, it must be pretty far away."

"Don't worry. We're only going to Martha's Vineyard outside Edgartown. One of our summer homes is there."

A summer home there, an estate with horses on Long Island, a penthouse on Park Avenue, a villa in Cannes. Reese had an impression those possessions only constituted the tip of an enormous iceberg. If Jamie didn't have a daddy who'd decided to break the cycle of emotional neglect that went with so much luxury, he could be suffocated by it all the way Nick had been.

He studied her for a moment. "Have you ever been sailing?"

She knew it was his favorite sport. "No. One time our family went to Wisconsin and we crossed Lake Michigan on the ferry in choppy conditions. None of us did well. That's the sum total of my knowledge of being on water."

A light gleamed in his eyes. "As long as you can swim, that's all I need to know. When we get out beyond where the breeze fills the sail, you'll find out you're a wonderful sailor."

"That's wishful thinking. I only hope I won't be imitating Jamie's bout of last weekend."

He chuckled. "You don't have the flu."

Reese knew Nick wanted and needed this outing, if only to take his mind off leaving Jamie with his grandparents. *Please don't let me get seasick.* When she saw the helicopter, another prayer went up about not getting airsick. She'd never been on one of those, either.

In the end she needn't have worried because Nick's cell phone rang before they even exited the limo. After he picked up, his gaze sought hers. She tried to read his expression as he listened to the person on the other end. It went on for a minute. After he hung up, he told Paul to turn the limo around and go back.

Her brows lifted. "Jamie?"

"He won't settle down. Anne says the nurse can't do anything with him, so if she can't, that's it."

Reese bit her lip. "I was afraid of that. Jamie worships you." She bet Nick's mother-in-law told him it was the nanny's fault for spoiling him and probably decried Nick ever removing Jamie from their house in the first place.

"Nothing could please me more," he declared in a satisfied voice. "Now we can take him with us. I'll call ahead for a cooler of food and drinks to be packed for us."

The burst of elation exploding inside Reese only lasted until she remembered her mother's last question to her. *"You've got a terrific head on those shoulders and broke off with Jeremy for a reason. I don't have to worry about you losing sight of your career plans just yet, do I?"* Not for the first time, Reese had to remind herself that she was just the temporary nanny. But the pain she felt at the thought of leaving this little family was becoming too much.

When they reached the mansion, Reese could hear Jamie's heart-wrenching sobs from the foyer of the mansion. They hurried down the hall to the dayroom and found the nurse pacing the floor with him. His in-laws stood around looking upset.

"Hey, sport? What's going on?" Nick walked over to the distraught-looking woman and took the baby from her arms. Jamie caught sight of his daddy and lunged for him before bursting into another paroxysm of tears. Reese could almost hear him saying, 'Why did you leave me?'

When he burrowed his head into the side of Nick's neck, Nick must have felt it deep in his heart. In a few seconds peace reigned. While Jamie clung to him, everyone in the room looked infinitely relieved.

"I think there's been enough excitement for one day. Why don't you come to the penthouse next weekend and we'll try this again."

"We'll be in Salzburg. Don't you remember?" Anne sounded indignant. "You and Erica went with us two years ago."

"I'm sorry. This new job of parenting has taken over my life. Call me when you're back and we'll make arrangements. Have a safe trip."

Jamie refused to leave his arms, so Reese picked up the carryall and diaper bag before they headed for the limo waiting outside the mansion. Once Nick got in the backseat with him, Reese's eyes zeroed in on the baby.

"Your cute little face is all splotchy from crying. Here's your pacifier. Do you want your rattle, too?"

His fingers glommed right on to it. He didn't fight Nick as he strapped him in the infant car seat.

"Crisis averted," he said to Paul before the older man shut the door. In seconds they were off.

Her eyes flew to Nick's. "That wasn't a pleasant moment back there."

"No, and there's not going to be another one like it again."

She covered Jamie's face with kisses until she got a smile out of him. "You're so worn-out, you'll probably sleep all the way."

Reese didn't realize how prophetic her words would be. He slept through the fabulous helicopter flight that took them to the famous little island off Cape Cod. They were set down at Katama Airpark only a few miles from Edgartown.

Nick took them to one of the harbor restaurants where they ate a delicious shrimp lunch. Afterward they walked around the historic part of the town and visited some of the shops. It wasn't until they reached the boat dock on the Wainwright's property that the baby's eyes fluttered open. He'd missed everything.

Reese found it so funny, she started to laugh. Nick joined in. He was still smiling when he transferred his son from the ramp onto the end of the immaculate, twenty-three-foot sailboat called the *Aeolus*.

"What does it mean?" she asked him.

"In Greek mythology, Aeolus was the god of the winds."

"That's beautiful." The white keel had a blue stripe. She thought of the little boat she'd bought for Nick and couldn't wait for him to open his present, but she'd put it off until after they'd finished sailing.

Excitement mounted in Reese to see all the boats out on the water. This was a day out of time, one to treasure before they went back to the city. But having Jamie with them was the reminder she needed to remember she was his nanny, nothing else.

Nick brought out two adult life vests and an infant life jacket. While he went about getting the boat ready and undoing ropes, she laid Jamie down on one of the benches and changed his diaper. He loved being bare and kicked his strong legs as if he was doing exercises. She laughed with pure pleasure before putting a fresh diaper on him.

With him propped against her shoulder, she went down to the galley. There was a microwave so she could warm his bottle. By the time she climbed the stairs with him, Nick had everything ready to go. She put the bottle down. Together they helped put Jamie's infant vest on, but she was unbearably aware of Nick and his potent masculinity. Their hands brushed, sending rivulets of yearning through her.

He kissed his boy's tummy before snapping everything in place. "I know you don't like it, sport, but that's the rule." He fastened him back in his carryall. "You'll get used to it."

With a speed that took her breath, Nick's gaze unexpectedly flicked to hers. "Now it's *your* turn." The message in his dark brown eyes was unmistakable. They traveled over her features and down her body, melting her from the inside out. She got this heavy sensation in her legs. Her hands felt pains that traveled up her arms.

His male mouth was like a vortex drawing her in. Thrilled and terrified because her desire for him was so palpable he had to know it, she put out her hands to take the vest from him so he wouldn't touch her. Instead his hands closed over hers, pulling her against him, sending a paralyzing warmth through her body.

"I'm going to kiss you, and I very much hope that you won't fight me."

She couldn't have if she'd wanted to. From the moment she'd climbed in the back of the limo and had discovered a man who surpassed her every notion of the ultimate male, she'd wanted *him*. It was that simple, and that impossible, but right now she couldn't remember the reason why and didn't want to.

In the next breath he found her softly parted mouth. Incapable of doing anything else, she melted against him and let herself go, craving the taste of him as he took their kiss long and deep. Oh… She'd never felt sensations like this in her life. He drew her closer in a quick compulsive movement. The vest fell to her feet, but she was barely cognizant.

It came as a shock to realize his hunger matched hers, sending fire licking through her veins. Reese felt the low groan way down in his throat before it permeated her body. As it reached her inner core, her helpless cry drew a response of refined savagery from him.

"You couldn't possibly know how beautiful you are." A fever of ecstasy consumed her with each insistent caress of his lips on her face, her hair, her throat. "I want to take you below," he whispered against her lips, swollen from the passion they shared. "If I've shocked you, I've shocked myself more."

She took an unsteady breath and eased herself out of

arms that were slow to relinquish her. The slight rocking of the boat didn't help her equilibrium. "What's really shocking is that I'd like to go downstairs with you," she admitted because total gut honesty was required right now.

"But after I broke off with Jeremy, I made a promise I wouldn't let anything get in the way of my goals. A man can make you lose focus. Who knows what could happen to me after a glorious day on the ocean in your arms. I—I know it would be wonderful," she stammered, "because I've just had a taste of you and crave more."

Nick's eyes narrowed on her mouth. He might as well have started kissing her again. She had to look away or she'd fling herself back into his arms.

"Your honesty is another quality about you I admire." Out of the periphery she watched his hard body lounge against the side of the boat. "What happened between you and Jeremy?"

"Probably the kind of thing that went wrong with you and Erica." She'd reached the tipping point and needed distance from this man who'd caused her world to reel.

Jamie wasn't fussing yet, but she knew his hunger had been building. She pulled him out of his carryall, then sat down and settled him in her arms to feed him.

"You mean you allowed yourself to drift into your engagement?" he asked in a benign tone.

Her head flew back. "Is that what happened to you?" she asked before she realized how revealing that question must have sounded. All along she'd been thinking Erica had to have been his grand passion because he could have had any woman he wanted.

"Why don't we concentrate on you and Jeremy first."

"He's not in my life anymore."

"Humor me anyway," he insisted.

"Well, we met at the bank where my father does business. That was the summer before I started at Wharton. We fell in love and dated until I went away, then we relied on emails and phone calls until we could be together. I went home at every vacation opportunity. He came to see me twice.

"Last fall he asked me to marry him and gave me an engagement ring. He knew I didn't want to get married before graduation, but when I went home at Christmas, he wanted to be married right away. No more waiting.

"I told him I would, but that we'd have to live apart while I was still away at school. That's when he gave me an ultimatum. Either I marry him before the end of the month and stay in Lincoln, or we break up."

The baby had finished his bottle. She pulled a receiving blanket out of the diaper bag and put it over her shoulder to burp him.

"I thought I knew him, but I didn't. It finally came out that he didn't want a working wife. He made enough money and wanted me to stay home so we could start a family. I told him I wanted children one day, but my education and work came first.

"I was amazed that my scholarship to Wharton meant nothing to him. He had a finance degree and aspirations to rise to the top, but didn't take mine seriously. It's too bad he didn't realize I meant what I said. It would have saved us both a lot of pain. I gave him back his ring and told him goodbye."

"Have you seen him since?"

"No."

"He's probably still waiting for you to change your mind."

"Then he's waiting in vain."

In the silence that followed, Nick reached for his life vest and put it on. Clearly he considered this conversation over. She'd learn nothing more from him about his marriage because he'd come out here to sail.

After their brief, intimate interlude that could have ended in her making the most disastrous mistake of her life, he was ready to head out to sea, the rapture of the moment forgotten. She had the gut feeling that the invitation to join him below wouldn't happen again on this trip or any other trips he planned in the future.

If he thought she was still feeling needy after her broken engagement and that's why she'd been an ardent participant in what they'd just shared, then let him go on thinking it. She didn't want him knowing her guilty secret.

To have fallen in love with her employer went against all the rules of being a nanny, but that's what she'd done. She was madly in love with Nick Wainwright. Between him and his son, she would never be the same person again.

No one could tell her Erica Hirst hadn't been desperately in love with him, too. You couldn't be in his presence five minutes without wanting any love he was willing to give. If anyone had *drifted* into a permanent relationship—if that's what had really happened—it would have been Nick.

Erica must have been shattered when he'd asked her for a divorce. Reese wanted to believe that the knowledge she was pregnant with Nick's child had brought her some solace in spite of her grief. If Reese had been in her shoes, she knew she would have grieved over losing Nick.

How tragic that she'd died. Tears pricked her eyelids. She loved their beautiful boy with all her heart.

"Reese?" His voice had a deep, grating quality. "Are you all right? I didn't mean to dredge up your pain."

Maybe it was better he thought Jeremy was the source of her distress, but nothing could be further from the truth. She shook her head. "You didn't. I thought you and I were having a simple conversation. Naturally our pasts would come up." She put the baby back in his carryall. "I think your son is on the verge of falling asleep again. Where shall we put him while we're out sailing?"

"Keep him right next to you. I'll do all the work, but put on your life vest first." He handed it to her.

Back to square one, the place where she'd gotten too physically close to Nick and had given in to her longings. Not this time around!

She slipped it on and fastened the straps.

"Are you ready?"

Reese nodded.

He walked to the rear of the boat and started the motor at a wakeless speed. Slowly they headed toward the water beyond the buoys. Once past them, he cut the motor and raised the white sail. A light breeze filled it and then there was this incredible rush of sensation as the boat lifted and skimmed across the water. She found it wasn't unlike the feeling of Nick kissing her senseless.

When she was an old woman, all she would have to do was close her eyes and remember the sight of the gorgeous, powerfully built man at the helm with the wind disheveling his black hair. For a little while she would relive being crushed in his arms and invited to visit paradise with him. That kind of joy only came once.

She dreaded for the day to be over, but the time came when Nick had to take them back to the port. Twilight had fallen all around them. After they'd floated alongside the pier and he'd jumped out of the boat to tie the ropes, she rummaged in the big diaper bag for the gift-wrapped package.

While he was still down on his haunches, she handed it to him.

"What's this?"

"It'll be Father's Day in a few hours. Before Jamie fell asleep, he asked me to give this to you. He told me to tell you he had the most wonderful day of his life out here with his daddy."

A stillness surrounded Nick before he undid the paper and discovered the sailboat. In the semidarkness his white smile stood out. He turned it this way and that. "The *Flying NJ?*"

"Yes. A Nick and Jamie partnership. He thought you might like to put it on your desk at work."

"Reese…" He stepped back in the boat. With his hand still holding his gift, he cupped her chin with the other, lifting her face to his gaze. "No one ever gave me a present like this before."

"That's because it's your first Father's Day and your son isn't very old yet," she teased to cover the intensity of her emotions.

He brushed his mouth against hers, melting her bones. "Where did you come from, Ms. Chamberlain?"

"The East 59th Street Employment Agency."

"My secretary did good work picking you. I'm going to have to give her a bonus."

"I'm glad she picked me, too. Jamie's...precious." Her voice caught before she moved away from him. She was in danger of begging him to take her below. If that happened, then a whole night alone with him would never be enough.

CHAPTER SEVEN

Two weeks later Reese entered the apartment building with Jamie after an afternoon of walking and shopping. The concierge called to her. "You have mail, Ms. Chamberlain."

She saw a postcard from Rich Bonner, his fourth, forwarded from the post office in Philadelphia to her temporary address here. His persistence irritated her. There was also a letter from Wharton. The school was no doubt reminding her of the test coming up in two weeks. She'd registered for it and would be taking it online.

"Thank you, Albert."

Once she'd tucked the mail in the sack, she went on up to the penthouse. Before she read anything, she had something more important to do. Jamie would be four months old in another week, but she couldn't wait for his birthday.

Her sister had one of those fold-out colorful quilts with the ends of a mobile sewn in. When you opened it and set it on the floor, the mobile sprang open. The baby would lie there on his back entertained with all kinds and colors of small blocks and shapes and mirrors dangling above him. When she'd been walking through the toy store, she saw one like it and had to buy it.

"You're going to love this," she told Jamie as she wheeled him down the hall to her bedroom. As soon as she washed her hands, she pushed him through to the nursery and changed his diaper in his crib. She left him long enough to wash her hands again, then hurried back.

The little Tigger clock she'd bought for him last week said it was five after four. Nick would be home any minute. She lived for this time of the day when he walked through the front door and said he was home. Today was Friday, which meant he'd be home for the whole weekend.

He was always the perfect employer, but since their outing on the boat when she'd come so close to making love with him, he hadn't touched her and the deprivation was killing her.

"Come on, sweetheart." She picked up the baby, pouring out all her love on him. "You're getting heavier, do you know that?" With a kiss, she knelt down on the floor with him where she could place him under the mobile on his back.

"There." A red ladybug hung from a coil so you could pull on it. She put it in his hand. His fingers tried to crush it and it sprang away. Reese laughed and put it in his hand again, thus commencing a game that had them both laughing. She was so involved, she didn't realize Nick had come in the room until he'd gotten down on the floor with them.

"This looks so fun I think I'll try it myself." His hip brushed against hers as he put his head inside to kiss his son.

Jamie was overjoyed to see his father. In the excitement his hands knocked several objects so they swung.

Reese was so excited to feel Nick's body next to her, she almost forgot to breathe.

His deep laughter rumbled through her, enchanting her. When he backed out, he suddenly pulled Reese closer so she was half lying on top of him with her face over his.

"A man could get used to looking up when there's so much to entice him." He undid the ribbon on her ponytail and her hair cascaded around her face. "I've been wanting to do this for weeks."

It was his fingers twining in her hair that opened the floodgates. With no immunity against the intensity of his desire, Reese couldn't help but lower her mouth to his, aching for the assuagement only he could give.

With slow deliberation he began to devour her. His breath was so sweet, so familiar, her senses swam. They kissed as if obeying some primitive rhythm. His lips traveled to the scented hollow of her throat. "You smell divine, do you know that? You feel divine."

"So do you." She let out a small gasp because the pressure of his mouth had changed, becoming so exquisite and loving, she would have fainted from pleasure if she weren't already on the floor with him.

He rolled her over on her back and kissed her passionately again and again until she couldn't tell where one kiss left off and another one began. Caught up in a euphoria such as she'd never known, she had no idea what time it was or how much time had passed until Jamie started to make hungry noises. Good heavens, the baby—

"He can wait for his bottle one more minute, or two, or three," Nick said in a voice raw with emotion, pressing another hot kiss to her mouth, each one growing more urgent than the last.

Reese agreed as she gave in to the needs building inside her. His charisma had drawn her to him from the start, but now it was his sheer, potent male sensuality that had ensnared her. The slight rasp of his jaw brought out a wanton side in her she didn't know she possessed. His hunger, never satisfied, was making her feel immortal.

Only Jamie's cries becoming louder had the power to bring her back to earth. "Nick—"

His answering groan of protest meant he'd been brought back, too. She felt his hard-muscled body roll away. Reese caught a glimpse of dark eyes glazed with the heat of their passion before he got to his feet.

She looked around, surprised to see his suit jacket and tie on the floor. He had to have discarded them in a hurry after he'd walked in. Reese lowered her head. What had she done? What was she doing?

Nick left the room with Jamie to get him a bottle. By the time she got to her feet, her body couldn't stop throbbing. She was completely dazed by emotions and feelings that had overwhelmed her. In a way it really frightened her. Nick had the power to take away her heart, soul, mind, will, *everything*—without even trying.

But it was *her* fault, not his. There was no force involved with him. All he had to do was touch her or say something and she was incapable of denying him or walking away. To do that, she would have to break her contract. But giving up Jamie would break her heart and leave Nick in a crisis until he found another nanny.

You've gotten yourself in a terrible mess, Reese.

In a druggedlike stupor, she picked up the sack and

almost threw it away before she remembered the mail inside it. After pulling it out, she tossed the bag in the wastebasket and looked at the postcard first. Laguna Beach.

Hey, beautiful— Wish you were here surfing with me. There are some waves rolling in with your name on them. By any chance did you get a letter from Wharton?

Reese stared at the unopened envelope in her hand.

I got one the other day. Email me either way, okay? Hope you are ready for the exam! Ciao for now. Rich.

She had no intention of contacting him, but she did have to admit she was curious about his mention of a letter. He wouldn't have said anything if all that was in it was the reminder of the exam coming up.

Nick must have carried Jamie out to the terrace to feed him. Thankful he'd disappeared to give her time to gather her wits, she wasted no time opening the letter. It was from the dean of her department no less.

Dear Ms. Chamberlain:

Two students whose academic achievement has set them above the rest of their graduating class have been given coveted internships for the coming fall semester. It is my privilege to inform you that you are one of those two remarkable scholars.

Congratulations, Ms. Chamberlain, on your outstanding record. I am proud and pleased to tell you that you have been placed with Miroff and Hooplan located on Broadway in New York City, as an analyst. You'll do research and make books, but more detailed information will be forthcoming from my office shortly.

I wanted you to receive this letter in plenty of time to find living accommodations and plan your finances accordingly.

Again may I express my personal satisfaction over your stellar performance here at Wharton. Miroff and Hooplan will be fortunate to have you.

Best Regards.

Reese pressed the letter to her chest. Miroff and Hooplan was on the top-ten list of brokerage companies in the nation. She couldn't believe it. This truly was a dream come true.

Was it the dean Mrs. Tribe had talked to when she'd been checking on Reese's background?

As for Rich, his question meant he'd received the other internship. She wondered where he would be working. All she had to do was email him and she'd find out. Maybe it was uncharitable, but she hoped it wasn't next door or across the street from Miroff and Hooplan!

Though an internship meant being on call 24/7 as a grunt, she would be a grunt in an exclusive brokerage house. She felt a shiver of excitement run thorough her. She read the letter over again. Her parents needed to hear about this. They'd loved and supported her all these years so that she could realize her dream. She owed them for many things, but especially for their belief in her ability to succeed. Now would be a good time to reach her mother.

After moving the quilt mobile away from the crib, she left the nursery for her bedroom to make the call.

"Where are *you* going in such a hurry?" Reese had been moving so fast, she'd almost run into Nick in the hall. Jamie was resting against his broad shoulder. After the way she'd lost it in his arms, she could hardly look at him yet without blushing or feeling the strong passion between them again. "When I stopped for my mail, Albert told me you received some, too. By the rate of your speed leaving the nursery, it must be important."

Nothing got past Nick. Nothing.

"Something from Jeremy maybe?"

Jeremy—

After kissing Nick as if her very life depended on it, her ex-fiancé had been so far from her mind, she'd forgotten he existed. Reese struggled for breath. On a burst of inspiration, she handed him the letter. She needed to prove to herself as well as to him that no matter how attracted she was to him, she was still on the path to forging a place for herself in the business world.

She felt the full force of his penetrating gaze before he scanned the contents. As she watched him, his demeanor began to change. He'd been so certain this was about her ex-fiancé.

When he lifted his eyes, she saw an expression of incredulity stamped across his striking features. "I knew you were a student, but I had no idea you were the caliber of scholar to have earned this kind of entrée into Miroff's."

"The letter came as a complete surprise to me," she said in a quiet voice. "I was about to phone my parents with the news."

There was a pause before he said, "When you asked me about the stock market, I understand now that it was no idle question." He didn't sound accusing exactly, but he didn't sound himself, either. She couldn't decipher his reaction.

"It wasn't an in-depth question, either." Reese felt strange having to explain herself to him. Until now there'd never been this void between them. She didn't understand it.

"Jeremy really didn't know the real you, did he."

Jeremy again. Why did Nick sound so cold? That was the only word that came close to describing his response. Anger or rudeness she might have tolerated, but this aloof side of him was something new. If they could just get on a better footing.

"Can I do anything for you or Jamie?"

He shook his dark head. "Now that I'm home, you're free for the weekend."

To hear him say that in an almost wintry tone of voice was like being banished to the outer darkness. This was pain in a new dimension. For once she didn't dare kiss Jamie.

"Before I forget, your house phone rang this morning. I picked up so it wouldn't waken the baby. Someone named Greg called, but he didn't leave a message. About an hour later a man named Lew phoned wanting to speak to you. When he realized you weren't here, he said he'd catch up with you at the Yacht Club tonight. If you need me to watch Jamie, I—"

"I don't," he broke in, "but I appreciate the offer." He handed her back the letter. When she took it, the postcard fell out of her hand. Nick grabbed it up before she could. If he'd looked for Jeremy's name before returning it to her, then he would be disappointed.

Summoning all her strength, she picked herself up off the ground mentally and smiled. "If something should change, I'll be in my room studying."

"For what exactly?"

"The G7 and G65." He knew what they were. Once upon a time he'd had to study for them, too. "My exam is coming up before the end of the month."

"I have no doubt you'll crush it." Why was there that glitter in his eyes? Just a little while ago they'd been glazed with desire.

"We'll see."

The quilt mobile Reese had bought for Jamie was another hit out of the ballpark. Nick sat in the rocking chair and leaned forward, watching his son play beneath it. All the objects stimulated him so much, it took him a long time before he fell asleep. That suited Nick, who needed time to wind down before he exploded with emotions so foreign to him, he didn't know himself anymore. This was Leah's doing.

—*I've found someone I believe will suit you and the baby.*

—*As long as she likes children and is a real motherly type and not some cardboard creation, I bow to your wisdom. Tell me more about her.*

—*You once told me you prefer to attack a new project without listening to any other voices first while you form your own opinion. I think that's a good philosophy, especially in this case.*

This case meaning a young woman who played dual roles to perfection.

Nick bit down hard. Reese had wanted a job that only lasted three months and she'd meant it! Jeremy-whatever-his-name was a fool for not having realized he'd never been in the running for the long haul.

But now that Nick had taken the time to calm down, he realized his anger at Jeremy had been misplaced. The fault lay in himself for assuming he could talk Reese into staying on as his nanny longer than just the summer. When he thought of her leaving now, he couldn't handle it.

Filled with fresh panic, he pulled out his cell and called his secretary.

"Nick? I'm glad you phoned. Greg, Lew and your father have been trying to reach you. He told me to tell you the time for the Yacht Club party tonight has been changed from six-thirty to seven. I left the message on your voice mail."

"Thank you." He shot out of the rocking chair and wandered through the joining door to his bedroom. "Leah? How many women did you interview for the nanny position?"

"Four. Does this mean Ms. Chamberlain isn't working out?"

His hand almost crushed his phone. "She's working out very well, but I'm thinking of the future."

"What happened to the Cosgriffs' nanny?"

"Nothing that I know of, but I've decided I don't want her to come."

"Would you like me to start looking again?"

"Not quite yet, but I am curious. How many applied?"

"I believe Mr. Lloyd said they had five hundred and forty applications on hand."

Considering the state of the economy, he shouldn't have been surprised. "How did you tell him to screen them?"

"I asked him to pick out the ones with the highest education."

He rubbed the back of his neck in surprise. "That was it?"

"Yes. Those with undergraduate degrees or higher still wanting to take a nanny job for only three months would have something else going on in their brain. When he gave me the four names, I started making calls, checking references.

"One of Ms. Chamberlain's professors told me she had a spark of genius in her. That was a plus. She came from a family with five siblings and was the youngest applicant of the four, which I felt was another point in her favor. You have to be able to move quick and get down on the floor with a baby."

A wave of heat flooded Nick's system when he remembered what he'd been doing on the nursery floor with her less than two hours ago.

"What tipped the scales in her favor?"

"You mean you haven't found that out yet?"

Another layer of heat poured off him. Leah knew him too well. They had few secrets. One thing he could count on was her honesty.

"Did you know she was given an internship as an analyst at Miroff and Hooplan for the fall?"

"Well, I'll be damned. Good for her."

Nick had found out all he needed to know. "Talk to you later. And Leah—"

"Yes?"

"Thank you."

Before Jamie woke up, Nick needed to do damage control.

Reese had changed into white cargo pants and a khaki blouse. When she heard the knuckle rap, she was on her way out with no destination in mind. She'd lived through a tumult of emotions this afternoon and needed to walk until she dropped.

Grabbing her purse, she opened the door. Nick stood there without Jamie, his arm braced against the door-jamb. She braved his penitent gaze and felt her heart thud because the darkness she'd felt from him earlier seemed to have gone.

He studied her with relentless scrutiny, as if looking for some sign that he might be welcome. "To my shame I've overstepped my bounds twice now. You're a very attractive woman, but that's no excuse for my behavior every time I get within touching distance of you. I swear that as long as you're in my employ, you have nothing more to fear from me."

His words filled her with pain, but relief, too, because it meant no permanent damage had been done. She eyed him directly. "I was a willing participant, so it's obvious I haven't exactly been afraid of you, Nick."

"Nevertheless is there the possibility that you would forgive me and we could start over? Whatever else went on with me earlier has nothing to do with you. The thought that you might decide to leave me and Jamie before time terrifies the living daylights out of me."

A small smile broke the corners of her mouth. "It terrifies me, too, because I need the money you're paying me."

One dark brow dipped. "Do you need it enough to come with me this evening? We'll be taking Jamie to a party?"

She folded her arms. "Why do I get the feeling this isn't just any party?"

"My parents expect me to marry again and have a woman picked out to become the next Mrs. Nicholas

Wainwright. Her name is Jennifer Ridgeway. I haven't seen her since her teens, but be assured her pedigree forms part of the framework of the upper crust. She'll be at the Yacht Club with her parents."

"I can see you're planning an all-out revolt."

"Yes." Reese could swear she saw fire in his eyes. "The sight of my son with his unsuitable nanny will dash every hope on all sides and make a statement that nothing else could do. It will be my virtual abdication from the family."

Whoa.

She felt Nick's conviction to her bones and knew tonight would change the course of his life and Jamie's forever. More than anything she wanted to be along to watch history being made.

"What should I wear?"

The lines darkening his face vanished. She saw his chest rise and fall due to the strength of his emotions. "How about that yellow outfit with a white ribbon around your ponytail?"

"I can do that. What about you?"

"No pedigreed member of the Yacht Club shows up in anything but formal dress. I'll wear a tux."

"And Jamie?"

A smile hovered around his compelling mouth. "His navy outfit with the Snoopy and his white high-tops. He'll be the first baby who ever made it inside the doors. If you're ready for Miroff and Hooplan, I know you'll be able to handle this crowd."

Her eyes suddenly moistened without her volition. That crowd included his parents, the two people responsible for bringing him into the world. She knew deep down somewhere he loved them because they *were* his parents. They'd bestowed every gift on him, given him every opportunity. There'd only been one thing lacking. She kept swallowing, trying to get rid of the thickness closing up her throat.

"How soon do you want to leave?"

"As soon as you can get Jamie and yourself ready. We'll be flying out to Long Island in the helicopter."

"I've had my shower. All I have to do is change clothes, then I'll take care of the baby and load his diaper bag."

He held her gaze. "One thing before we leave."

Adrenaline caused her heart to pound hard. "What is it?"

"I couldn't help but see the name of the person who sent you the postcard. Who's Rich?"

"My study partner at Wharton."

Nick cocked his head. "Does he measure up to your brilliance?"

Since emailing Rich a little while ago, Reese decided she'd better tell him now. "His full name is Richard Bonner."

His brows knit together. "That sounds familiar."

"It's because he just received word from the dean that he's been chosen to do an internship at Sherborne and Wainwright this fall."

He gave her an incredulous stare. "For years my uncle Lew has been in charge of choosing the interns. If they're not bright enough for him, he won't take one."

"Then there you go. Rich is the original whiz kid. He's apoplectic with joy about being chosen to work for the top company in New York. In case you're wondering, he has no idea you're my employer and I have no intention of ever telling him. Just imagine how crazy that would have been if you'd been stuck with me for a second round."

"Crazy doesn't begin to describe it," he ground out.

Two hours later the helicopter started to make its landing. Nick turned to her. "Welcome to The Sea Nook Yacht Club, listed on New York's Historical Register. Former home to the tall ships on Long Island's Gold Coast. Members only."

As it set down, Reese found the sight of the sprawling Tudor/Elizabethan estate overlooking the ocean surreal. Sailboats and yachts with pennants fluttering dotted the marina and beyond. To her, the world Nick had inhabited all these years was just as fantastic in its own way as Middle Earth or the Land of Oz.

Jamie reached for her after they climbed out of the helicopter. She held him as they walked next to Nick, who carried the baby's carryall and diaper bag across the grounds to the entrance. He looked adorable in his little navy suit. One day he would grow up to be as fantastic-looking as his gorgeous father, whose appearance in a black tux blew her away.

Nick had told her he wanted to arrive before anyone else. He preferred that his parents make the entrance with the Ridgeways instead of the other way around. The sight of Nick already installed with his nanny and child would set the ground rules in concrete for the future.

The club had its own concierge, a burly man complete with beard, dressed like a proper sea captain in a smashing blazer and slacks. He swept across the enormous foyer with a smile on his face. "Good evening, Mr. Wainwright."

"How are you, Max?"

"Very well indeed. It's been a long time since we last saw you here. May I take this opportunity to tell you how sorry I am about the loss of Mrs. Wainwright? It was a shock to everyone."

"Thank you."

"You're the first of your party to arrive. We've put you out in the conservatory. Your father wanted the best view and we were able to accommodate him."

"Thank you."

The man's gaze flicked to Reese. "On vacation are you, miss? I'm sorry, but only members of the Yacht Club are allowed inside. You're welcome to stroll about the grounds with your child, of course."

Nick's eyes caught hers for a moment. She saw a wicked gleam of amusement in their dark depths. He was enjoying this. "She's with me, Max. Ms. Chamberlain is my nanny and this is my son, Jamie. He's just out of the hospital and won't be separated from us yet."

Reese had to give the host points for his aplomb in an awkward situation he'd most likely never had to deal with before. She could hear him trying to decide how to handle this. He cleared his throat. "Of course. Go right on out."

"Thank you, Max."

Reese had to put up with unfriendly stares and lifted brows from the beautiful people decked out in formal attire. Nick appeared oblivious. He led her through some tall paneled doors to another section of the club, which had to have been someone's spectacular estate at one time.

They came to a private room with high paneled ceilings, all of it surrounded by floor-to-ceiling glass windows, a modern innovation. It was almost like being on the water. He pulled out a chair where he put Jamie's carryall, then fastened him in it.

Reese sat down next to the baby. "I believe if I were prone to it, I'd be seasick about now."

A heart-stopping smile broke the corner of his mouth. "It's been known to happen in this room."

"What's the history of this place?"

He took a rattle from the diaper bag and handed it to Jamie, who claimed it in a fist and put it directly in his mouth. They both laughed.

"My mother's ancestor, Martin Sherborne, was an English sea captain in the early 1600s who traded in all sorts of lucrative things that brought him wealth. When he bought up a lot of the land around Sea Nook and had this place built, the colonial governor of New York conferred the title of Lordship of Sherborne on him.

"Eventually his grandson donated this place to the Sea Nook Township and built Sherborne House where my mother grew up. It's located about ten miles from here. The estate borders Wainwright Meadows, known for its horses, where my father was born."

"How did they amass their wealth?"

"His ancestry developed tools for steam engines. Their manufacture proliferated beyond anyone's expectations. For those who live here, Sea Nook is known as Little England."

The sommelier approached, wanting to know their preference of wine. Nick turned to her. "Nothing for me," she responded.

"We'll both wait," Nick told him.

Reese leaned over to kiss the baby. "Did you hear all that your daddy said, Jamie? You could have been its newest prince," she teased, but she shouldn't have said anything because she saw Nick's jaw harden.

"*Could have* is exactly right. Don't look now but my cousin Greg has just arrived. It appears he's alone. He and his wife live at our property in the Hamptons. They're having difficulties right now."

Add one more property to the growing list. "Are you close to him?"

"No, but he works in the office and so far we've managed to get along."

"That's something at least."

When Nick smiled like that, she couldn't breathe. "At least," he drawled. "I'm afraid I've overloaded you with too much information."

"Not at all. It's like attending an on-site live college course covering the aspects of upper-class society in Colonial America. I wouldn't have missed it for the world."

"Greg!" Nick stood up and shook his cousin's hand. He was dark like Nick, a little shorter and heavier. "This is Reese Chamberlain from Lincoln, Nebraska. Reese, this is Greg Wainwright, one of the vice presidents of the brokerage."

"How do you do, Greg." She extended her hand, which he shook. Nick's cousin couldn't take his eyes off her. Nick didn't blame him. Anyone seeing Reese with that oval face and high cheekbones would call her a classic beauty. In the candlelight her light blue eyes let off an iridescent glow.

"Come around and say hi to Jamie."

His cousin's gaze shifted to the baby, but he didn't move from his stance. He flashed Nick one of those looks that said he needed to speak to him in private. *Not this time.* Nick had an idea what it was all about. In fact he'd been anticipating it.

"Won't you sit down? Or are you waiting for Uncle Lew?"

Greg shifted his weight, a sign that he was losing patience. "I need to talk to you alone for a minute. I tried to reach you earlier."

"I'm aware of that. You can say anything you want in front of Reese."

"Father sent me in here to talk sense to you."

"What sense is that?"

"This is a special dinner party." His brows lifted. "Max has let everyone know the…three of you are here," he said in a quieter voice.

Good. "Let's call a spade a spade. This was planned so the widower could meet wife number two, but my life has changed since Erica's death, Greg. No one owns me."

His face closed up. "Then I'm afraid you'll be dining in here alone."

"My parents should have thought of that before they tried to maneuver me into something that would hurt the Ridgeways. The fact is, no one consulted me. I intend to enjoy my dinner with my son and Ms. Chamberlain. You can tell that to Uncle Lew in private. What he tells father is up to him."

Greg studied him through new eyes. "What's happened to you?" It was a genuine question, requiring a genuine answer.

"The truth? I became a father, but I discovered I want to be a dad. Ms. Chamberlain is teaching me how."

His cousin seemed to have trouble articulating before he nodded to Reese and walked out of the room.

"Nick—"

The tremor in her voice was one of the most satisfying sounds he'd ever heard.

"The swordfish here is excellent by the way. If I order it for you, I promise you won't be disappointed."

CHAPTER EIGHT

FOR five solid days starting the next Monday, Reese took Jamie with her every morning and afternoon to hunt for an unfurnished studio apartment near Miroff's located on Broadway and Seventh. She needed one close enough to walk to her job.

By midafternoon she finally found it six blocks away above a small bookstore with signs saying that it was going out of business. You had to enter the store and walk to the back where there was a circular staircase leading to the studio. Both were owned by the bank.

She couldn't allow herself to think about where she was living right now. Moving from Nick's thirty-million-dollar penthouse to the tiny hole-in-the-wall that had no AC would be like going from the proverbial sublime to the proverbial ridiculous.

In order to hold it, she arranged for a six-month sub-lease starting now, even though the two guys living there wouldn't move out until the end of August. She would buy a futon and use it for a bed. Reese wouldn't need anything else since she'd be slaving day and night at the brokerage. If she was careful, the salary Nick paid her would cover the rent through January.

The small stipend she received from Miroff's would

have to be enough for her food and any other incidentals. But at least she'd taken care of her housing problem and could spend the next week studying for her exam coming up a week from today. With a sigh of relief she phoned Paul and asked him to drive her and Jamie to the park.

"This is more like it, huh." She gave him a bunch of kisses before carrying him over to the pond. "You like these sailboats?" In her mind's eye she could see the larger sleeker ones and yachts moored at Sea Nook. That night had marked another change in Nick. He seemed charged by a new energy.

Throwing off the yoke of his other self acted as some kind of catharsis. Twice this week he'd come home early, pulled on a pair of jeans with a T-shirt and made dinner. He put Jamie in the swing to watch him and held long conversations with him. When everything was ready, he'd invite her to eat on the terrace with them.

He cooked steaks and potatoes both times, reminding her of her father, who was a meat and potatoes man, too.

"Oh—my phone's ringing. Let's find out who it is." She pulled out her cell, but didn't recognize the name on the caller ID. After a slight hesitation she clicked on.

"Hello?"

"Ms. Chamberlain? This is Albert."

"Hi, Albert!"

"Sorry to disturb, but you have a visitor and I knew you'd gone out. He says it's urgent that he sees you. His name is Jeremy Young."

Reese closed her eyes tightly. She didn't blame her ex-fiancé for coming all this way without telling her. If their situations were reversed and she couldn't let him go without trying one more time, she would do the same thing. Her dad had probably told him about the internship and he'd made up his mind to talk to her again in the hope she wouldn't take it.

But it was no use. Their romance wasn't meant to be. Her plans for the future were set. She was so close now.

And then of course there was Nick. Every living moment with him meant falling deeper and deeper in love. She wouldn't be with him much longer, but it didn't matter. He'd colored her life forever. Nick and Jamie had her heart. All of it.

"I'm leaving for the apartment right now. Would you mind letting him in the penthouse? He's flown all the way from Nebraska and will appreciate freshening up before I get there."

"I'll be happy to."

"Thank you."

She hung up. "Let's go home, Jamie. We've got company."

When she pushed the stroller into the apartment a short time later, Jeremy stepped in the foyer from the living room.

"Reese—"

His was a dear face. Familiar, yet she couldn't conjure any feeling for him. Six months ago she couldn't have imagined not flying into his arms.

"It's good to see you, Jeremy." He was an attractive six-foot blond with dark blue eyes. He wore jeans and a button-down shirt with the hems out, his usual style when he wasn't in a business suit. But the wide smile that had been his trademark was missing. She saw pain in his eyes.

"You're not angry I just showed up?" he asked with an edge.

"No. How could I be? I'm only sad that you spent your time and hard-earned money for nothing."

"That's a matter of opinion. I've had some time to think since your dad told me you got that internship. I'd like to talk to you about it."

"Of course. Come out on the terrace with me and Jamie." She pushed the stroller through the apartment.

The second she opened the sliding door and they walked out, he let go with a long, low whistle. She watched him walk over to look out on the city. "My hell... I know there are people in the world who live like this, but to see it all up close makes me think I'm hallucinating."

"I've done a lot of that myself." She put Jamie on the lounger and changed him. Jeremy returned as she was snapping his suit.

"He's a cute baby. How old is he?"

"Four months."

"How much longer will you be here?"

"Until the end of August. That's when I start at Miroff's."

"Reese," he whispered. "I'll move to New York and get a bank job. If you're determined to be a career woman, then so be it. I don't want to lose you."

She hugged Jamie to herself, needing a minute to comprehend what he was saying. Reese could only imagine what it had taken for him to come to her like this. She needed to be so careful, but whatever she said, he was going to be hurt.

Taking a fortifying breath, she faced him. "I'll always love you, Jeremy, but I've had months to think about everything, too. Your instinct is to be the provider and come home to a wife who takes care of you and your children. A lot of men are like that. It's a wonderful instinct.

"What's wrong is that you met a woman like me who needs intellectual stimulation beyond mothering. I'd like to believe that in time I can do both. If we did get back together again, I'm sure it wouldn't be long before you'd start resenting me and I'd get upset with you because I would know I wasn't making you happy. It just wouldn't work."

"You're different than before," he said on a burst of anger.

She pressed her lips together. "I've had to put you away. It wasn't easy."

"But the point is, you *have* let me go."

"Yes," she answered honestly. This tearing each other apart was exactly what she didn't want to happen. "Jamie needs his bottle. I have to get it from the kitchen." Jeremy followed her. She took it out of the fridge and warmed it in the microwave.

"Has the baby's father made moves on you already?"

"Jeremy—please let's not do this."

"That's what you say when you want to avoid the issue."

She took the bottle out of the microwave. "I think you'd better go."

"No wonder you don't want to work anything out. There's nothing to stop you from staying on here permanently. You live in a virtual palace with New York at your feet. The money he's paying you is probably more than I make in a year at the bank."

Reese held the baby in her arms and fed him, praying Jeremy would see the futility in this and leave.

"Anyone home?"

Nick's deep male voice preceded him into the kitchen. She was sure Albert would have told him Jeremy was up here. Nick had announced himself in order to warn her he was on his way in.

The look on Jeremy's face reminded her of the Hirsts' expressions when they'd walked in the kitchen and had come face-to-face with Reese. Nick was a breed apart from other men. His polish and sophistication couldn't be denied. Besides his compelling physical attributes, there was something else you felt just being in his presence.

"Nick Wainwright?" She tried to keep her voice steady. "This is Jeremy Young."

Always the urbane host, Nick extended his hand. "It's nice to meet you, Jeremy."

"Likewise, Mr. Wainwright. You have a cute son."

"Thanks. I think so, too. Please excuse me for interrupting. I came to find him so we could play for a while." His eyes darted Reese an enigmatic glance before he lifted Jamie out of her arms. The baby was still drinking his bottle. "We're going out to the terrace, aren't we, sport."

Quiet reigned after his tall, hard-muscled body left the kitchen. Jeremy's eyes narrowed on Reese's upturned features. "Well...*that* just answered every question."

"Jeremy—" she called after him, but he was out of the kitchen and the penthouse like a shot.

He'd given her no choice by showing up without having called her first. How she hated hurting him. But if meeting Nick convinced him Reese was involved with her employer, then it had to be a good thing. Otherwise

Jeremy would go on hoping for something that could never happen.

She rubbed her arms, feeling at a totally loose end. She was too tired from walking so much to go out again, but if she stayed in, she knew she wouldn't be able to study. Nick needed his time with Jamie. That left TV. Maybe a good film was on.

In the end she didn't bother to turn it on. Instead she flopped across her bed in turmoil. Five more weeks to go, but Reese was in trouble. The ache for Nick was growing intolerable.

She flung herself over on her back. Somehow she would have to find a way to be around Nick every day and not let him know the kind of pain she was in.

An hour later hunger drove her to the kitchen where she found him making ham-and-cheese sandwiches. She felt his gaze scrutinize her. "Do you and Jeremy have plans later?"

She shook her head. "He'll probably be back in Lincoln by tomorrow."

"Did you know he was coming?"

"No. His arrival was a complete surprise. Albert called me while Jamie and I were at the park."

He pursed his lips. "Then let's eat. Grab us a couple of colas from the fridge and we'll go out on the terrace."

"That sounds good."

He reached for a bag of potato chips. Together they carried everything outside to the table. After they sat down, she opened her cola and drank almost half of it, not realizing how thirsty she was.

Nick relaxed in the chair, extending his long legs in front of him while he swallowed two sandwiches in succession. "Leah and I had a conversation the other day. When she chose you for the nanny, there were three other women who could have done the job. One of them is probably still available to work. But even if they've all found other employment, there'll be someone else."

A sharp, stabbing pain almost incapacitated her. "Why are you telling me this?"

"Because you need to be free to work things out with Jeremy. The man didn't fly all this way unless he were still terribly in love with you. I saw the look on his face. He couldn't say what he had to say with me walking in on him. If you go home now, it's possible you'll straighten out your differences and end up getting married."

Nick's last stab had dissected her heart. "You mean the way you and Erica straightened out yours?" Her pain had to find an outlet. He might just as well have been her patronizing uncle Chet patting her on the head and telling her she was too pretty to study so much. The guys would be intimidated.

He stopped eating and sat forward. "I was never in love with her."

The bald revelation was swallowed up in her pain because he wasn't in love with Reese, either. Not even close or he couldn't have suggested she abandon Jamie and follow Jeremy home.

In a rare display of sarcasm she said, "Well, that's an excellent explanation for why your marriage fell apart. Jeremy and I have irreconcilable problems *now,* and would never make it to the altar."

"Love is a rare thing," he came back in a mild mannered voice, the kind that set her teeth on edge. "You had that going for you once. He hasn't given up. It appears to me that anything's still possible."

"Not when he doesn't want a working wife."

"Would it be so terrible if you compromised in order for the two of you to be together?"

"Terrible?" she cried. "It would be disastrous."

"Why?"

"Because then neither of us would be happy." She shook her head. "You really don't understand. Let me ask you something. After you'd studied all those years to make your place at Wainwright's, what if Erica had said, 'You don't need to go to work now, Nick. Stay home with me. I have enough money to take care of both of us for a lifetime.'"

His lids drooped so the black lashes shuttered his eyes. "You can't use me or Erica for an example."

The first sparks of temper shot through her. "Why not? Blue bloods still make up part of our world, albeit a tiny percentage of the population."

She watched him squeeze his cola can till it dented. "Because for one thing, the kind of love that should bind a man and woman didn't define our relationship."

"Supposing it had?"

Nick didn't like being put on the spot. It only made her more determined to get her point across.

"What if you'd both been crazy about each other and she'd told you she wanted you to be home with her and the baby. Several babies maybe. What would you have said?"

His hand absently rubbed his chest. "It's an absurd question, Reese."

"Of course it's absurd to *you*. You're a man, right? And in the world you've come from, a man is better than a woman." She jumped to her feet, unable to keep still.

A white ring of anger had encircled his lips, but she couldn't stop now. "It would be purgatory for you if you couldn't get up every morning of life eager to match wits against your competitors.

"I heard your whole genealogy the other night at the Yacht Club. You come from an ancestry that made things happen. Like them you live to pull off another million deal today, and another one tomorrow, and all the tomorrows after that. It's what makes you, *you*."

He pushed himself away from the table and stood up. "And you're telling me you feel the exact same way?"

She let out a caustic laugh. "That's inconceivable to you, isn't it. *Moi?* A mere woman who has that same fire in her? Impossible. A woman who wants to make a difference? Unheard of, right?"

"Frankly, yes," he said in a voice of irony, "particularly when I see the way you are with Jamie. No one would ever guess you weren't his mother."

"You're not even listening to me because in your eyes a woman can't be both." She circled in front of him. "Let me tell you something about yourself, Nick. Though you've come a long way to rid yourself of the shackles imposed by thirty-four years of emotional neglect, you'll never be a man who could compromise on something so vital to your very existence as your work."

The glitter in those black depths should have warned her, but she was just getting warmed up.

"Yet you hand out advice to me and suggest I go home to patch things up with Jeremy as if my problem is nothing more than a bagatelle that can be swept under the rug. Be a good girl and do what girls are supposed to do, Reese. Let Jeremy take care of business so you can take care of his babies. Compromise for the sake of your love.

That's great advice, Mr. Wainwright, as long as *you're* not the one being forced to do the compromising."

"Are you finished?" he asked as if he'd grown tired of her tantrum. She couldn't bear his condescension.

"Not quite," she fired back. "One day I intend to open my own brokerage company right here in New York and be a *huge* success. In the meantime I'm contracted with you to take care of Jamie until I start my internship at Miroff's. For your information I never renege on my commitments, unlike you who would send me back to Nebraska on the next flight without a qualm."

She paused at the sliding door. "If you need me, I'll be in my bedroom studying."

Nick buzzed his secretary. "Leah? I'll be in Lew's office for a while." He'd done a little research and had requested this conference. "Hold my calls." If Reese needed him, she'd phone his cell. But she didn't need or want anything from him.

He still had the scars from their scalding conversation of three weeks ago. Nothing about their routine had altered since then, but the atmosphere had undergone a drastic change. When they talked about Jamie, everything was civil, but the gloom that had enveloped him after Erica had died couldn't compare to the darkness enveloping him now. A wall of ice had grown around his nanny. He couldn't find her anywhere. Her love and animation were reserved exclusively for his son.

Unable to take it, he'd gone off to Martha's Vineyard with Jamie every Friday afternoon. They'd sailed the whole weekend. Sunday nights he returned to the penthouse, always finding her bedroom door closed. He'd see the light beneath and know she was in there.

Today he knew she was taking her online exam.
When he'd told her he would stay home to keep Jamie
occupied, she'd told him it wouldn't be necessary. She'd
handle both just fine, underscoring her assertions made
during their heated exchange earlier.

On that black night Reese had delivered some salvos
he'd never seen coming. Stunned by their impact, he'd
barely functioned since then. This morning he'd found
himself floundering in a dark sea and knew he couldn't
go this way any longer.

The emotional temperature was distinctly cooler
in his uncle's office. Lew sat at his desk, more or less
squinting up at Nick as he walked in. Nick had committed the unpardonable at the club for which he'd been
collectively shunned by the family.

That didn't bother him, but it had thrown Lew out
of his comfort zone. The business Nick was about to
conduct with him would dissolve what little relationship they had left. This meeting would supply the final
punctuation mark.

"What was so important I had to tell my secretary to
cancel my last two appointments for the day?"

Nick sat on the arm of one of the leather love seats.
"I'm resigning from the company effective immediately
and wanted you to be the first to know, besides Leah, of
course."

"What?" Suddenly the mask of implacability fell
from his face to reveal a vulnerability Nick had never
seen before. "You haven't told Stan? Not even your
father?"

"No. I'll leave that to you since you're closest to
them."

"But you *can't* resign—this place would fall around our ears without you."

A genuine emotion for once. Who would have believed?

"I've named Greg as my replacement in the resignation letter I gave to Leah this morning. It's been dated and notarized. Your son has earned the right to head the firm. I've earned the right to do what's best for me."

He shook his head, clearly aghast. "What are your plans?"

"I'm keeping those to myself for the time being. This is my last day here. Except for a few personal items I'm taking with me, my office is ready for Greg to claim. My accounts are now his. Leah will stay on as his private secretary to make certain there's a smooth transition."

His uncle rose slowly to his feet. "Are you dying of a fatal disease?"

Nick made a sound in his throat. Illness was the only reason Lew could possibly imagine for one of the family to do something unprecedented and heretical.

"In a manner of speaking, but that's confidential. I'll be seeing you." He got up from the chair to shake his hand. His uncle's response reminded him of a person who'd just gone into shock.

On Nick's way out he stopped by Leah's office. "Is everything done?"

"It is."

"Did you get everything I needed?"

"It's all there in your briefcase. Paul's waiting out in front."

"You're the best friend a man ever had." The fact that it was a woman didn't escape him.

He slipped her an envelope with a check in it made

out to her, gave her a hug, then rode down the elevator and walked out of the building as if he had wings on his feet. A few minutes later he walked in the door of the penthouse feeling as if he'd been given his get-out-of-jail-free card.

"Reese?"

When she didn't answer, he headed for the terrace. The second he opened the sliding door he could hear her laughter. Over the hedge he could see her and Jamie in the pool. She'd pinned her ponytail on top of her head and was pulling him around on an inflated plastic duck. Evidently her exam was over and she'd decided to let off some excess energy. She was a knockout in that tangerine-colored bikini.

Since Reese hadn't seen him yet, he dashed back to his bedroom and changed into his swimming trunks. On his way out he grabbed a couple of bath towels and headed for the pool once more.

To his delight she and Jamie were still moving around in the water. She sprinkled his tummy several times, provoking little laughs from him. Would the day might come when she'd do that to Nick, but it would be more than laughter she'd get in return.

He dived in the deep end and swam underwater on purpose where he could feast his eyes on her long, gorgeous legs. They were an enticement he couldn't resist, but he *had* to.

A few feet from her, he surfaced and heaved himself up on the tile. She was all eyes when he came out of the water. *"Nick—"*

Yes, Nick. For a split second he could have sworn he saw longing in them before she turned to Jamie, who'd become her shield. "How was the exam?" His eyes were drawn to the small nerve throbbing at the base of her throat.

"Maybe I had a different battery than others who've taken it, but it wasn't as hard as I'd thought it would be."

"I'm sure you're glad it's over."

"Definitely." She twirled the duck around so Jamie could see him. "He's been waiting for you to come home."

What a sight! Her blue eyes were more dazzling than the water. He slid back in the pool and swam over to his son.

"Look at you having the time of your life out here." Jamie almost fell out of the floater trying to get to him. With a laugh, Nick caught him up to his shoulder and kissed him. While he was enjoying his son, Reese did a backflip and swam to the other end of the pool to get out. It was a good exit line, but he wasn't about to let her get away with it.

"Reese?" She looked back at him as she was about to walk off. "Whatever your plans are this evening, I need to talk to you first. Give me ten minutes and I'll meet you in the dining room."

"All right."

When she'd gone, he looked down at Jamie. "We've got to get out and dressed, sport. Tonight's kind of important." He swam over to the steps and climbed out. After wrapping him in a towel, he headed for the nursery and put him in a diaper and shirt.

Since he seemed content, Nick let him stay in the crib with his pacifier. Then he went to his bedroom to shower and change into trousers and a sport shirt.

Fifteen minutes later he gathered Jamie and the

swing. Reese was already waiting for them at the table in the dining room with her ponytail redone. The waiter had already brought their meal and had set everything up.

With Jamie ensconced in the swing, Nick was able to concentrate on Reese, who'd changed into a pale blue cotton top and denims. "Do you like lamb?" He lifted the covers off their plates.

"I love it."

"Then I think you'll enjoy Cesar's rack of lamb." So saying, he poured both of them water before starting to eat.

She followed suit. "Sounds like you're celebrating."

"I thought it sounded like a good idea. Your exam is over, and a Greek friend of mine named Andreas Simonides has invited me to spend some time with him and his wife, Gabi, on the island of Milos in the Aegean. We met a few years ago when we were both single and did some sailing together. He has stayed here at the penthouse on several occasions. He's married now with a three-month-old baby girl himself and is anxious to meet Jamie. So I told him I'd come."

"That sounds exciting." She was doing her best to act pleased for him, but she'd been with him and Jamie every day for weeks now. The thought of a separation caused such a great upheaval inside her, she could hardly breathe from the pain.

"I think so, too."

"When are you leaving?"

"Tomorrow morning."

That soon? "How long will you be gone?" She fought to keep her voice steady.

"Two weeks."

She didn't have time to hide her shock.

"Now that I've got Jamie, I feel like a long holiday. You'll be coming with us of course. His wife is an American, which will be nice for you."

Reese and Gabi sat in deck chairs on the patio surrounding the pool of the Simonides villa, watching the babies in their swings. Little Cristiana was as golden-blonde as Jamie was dark headed. They looked adorable together. Reese had never envied anyone until now, but she envied Gabi, who had Andreas's love and his baby.

Moaning inwardly, she looked all around her. The Simonides' family retreat was so gorgeous, it was beyond impossible to describe. A myriad of white, cubed-styled villas were clustered against the cliff abounding in flowers of every color and greenery all the way down to the water. There the white sand merged with an aquamarine ocean that took your breath.

This morning the men had gone fishing early, but they'd promised to be back by lunchtime. Reese's holiday would have been heaven on earth if she and Nick were lovers, but such wasn't the case. Nick had behaved like the perfect employer, albeit a kind, generous one. But he'd kept his distance and had given her plenty of time off so she could enjoy herself without having to tend Jamie every second.

Gabi was a sweetheart. She'd been the manager of an advertising agency back in Alexandria, Virginia, so they had a lot in common. The two of them had taken to each other at once and had flown to Athens several times to meet other members of the Simonides clan. They shopped and went to the opera, but for the most part, the time was spent on Andreas's fabulous gleaming white luxury cabin cruiser probably forty to forty-five feet long.

With the babies, the four of them visited all the wonders of the island. They walked through the little villages, ate local food, swam at the unique beaches and soaked up the Grecian sun in absolute luxury. But this idyllic time was fast coming to a close. Tomorrow they were due to fly back to New York.

True to their word, Nick came out on the patio with Andreas, both in shorts and nothing else, just as lunch was about to be served. The latter kissed his wife soundly before pulling Cristiana out of her swing to kiss her.

Writhing with unassuaged longings, Reese got up and slipped on her beach jacket while Nick grabbed Jamie and got into the pool with him. When they emerged and everyone was seated around the patio table eating, Nick glanced at her. "I've made arrangements for one of the maids to tend Jamie this afternoon so I can take you to a beach you haven't seen before."

"It's our favorite spot on Milos," Andreas said, covering his wife's hand.

"That sounds wonderful," Reese murmured, though something inside told her she'd be a fool to spend that much time alone with Nick. But she didn't want to argue in front of their hosts who'd been so fabulous to them, she'd never be able to repay them.

"Good. You're already in your bathing suit, so as soon as you've finished eating, we'll go."

Reese swallowed the last of her iced lemon drink and got up to give Jamie a goodbye kiss. "Be a good boy. We'll be back soon." The baby got all excited. His reaction warmed her heart.

"We'll go down this path." He started ahead of her. They zigzagged down to the private pier lined on both sides with various types of boats. Nick headed for a small jet boat they hadn't ridden in yet.

When he helped her to climb in, she felt fire shoot up her arm. This really wasn't a good idea, but she'd said she would go. Somehow she needed to turn off the hormones. To her chagrin she didn't know how.

Nick was so at home on the water, you would have thought he lived here year-round. After handing her a life jacket and telling her to put it on, he untied the ropes and they backed out into the blue bay. Once they got beyond the buoys, they sped through the glasslike water of the Aegean. Glorious.

When he turned his head and smiled at her, she was in such a euphoric state, she felt as if they were flying. "There's no beach in the world like the one you're going to see."

"I can't imagine anything more beautiful than the ones we've been to already."

"Papafragas is different. Have you had a good time so far? Feel like you've gotten away from all your studies and worries?"

Her lips curved into a full-bodied smile. "A good time?" she mocked. "That's like asking me if I've been having a good time in paradise."

"There are levels of excitement, even in paradise."

She averted her eyes. Yes. To be loved and make love with Nick would be the pinnacle, the only part of paradise she would never know.

They eventually drew close to another part of the island. Nick cut the motor and the momentum drove them toward a cave opening.

"I feel like a pirate."

He flashed her a penetrating glance. "Andreas tells me they used to roam these waters. We'll swim from here." Nick got out of his seat and lowered the anchor. "If you get tired, you've got your life jacket on to support you and I'll take us the rest of the way."

At the thought of him touching her one more time, adrenaline shot through her system, driving her to her feet. Without waiting for Nick, she leaped off the side and headed through the cave opening. Once beyond it she realized it was a long, natural, fjordlike swimming pool surrounded by walls of white rock.

"This is fantastic!"

"This is fantastic!" came the echo. She laughed in delight.

He caught up to her and they did the side stroke as they headed for the other end. His dark eyes held hers. "There are half a dozen caves in here. If we had more time, we could explore them."

Time. Her enemy.

Another fifty yards lay a strip of warm white sand from the sun finding its way down between the walls of rock. Nick reached it first and pulled her onto the sand. They both turned over to lie on their backs.

"You were right, Nick. This beach is incredible."

"Andreas said he used to come here with his brother Leon to play space aliens."

Her laughter rang out over and over because of the echo. "I love it here!" she cried. Again, her words reverberated, *Love it here, love it here, love it here.*

"You sound happy, Reese."

"Not happy. Something so much more, but there is no word in English for what I'm feeling right now."

"Then you admit you needed a vacation, too."

She let out an exasperated sound. "You know I did. I've been in school for so long, I almost forgot what it's like to play. Of course there's playing, and then there's the Wainwright-Simonides way of having fun."

This time Nick's deep, rich laughter resounded against the walls.

Reese smiled at him. "You sound like King Poseidon in here, coming up from the sea for a breather because he's happy, too."

"I am. When I think of the dark place I was before I hired you, I can't relate to it anymore. I have you to thank for that. There's no way in this world I'll be able to repay you for showing me how to be a dad to my son."

Her eyes filled with tears she fought to hold back. "You just have by giving me this trip. Andreas and Gabi are the nicest people I've ever known. It's been an experience I'll cherish all my life."

"I'm glad then," he said in a husky voice. Quick as lightning he rolled on his side, bringing him close to her. "Reese—" He put his hand on her arm, but she wasn't destined to succumb to her needs because four people had started down the rocks from the surface on their end of the beach and their voices were already making echoes.

She heard a groan of protest come out of Nick before he got up and pulled her to her feet. His eyes fused with hers. "A serpent has entered Eden. Let's go."

Much as she hated the intrusion, those swimmers had probably prevented her from confessing all to Nick and begging him to make love to her. She'd passed up her chance when they'd gone sailing at Martha's Vineyard.

This time she wouldn't have had the willpower to deny herself or him anything.

Other swimmers were pouring in at the other end of the cave entrance. Apparently it was a very popular place in the late afternoon. She and Nick had been lucky to have it to themselves for as long as they did.

On the other side of the rocks were two more boats with even more people jumping off to enter the cave. They asked questions of Nick in Greek. It gave her time to hurry around the end of their jet boat and climb the ladder before he could touch her. The unforgettable memories were storing up like mad.

During the trip back, Nick was unusually quiet. She was glad, because she was in no frame of mind to make small talk. It was good they were leaving in the morning. She couldn't take any more of this kind of togetherness, knowing it had no future.

As soon as they pulled up to the pier, she told him she was anxious to shower. After that she would relieve the maid of taking care of Jamie and would see him at dinner.

It turned out to be a big family affair with many of Andreas's family in attendance. So many children. So much love. All of them belonged to each other except for her and Nick.

Reese was actually glad when morning came and the three of them left in the helicopter for Athens. Once they were back in New York, they would return to their normal routine. Nick would go to work and Reese would continue to love the baby and take him everywhere with her until…

She couldn't think about *until*. The thought of moving to that tiny little room and starting her internship without them was anathema to her.

CHAPTER NINE

REESE had endured a terrible last night on Milos. She'd finally fallen asleep on a wet pillow. By the time they were in flight on Nick's private jet and she'd given Jamie a bottle, she was so tired, Nick took the baby from her and told her to go to sleep.

She didn't waken until the fasten-seat-belts sign flashed on. Jamie was strapped in his carrycot in the other club seat sound asleep. Reese looked at Nick.

"I'm sorry I slept so long."

"Evidently you needed it." He was staring at her rather strangely. She didn't understand.

"Is there something wrong?"

"Not at all."

Maybe it was her imagination. After leaving Greece, it was probably hard for him to come back to the penthouse, which was a huge reminder of the sadness he'd lived through during the past year.

The jet touched down and taxied to a stop in front of the private hangar. Out the window she saw Paul leave the limo and walk toward them. With Nick, everything ran like clockwork.

She undid her seat belt and stood up to stretch. Paul came on board and nodded to her before carrying Jamie off the jet. When she turned to Nick, he smiled. "You look rested."

"I am. How did Jamie do during the flight?"

"He was perfect."

"That's good." Why was he standing there, looking at her in such an odd way again?

"It's because of the expert care you've given him. He's thriving because of you. Now it's time for you to have a few weeks to yourself before you start your internship at Miroff's. My pilot has instructions to fly you to Lincoln as soon as I get off."

What? Her world started to reel.

"Andreas and I talked about it and thought it best that both you and Jamie have a clean break from each other. He's had maids and a housekeeper fussing over him while we were in Greece. Hopefully he'll adjust to the new nanny Leah has found for me. Since I don't have one complaint about you, I'm going to trust her judgment again."

He was sending her back to Nebraska, just like that?

"Please accept my gratitude for all you've done by accepting this last gift. As your employer, I have the right." So saying, he reached in his pocket for an envelope and handed it to her. "Inside this is an airline ticket for your flight when you come back to New York in two weeks."

Her mouth had gone dry to the point it was impossible to swallow. "I couldn't take it."

"If that's your decision, but I wish you'd reconsider." He took it and tossed it on the seat of the club car next to her. "The return date has been left open in case you didn't plan to arrive until the day you start at Miroff's.

Since I put your full salary for the three months speci-
fied into your account the day you came to work for me,
I don't think I've left anything out."

No. Nothing. Absolutely nothing.

"I instructed Rita to pack the rest of your belongings.
Paul brought them to the airport. They're being put on
board right now. Since I'm sure your parents would want
to know you're coming, why not phone them before the
pilot's ready to take off?"

"I'll do that," she answered numbly.

"If you need anything, just ask the steward."

"I will. Give Jamie a goodbye kiss for me."

"Of course." He studied her for a moment longer.
"Miroff's is going to be lucky to get you. Have a safe
flight."

"I can't face the family tonight, Mom. Yesterday when I
got home, I thought I could." Reese had been shucking
the corn while her mom finished fixing the green salad
for the barbecue. Her dad was outside getting the grill
warmed up. The whole family would descend en masse
in a little while.

"I know you're absolutely devastated, but that's the
very reason why you need to."

Tears gushed down her tanned face. "You'll never
know the pain I'm in. I honestly thought Nick had fallen
in love with me, too. I'm such a little fool I can't believe
it."

Her mom flashed her a commiserating look. "You
know what you're going to have to do?" She sliced two
rows of tomatoes and onions in perfect sections. "Put
this experience behind you. I realize that's easy for me
to say, but in a way he's done you a great favor. Another

two weeks of togetherness would have made the parting nearly impossible. You have to think of Jamie."

"You're right." She wiped her wet cheeks with the back of her hands. "Nick could see how attached I've become to him. I love that little boy. He's so cute and darling, you have no idea."

"I'm sure he loves *you*. The hospital visit bonded you."

"I know," she said in a haunted whisper.

"Thanks to Nick's generosity, we have two weeks to talk this over without you having money worries or deadlines."

At any other time in her life Reese might have echoed her mom's feelings, but it was agony being away from Nick. Every time she thought about him and Jamie, she got this pain in her chest and could hardly breathe.

"Do you have pictures of them?"

"Yes. I had doubles made up for his baby book and kept some for me. I'll get them." She dashed through the house to her bedroom and grabbed the packet off her dresser. "These are the ones I took of them the day we put the nursery together. And here are some I took while we were on Milos."

Her mom wiped her hands and studied them. When she lifted her head, she took a long time before she spoke because her lovely gray-blue eyes said it all. "I think your pain is going to take a long time to go away. It's a good thing you'll be working so hard at Miroff's."

Her mom was right. She needed family around. Her sister Carrie would be here soon with her two children. The distraction would help, but then everyone would go home after the weekend was over and Reese would once more be a prisoner to her memories.

She didn't know how she was she going to make it through tonight, let alone the rest of her life without him and Jamie. But to her shock, she was still alive the next day and the day after that. Her dad put her to work at the lumberyard, which saved her life. She answered phones and did odd jobs for him.

On Friday of the second week her mom phoned the office. "I'm glad you answered it. An express-mail envelope just came for you. I had to sign for it." Reese's heart began to thud. Intellectually she knew it wasn't from Nick, but her heart was crying out otherwise. "Do you want me to open it?"

"Please. It could be my exam results, but I thought they'd just send my score online."

"Well, you *are* their top student."

Reese smiled to herself in spite of her pain. "I'm the luckiest girl in the world to have a cheering section like you, Mom. What's in it?"

"A letter from Miroff and Hooplan." Reese had been waiting for final instructions from them, but her disappointment was so acute that it wasn't from Nick, she sank down in the chair. "Do you want me to read it?"

"Yes. I need to know when to make my return flight."

"Let's see. It's very short. 'Dear Ms. Chamberlain, congratulations on your new appointment. Please report to our office on Monday, August 29, at 9:00 a.m. for an orientation that will last until 4:00 p.m.'"

"That's two days sooner than my studio apartment will be vacant—"

"Don't worry. Your father and I want to pay for a decent hotel for you to stay in until you're settled."

"You're wonderful. Thanks, Mom."

"It says, 'We look forward to working with you. Sincerest Regards, Gerald Soffe, Vice President of Internal Affairs.' Well, honey, that makes it official."

The taxi dropped Reese off in front of Miroff's on Broadway. She'd decided to dress in a summer two-piece suit in a melon color. Maybe she could get away with a ponytail later on, but today she wore her hair down. It fell from a side part and had a tendency to curl in the humidity.

She paid the driver and went inside carrying her brief-case that held her laptop. "I'm Reese Chamberlain. I was told to report to Mr. Soffe," she told the receptionist.

"Second door down the hall on your left. He's expecting you."

"Thank you." She started for her destination, realizing she didn't feel the excitement she should have. For the past two weeks she'd been in a depressed state. Coming back to New York had made it worse.

When she spotted his name and title on the door, she opened it and walked in to find another receptionist, who lifted her red head. "You must be Ms. Chamberlain."

"Yes."

"Go right on in."

"Thank you."

The second she entered the man's office, she saw a familiar figure seated behind the desk and let out a cry.

It was Nick!

He'd kept his dark tan since their return from Greece and his black hair had grown longer. In a dove-gray summer suit with a darker gray shirt and no tie, he was gorgeous beyond belief.

"Hello, Reese." His eyes played over her slowly, missing nothing from her head to her low heels. "Come all the way in and sit down."

He didn't need to tell her that. By the time she reached the nearest chair, she was out of breath and her legs no longer supported her. "H-how's Jamie?" she stammered like a fool.

"Other than missing you, he's perfect."

She'd started trembling and couldn't stop. "What's going on? Where's Mr. Soffe?"

"He's a professional friend of mine. I asked him to make himself scarce while I talked to you first."

Maybe she was hallucinating. "Why would you do that?"

"When my uncle Lew assigned Rich Bonner to be the fall intern, he made a mistake. You were the top candidate from Wharton's, but as you know, blue bloods don't consider women equal to men, so he chose Mr. Bonner, who'd been ranked second highest in his class."

Reese wanted to die. "You'll never forgive me for that, will you. Don't you know how sorry I am?" she cried out emotionally.

His eyes flashed dark fire. "You have nothing to feel guilty about. Why would you when it was the truth! I straightened things out with Gerald. He's been in contact with Mr. Bonner, who will be coming to work for Miroff's in a few days."

With those words, Reese felt as if she was in a strange dream where nothing was as it should be. "Don't think I don't appreciate what you've tried to do for me, Nick, but I don't want anything changed, because I have no intention of working for your corporation. Even though

I was a woman, Miroff's took me on. I plan to make them very happy with their choice."

He studied her for a tension-filled moment. "In that case you'll have to walk across the street with me while we visit with Greg, Uncle Lew's son. You met him the night we had dinner at the Yacht Club. You need to tell him what you just told me. Then he'll make it right with Gerald and your friend Rich."

Searing pain drove through her to think that in the future she'd be working across the street from Nick. She couldn't bear it.

He came around the desk and picked up her briefcase. "Shall we go?"

How many times had she heard him say that before in connection with Jamie. Like déjà vu she left the building with him. Whenever they walked together, she had to hurry to keep up with his long strides. They maneuvered the crowded crosswalk and eventually entered the tall doors of his family's firm.

Nick nodded to the foyer receptionist and continued to the elevator. "Greg's in his office waiting for us." They emerged on the third floor and entered a door marked Gregory Wainwright, President.

President? But *Nick* was the CEO.

Before she could ask what it meant, Leah Tribe was there to greet her. "We meet again, Ms. Chamberlain."

But Mrs. Tribe was *Nick's* secretary. What was going on? "How are you, Mrs. Tribe?"

"I couldn't be better. I hear you're going to be working for us. How do you feel about that?"

How did she feel? "I'm afraid there's been a mistake. I need to talk to Mr. Wainwright."

"Oh—" The secretary looked surprised. "Go right on in. He's expecting you."

Nick slanted her a glance she couldn't read. Still carrying her briefcase, he led her inside the inner door.

Reese remembered Nick's cousin, who got to his feet. He was a man in his thirties who bore a slight resemblance to Nick, though he was shorter and less fit looking.

"Greg? You were introduced to Ms. Chamberlain before. Apparently there's been a mistake. She intends to stay with Miroff's and you'll be getting Mr. Bonner as planned."

His cousin looked completely thrown, but before he could say anything there was a buzz, then Leah Tribe's voice came over the intercom. "I'm sorry to bother you, Mr. Wainwright, but Stan needs a minute of your time for something that can't wait."

"I'll be right there, Leah. Nick?" He turned to him. "If you'll keep Ms. Chamberlain occupied, I'll be back as soon as I can."

The door shut, enclosing the two of them in a silence so quiet, she was sure Nick could hear her heart hammering. He took his seat behind the desk. She found a wing chair opposite him and sat down.

"Did they let you go because of what happened at the Yacht Club?"

"No. It was my choice. In fact I stepped down before I left for Greece with you and Jamie."

"Why?" she asked in shock. "I don't understand."

He stared at her for a long time. "Because I wanted to be free. You see…I'm getting married right away. You could say I'm starting a new life."

Reese thought she would faint, but she wouldn't let

him know how his news had affected her. "Someone you've known for a long time?"

Nick cocked his head. "Do you remember the day you stepped into my limo for the first time?"

She frowned. "Surely you don't need an answer to that question."

"Surely you shouldn't have had to ask me that question at all," he fired back. "Who else would I marry but *you*."

Blood hammered in her ears. "Be serious, Nick," her voice trembled.

"I would never be anything else *but* with the woman who's about to become my wife and Jamie's legal mother. We took a vote while we were on Milos and decided it was you or no one. Andreas and Gabi seconded the motion."

Reese shook her head. "I'm so confused I must have missed something. I'm going to work at Miroff's. How could you think I would be your wife?"

"It's possible to be both. You convinced me of that a month ago during one of our more scintillating conversations. Here's my proposal. We get married in Nebraska and honeymoon there. I want to meet your family. Then we'll come back to the penthouse and you start work. I'll be a stay-at-home daddy during your internship."

She couldn't possibly be hearing him correctly.

"When you're through at Miroff's and graduate, we'll take care of Jamie together while you decide where and how you're going to start your own brokerage firm. You'll be doing it all on your own. When you're ready to take on a partner, I'm your man behind the scenes."

"Nick—"

"We'll get my office set up in the other bedroom

at the end of the hall like you wanted to do in the first place. I'll work for you at home. I'm counting on you being a huge success because you're going to be the one bringing in the money for both of us, starting with the stipend you'll make being an intern. You see, I've signed away my entire inheritance to the family."

Her gasp reverberated in the room.

"The money I earned myself allowed me to buy the penthouse. But it represents my old life with Erica. When your company gets off the ground, I want to sell it and buy us a house outside the city. Somewhere in a residential neighborhood where Jamie and another brother or sister can play with other children on the block and have a dog. The rest I'll invest for our children's future."

"Oh, darling—"

Reese flew out of the chair and around the desk. Her feet never touched the ground before she landed in his arms. She threw them around his neck, so deliriously happy she couldn't talk. Instead she started sobbing. "Nick— I love you and Jamie so terribly. You just don't know—"

"Tell me about it," he whispered into her hair, crushing her to death.

Neither of them was aware Mrs. Tribe had come in until they heard her voice. "I like what I see, you two. I like it very much."

Nick lifted his mouth from Reese's. "Thank heaven for you, Leah."

When the door closed, Reese urgently pressed her mouth to his again. She couldn't get enough and never would, but her euphoria was interrupted once more. This time she heard a baby crying, but it had lost its newborn sound.

"Jamie?"

"Who else? He's living for you to hug and kiss him, but this is one time he's going to have to get in line."

Miroff's closed down for Christmas on the eighteenth, which would be Reese's last working day as an intern. But when she approached Gerald a few days before and told him she had a special surprise for Nick that required the last day off, her boss was happy to give it to her.

In fact he handed her an enormous bonus for her outstanding work. Then he offered her a job with his company. She hadn't expected either offering and was overwhelmed.

After expressing her gratitude, she told him she couldn't accept the offer because she and Nick had other plans. But she thanked him with a big hug, which he reciprocated, and she gave him his Christmas present. It was a box of chocolate truffles from his favorite candy shop. She'd given the same gift to Leah.

On the seventeenth, she kissed her husband and son goodbye and pretended to leave for work. Paul was waiting for her out in front of the apartment building as always. When she climbed in the limo, she asked him to drive her to the studio apartment she'd leased in August. Unbeknownst to Nick, Paul had been bringing her here most every working day on her lunch break for the past four months.

When she got out of the limo into the freezing cold, she walked up to the window. He put it down. "This is for you. Merry Christmas." She handed him the gift she'd had engraved for him. It was a gold ring with a stunning black onyx stone. Inside it read, Ever Faithful.

"I don't know what Nick and I would do without you." She smiled. "Until later."

He winked. "I can't wait to see Nick's face when I pull up with him."

"I'm living for that, too."

When he drove off, she walked toward the entrance of the former bookshop with so much excitement, she could scarcely contain it. A large, classy-looking black-and-white-striped awning gave the storefront a whole new look and caught the eye of every passerby. Her eyes traced the formal gold lettering on the squeaky-clean glass door with a stunning holly wreath hanging above.

Chamberlain & Wainwright Brokerage.

For the rest of the day she wrapped presents and put them under the lighted Christmas tree in the center of the room. By two o'clock everything was ready upstairs and down.

With her pulse racing, she reached for her cell and phoned Nick.

"Reese?" She hadn't heard that tinge of anxiety in his voice for a long time.

"Hi, darling."

"Is anything wrong? You don't usually call me this time of day."

"Everything's fine. I'm just tired and feel like leaving early. Gerald gave me the time off. I thought if you and Jamie came and picked me up, we could have an early dinner at a cozy little place I've found."

Whenever Nick worried, he was always quiet before he responded. "We'll come right now. Are you sure you're all right? You've been working so hard you've knocked yourself out."

"No harder than you. How's our boy?"

"He's been trying to stand up, but keeps falling down."

"I have no doubts he'll be walking sooner than most children his age. Come soon? I miss you both horribly."

Convinced something was wrong, Nick phoned Paul and told him to bring the car out front. Getting up from his office chair, he rushed down the hall to the nursery. Jamie wasn't due to wake up from his afternoon nap for another half hour, but it couldn't be helped. It wasn't like Reese to call in the afternoon. That's when she was normally in conference with the staff.

"Sorry, sport." Jamie was still half-asleep while Nick changed his diaper and put him in his blue snowsuit with the white fake fur around the edge of the hood. He grabbed a couple of bottles of formula and put them in the diaper bag. Once he'd shrugged into his overcoat, they left the penthouse for the limo.

As far as he was concerned, this ought to be her last day at work. His wife was a dynamo and needed to slow down. They could go get a Christmas tree in a few days after she'd had a rest. Deep in thought, it surprised him to discover they'd turned off Broadway at Seventh. It had started snowing. What was going on?

He spoke into the intercom. "Paul? Did you have to make a detour?"

"No. Your wife phoned and asked me to drop you off at the restaurant to save time. It's only a few more blocks now."

Nick frowned. "Did she sound all right to you?"

"Perfectly."

He glanced out the window, not seeing anything

because Reese's call had disturbed him. Pretty soon they pulled to a stop in heavy traffic. Nick climbed out and lifted Jamie's carryall from the car seat. Paul came around and handed him the diaper bag.

When he looked around he said, "I don't see a place to eat anywhere. Are you sure you have the right address?"

"It's right there in front of you, Nick."

All he could see was a business of some kind. He brushed the flakes off his lashes. On the awning he saw the words *Chamberlain & Wainwright Brokerage.*

Suddenly he could feel the blood pounding in his ears.

His gaze darted to the front door with the same words done in gold lettering. Through the falling snow a Christmas tree with dozens of colored lights beckoned him from behind the glass.

"How long have you known about this?"

"About four months."

"You've been helping her?"

He nodded. "Driving her to and fro on her lunch hour. She gave me this." He held up his hand to show him the ring he was wearing. "There was an inscription." When he told Nick what it was, Nick felt this thickness in his throat. There was no one more exciting, more thoughtful, kind and full of surprises than his beloved wife!

"Thank you for helping her, Paul."

"It's been a pleasure. I'll be around when you need a ride home."

He started for the door.

Reese couldn't wait any longer and opened it. "Merry Christmas early, darling."

Nick came inside and shut the door, bringing the cold

in with him. She held her breath, waiting to hear what he would say and think. The first thing he did was put the carryall with Jamie in it on the floor and crush her in his arms. She got a face full of snowflakes, but she didn't care.

"I don't know how you did it," his deep voice grated, "but you *did* it."

"I hope you won't be upset I put your name on the door, too, but I am a Wainwright now."

"You most definitely are, my love. If you hadn't put it on there, I'd have been devastated."

"Oh, Nick—"

Their mouths fused in rapture. They clung for a long, long time.

"Mr. Soffe gave me a bonus," she explained when he let her come up for breath. "It was enough to buy all the office equipment and furniture."

"Where did you find this place? How did you manage it?"

"When I leased the upstairs part thinking I'd be living here while I worked at Miroff's, the place was going out of business. Mr. Harvey from the bank was one of the clients I've been working with at the brokerage.

"I told him my idea for my own plans and he was willing to give me a lease and a loan to refurbish the whole place without a cosigner. That's because of you, darling. But I have to make good this time next year to pay it back. Now I'm terrified!"

Nick laughed for joy and swung her around. "Of what? I'm convinced you can do anything! Trust my wife to pull all this together."

"I used part of the money you paid me to hire Toni to do the painting."

"The waiter? You're teasing me."

"I hope you're not upset about that. He paints houses and apartments on the side part of the week to earn money while he's at night school. He attached the awning for me, too. I think he did a wonderful job."

His dark eyes roved over her face before he covered it with kisses. "I think *you're* wonderful."

"Thank you for being there for me every step of the way. I've never known such happiness in my life. Now I want to make you happy. Take off your coat and follow me upstairs."

While he removed it, she undid Jamie from the carryall. "Don't you look so cute in your snowsuit? I could eat you up. Yes, I could." She kissed his neck while she took it off. He laughed over and over again as she kissed one cheek, then the other. "I love you, little guy."

She looked up to see the love light in Nick's eyes. "Come with me."

The three of them ascended the winding steps to the studio. Reese had bought a playpen, which she'd set up next to the double bed. She lay Jamie in it and handed him a ball just his size. "With the tiny kitchen to one side of the room, there's hardly any space left to maneuver."

"I like it when we're so close nothing comes between us," Nick whispered against her neck. He slid his arms around her hips and before she knew it, they'd fallen on the bed together. "I love this innovation, Mrs. Wainwright."

"I figure it will come in handy for small naps in the next seven and a half months."

"What are you talking about?" he murmured, burying his face in her neck.

She smiled secretly. "Why, Nick Wainwright—imagine the financial prince of Park Avenue having to ask a question like that."

He lifted his head to look down at her with fire in his dark eyes. "The *what?*"

"You heard me. That's my mom's secret name for you. You *are* known to have a computer brain that catapulted you to be the former CEO of Sherborne and Wainwright. No one would believe it if you couldn't calculate the significance of a simple number like 7.5."

His black brows furrowed.

"Maybe if we go downstairs and open a few presents, you'll understand."

"Give me a hint now." He claimed her mouth again in a deep kiss that went on and on.

"Even though we won't need it until July, I got it on sale now. It goes in the limo."

More silence, and then she heard his sharp intake of breath. He sat all the way up. If she'd been worried, she didn't have to be. On his handsome face she saw the eager, tremulous look of joy, making him appear younger.

"I've made you pregnant?" he cried. "But you went on the pill."

"No, I didn't. On our honeymoon there was a night when you told me you had this dream about giving Jamie a little brother or sister right away, so he wouldn't grow up alone the way you did. Of course you knew it wasn't possible you said and brushed it off as if it were nothing.

"After you went to sleep, I thought about it all night long and knew you were right. I grew up with siblings and can't imagine being an only child. I didn't want that for Jamie, either."

His hands cupped her face. "You've been to an ob-gyn?"

"Yes. He's one Leah recommended. I really like him. He said everything looks good."

"Reese—"

He lay back down and ran his hand over her stomach. "I can't believe you've got our baby in there."

"You're really happy about it?"

A sound escaped his throat. "What a question."

"I'm glad because I am, too. Ecstatic! We'll figure it all out."

"After taking care of Jamie, what's another one."

She laughed and rolled into him. "For the man who didn't know how to diaper a baby, you'd win the father-of-the-year award now. I sent for something special for you to celebrate. Why don't you go downstairs and get it. It's the carton with the red ribbon tied around the middle."

"I'll be right back." In a minute he'd returned.

She raised herself up on her elbow. "Go ahead and open it."

Like a little kid ripping at his Christmas present, he tore off the paper in no time. "What's this?" He lifted out the bottle. "Deer Springs Wine from Lincoln." His gaze flicked to hers. A smile lit up his face. "They produce wine in Nebraska?"

"It *is* pretty amazing. Pretty good, too. The label will tell you it comes from a hearty grape called the Edelveiss that can withstand the cold, the heat and the prairie winds."

His eyes glazed over. "That could be a description of

my Nebraska nanny who withstood everything thrown at her and is now a Seventh Avenue broker to be reckoned with." He walked to the kitchen and found a supply of paper cups she'd put out. After he removed the cork, he poured himself some.

Then he walked back to the bed and sat next to her. "*Salut*, my pregnant love," he spoke in a deep velvety voice. "May our partnership last forever."

"I'll drink to that one day. I love you, Nick. To *forever*."

Nanny to the Billionaire's Son

BARBARA McMAHON

Barbara McMahon was born and raised in the South, but settled in California after spending a year flying around the world for an international airline. After settling down to raise a family and work for a computer firm, she began writing when her children started school. Now, feeling fortunate in being able to realise a long-held dream of quitting her 'day job' and writing full time, she and her husband have moved to the Sierra Nevada mountains of California, where she finds her desire to write is stronger than ever. With the beauty of the mountains visible from her windows and the pace of life slower than the hectic San Francisco Bay Area where they previously resided, she finds more time than ever to think up stories and characters and share them with others through writing. Barbara loves to hear from readers. You can reach her at PO Box 977, Pioneer, CA 95666-0977, USA. Readers can also contact Barbara at her website: www.barbaramcmahon.com.

Chuck Nash, for always being there for me.
I love you, Daddy.

PROLOGUE

SAMANTHA DUNCAN lifted the crumpled card from the floor. It had fluttered in the air when she dumped the deskside trash can. Smoothing it out on the flat surface of the mahogany desk, her fingers traced the embossed print, complete with gold emblem at the top. It was a ticket to Atlanta's Black and White Ball on New Year's Eve. The thick, creamy paper screamed expensive, as did the fancy script. Of course tickets to the ball went at five hundred dollars a pop, so they should look elegant.

And the owner of this one had crumpled it up and tossed it away. For a moment her imagination sparked. She'd love to go to a ball, dressed to the nines, flirt with dashing captains of industry, or trust-fund men who never had to work two jobs to make ends meet.

She held it over the large barrel that held the floor's trash, hesitated a moment, then slid it in her apron pocket, righted the trash container and continued with the task of dusting and vacuuming the office of the CEO of McAlheny Industries. It probably meant nothing to the man. He was one of the top-ten wealthiest men in Atlanta, maybe even the East Coast. A mere five hundred dollars would be a pittance to him.

As she worked, she furthered her image of herself at the ball, just like Cinderella. She'd be wearing a fabulous designer creation. Men would fall over themselves asking her to dance. She wouldn't sit out a single one. And she would be dazzling in her witty repartee.

The food was rumored to be to die for. She had a sweet tooth and couldn't help wondering, would the desserts be beyond fabulous? She'd love to have crème brûlée or a super-rich chocolate torte.

"Ready to move to the next floor?" One of her coworkers waited at the door. Sam glanced around the pristine office and nodded. The bubble popped. She was tired. The good news was she only had another five offices on the next floor to clean and she'd be finished for the evening.

It was hard to work all day at her regular job then put in six hours cleaning offices, but she needed the money in the worst way. She'd been lucky to get this job. Still, it was Friday night. Once finished, she'd have two days to sleep in, nap and get ready for the next workweek.

Not for her the promise of a Cinderella ball. She knew her limitations. After Chad, she knew better than to daydream about men dropping at her feet. The reality was always there to face as soon as they met Charlene.

Saturday morning Sam slept in until nine. Not super late, but late enough for someone who usually rose before seven and was at work by eight.

She donned on her robe, slipping the ticket in her pocket, and went downstairs. Her sister was in the small study she used as her office, typing away. Sam paused at the door.

"Did you eat already?"

Charlene looked up and shook her head. "I waited for you. I was hoping for blueberry pancakes."

"Sounds good," Sam said. She headed for the kitchen. Feeling slightly depressed when she entered, she glanced at the patched wall where the old oak tree had crashed through during Hurricane George. The damage remained, awaiting funds to repair it. Sighing softly, she quickly moved to gather ingredients to make the pancake batter, using the small, two-burner camp stove they were making do with. Once she had enough money, they would get the kitchen repaired and at that point she was buying a top-of-the-line gas range.

Charlene rolled into the kitchen.

"Want any help?" she asked.

"No, I've got it. Why are you working on Saturday? I thought you tried to get everything done during the week."

"I know, but I got caught up in quilting on Thursday and so am behind a bit. I need to be caught up by Monday." Charlene was a medical transcriptionist for a local physicians' clinic. She worked at home and normally her income plus Sam's kept them afloat. The hurricane had caused them to dip into their small savings, and still repairs remained waiting to be done.

"Oh, look what I brought home," Sam said, pulling the invitation from her robe pocket and tossing it to her sister.

"Pretty," Charlene said, looking at it. "I didn't know you got a ticket."

"I didn't. It fell out of the trash at one of the offices last night. I brought it home for you to see. Really posh, don't you think?"

Charlene toyed with it, glancing at Sam from time to time as Sam flipped the pancakes and dished them up. As soon as Sam sat, Charlene said, "You should go."

"Where?"

"To the ball, of course." She tapped the edge of the invitation on the table. "It's obviously not being used by anyone."

"Someone paid big bucks for that. I can't use it," Sam pointed out, pouring on the maple syrup.

"Why not? Whoever bought it changed his or her mind and tossed it. Think of it as recycling." Charlene began to warm to her idea. "I think it would be the perfect chance for you to go out and have a great time. Something you haven't done much of since the hurricane."

"Once we get all the repair work done, I'll start dating again. Right now, I'm too tired."

And dating wasn't all it was cracked up to be. Sam had fallen in love in college, only to have her boyfriend let her down when the accident claimed her parents' lives and injured her sister so much. He couldn't face having to deal with a paraplegic as part of his family. For a moment she remembered the crushing scene right after he visited Charlene in the hospital with Sam.

Don't go there, she warned herself. Chad was in the past. She had the future to think about. It was only once in a while that she thought about how her life would have been had that drunk not crashed into her family's car and altered all their futures.

She dated occasionally, but usually once the man found out she had a disabled sister, one who could not live on her own and would always need some assistance, he faded away. Or vanished instantly as in the case of her most recent foray into dating last August. She still had hopes of one day finding the perfect man, someone who would love her to distraction, and be able to handle having Charlene as a part of their lives.

In the meantime, Sam had other priorities. Like getting enough money to repair the kitchen and quit the nighttime job.

"I bet Margaret would let you borrow one of her gowns," Charlene said.

Sam looked at her sister. "You're not serious."

"What have I been saying? Of course I am. Think about it. The Black and White Ball is the most exclusive charity event in Atlanta. They sold out last Thanksgiving for the New Year's Eve event. It's in three days' time. You found the ticket. Think of it as serendipity. I think you should go."

"The ticket isn't mine," Sam protested. She couldn't help remembering her daydream of the previous night. She'd love to go to something so elegant. To be carefree and pretend all was right with her world.

"It'll just go to waste if you don't use it," Charlene argued. "No will know how you got it. No one would care. The charity obviously already has the money. I'll call Margaret right after breakfast."

Sam toyed with the idea. It would be wonderful to have a special memory to look back on. And when would she ever be able to spend five hundred dollars on a ticket to a dance?

Not a dance—to an elegant ball.

"Maybe—if Margaret has a dress. It has to be black or white, remember. That's the whole premise of the ball." The more Sam thought about it, the more she wondered that even if she did go, she'd be spotted for an imposter in an instant. Still—it did seem a shame to waste the ticket. Should she throw the decision to fate and leave it up to seeing if Margaret had a suitable gown?

CHAPTER ONE

SAMANTHA entered the luxurious lobby of the Atlantian Hotel with a mixture of excitement and trepidation. Her pace slowed as she looked around, taking in every detail. The spacious lobby was amazing, ceilings that soared at least twenty-five feet supporting crystal chandeliers that sparkled and gleamed with light. The floor alternated glowing hardwoods with lush Persian carpets centering seating arrangements of plush sofas and deep easy chairs. Sidestepping from a direct line to the ballroom, she deliberately walked on one of the crimson carpets, her heels sinking in dangerously. Glancing around to make sure no one was watching, she savored the luxury, smiling in sheer delight.

She felt like a schoolgirl let out into the real world for the first time. Only this was not her world. Elegant hotels, fabulous balls, expensive gowns and jewels were only things she normally read about. This was a first—to actually be participating. She couldn't believe she'd actually let Charlene talk her into attending.

Samantha assumed an air of casual sophistication and crossed to the cloakroom hoping she appeared as if she attended events like this routinely. She checked in her coat, her practical wool a poor showing beside the cashmere and silk.

Clutching her small purse and purloined ticket, Samantha

raised her chin and walked to the huge double doors opening into the ballroom. Atlanta's Black and White New Year's Eve Ball was one of the most prestigious charity events of the winter season. A recent tradition, its goal was raising funds for the Children's League while celebrating the beginning of each new year. With such sponsors as Gideon Fairchild and Vanessa Winters, it attracted the crème de la crème of Atlanta society. And tonight Sam was mingling with them all!

Samantha smiled at the white-gloved man at the door checking the coveted tickets. She showed hers wondering if he'd immediately recognize she should not be here and block her entry.

He merely glanced at the embossed ticket and said, "Table twenty-one is near the dais."

She nodded and entered the enchanted ballroom. Her gaze moved around the room taking in every lavish decoration. White lights sparkled from a dozen chandeliers reflected in the antique mirrors that lined one wall. Even more gorgeous than the ones in the lobby, the crystal illumination offered a rainbow of colors matched only by the glittering jewels displayed by guests.

Round tables were set with fine linens, bone china and real silverware. Small, discreet signs with table numbers sat in each center. Waiters circulated with champagne, filling flutes expertly. Uniformed waitresses offered hors d'oeuvres. People were already sitting at some of the tables, even more were roaming around greeting friends. Sam took her time sauntering through the lavishly appointed room. She felt like Cinderella at the ball. She didn't know anyone here, but that wouldn't dim her excitement.

People smiled at her and she returned the silent greeting with an answering smile and slight nod. Her gaze moved to the dais where a table for those sponsoring the event was already filling up. There she recognized one or two famous residents of the city from photographs in the newspaper.

True to the nature of the event, everyone wore either white

or black or a combination. The men looked superb in their dark tuxedos. Occasionally she'd spot one wearing a white dinner jacket. Young and old alike looked more polished and debonair in a tux. She wished there were more events that required formal attire. Not that she'd likely attend any of those, either.

The gowns the women wore were fantastic. The only colors were the jewels that sparkled at throats, ears and wrists. Her own string of pearls seemed subdued in comparison to the emeralds and rubies and diamonds that predominated. But they had belonged to her mother and she loved them. She could only pretend so much.

Normally when Samantha thought about white gowns, she envisioned wedding dresses. Not tonight. The creations ranged from sleek and sophisticated to almost indecent. More black gowns were present than white, but all were obviously designer creations.

Her own gown blended in perfectly. On loan from her friend Margaret who owned a vintage clothing shop, the white satin strapless bodice gradually faded into gray then black at a wide band at the bottom of the floor-length skirt. It was more than fifty years old, but had been lovingly cared for and Sam felt as comfortable in it as she would have in one of today's couture gowns. Because of its age, there was not a high likelihood of seeing another like it tonight.

She felt like a princess and held her head even higher to show off her gown. She had never worn anything so elegant before. Her hair, normally worn down or tied back in a ponytail, had been done by her sister into an upswept loop with a few curls cascading down her back. She repressed the urge to twirl around in giddy delight, feeling excited like nothing before. There would be dancing after the dinner. Would she get a chance? An assessing look around her showed most people seemed paired. Sighing softly, she made up her mind to enjoy every moment—whether she danced or not. It was unlikely she'd ever have another opportunity to attend a Black and White Ball.

"Champagne?" A waiter stepped close, a tray of filled flutes in his hand.

"Thank you," she said, taking a glass. When he'd passed on, she took a tentative sip. Mmm. Another sip. Champagne was not normally in her budget. This was delicious.

Before she could move, a man stepped in front of her.

"I'm sure we have met," he said with a grin. He sipped from his own flute of champagne and from the slight swaying on his feet she wondered how much he'd already had.

"I'm afraid not," she said with a smile.

"Fred Pearson. At your shervice." He shook his head. "Service."

He reached out and caught her arm. "Here alone? I am. Don't like to come to these events alone. Too shhhtupid, ya know? But I recognize you. I'm sure we have met."

"No. I'm Samantha." She didn't want to be rude but Fred was impeding her way to her table and she caught a couple of people looking at them. The last thing she wanted was anything to call attention to herself. What if someone questioned who she was and when she'd bought the ticket?

"I need to get to my table," she said, hoping he'd release her.

"Ah, my table is right over—" He looked around, peering at the numbers on the nearby tables, still holding on to her arm.

Sam began to wonder if it were to keep him upright.

"—somewhere," Fred ended, obviously giving up on finding his own table. "Do you want to dance?"

"The music hasn't started yet," Sam said, trying to pull away without making it too obvious.

Fred glanced around again, finishing the last of the champagne in his glass. "It'll start soon."

"I think dinner is first. It was nice to meet you. I need to get to my table."

"My table is around here somewhere," he said, stumbling a step as he turned to look around, almost pulling Sam off her feet.

"There you are. I was thinking I'd missed you."

Sam looked to her left where another man in a tux spoke to her. He looked at Fred.

"You need to let her go. I'll take over now," he said.

"Oh. Thought she was lost," Fred said, swaying a little. He looked at his hand holding Sam's arm and slowly released it. "Think I need another drink."

"I think we don't belong here," her rescuer said. A warm hand grasped her upper arm and urged her quickly to the left. Guiding her through tables and making a way through the couples standing in conversations, she was soon whisked to the sidelines.

She turned and looked properly at her rescuer—and promptly caught her breath. Her heart fluttered, her breathing stopped. He was gorgeous, tall and dark and breathtaking. He just oozed sex appeal. She'd read about that before, but never experienced it. Now she knew what the books meant. Feeling slightly light-headed, she finally remembered to breathe.

He was so tall, her head barely cleared his shoulder. Wide shoulders that gave a new meaning to wearing a tux made the suit look as if it were designed with only him in mind and the ruffles on the shirtfront served to highlight his masculinity. His hair was cut just long enough to entice a woman's fingers to thread through and dark eyes were framed by lashes a starlet would envy. His jaw was rugged. His sensuous lips curled into a slight smile, which showed a dimple indenting his left cheek. His gaze was firmly focused on her. Oh, dear, had he said something?

She blinked and looked away, her heart pounding. Good grief, she never paid attention to such things. Did coming to a ball like Cinderella give rise to Prince Charming expectations? She almost laughed, except she felt giddy with her conflicting emotions.

"Are you all right?" he asked. For the second time?

"I certainly didn't expect a confrontation at this ball," she murmured, glancing back to where Fred was making his way through the crowd. "Do you think he'll be all right?"

"Probably. But you never know with Boozer."

"Boozer?" she repeated.

"Fred's nickname. Rumor has it he drinks bourbon for breakfast. He's already three sheets to the wind and he's only just arrived. Stay clear of him."

"I shall. If I had seen him coming I would have gone the other way. Thank you for rescuing me."

"My pleasure."

A waitress stopped by them, offering tiny crackers covered with caviar.

Samantha hesitated. She had never tried caviar before and had heard mixed reviews from friends who had.

Her companion had no compunctions. He took a couple, then looked at her.

"Not having any?"

"I'll try one," she said, feeling daring. But with her small purse and the ticket in one hand and the other holding the champagne, she wasn't sure how.

He solved that dilemma. "May I?" he asked. He fed her one, his fingers barely brushing her lips. She didn't even taste the caviar, her whole being was riveted on the reaction to his barely felt touch. She shivered slightly, but not due to cold. She gazed up into deep brown eyes and felt her bones weaken even as every cell seemed to stir in anticipation of more. Oh, help, she was in trouble.

"Another?" he asked, offering a second.

She nodded and he fed her again. This time she paid attention to the strong taste by looking away.

"Mmm," she said, wrinkling her nose. She was not sure caviar would ever become a favorite.

He laughed and took another cracker for himself before the waitress moved on to the next guest.

"Not your thing, I take it," he said as he popped the hors d'oeuvre into his mouth.

Sam shook her head, her gaze on his lips as he chewed the tidbit. *Get a hold of yourself!*

"I'm glad I got to sample it. Now I know I don't have expensive tastes," she said.

"Is this your first time here?"

She nodded.

He glanced around. "Will your date know where to find you?" he asked.

"I came alone. I think Fred—Boozer—picked up on that." Did that make her sound odd? Should she make up something about her date getting sick at the last moment or something?

"So did I. If you are ready to find your table, I'll escort you," he said genially.

She smiled, suddenly feeling like anything could happen tonight. Taking another sip of her champagne, she wondered why a man who looked like he did had come alone. Maybe his date really had got sick.

"Your wife was unable to attend?" she asked, fishing for an answer without being too obvious—she hoped.

"I'm not married." His demeanor changed, instantly becoming somber.

Bad topic. She swept her arm toward the dais. "Mine is table twenty-one. The doorman said it was near the dais."

He paused for a moment, staring at her. "How interesting. That's my table also."

She went on alert. For a moment tension rose. Surely he didn't think she had deliberately set out to sit at his table? He had rescued her after all. Yet his reaction had definitely been odd. She still had the ticket out and showed it to him. He inclined his head slightly and gestured for her to walk toward the front of the large ballroom.

"My friends call me Mac," he said, placing his hand at the small of her back as they wound through groups of guests chatting and laughing with enjoyment of the evening.

"Mine call me Sam. Short for Samantha," she murmured, her heart pumping wildly—from his touch, or adrenaline, or just plain old fear of exposure, she wasn't sure. No one had challenged her so far. She should feel safe. But she couldn't help glancing around to see if anyone was paying special attention to her. Apparently not.

"Mac and Sam, sounds like a rock group or something," he responded. Twice he spoke to people as they wound through the conversing groups, but he didn't stop to introduce Sam.

The tables were set for eight. A couple was already seated at table twenty-one when Mac and Sam reached it. Everyone introduced themselves with first names as Mac seated Sam then took the chair beside her. It was obvious the others thought they had come together. She waited for him to deny it, but he ignored the assumptions.

By the time the salad was served two others had joined them. Conversation became general and Sam relaxed as the meal progressed. It looked as if her gamble had paid off. She could give herself up to the sole purpose of enjoying the evening and no longer worry about discovery. How long had it been since she'd gone out for fun and nothing more?

Longer than she cared to remember, thanks to Hurricane George.

Mac was a perfect partner for dinner. He spent his time talking with her and the woman on his other side. Two places remained empty at the table. How odd that those people had not used their tickets. Or had they, too, been trashed? The sponsors of this event had declared it to be a sellout. Was that just hype, or had something at the last moment prevented some ticket holders from attending?

When the final dinner plates had been removed and coffee served, the waitstaff quietly vanished and the night's speaker was introduced. The speech was short and poignant, urging everyone present to take up the cause of the Children's League and to be generous in support for disadvantaged children.

Then the wall to the right began to fold into panels and open revealing the dance floor and the orchestra providing the music. Along one wall a buffet table lavishly displayed desserts of all types. Two large open bars flanked the buffet tables. The rest of the room sparkled beneath the crystal chandeliers that illuminated the space, dimmed slightly to provide a sense of intimacy in the huge ballroom.

The music began and Mac turned to Sam. "Care to dance?"

She nodded, her heart kicking up again. She had hoped to have a chance, but hadn't expected such a dashing partner. As they walked to the dance floor, she noticed the covert glances given them. All for Mac, she knew. She smiled, delighted to be in the company of the best-looking man in the room.

In seconds they were on the dance floor moving to the waltz the orchestra played so well. So far so good. She'd enjoy her dance and then leave. It wasn't so awkward eating with a group but once dancing began, couples would rule the event.

As Mac continued to sweep her around the dance floor effortlessly, she forgot about the fear she'd be exposed and escorted from the ball. She could only see Mac, smell the enticing scent of his aftershave, relish the strength of the muscles beneath his jacket. He danced divinely and Samantha felt like a kid in a candy store. She loved to dance. With a sister confined to a wheelchair, however, she cherished it even more, though she rarely went to dances. Which made tonight especially delightful. Closing her eyes, she moved with the music, relishing the sensations that seeped in. Mac was an excellent partner. It had been far too long since she'd gone out for the sole purpose of enjoying herself. Perhaps it presaged a better year in the offing. She hoped so.

"You're very quiet," Mac said midway through the waltz.

"I'm enjoying myself immensely," she said with a quick glance up. His dark eyes were mesmerizing. Seconds spun by. She wanted to trace that slight dimple in his left cheek. Wanted to shift her hand from his shoulder to his neck and feel the warmth of his skin. She wanted to learn more about the stranger with whom she danced so superbly. The night was full of magic and she savored every moment. All too soon it would end and she'd be back to her day-to-day routine.

She knew she was on borrowed time, but a few stolen moments of dancing with Mac were worth any risk. If anyone official made a beeline toward her, she'd dash out of one of the doors and vanish into the night.

"There aren't many New Year's Eve parties these days that have a full ballroom and the music to go with it," Mac commented.

She nodded and murmured in agreement. She knew the ball's primary goal was to raise money, but more than anything else, it provided an elegant evening to all who attended. What a way to end the old year and usher in the new.

"Are you from Atlanta?" Mac asked.

"Born and bred," she said, giving up the quiet to respond. He was trying to talk and she was acting like a tongue-tied schoolgirl. *Get with it, Sam.* "You?"

"Born in Savannah, came here a decade ago."

"Savannah has a lot of charm. Atlanta is the New York of the South—dynamic and exciting—but perhaps it's not as charming as Savannah."

"It suits me to a T," he said.

Sam smiled and wondered what he did, where in the city he lived. What part of living here he liked best.

She wished she could say Atlanta suited her. She glanced over his shoulder, feeling the sudden aching longing for the path she once thought she'd take. Her dream of becoming a national park ranger and living in some of the western parks with wide-open spaces and nature's bounty evident everywhere had ended with the car crash that had changed her life.

Instead she was surrounded by glass and concrete and heavy traffic. And she hated almost every moment.

The music ended, but Mac kept hold of her hand.

"Since you came alone, as did I, would you care for another dance?" he asked.

"Thank you, I'd like that." She felt a tingling in her hand where his clasped hers. For a second or two she could almost imagine they were on a date together. That he was interested in her and wanted to see her again. They'd ring in the New Year together and then slip away to a quiet place just for the two of them.

But even if he asked her, she'd have to say no. Before long it would be midnight and time to leave. Even if they did spend some time together, once he met Charlene, he'd pull back like the others. The perfect man who would sweep her off her feet, loving her as no one ever had before, and committing to a life together forever, just didn't exist.

Forget commitment, she admonished herself. Until it was time to leave, she should squeeze out every last bit of fun.

When the music began again it was a faster beat. The dancing wasn't as conducive to conversation, which suited Sam. She liked dancing with Mac, but knew it was a night out of time. Monday morning she'd be back at her desk at the Beale Foundation and that night working with the cleaning crew at the towers.

When the song ended, Mac once again touched her, this time at the small of her back as he guided her from the floor. He was a sensuous man, and she felt cherished and feminine. She hadn't been touched like that in a long time and she'd never felt this way before.

"Want something to drink?" he asked, nodding toward the bar.

"As thirsty as I am right now, the only thing would be water," she said.

"Iced sparkling water it is," he said as he escorted her toward one of the large bars serving the guests. The line moved quickly. Sam watched the dancers on the floor, glancing back to the dining tables. More people were standing around talking than dancing. She would have taken advantage of the orchestra and not merely talked with friends. She didn't want to miss a beat.

"Here you go," he said, handing her a tall glass of ice and sparkling water. She drank quickly, glad for the refreshment. He'd also asked for water and finished before she did, guiding them to where a tray for empties stood. Sam drained her glass and put it down beside his.

The lights dimmed and another slow song began.

"Another dance?" he asked.

She hesitated. But temptation proved too strong.

"I'd love one more," she said.

Once they were circling the floor, Sam wondered if her imagination was playing tricks or if Mac held her even closer than before. Not that she minded. She rested her forehead against his jaw and closed her eyes again. Dancing like this was pure heaven. The shimmering feelings that swept through her only added to the magical feel of the night.

"Having fun?" he asked softly.

"The best time," she replied, realizing it was true. She was so glad she'd come.

"Me, too. More than I expected."

She pulled back and looked at him. "Why's that?"

"I thought this more of a duty event—show up, be seen, go home. You're an unexpected bonus."

She smiled. "I don't think I've ever been called a bonus before."

His phone vibrated. She could feel it as they danced.

He stopped and pulled it out, glancing at the number

calling. "Excuse me, I need to take this." He guided them to the edge of the floor as he flipped open the phone and spoke.

"Tommy? What's up? Why aren't you in bed?"

Sam watched the others dancing, but listened to the man talking. Was the call from a child?

A few moments later Mac hung up. "Sorry about that. Tommy's my son—he wanted to wait up to wish me Happy New Year, but has to go to bed now, he's too tired to stay up."

"Oh." Sam had not expected something like this. "I thought you said you weren't married," she commented, suddenly wary.

"I'm not. My wife died three years ago. Today proved to be a hard day. Our longtime housekeeper is leaving in the morning and Tommy's never known anyone else. I have a new person starting Monday, so for a few days we'll be batching it ourselves."

Sam nodded, her perception of Mac undergoing a subtle change. While he was still wildly attractive, any fantasy she might have had of them becoming a couple came to an abrupt end. She had her own baggage and couldn't see herself taking on another's. Not that children weren't delightful and a blessing, but she was already tied down. She would never achieve her dream if she became entangled with children.

"How old is he?" she asked, curious despite her resolve.

"Just three. It's a cute age."

She smiled. She wouldn't know; she didn't have the occasion to be around many young children. Her work was with disabled adults, not kids.

The music was still playing, and he took her back into his arms and they moved onto the floor once again.

It wasn't fair, Sam thought as she rested her head against him again. She wanted one fantasy evening and now that was no longer the same knowing Mac was a father and so involved with his son he'd answer a phone call in the middle of a dance.

But wouldn't she if Charlene called?

Family came first. Sighing softly, she tried to capture the sparkle from earlier. It wasn't hard being held in Mac's arms. Soon she once again pretended it was just the two of them dancing on a cloud. The music was the perfect tempo; the feelings evoked were nostalgic and warm. Unlike the experience of being held in this man's arms. She felt as if she were on the edge of a cliff—one step could send her flying, or crashing to the bottom.

When the song ended, she looked up as the countdown to the New Year began.

Ten, nine, eight…

People around the ballroom began the chant. Sam could feel Mac's arms tighten slightly as the lights dimmed even more.

…five, four, three…two…one.

Balloons popped, confetti showered down and the band began the strains to the familiar "Auld Lang Syne."

"Happy New Year, Samantha. May all your dreams come true," Mac said and kissed her.

After the first second of surprise, she relaxed. His lips were warm and seeking. She closed her eyes and relished every nanosecond. She'd met him only a few hours earlier, but it seemed entirely right to return his kiss to bring in the New Year. Her heart pounded and her body quivered in anticipation. Heat swept through her. Was this the beginning of a great year? Would she ever see him again?

He ended the kiss when the band started to play a different tune. It took a moment for her to come down to earth. Once again he led and Sam tried to get her spinning senses under control. She never did things like this. She was practical, not given to girlish dreams and foolish hopes. Still, without thought, she smiled and snuggled just a little bit closer. She felt cherished, special, connected—as if they were a couple. A woman could dream once in a while, couldn't she?

At the end of that song, the music tempo picked up and Sam pulled back. It was getting late. She should leave, however reluctantly.

"Another drink?" he asked as they walked from the dance floor.

"That would be lovely," she said. This time the line at the bar wasn't as long and in only moments they each had a glass of champagne. He touched his glass to hers.

"Make a wish," he said.

She did, for the future to be brighter than the past. Sipping, she smiled at him.

"Is that a tradition I don't know about?" she asked.

"In my family it has been. Weddings, christenings, whatever— when we serve champagne, we make wishes. Why not?"

She was charmed. If they had met in other circumstance, she would ask about his family, about other traditions they shared. But this was not her milieu. She was more the jeans-and-sweatshirt type, not one for designer clothes. Mac was perfectly at home, even speaking to people she only knew from the newspapers. Movers and shakers of Atlanta's vibrant business community.

"Shall we sit this one out?" he asked.

"You needn't spend the entire evening with me," she said reluctantly. She didn't want him to feel she was monopolizing him. And she had to leave. In a few more minutes. She'd claim just a bit more time before walking away.

"If not you, then who?"

She looked around. The only single woman she saw looked old enough to be his grandmother.

He caught her direction and laughed, leaning closer to speak softly. "She's not my type. I like pretty brunettes with chocolate-brown eyes."

Sam could scarcely breathe. He was too close. If she turned her face, her lips would brush his cheek. Suddenly she longed to kiss him again, to feel the stirring emotions his touch brought. Was he flirting with her?

She dare not take that for granted. *Remember your real life,* she admonished herself silently. Yet it seemed so far away this evening. In the normal course of events, she could never have spent five hundred dollars for a ticket to tonight's ball. She didn't move in these social circles. She was a working woman, with a dependent sister, an ancient house and no chance to change things in the near future.

He held out her chair and she sat, glad for the glass of champagne to hold on to, and to study to avoid looking at him. He couldn't read minds, could he?

"I'm sorry your wife died. That must have been awful," she said.

"It was." He sat beside her, angling his chair slightly for more room. "Chris was only twenty-eight. Who'd expect anyone to die that young?"

"That's tragic," she replied sympathetically.

"She left me with Tommy. If it weren't for him I don't know if I would have made it. But he needed me as an infant, and he needs me even more now."

The brief glimpse of Mac's personal life touched her. He appeared successful and confident with everything going for him. Who would suspect such a tragedy had befallen him?

"Hey, Mac, I didn't know you were coming. Thought you said you wouldn't make it." A couple stopped by the table and greeted him. He rose and shook hands with the man, kissing the woman on the cheek. "I changed my mind. It's a nice event, and a good cause."

The woman looked at Sam and then at Mac. "A change from your usual style?" she asked in a teasing tone.

Sam looked away. He was not *seeing her,* either. This was getting awkward. Maybe she should take this opportunity to leave, much as she hated for her special evening to end.

Another couple walked by and the first stopped them.

"Jerry, you wanted to meet Mac McAlheny, here's your chance. Mac, this is Jerry Martin, head of Windsong Industries. I'm surprised you two haven't met before."

Samantha instantly went still. Oh, no! The CEO's office of McAlheny Industries was where she'd found the ticket, crumpled in the trash. Her heart raced.

Ohmygod, she'd been dancing with the man! Talking with him. Kissing him.

She had spent the evening with Mac McAlheny!

She had to escape before he realized she'd taken the invitation from his office. She hadn't exactly stolen it—it was trash after all. But she wasn't sure the CEO of one of Atlanta's fastest-growing high-tech firms would see it that way.

She looked at the door across the room in panic. She had to leave. Right now.

"Excuse me, I need to find the ladies," she said, pushing back from the table. Her eyes met Mac's. She wanted to smile, but was afraid to do anything but escape while she had the chance. To be discovered at this late date would be beyond embarrassing.

Weaving her way through the tables and the people standing around talking, she quelled the temptation to run. She kept taking deep, slow breaths to ease the screaming panic that assailed her. Once she reached the lobby she almost broke into a run to the cloakroom. She retrieved her coat and put it on as she hurried out into the rainy night. Escape was the only thought in her mind.

The doorman called a cab and she was ushered in like royalty. She'd avoided discovery. She sighed with relief and glanced back through the rain-drenched window, but saw only the glittering lights and the doorman in his fancy uniform.

"Goodbye," she said softly. Her magical evening had ended.

CHAPTER TWO

MAC listened to Jerry talk about one of the deals he had pending all the while trying not to look around to see if Sam had returned. It seemed like a long time since she left, but it could be because he'd rather be with her than the young man going on and on so tediously about something that held no interest for Mac. His friends waited patiently for Jerry to wind down. How long could the man continue? Mac glanced back to the door. Still no sign of Samantha.

When Jerry and his wife finally moved on, Peter shook his head. "Sorry about that. He said once he'd like to meet you, but he does get enthusiastic about his work."

"Much like you do, darling," his wife said. She tilted her head slightly when Mac checked his watch and glanced at the double doors across the room.

"Where did your date go?" she asked.

Mac almost corrected her, but thought better of it. If it got back to his latest ex-girlfriend that he was seeing someone else, maybe she'd finally get the message and stop contacting him.

"Ladies' room, I believe," he said.

"She's quite different from Teresa," she said.

"Teresa and I are no longer seeing each other."

"So you've found someone new already?"

Mac took a breath. Cindy was a noted gossip. He didn't

mind her telling Teresa he was off the market, but he had no intention of offering up Sam as a replacement.

"Let's just say I'm footloose and fancy-free."

"With no intention of getting married again," Cindy said. "That either says marriage was hell with Chris or so beyond marvelous you can't imagine ever duplicating it."

"You never met Chris," her husband said uneasily, as if picking up on Mac's reaction. "She was quite a woman."

Mac felt the anguish of her death anew. Four years ago, had they been able to afford it, Chris would have loved to attend the Black and White Ball. But his company had only moved into the big time after her death. He found it ironic that she had worked as hard as he to build McAlheny Industries, yet had died before it expanded to the successful firm it now was.

"Well, darling, we both know Mac has so much charisma that women naturally want his attention. And saying he will never marry again sets up a challenge some women can't resist."

"Or it could be that's simply the way I feel," he murmured, wondering how rude it would be to just turn and walk away from Cindy. He wanted to spend more time with Sam.

Cindy laughed. "So you say. You've made billions with your business. Still—" she studied him for a moment "—I'm telling you, women would be interested even if you were flat broke. Something about your eyes, I think."

"I doubt it."

"So did Teresa want a ring on her finger?" Peter asked.

"Apparently. She didn't take to heart my telling her that I wasn't marriage material. Why is it when a man's honest and up-front, women try to change his mind? She's beautiful, but she's not someone I want to grow old with."

Chris was the woman he'd always thought he'd grow old with. No one could take her place. But the past couldn't be changed. The aneurysm had caught everyone by surprise.

She'd been far too young to die. But much as he'd railed against fate, she had not lived to enjoy the fruits of their labor—or their son.

His goal now was to make a difference, for himself and Tommy. His business provided employment to more than a hundred people. He contributed lavishly to several charities, including the Children's League. Not bad for a poor kid from Savannah.

He glanced at his watch. How long did a woman need? The champagne in her glass would be warm by the time she drank it.

"Who's your date?" Peter asked.

"I just met her tonight," Mac said.

"A blind date? Oh, my," Cindy said with a laugh. "Imagine that."

"Imagine," he said dryly. He felt no obligation to explain anything to Cindy.

"Come along, darling, the music is starting again and I want to dance," Cindy said with an air kiss for Mac. "Good luck with your blind date."

As the minutes ticked by, Mac began to suspect Sam wasn't returning. He idly watched the dancing. Glancing around caused a waiter to appear with another glass of champagne. How the Children's League made money when they spent so lavishly on the ball was beyond him. But he knew donations poured in for this charity.

He looked at the table. Sam's ticket lay near the center. Was she unable to return because she didn't have it with her? He reached for it and rose. It wouldn't hurt to check to see if she was trying to convince one of the men at the door she was supposed to be here.

No sign of her when he entered the lobby. Those that had been checking tickets were no longer there. Maybe once the dinner finished, it didn't matter as much if anyone crashed the party.

He positioned himself where he could see the restroom

doors and waited. After fifteen minutes he knew Sam wasn't coming back.

He debated returning to the ball but decided he'd made an appearance, supported the charity with money. Kissed in the New Year. He could go home.

His housekeeper of several years was leaving in the morning and his little boy knew no other mother figure. Mac needed to be there for Tommy. There were two agencies searching for the right live-in housekeeper/nanny and he hoped they found someone soon. Mac didn't want his son to grow attached to Alice Horton, who started on Monday, only to break the tie with her when a more permanent arrangement could be found.

Mrs. Horton was not the solution, but a temporary fix. She had been a nanny for decades and, while sounding a bit strict, she came with impeccable references. He hoped Tommy would accept her until a new housekeeper could be found.

It was still raining when Mac gave the valet attendant his parking ticket. A good night to be home.

Or with an interesting woman who seemed dazzled by the ball yet content to simply enjoy it without flirting every moment or making sultry and suggestive comments as Teresa would have done. Samantha—Sam had made no moves on him after his impulsive kiss at midnight. Yet she'd returned his kiss with passion.

Getting behind the wheel, Mac was surprised to realize he'd enjoyed the evening. He'd gone out of duty and ended up having a good time—no, more than a good time. Sam intrigued him. That was a first. Since Chris's death, he'd made up his mind to remain single and focus on raising his son, and a chance encounter at a dance wouldn't change that. But he couldn't help thinking about Sam as he drove home. Her hair had gleamed in the light, artfully arranged and feminine. For a moment he wondered what she looked like with it in disarray, swirling around her face. Her cheeks had been tinged with color—natural, not cosmetic. But it was her chocolate-brown eyes he remembered the most. They showed her emotions, and twice he was convinced he'd seen awareness in them, as if for a few seconds she saw him as a desirable man.

Her lips had been sweet and her kiss memorable. Mac realized it had been a while since he'd felt anything when kissing someone. Teresa was beautiful, but cool and detached. Dating her had not changed his mind about wanting a new life partner. He doubted anything would.

Still, a few evenings spent together didn't mean a lifetime commitment.

Only—Sam had left with no way for him to contact her. Had it been deliberate? Had he misread the signs? He would have sworn she had enjoyed herself.

Yet she'd waited until he was occupied with Peter and Cindy and then cut out. If she'd felt any connection between them, wouldn't she have made sure he knew how to contact her?

As he pulled into his driveway, the full situation hit him. He wouldn't be going out for quite a while—not until he had a live-in nanny who would be home with Tommy. Until then, Mac had to be home each evening by six, the time Alice Horton left per their agreement when he hired her because Mrs. Horton taught an adult education class and had to be at her school by seven Monday through Thursdays.

Just as well. Dating had not played a big part of his life since Chris died and he liked spending time with his son.

But it would take a while to forget that kiss with Sam. He had tried to move on after grieving for Chris, only no one had come close to replacing her in his life. Sam was nothing like his wife, yet he could almost taste her on his lips. He remembered the warmth that had crashed through him when she'd returned the kiss. Another one or two of those wouldn't hurt. It would prove he was still living and capable of moving forward. Chris would have wanted that.

* * *

"So, how was it?" Charlene asked as soon as Sam entered the kitchen the next morning.

Sam smiled at her sister and went to pour herself some hot coffee. She'd slept later than normal because it had taken a long time to fall asleep after her magical evening. Thankfully today was a holiday, or she'd be a zombie at work. Home before one, it was actually after three before she stopped reliving every precious memory of Mac McAlheny.

"It was fabulous, how else?" she replied, turning and leaning against the counter. She glanced down at her bunny slippers, a fun Christmas offering from her sister. She sighed softly. She was much more a bunny-slipper kind of gal than elegant socialite.

"For one evening I felt like Cinderella," she said slowly.

"You looked so marvelous," her sister said.

"You told me that before I left," Sam commented, grinning. She had felt marvelous. "The hotel was fabulous. I saw lots of people who are in the newspaper all the time. The mayor was there, and our representative. The food was to die for. And I had the best dance partner in the world. Tall, dark and handsome—and he could dance better than Fred Astaire, I believe." She ended, mentioning one of Hollywood's most famous dancers she and her sister enjoyed watching in old black and white movies.

"Ooooh, do tell all!"

Sam put some bread in the toaster and began to relate every delicious memory of the previous evening to her sister. She ended with her dances with Mac.

"We danced, then I left."

"That's all?" Charlene clearly wanted more.

"Actually the tall, dark and handsome stranger turned out to be the man from whose office I got the ticket. What are the odds of that happening? Once I realized that, I left before he figured it out. I consider that a lucky break. I was worried half the evening that someone would spot me as an imposter and have me thrown out."

"You didn't do anything wrong. The ticket had been thrown away. You were just recycling," Charlene said.

"Which was the argument you used to talk me into going. And I'm glad I did, but the longer I stayed, the more chance there was of someone asking how I came to acquire a ticket."

"No one would have been so rude. And your dress fit in, didn't it? You'll have to tell Margaret all about it."

"You should have seen the designer creations there. But I held my own. It's a lovely gown and I'm so glad she trusted it to me. What if I had spilled champagne on it or, worse, caviar?"

Charlene laughed. "My sister, the champagne and caviar girl."

"Well, champagne maybe. I don't think I'll be eating caviar again." Sitting at the table, she finished her toast, still feeling the warm glow from the night before. She'd had a fabulous time. If only she could have afforded to buy a ticket on her own and gone without a care in the world. The party had ended too early for her and would never be repeated.

She'd relished the sensations she experienced wearing that shimmery satin dress. It would take a long time to forget the feelings of elegance and sophistication. A magic beginning to the New Year.

And a kiss to welcome it in. She hadn't had that in a few years, either.

She glanced up, at the coat hanging from the nail on the plywood at the back. She'd hung it on one of the nails last night to let the dampness dry.

"At least that's good for something," she muttered.

"Hey, we're warm and dry," Charlene said.

"Dry anyway. It's drafty in here. And I'm so tired of using a camping stove for cooking instead of our old gas range. It'll take weeks to finish paying off the roof before we can start saving for this repair. It's already the worst part of winter. Do we want the back wall open to the elements now? The house is hard enough to heat in winter without losing a wall for a few days." She sighed. She was back to reality with a vengeance.

Charlene gazed at the damaged space patched by panels of plywood. "It could have been worse—we could have been in here when the tree crashed through."

"We were too busy trying to stem the flood of water coming in through the attic when parts of the roof blew off," Sam reminded her. The hurricane that had freakishly blown into Georgia last September had wreaked havoc in a wide swatch of the state, including this southside of the state capital. Their roof, more than a hundred years old, had not stood up to the gale force winds. Nor had the huge old oak trees that fell beneath that force when the soil became saturated with all the water that rained down for days. Only one fallen tree had damaged the house, thank goodness. But it had done a tremendous job of taking out most of the back wall.

Insurance covered a portion of the repair costs but it was up to Sam to earn the extra money needed to finish the repairs and get their home back in order. Charlene did the best she could, but there was a limit to her work as a transcriptionist.

"Happy New Year, Sam," Charlene said, raising her mug.

Sam clinked hers against her sister's and smiled. "Happy New Year, sis."

She felt her eyes fill with tears and blinked, looking away. Only a short time ago she'd been kissed into the New Year.

"So are we going to make New Year's resolutions?" Charlene asked.

"We do each year, why should this one be different?" Sam asked, hoping her sister didn't see her distress.

"Then, I resolve to make a push to sell some of my quilts," Charlene said.

Sam laughed. "You say that every year." There was nothing

wrong with her life. She should be grateful it was as full as it was.

"This time I mean it. I'll force myself. It's not right that you have to do everything for me. I'm capable. The damage from the hurricane shows me how close to the edge we live. I need to do something to contribute to the unusual expenditure, not be a drain."

"You're not a drain. You have your job and I have mine."

"Face it, Sam. If I can get some of these quilts sold, it would help a lot and make your time working that second job shorter."

Her sister had been confined to a wheelchair since the accident nine years ago. Charlene would never walk again, nor dance, nor enjoy all the freedom that Sam took for granted. But she pulled her own weight with her home-based job and as a hobby made beautiful quilts. Some were the traditional kind that went on beds. But more and more she was doing artistic work—quilted pictures and clothing. Sam had two of her quilted vests and always received compliments when she wore them.

"And you should resolve to go back to school," Charlene said before Sam could think up a single resolution.

"I have a full-time job and am working nights until we get the house repaired. When do you suggest I consider attending classes and studying?" Sam asked. She loved the courses she took at one of the local colleges. It was taking far longer than she originally expected to get her degree, but she drew closer each year.

"I don't know, but you need to put that as a resolution. If I could sell a few quilts for enough money, we could catch up on the bills and arrange for the repairs."

"You do that and I'll look into college again." She rose and went to the sink to run water in her cup, not wanting Charlene to see how fragile her control was. She longed to return to college to finish her degree. She had less than a year's worth of classes left. Once she had her B.S., she would apply for a job with the National Park Service. She'd have to make sure she could afford living arrangements for her and her sister if she got selected. But if they could renovate this house, they could either sell it, or rent it out when they moved west. It was the only legacy their parents had left them. It was a mixed blessing, now, with the hurricane damage.

"I'll need help," Charlene said.

"With what?" Sam turned to look at her sister. She was so pretty and seemed so small tucked in that chair.

"Getting contacts. Finding someone willing to buy the quilts," Charlene said.

"Doesn't your quilting guild have contacts?"

"Not really. Everyone there dreams of selling their work for fabulous sums and becoming famous and rich. I think the patterns are a better aspect to focus on. I have quite a few I designed, you know."

Sam hadn't a clue how to market her sister's quilts. But she could find out. This was the first time Charlene had sounded like she was serious, rather than simply indulging in wishful thinking, so Sam would be as supportive as possible.

"And you should date," Charlene said. "You still have weekends."

Sam blinked at that. "What? Where did that come from?"

"You haven't gone out on a date since the hurricane. You don't have to stay home with me all the time," her sister said candidly.

"Charlene, you know I only have the weekends to catch up on chores and get some rest. Besides, I don't have anyone in mind right now. Jason at work asked me, but I don't see myself and him having anything in common except the Beale Foundation, and I don't want to talk business on a date."

Charlene bit her lip. "Well, once things turn around."

"I can't conjure up dates," Sam said, her mind instantly bringing Mac's face to the forefront. He'd be the last person she'd date. What if he found out about the ticket? How embarrassing that would be!

"But if you go places where men are, you could meet some interesting ones and get asked out."

Sam had met a very interesting man last night. Only circumstances conspired to make sure they never met again. She wasn't sure whether she wished she'd never used the ticket or not.

"Okay, the next time a presentable man asks me, I'll go out." The chances of that happening were slim to none, so she felt safe making the commitment.

"Until then, you can help me sort through my stuff and see which quilt would be the best to start marketing," Charlene said.

Mac and Tommy stood on the porch waving Louise farewell. The little boy still didn't grasp the full extent of the departure. He would begin to get it when Louise wasn't there to prepare dinner or tuck him in. And again when a new nanny arrived.

Tommy had his arm around Mac's neck and waved with his other hand. "Bye-bye," he said.

Mac waited until the car was out of sight before heading back inside. It was cold, but the rain had stopped during the night.

"Want to go to the park later?" he asked as he put Tommy down.

"Yes!" The little boy raced around in excitement. An hour or so at the park would burn off some of that energy.

Louise had left a casserole for dinner, so that left only lunch to prepare—something Mac could handle. But the next few weeks were going to see a lot of changes.

He went to his room to get his keys. He'd emptied his pockets last night, placing the contents on the dresser. Keys, billfold, tickets. Both his and Sam's. He picked them up to drop them in the trash when he noticed the numbers were sequential.

For a moment he stared at them. One was crumpled as if someone had balled it up and tossed it into the trash. From where it had been retrieved and used?

Was this the ticket he'd bought for Teresa and tossed away when he decided to break it off with her? For a long moment he stared at them, trying to come up with another scenario. How had Sam gotten hold of his discarded ticket?

Mac McAlheny arrived late at work on Monday—an unheard-of event. The new nanny had shown up on time, but Tommy had taken an instant dislike to her. Mac had stayed with his son until he had calmed down and agreed to give Mrs. Horton a chance. The woman wasn't precisely warm and loving, but was competent, as Mac knew having interviewed her twice and checked her references. She had also come highly recommended. Mac hoped she and Tommy would get along until he could sort out a more permanent solution.

"Good morning, boss," Janice said. His secretary had been with him from the beginning and knew as much about the business as he did. "Late isn't your style," she commented, following him into his corner office.

"Domestic problems, I'm afraid. Tommy didn't take to Mrs. Horton."

"Poor kid. It has to be hard on him changing like that," she said. Placing two folders on the desk, she leaned one hip against the edge. "Anything I should know before the day starts?"

They often began the day going over his appointments and reviewing updates on projects.

"Who does the cleaning of our offices?" Mac asked, glancing at the folders.

"Whoa, where did that come from?" She glanced around at the immaculate room. "Are you unhappy with the standard of work?" she asked.

"Just curious about something," Mac said. The more he

considered the idea, the more he began to think it held merit. Sam had somehow obtained the invitation he'd thrown away. The only way he could picture it was if someone from the cleaning staff had taken it. Had he or she then sold it? Or had that been Sam herself? He'd realized how little he knew about her when he tried to figure out how she'd obtained the ticket.

"The building owners arrange for that. It's in our lease they'll take care of it. If you want, I can find out who they hire."

"Please do. And then call the two employment agencies looking for a housekeeper for me and find out why there isn't one qualified woman in all of Atlanta who would like to have a live-in job keeping house and watching one small boy."

"Got it, boss." Janice headed for her desk.

Mac glanced at the phone messages, and began to return some calls. As soon as Janice had the information he needed, he'd put work on hold and track down Samantha-my-friends-call-me-Sam.

While he didn't want to think about people going through his trash, he suspected that's what had happened. Did Sam work as a cleaner? Employment these days was difficult to find, even for skilled workers.

He tossed aside the paper he was reading and leaned back in his chair. He'd been intrigued by her the entire evening. She was one of the few women under forty who hadn't tried to flirt, hadn't hinted she'd be available if he ever called. Hadn't made a big deal out of a New Year's kiss. Hadn't practically invited herself back to his place.

He remembered at the table when she'd turned from him to talk with the man on her other side. It was an unusual experience for Mac in recent years. Ever since Chris died and the company had taken off, he felt he'd become prey for determined single women. He'd shared everything with Chris— hopes, dreams, pet peeves. Now it seemed his unexpected wealth had become the most important part of his personality.

Except to Sam.

Even when he'd held her while dancing, she had not flirted. He could tell she truly enjoyed herself. Unself-consciously. Her smile had been genuine, lighting up her dark eyes. Her hair was also dark, so unlike Chris's blond mane.

He frowned. He wasn't comparing his wife with other women. There would never be anyone to take her place in his heart or his life.

The phone buzzed; it was Janice.

"Jordan Maintenance keeps this building clean," she said. "Want the number?"

"Yes." Mac jotted it down and then called the firm. In only moments, he had Samantha's last name, Duncan. The firm would not give out personal information but had let that slip. The owner, Amos Jordan, was quite flustered to have one of the building's tenants call. Mac normally would not have even mentioned the situation, but he hoped to learn more about his mystery woman. Mr. Jordan revealed nothing else and assured him the cleaning staff was of the highest caliber.

Hanging up frustrated, Mac reached for a phone book. No Samantha Duncan listed in Atlanta. Damn, how was he going to find her? Camp out tonight and wait for the cleaning staff to arrive? He couldn't do it—he had to get home for Tommy. But he'd find a way.

"But, Mr. Jordan, I didn't steal anything," Samantha tried to explain to the boss of the cleaning crew she worked for. The cleaning position, though not really a job she relished, had nonetheless been a lifesaver in providing much-needed cash with minimum training.

Now she'd been accused of theft and was being fired!

"The client was displeased. I have the reputation of my company to consider. I thought I could trust everyone, but to find someone of your caliber stooping so low is more than I care to deal with," he said.

"It was in the trash," she interjected.

"If important papers were in the trash, would you take them and sell to the highest bidder?" he asked.

"Of course not!"

"How could I trust you? If you take one thing, you could take another."

Sam rested her forehead against her palm, her elbow on her desk. Thank goodness the door to her tiny office was shut. She couldn't bear for anyone to hear this conversation.

"Please, Mr. Jordan, there was no harm done. It was trash. I was recycling," she said, giving the airy excuse Charlene had used. It was stupid. She shouldn't have done it. She wouldn't have done it if she'd been thinking clearly, but the chance for a wonderful night had proved too alluring.

And now her dream man from the ball had accused her of theft. She felt sick—not only for the accusation, but because he thought that of her. She knew she'd never run into Mac again—their worlds were light-years apart. But she wished he'd been left with a pleasant memory, not one tainted by his thinking she'd stolen something.

"I regret the situation, although I have no choice but to fire you. I will also not provide you with a reference," Mr. Jordan said heavily.

Sam took a deep breath. "I understand. Thank you for the opportunity to work for your firm," she said. She recognized the inevitable when she saw it.

"Damn," she said after hanging up the phone. She sat up and gazed out the narrow window where the sun was shining. How ironic. On the most fabulous night of her life it had been pouring rain. Now the worst thing had to happen and the sun shone.

Not the worst—that would be if Mac McAlheny made the entire situation public.

"Oh, no," she groaned quietly. She couldn't have her reputation smirched. It would jeopardize her job at the Beale Foundation.

When she thought about it, really considered it from his point of view, she could concede he had a point. Those tickets went for five hundred dollars each. Just because it had been tossed away didn't negate its value. And she'd used it as if it had been given to her.

She was stricken with remorse. It had seemed like a lark. First to find it and take it home to Charlene to show the embossed script, the fancy gold seal. Then to fantasize about attending. The actual borrowing the dress from Margaret's boutique and going now seemed like the dumbest thing she'd ever done.

Closing her eyes, she could still see Mac's eyes as he gazed down into hers as they danced. Their special kiss. Her heart rate increased thinking about it. The image dissolved as she remembered he had filed a complaint with the owner of the cleaning company.

What could she do to make amends? Send him a check to cover the cost of the ticket? And where would she get that kind of money? The entire reason she had a second job was that she was about at the end of her rope. They needed a large down payment for the carpenter to begin work on renovations to the back of the kitchen.

Charlene's salary didn't cover all her expenses, much less unexpected surprises.

Samantha's job at the Foundation didn't pay much—no job in nonprofit companies did. She'd have to find something else. Leave the work she enjoyed, the cause she embraced, for something a bit more mainstream and financially beneficial. Definitely more financially beneficial.

A job she probably wouldn't like. But she'd started at the Foundation not wanting to work for them—or in any business in Atlanta. Her dream had been so different.

But reality didn't allow for dreams. She had a house—for which she was grateful. She had her sister to care for. She had to make the most of what she had and not bemoan a future that wasn't to be.

"Double damn," she said, pounding her desk once with her fist. She had to do something—but what?

Sam fretted all morning. She didn't know if Mr. McAlheny would contact her, though Mr. Jordan had assured her he had not given out any information. But how hard would it be for a man with Mac's influence to find out her name and address? Then what?

She called home.

"Hello?" Charlene answered.

"Any calls for me?" Sam asked. She knew it was an odd request; her friends knew she worked days and called the Foundation if they really needed to get hold of her during business hours.

"Here?" Charlene asked.

"Just a thought. Don't give out my work information to anyone, okay?"

"As if I would. What's up?"

Sam debated not telling her sister, but it would come out eventually. "Mac McAlheny found out I used his ticket and called my boss at the cleaning service. I was fired."

"What? Why?"

"For indiscretion," Sam said softly. She still couldn't believe it.

"So if he threw away a fan and you fished it out of the trash, that would be a problem? That doesn't make sense. We were recycling. People do it all the time. Throwing something away ends ownership."

"I guess a case could be made for that," Sam said. "But Mr. Jordan didn't see it that way."

"So now what?"

"I look for another job and hope Mr. McAlheny doesn't come breathing down my neck."

"Gosh, sis, I'm sorry. I know I urged you to use the ticket. I never expected you to lose a job over it. Can I do anything?"

"Pray I can find another part-time job soon."

The rest of the day Sam alternated from nervousness every time her phone rang, to panic about where she would find a second job to help pay off their debt.

Just before leaving that evening her boss popped his head in through her open door.

"You remember the business luncheon tomorrow, right? I'm hoping my speech will loosen some wallets. I want you and Pam there to handle any donations we may get."

Sam nodded. "I've had it on my calendar for weeks, ever since you told me, Tim. We'll both be there from eleven-thirty on. Maybe some of the guests will take a brochure or some- thing prior to lunch and offer a few thousand dollars on the spot."

"That's always a hope."

Raising funds for worthy charities was getting more diffi- cult. There were so many deserving organizations, but with companies tightening their belts to make sure their bottom lines continued to be robust, available corporate donations were drying up. Sam's boss, Timothy Parsons, had been scheduled to speak at this luncheon for weeks.

Sam liked attending events like this since it gave her an op- portunity to discuss the wonderful work of their Foundation with people who may not know about it. While not her first choice of professions, her work at the Foundation was impor- tant to her.

Nothing untoward had happened the rest of the day. Anonymity should prove enough protection—she hoped.

That evening shortly after dinner was finished, Sam studied the want ads in the paper. Most were for day jobs or required specialized training. It was depressing how few jobs there were that she could do, and even more so how few part- time jobs. Nothing popped out at her.

Charlene was in her studio, as they called the former dining-room-turned-quilting-haven. Her sister was so talented in that area maybe Sam should look at marketing the quilts until another part-time job appeared. It would be wonderful if Charlene could overcome her shyness and sensitivity to being in a wheelchair and sell some of the lovely works she'd created. Not only for the much-needed income, but as a boost to her sister's self-esteem.

How did one go about marketing quilts besides visiting specialty shops and seeing if the owners would take them on?

The worry that she hadn't heard the last of the purloined ticket nagged at her. If Mac wanted to make an issue of her using the ticket, she'd pay him the cost of it. She wasn't sure how she'd come up with the money on short notice, but there had to be some way. She tried to think of something of value they owned that she could sell.

Charlene rolled her chair into the kitchen. She took out some juice and went to the lower cabinets where they stored dishes. Glancing at Sam, she frowned. "No luck?"

"Huh? No, none. How's the vest coming?"

"Just about finished. Then I want to bind the wall hanging of the garden scene."

It was common for the women in Charlene's quilting guild to donate some of their work to the annual Beale Foundation Boutique that the Foundation hosted each December. All proceeds went to the Foundation. Sam privately thought her sister's work the best of the bunch, but Charlene received none of the money her creations brought in. If only she could find a steady buyer for her work. The garden scene she referred to was a picture quilt and Sam thought it was stunning.

But she knew better than to expect some fairy godmother to show up out of the blue to buy all Charlene's quilts.

"Want to rent a movie for Friday night?" Sam asked, folding the newspaper and putting it aside.

"I'm going to Betty's for dinner and to see her new quilt. She used my pattern and I want to see how someone else interpreted it. She's picking me up at six. I forgot you won't be working nights anymore. Want to join us? I'm sure she wouldn't mind," Charlene said.

"I'll pass." It wasn't often her sister went out. When Sam had worked for Jordan Cleaning, her evenings were full. Now she had a break. For a moment she wondered if it would be too late to enroll in spring classes at the local college.

No, she was being stupid to even consider it. She had to find something to supplement her income to afford their repairs. Maybe she could find another evening job this week and be busy again by Friday. She went back to studying the ads.

CHAPTER THREE

WHEN Sam entered the large restaurant, which hosted the business luncheon, she was immediately surrounded by people she knew. Caroline Bentley's law firm donated regularly to the Beale Foundation. She was accompanied by one of her law partners, Ted Henley. Then Sam greeted two CEOs of companies who also routinely gave funds to the Foundation. She enjoyed catching up on snippets of news as she worked her way to the table assigned her. Her counterpart, Pam, and their boss, Tim, were sitting at separate tables, so between the three of them they could speak to more guests.

There were twenty tables of eight set up. A nice turnout, Sam thought as she took a chair with her back to the lectern. She already knew what Tim had to say; this way she could judge reactions while he talked.

Things settled down shortly after noon when everyone took a chair and the meal began. As the waiter was placing the salad in front of Samantha, she looked up—straight into the eyes of Mac McAlheny!

He sat at the next table over, in her direct line of sight. He lifted one eyebrow at her, but could not do more across the distance.

Flustered, Samantha looked at her plate. Good grief, what was he doing here? She peeked again to see him still watching her. She hadn't a clue he'd be one of today's guests. Would he cause a scene? She couldn't tell anything from his expression and she wasn't sure she wanted to find out. Could she somehow find an excuse to leave? He didn't know she worked for the Beale Foundation. Maybe he'd think she was the CEO of some firm he didn't know. All he knew was she once worked for Jordan Maintenance.

The man at her left spoke and she gratefully grasped the diversion. She made a special effort to engage each person at her table, giving information about the Foundation in practical terms, resisting the temptation to look over at the other table again. But it was an effort and she felt her nerves on edge the whole time. Mac was watching her. Some sixth sense made that clear. How far would he go in a public forum like this? She didn't want to put it to the test.

When Tim was introduced, some people shifted their chairs slightly for a better view of the keynote speaker. She risked a glance at the other table. Mac's gaze was narrowed and focused directly on her. She shifted slightly so she wasn't in his line of sight. Listening to Tim with only partial attention, she glanced around for the nearest exit. When the luncheon finished, people would be leaving, chatting, creating a barrier between her and Mac. She could zip out through the exit on the side before Mac confronted her.

Samantha was ready to make her move as soon as Tim finished. She quietly gathered her purse and tote that carried pamphlets for the Foundation. She'd already distributed most of them before lunch. The applause was heartfelt and she was pleased Tim's speech had gone over so well. But now—

"I must admit his speech pushed me over the top," the man next to her said. "I'd like to discuss a donation. I like the idea of a perpetual gift, one that keeps generating income over the years. If our own fortunes continue to increase, we could add to the gift each year. And if not, the Foundation would still get income from the initial grant in the name of our company. Are you the lady I talk to?"

Samantha sighed softly. No escape.

Smiling brightly, she put down her purse and tote. "I sure am, Mr. Hadden. And the Beale Foundation would be grateful for any donation, but a gift that keeps giving is especially appreciated." She dug into her tote for the proper pamphlet explaining gifts-that-keep-giving and handed it to him. "As you can see, you have a choice of ways to do this. I can run some numbers if you give me an indication of how much you wish to donate."

Her body went on alert. Without turning, she knew Mac stood right behind her. She longed to turn and glare at him for disturbing her peace through lunch. Maybe if she continued to talk with Mr. Hadden, Mac would get tired and give up.

Ha, who was she kidding? She knew CEO types; they were focused and persistent. Ruthless, some said. A man didn't build a company being easily dissuaded.

"I'll have to talk to my chief financial officer, but I was thinking something along one or two million to begin with. This is a good year for us. I like the way your Foundation works," he said.

Two million dollars was a huge donation. Samantha had to keep talking. Would Mac please, please, please leave?

"In addition to accepting donations, we'd also like to encourage businesses to hire people with disabilities. There are many tasks that are easily handled by people with some limitations. I know a deaf woman who works with data entry and analysis. She's a whiz at it. Another young man who has strong computer skills is working in an electronic engineering firm. He's been working for only a few months and has already received a promotion because of his excellent work. One older woman in a wheelchair is perfect at customer service. She is on the phone all day and has improved the company's image of customer caring. She received a bonus at Christmas that almost equaled her annual salary. Please, give some of our registered prospects a chance," she said.

Sam handed Mr. Hadden three more pamphlets. "Many people don't look beyond the obvious disabilities to the true talents of people who are slightly different."

"I'll have my HR people look into that as well," he said.

"I'll take a couple of those brochures," said one of the other CEOs at her table who had been listening.

She thanked them all and then, unable to put it off, gathered her things and rose. Please don't let him make a scene here in front of potential donors, she prayed, scrambling around for an excuse that would get her off the hook.

A warm hand lightly grasped her arm and turned her gently. Not unlike the other night. But this time she wasn't moving away from danger, but directly into it.

"Hello, Samantha Duncan," Mac said.

His voice sounded as warm as honey on a summer's day. A quick glance up at his face assured her she'd not forgotten a single thing about him. His dark eyes were just as compelling. That slight dimple in his left cheek called to her. She still ached to trace the indentation, feel the texture of his skin. Fisting her hands to resist, she forced a smile.

"Hi." Her heart pounded. Her skin felt too tight. People chatted as they made a general exodus from the restaurant. The waitstaff was clearing tables and moving some of the furnishings to reconfigure for their normal seating. She felt caught like a fly in amber.

"I listened to your brief discourse about the Beale Foundation. Have you worked there long?" he asked.

She could hardly concentrate, with his hand holding her and her worry he'd accuse her of theft. The delightful sensations that swept through her made her want to lay down her purse and put her arms around him. Would he kiss her as he had on New Year's Eve? Or threaten her with the police? Was stolen property valued at five hundred dollars a cause for misdemeanor or felony?

Get a grip, she admonished herself. He was not going to

have her arrested. At least she hoped not. If he wanted to, he would have already taken action. She tried to quell her rioting nerves with that rationale.

"More than eight years," she said, hoping the trepidation didn't show.

"Interesting," he said.

"Perhaps your firm would like to give a donation or hire a partially disabled person," she said brightly, trying to ease her arm from his grip. His fingers tightened slightly.

"It went well, don't you think?" Timothy Parsons said as he strode over to join Samantha. Pam came over and both looked expectantly at Mac.

Samantha wanted to sink through the floor, disappear and never have to face any of them again. She gave in to the inevitable.

"Timothy, I'd like you to meet Mr. McAlheny. This is my boss, Timothy Parsons, and my coworker, Pam Barnnette."

"Good to meet you," Tim said, reaching out to shake hands. Mac was forced to release Sam's arm in order to return Tim's greeting. She sidestepped out of reach and stood halfway behind Pam, resisting the temptation to turn and run for her life.

"I'm impressed by the work your Foundation does. I was hoping to get some time with Samantha to discuss it further," Mac said smoothly.

"Excellent. Carry on. I'll see you back at the office," Tim said to Sam. In only seconds he and Pam left her alone with Mac.

Traitors. Only they didn't know how much she did not wish to be left alone with Mac McAlheny.

Once the others were out of earshot, she glared at him. "If you really wish to discuss the Beale Foundation, Tim would have been a better choice. He's the head of our Ways and Means Division."

"After eight years on the job, I expect you know as much

as he does. Which raises the question, what is an accomplished businesswoman like you doing cleaning offices?"

He was going to challenge her on the ticket. At least he'd waited until they were virtually alone. She didn't count the busboys moving about their tasks.

"I need the money."

"Ah, to fund an extravagant lifestyle," he said smoothly.

"Hardly," she returned with a short laugh. "To fund the consequences of Hurricane George."

She caught the change in his attitude. His mocking ceased and he looked almost thoughtful. Yeah, right, like that was going to happen. Men like Mac never had to count pennies or worry about how to make needed repairs. She'd bet Hurricane George hadn't dented his place, much less caused major damage which exceeded his ability to repair.

"So maybe you can tell me more about the Beale Foundation over dinner," he said.

She blinked at the unexpected comment. Turning, she began walking toward the exit. "If you really want to discuss contributions, I'd be happy to do so, but I suspect that was just a ploy to get rid of my boss." She took a deep breath. "I know what you really want."

"Oh?" Mac felt a kick of amusement. He'd been stunned when he looked up from the luncheon program and found himself staring at Sam. He normally did not believe in coincidence. When he wanted something, he usually had to work to get it. He'd had no luck in finding out more about Samantha than her last name and had begun randomly calling a number of the Duncans listed in the Atlanta phone book to no avail. With a bit more patience, he could have saved himself a lot of trouble.

He refused to closely delve into the reason he'd gone to such lengths to find her. Here she was, of all places. It hadn't made sense at the onset.

He'd watched her during the entire time he ate. She looked

polished and professional and seemed to relate well to the people sitting at her table. Twice she'd glanced his way. Once she reminded him of a doe caught by headlights—she'd looked downright stricken. The other glance had been more surreptitious, as if verifying he was still there.

Once the after-lunch speech finished, he made directly for his quarry and been impressed with her discussing huge grants with Hadden. He knew the man only by reputation, but she'd handled him perfectly.

"So what do I really want?" he asked after a few seconds of silence. Tension seemed to radiate from her. He leaned a bit closer to better hear her.

"Retribution for taking the ticket. It was in the trash, you know," she added quickly.

"Retribution? It was indeed in the trash. I bought it for someone, then ended that relationship. Having no further need of it, I tossed it. I haven't a clue what you mean by retribution."

"For me to pay for it or something," she muttered, picking up her pace. They reached the doors to the outdoors and Samantha sailed through, stopping short when a gust of cool wind blew right in their faces.

"I'll get a cab," he said, gesturing for one as it approached.

Before she could argue, he ushered her into the vehicle and climbed in beside her. She scooted to the far side, probably wishing the space was larger.

"Where to?" the driver asked.

Mac looked at her.

She gave the driver an address and then threw Mac a wary glance. Was there some hidden message in that?

He studied her for a moment. She apparently thought he was out for some kind of payback for the ticket. Was that all that was keeping her from at least being somewhat glad to see him? He frowned. He didn't care if she were glad to see him or not.

He almost laughed, for the situation was proving farcical.

For the past three years every time he turned around another woman was waiting to pounce. Now he'd found someone who rebuffed his every move. Cindy would have to revise her estimate that Mac had charisma after all.

"I can't pay back the ticket at this time," she said primly.

"Forget the damn ticket," he said. "It's not important."

"After you got me fired over it? I don't think so!" Sam retorted indignantly.

"*Fired?* What are you talking about?"

"Didn't you call Mr. Jordan and accuse me of stealing the ticket?"

"Of course not. That is, I called him, but only to find out who you were. I hoped to find out some way to locate you. I realized eventually that you weren't coming back to the table on New Year's Eve. Your ticket was still on the table and it was the next one issued after mine. I put two and two together and tried the cleaning service. How else would you have suggested I find out how to contact you?"

"Well, Mr. Jordan took it wrong, because he fired me Monday morning, and I really needed that job."

"Cleaning offices? I thought you worked for the Beale Foundation."

"I do, but the pay is not the greatest. After George ripped off the roof of the house and caved in the back with a huge oak that crashed in under the force of the wind, money has become more important."

"Didn't you have insurance?" he asked, surprised to hear the reason she had to take a second job.

"Only partially. I didn't know I was supposed to update it periodically as property values rose. So it covered some, but not the full amount."

"Hence the second job?"

"Which I no longer have, thanks to you," she said, flaring at him.

"That was *not* my intent."

"Gee, that's good to know. You got me fired all the same."

"So come to dinner with me and donate the savings in your food bill to the house fund," he said whimsically.

"What?" She stared at him.

Mac watched her expression. There was something about Samantha Duncan that intrigued him. How many women did he know would take a second job to pay for something without whining or looking for sympathy? Or even a handout once they realized he had money to burn.

"Why did you want to find me?" she asked, her eyes narrowing as she gazed at him.

"To see you again. Come to dinner Friday."

"Since I probably would have had a sandwich on Friday night, I'm not sure the sixty cents or so it would save me to eat with you will help a lot," she said.

He was hard-pressed not to laugh. "I'll double the savings."

"This is all a joke to you, isn't it?" She glared at him.

"No. Have dinner with me and we can discuss ways for you to get that money you need for repairs."

She glanced around as the cab slowed. They had reached their destination.

Mac didn't know why it was important she agree to see him, but it was.

"So you'll have dinner with me Friday?" he pushed.

She shrugged. "Why not. It's not like I have a job to get to anymore."

Mac had had more enthusiastic responses to budget meetings, but he'd take what he could get.

"I'll pick you up at seven," he said.

"I'll meet you at the restaurant," she countered instantly. "I don't know you, Mr. McAlheny. I prefer to keep meetings in a public place and keep my home life separate."

The cab swooped into the curb in front of the small office building that served as headquarters for the Beale Foundation.

"Thank you for the ride," she said, lifting her tote and handbag.

"Francesca's on Monteith Street, seven o'clock," he said, getting out and assisting her to the sidewalk. "And it's Mac, remember?"

"I'll be there," she said and turned without another word to enter the building.

Mac watched her for a moment. As he entered the cab, giving the driver the address for McAlheny Industries, he considered how dating Samantha would be different from seeing Teresa. Samantha Duncan was unlike any other woman he'd met. She didn't seem impressed with him or his company. In fact, she was downright mad at him. How was he to know a simple inquiry would result in her dismissal?

She was as unlike Chris as anyone he'd known—not that it mattered in the long run. He wasn't looking for a relationship that lasted for any duration. He had a business to run and a son to raise.

For a few weeks, maybe they could share some good times together.

Was he getting jaded? Date one woman for a short time then move on?

Yet what choice did he have? He was not planning to have his heart ripped out again by falling in love and having it end abruptly through death. Life was chancy enough without putting himself in situations that could hold him hostage to fate.

By Friday afternoon, Sam was a nervous wreck. She had not come up with an excuse to avoid dinner with Mac. Maybe something would happen to make the engagement impossible. She tried to quell the escalating kickboxing butterflies by repeating it was only a meal with a prospective donor to the Foundation. The discarded ticket had been discussed and he'd surprised her by inviting her to a meal rather than threatening her with the police.

On the other hand, if he hadn't talked to Mr. Jordan, she would be working tonight and not going to dinner at one of the best Italian restaurants in Atlanta.

A dusting of snow had covered the city yesterday and some traces lingered in spots. When Sam left the office, night had fallen and the glittering streetlights reflected on the patches of snow, glistening white in the dark. She found a parking place just a block away and entered the restaurant promptly at seven. She immediately spotted Mac leaning casually against one of the walls in the lobby, watching the door. He pushed away when he saw her and walked over. The butterflies increased their activity. She drew in a deep breath. She could handle this.

"Hi," she said, suddenly feeling shy.

"Hi yourself," he said. "Want to check in your coat?"

"Yes." She slipped out of it before he could help her and handed it to him. This wasn't the Black and White Ball. She needed to keep her wits about her. He stepped to the cloakroom and checked it in. He tucked the ticket in his pocket. No escape that way tonight, she thought.

"Our table's ready, I told them you would be here at seven," he said, guiding her into the large dining room. The maître d' greeted them both and led them to a small table near the far wall. Most of the tables were already occupied. A large Reserved sign sat in the center of theirs, which was swiftly whisked away.

"How did you know I'd be on time?" she asked when seated.

"You're the type."

"What type?" She glanced at the menu, her mouth watering at the selection. His words caught her by surprise.

"Competent, businesslike, not someone to waste time— your own or someone else's," he said while also studying the menu.

Sam wondered if she liked the assessment. It sounded

boring and dull. Which she probably was. Who had time to develop exciting traits with all her responsibilities?

When she looked up, his gaze was fastened on her.

"What?" she asked.

"I wasn't sure you'd come," he said.

"You told my boss you wanted to discuss the Foundation. Besides, this beats a tuna sandwich."

Knowing he wasn't as certain about her joining him made her feel better about the evening. Despite his wealth and standing in the city, he had human doubts just like she did. She tried to keep that thought in the forefront of her mind.

They began discussing the Foundation's goals and the question came up about how Samantha had started work there.

"So Charlene is the real reason I'm there today," she finished, after giving him a brief recap of the car crash that had killed her parents and rendered her sister paralyzed from the waist down.

"A lot of responsibility for one so young. You must have been only about twenty-one when it all fell on you," he said.

"Actually I was nineteen. I had to quit college and find work fast. We were lucky in one way, however. The house had mortgage insurance and upon my dad's death, was paid in full. So housing is one expense we don't have to worry about."

"But you worry about others?"

She shook her head. "We're not here to listen to my woes. Are you going to donate to the Foundation or not?"

"Persistent, aren't you? Yes, McAlheny Industries will give a perpetual gift, like Hadden."

His cell rang. Checking the number, he frowned. "Excuse me," he said, answering the call.

From his side of the conversation, Samantha could tell it was from a babysitter. She remembered Mac had spoken to his son at the ball. She couldn't hear the other end of the conversation, but it was obvious the little boy wasn't happy about his dad being gone. Mac talked to him for a few minutes, ending with, "I'll see you in the morning as soon as you wake up, okay?"

He replaced the phone in his pocket. "Sorry about that."

"That's okay," Sam said.

"Do you remember I told you at the ball that we just lost our longtime housekeeper and nanny? Well, Tommy doesn't like the new one I've hired. She's daily and only agreed to stay longer tonight as a special favor. I need a live-in nanny fast and so far none of the agencies I've contacted can locate a suitable one." He looked at her again.

"What?"

"After we spoke the other day, I called Jordan Maintenance and spoke again with Amos Jordan. You're right, it's my fault you lost that job. I have one to offer you in exchange."

Sam just looked at him. Instead of making an issue of the ticket, he was offering her a job? What was he up to?

"I'm listening," she said after a moment.

"I'm looking for a live-in housekeeper—"

"I'm not interested." Good grief, live with the man? She'd never get any sleep. She was having enough trouble these nights dreaming about their dances, that special kiss. How could she possibly consider working for him?

"Hear me out. I have a woman coming in from seven in the morning until six at night. But she leaves promptly at six, unless we make prior arrangements like this evening. I can't get away from work at a set time every night. I need someone to watch Tommy from six until I get home."

Sam nodded, feeling a spark of anticipation. "So you're offering me a babysitting position until you hire a live-in nanny?"

"Seems the least I can do to make up for your job loss." He mentioned a sum above what she had been earning at the cleaning service.

"How late do you work?" she asked. Jordan had paid her for six hours of work each night.

"Sometimes as late as ten or eleven. Most nights I try to get home before Tommy goes to bed at eight."

"Hourly rate?" she asked.

"Flat fee per week, some nights you may be there until almost midnight. Most nights you can leave before eight."

If most nights proved true, she'd be receiving more than she received before for only two hours of work each day. How hard could it be to watch a three-year-old for two hours?

She was undecided. Wary of a deal that sounded too good to be true, she was tempted by the income. And fewer hours would mean she could work with her sister to devise and implement firm plans for marketing Charlene's work this year.

But to work for Mac McAlheny? She wasn't sure that was wise. He affected her on a primal level. Could she work for him and not want something more?

"I've never worked with children before. Surely you could find someone else better suited."

"Come meet Tommy, see what you think," Mac said.

Sam considered the offer. It sounded perfect. If things would once go her way, she could get the repairs finished and paid for and resume her night school college work. She was so close to her degree and eventually the career she longed for. That's what she had to do, keep her eye on her goal and not get sidetracked by a gorgeous man looking for help with his child.

Sam hesitated a moment, then nodded. "Okay, I'll meet your son and see where we go from there."

Mac smiled with satisfaction. He would get to see more of Samantha Duncan—and find out exactly why she caught his interest. The current situation was perfect for hiring her. It would atone for causing her to lose her job and help him out after Mrs. Horton's rather strict rules. He had an idea Sam would be good for Tommy. And, perhaps, for him?

CHAPTER FOUR

SAMANTHA drove home thoughtfully. She wasn't sure if she understood why Mac McAlheny had offered her a job. She tried to analyze it from all different angles. She didn't think he was angry she'd taken the trashed ticket. In fact, he seemed content to talk about a variety of subjects at dinner—including a perpetual grant for the Beale Foundation.

But his job offer had come totally out of the blue. Why had he made it?

She'd never worked with small children. Could she be what Tommy McAlheny needed? For the most part they would only spend a few hours together before the little boy went to bed at eight. How hard could that be? Then she'd just need to be there until Mac returned.

But what about weekends? He'd mentioned he'd need her to watch his son occasionally on the weekends when he had to travel or work on a special project. He had not said anything about watching his son while he dated—but Sam knew that would be part of it. She frowned when she thought about him taking someone out for dinner and dancing. She couldn't possibly consider him *hers,* but even she knew that New Year's Eve kiss had been special. Even now, several days later driving a car through the dark streets, she could almost feel the sensations that had zinged through her with his kiss.

"This is strictly a job," she said aloud as if to dispel the memory.

Charlene was not home when Sam arrived. It was unlike her sister to be out so late. Sam hoped it meant she was having fun at her friend's house. Normally Charlene invited friends to their home, which was set up for wheelchair access to everything on the first floor. It was hard for her to get in and out of cars and maneuver in other homes that weren't wheelchair friendly.

Sam changed into her warm nightgown, donned her robe and slippers and went down to fix some hot chocolate. She was just about to go upstairs when her sister returned so she veered to the front of the house to greet her.

"Hi," Charlene said, turning in the doorway to wave at a departing car. She closed the door on the cold and spun around to face Sam.

"You must have had fun…you're so late getting back," Sam said with a smile.

"We had a ball. Talked and compared notes on quilting. She showed me what she'd done using my pattern. It turned out great. How was dinner?" she asked as she pulled her jacket off.

"I'm not sure. I went thinking we would be talking about the Foundation, but I got an offer of a different kind. I may end up watching a small child for a few hours each evening."

"How did that come up? I didn't know you knew anything about taking care of kids," Charlene said.

Sam took her sister's jacket and hung it on the lower of the closet poles and picked up her chocolate she'd placed on the small entry table. "Want some hot chocolate?"

"No, I'm full from Betty's meal. Spill."

"It's not a sure thing yet—I'm to meet the little boy tomorrow. If we hit it off, I'd start Monday after work. It's still an evening job, but when else can I find a second job?"

"Should beat cleaning offices for six hours a night.

Maybe you can rock him so you sit for a while," Charlene said with a smile.

Sam sipped her beverage. "I'm not sure three-year-olds like to be rocked. That's more for babies. We'll see. He may not like me." Then what would Mac do?

"I was heading for bed." She wanted to think about their dinner and the commitment she'd made.

"Me, too. I had fun tonight, but I'm tired. Good night, sis."

Sam climbed the stairs to her bedroom as Charlene headed down the hall to hers. She hadn't told Charlene all the details and wondered why. Perhaps because she wasn't sure about the job. Yet despite the uncertainty, she felt a spark of excitement.

She'd get to see Mac again. Get to learn a bit about his personal life and meet his son. The child he'd had with his wife. Was he over her death yet? Did he keep her pictures around for this son to see?

And what all would he expect of his son's nanny? Could she live up to his expectations?

She sure hoped so.

Mac lay in bed. The dark was complete except for the faint spray of stars he could see from one of the windows. It was late and he should be asleep. But he was thinking.

Mrs. Horton was competent, but more old-fashioned and strict with schedules. Tommy seemed to be subdued around her. When Mac questioned her about their evening, she'd said only that Tommy had gone to bed right on time. As if she'd allow anything else.

Would his son like Sam?

What was there about her that had him making such a ludicrous job offer out of the blue? She'd been worried about the blasted ticket—afraid he'd be upset she'd used it. He considered her finding it an act of providence. Now he'd wanted a way to see her again.

In a few weeks, hopefully sooner, he'd find the perfect live-in housekeeper and not need for Sam to babysit Tommy.

But until then, he'd see her almost every day. Surely in a short time he'd grow indifferent to her and move on?

He turned his head slightly, not able to see in the dark the photograph of Chris that sat on his bedside table, but knowing it was there. She was laughing, the delight of her happiness shone through in that candid shot. He missed her so much. But it was becoming harder and harder to feel her with him. Her laughter had enchanted him yet its echoes had long ago faded. Her blue eyes would forever live on in Tommy. But tonight, instead of seeing her, he saw Samantha Duncan. Her face danced in his mind anytime he closed his eyes.

He hoped he hadn't made a mistake hiring Samantha. But when he'd heard about the damage the hurricane had done, and realized his call had gotten her fired, it was the first thing that came to mind as a way to help. She might go after funds for the Beale Foundation, but Sam wasn't one to take charity herself.

Mac threw off the covers and grabbed a shirt to pull on over the shorts he slept in. He wasn't getting any sleep thinking about Sam. Maybe he'd put in a few hours catching up with e-mail. She'd be here tomorrow and he couldn't wait to see her in his home.

The next morning Samantha dressed in warm jeans and a thick cable-knit white sweater. She had debated for a while about what to wear to meet Tommy. Hearing the echo of her mother's voice, *start as you mean to go on,* she eventually just wore what she was comfortable in. She'd probably be down on the floor playing with the little boy; no sense wearing dress slacks for that. Be yourself, was another axiom from her mother. People will either like you for who you are or not. But you'll never have to worry they are your friends only because you are acting like someone you are not.

She was not some glamorous socialite who traveled in exalted circles in Atlanta. She was a working woman who had a dream to move west. It might be an impossible dream, but it was all hers.

Charlene had prepared waffles for breakfast, with warmed maple syrup and spicy sausages. Sam headed for the coffee first, however.

"Looks great," she said as she sat down.

"I heard you moving around so knew how to time the meal," her sister said as she rolled into her place at the table. "So what time do you go?"

"Ten o'clock. I think if I hit it off with the little boy, I'll stay for a bit while his father is there, so Tommy can get to know me. The longtime housekeeper they had left last week and Tommy isn't so fond of the new nanny. She leaves at six each evening, so I'll just have time to get there immediately after work."

Charlene looked at her. "Where's the mother?"

"She died when the little boy was a baby."

"How sad. Goodness, she couldn't have been very old. I hope you get the job, sis. You'll be perfect at it. Look what good care you take of me."

Sam shook her head. "You make it easy for me. And you could sell those beautiful creations you make to bring in money. We really have to do something about marketing them this year."

Charlene nodded, not looking as confident as she had on New Year's Day.

Sam felt the edgy nervousness increase as she drove to Mac's home. She wanted to make a good impression on the little boy and had stopped at a toy store to buy him a picture book. She didn't know if it was in order to bring a present. Would Mac think she was trying to bribe his son into liking her?

He'd be right.

Vacillating from wishing to clinch the job to panic at taking care of a small child only added to her nervous state. One way or the other, she'd soon know if she had the position.

She studied the house when she turned into the driveway. It was large, built of stone, with soaring peaked roofs and a huge front lawn. From the treetops she could glimpse behind the garage, the backyard was probably even larger. Still, for the home of one of Atlanta's richest men, the house wasn't that opulent.

In two minutes she knocked on the door, rubbing her palms against her jeans, trying to quell the jitters.

Mac opened the door and for a moment she forgot to breathe. He'd been gorgeous in a tuxedo. Looked sophisticated and dynamic in a business suit, but wearing casual attire had her heart beating even faster. From the navy crewneck sweater to the dark cords and black boots, he oozed sex appeal. Maybe this had been a mistake. His eyes drew her attention. They were dark and deep and so intriguing. She wished she was coming for an entirely different reason.

"Good morning," she said. Her voice sounded rusty and she cleared her throat.

"Right on time," he said, opening the door wider so she could enter.

A small boy stood on the stairs, staring at her with wide eyes. He ran down the last few steps to his father, encircling one leg and peering around at Sam.

She smiled at him but kept her distance. "Hello, you must be Tommy. I'm Sam."

"Sam-I-am?" he said, quoting from *Green Eggs and Ham* by Dr. Seuss.

"No, not that Sam. I know your daddy and he said you needed someone to come watch you after your nanny goes home each day."

"When Mrs. Horton leaves and before I come home, Sam will stay with you. Remember I explained that?" Mac said, reaching down to pick up his son. The two males turned to look at Sam. Tommy studied her gravely.

"I brought you a present," she said, offering the wrapped book.

"You didn't need to do that," Mac said. He looked at Tommy. "What do you say?"

"Thank you." He gave a big grin and reached for the package.

Sam's heart about melted. The little boy had the same dimple in the same place as his father. His blue eyes were unexpected with his daddy's dark ones. His mother must have given him those eyes. She wondered if his mother had been a blonde as Tommy had a head full of blond curls. She glanced at Mac. He was Tommy's father...she could see the strong resemblance—except for the coloring.

"You are very welcome," she said in response to Tommy's thanks. "I hope you like it and that you don't already have it."

Mac took Sam's jacket and hung it in the closet, all the while juggling Tommy and the big book.

"Let's go into the family room. Tommy's toys are there," Mac said, leading the way down the hall.

Sam glanced into the large living room as they passed—a huge fireplace dominated the far wall with windows flanking it. The furnishings looked oversize and comfortable. Still, it was lovely. Far more spacious than the living room in the house she and Charlene owned. When she entered the family room, Sam was pleasantly surprised by how homey it looked. Kid friendly, yet designed with adults in mind as well. There was a breakfast nook between it and the open kitchen.

"This is beautiful," she said, putting down her purse and sitting on the edge of one of the sofas.

Mac sat on the one at a right angle to the one she sat on and put Tommy on his feet. In only seconds the wrapping paper had been torn off and he showed the book to his dad.

"Something to read later," Mac said. "Thank you."

"Wanna see my truck?" Tommy asked Sam.

"Yes." She watched as he ran halfway across the room and picked up a large toy truck and raced back to her, offering it for her inspection. It set the tone for the day. He was an open and friendly little boy whom Sam thought she could manage for a few hours every evening.

Mac leaned back on the sofa and watched as Sam and his son grew acquainted. He'd wondered all last night what he'd been thinking when he asked her to watch Tommy. He wasn't so impulsive as a rule. He had inquiries out at two leading employment agencies in town, yet had hired a virtual stranger to watch his son with no background check, no references. Only his gut feelings.

Not that Mrs. Horton wasn't a stranger—but she'd come with loads of references. He knew next to nothing about Samantha Duncan except that he was attracted to her. Looking at Sam had him thinking about kisses and dancing cheek to cheek and even lazy evenings watching a television movie complete with fire in the fireplace and shared popcorn.

Whoa—where had that fantasy come from? She was trying out for the role of his part-time nanny, not his lover.

He rose suddenly and they both looked at him in surprise.

"I just remembered something I need to do. I'll be back in a little while." He waited for a moment in case Tommy didn't want him to go, but when his son turned back to Sam, he left. Entering his home study a moment later, he closed the door and glared at the picture of Chris on the credenza. "Why did you have to die and leave us?" he asked. It was a question he'd asked often over the years. "It makes life so much more difficult," he said.

But her sunny smile did not seem to take in the difficulties he faced. She would forever be happy and beautiful and young. He'd have to find his way alone.

"It's not like I'm going to fall in love again," he explained as he walked over to her picture and picked it up. "It's just chemistry. She's pretty, I'm lonely. It's nothing like what we had." They'd shared dreams together, worked together to build a marriage and a business. When their son had been born—for a few brief hours they'd thought they had it all. But she had died before she could leave the hospital after Tommy's birth. At least he had the comfort of knowing everything had been done to try to save her. He would have forever wondered about that if she'd died at home.

Mac studied the picture for a long time. In the back of his mind he knew he was running scared. Chris would not have wanted him to be lonely. She'd loved life and embraced it fully. She'd probably whomp him on the arm and say, *go after what you want.*

But her death had crushed something inside him. Trust. An ability to believe in the future. Work gave him an escape and when he concentrated on the problems and challenges of building McAlheny Industries, he felt alive. When faced with the loneliness of the nights in bed, he felt half dead. Only his son kept him from devoting all his time to work.

"You would have adored our son," he said softly to the picture, setting it gently back on the credenza and turning to see what he could do for a little while, giving Tommy time to get to know Sam at his own pace. He hoped he was doing the right thing hiring Sam.

For a moment, he wondered if it were the right thing for Tommy, or for himself.

After Tommy finished explaining the truck and all it could do, in which Sam understood about one word in three, he picked up the new book and said, "Read me?"

"Sure thing." This she could handle.

He handed her the book and then lifted his arms. Sam pulled him into her lap and opened to the first page. In only a moment they began a new story about Thomas the Tank Engine. She'd bought it in honor of Mac's Tommy.

Sam was surprised at how easily the child accepted her. Was it because he knew his father was home? Or would they be able to spend their evenings harmoniously, too? She hoped so. He leaned trustingly against her as she read. Sam had never read children's books to kids before. She was two years younger than Charlene. Had her sister read to her? She didn't remember.

The story was soon finished and Tommy asked for it again. Amused, Sam complied. By the fourth time he asked, she asked him if he had other stories, or wanted to play a game.

He struggled off her lap and went to the cupboard near the fireplace. Opening it, he took out three books and ran back, offering them to Sam.

The morning passed swiftly. Once in a while Sam wondered what Mac was doing, but she was enchanted with Tommy and had fun keeping up with him.

"Can we go to the park?" he asked.

"Is there a park nearby?"

He nodded and ran to the front of the house, opening the closet door. "Jacket."

Sam followed, wondering where Mac was and if she should be taking Tommy out into the cold.

Mac had obviously heard them and stepped out of a room opposite the living room.

"Going somewhere?"

"I wondered where you were. Tommy wants to go to the park. Is that something he does?"

"We go frequently on the weekends when the weather's nice. I'll go with you, show you where it is. If you work on a Saturday, you'll want to go to the park and let him run. It burns off some of that energy. And then he'll take a long nap to boot."

"Ah, tricks of the trade," she said, glad for any hints she could get.

The walk to the park took five minutes. Sam paid strict attention to the way in case she did bring Tommy on her own. Mac kept hold of his son's hand and would not let him run on the sidewalk, though Tommy asked several times. Once they reached the grassy area near the playground, Mac let him go and the little boy ran straight for the slide.

"He's adorable," she said as they followed more slowly. There were other children and parents at the park. Benches were placed on the perimeter of the playground in locations that gave good access to the various play structures. The slide Tommy ran for was a curved one. Sam saw three other slides of various sizes, in addition to swings, seesaws, balance beams and a fort with cargo netting on one side and a fire pole on the other. There was even a suspension bridge between two platforms.

"He won't fall, will he?" she asked, already a bit wary of the relative height of the slide in comparison to the small child.

"He's played on it many times. If he does fall, we'll just hope he doesn't get hurt."

"I wouldn't want him to fall," she protested.

"I don't, either. But I'm not going to coddle him and deny him a chance to explore his own boundaries. This park is safe. The mulch beneath the playground equipment is several inches thick, cushioning any falls. It scared me to death the first few times we came, but I'm getting better," he said with a wry grin.

Sam felt her insides melt at his look. She nodded and turned back to watch Tommy. She wasn't so sure she should take this job. Anytime she was around Mac she wanted to be the center of his attention. She relished the special feelings she experienced when he looked at her. His grin turned her upside down. He made her feel things she'd never felt before.

Not that anything could come of it. She had her sister to consider. In the past anytime a man got interested in her, he'd meet Charlene, take one look at the wheelchair and soon thereafter vanish from her life. Charlene hated it, knowing she was the cause. Sam hadn't felt a tremendous loss at any time since Chad. That had been hard to take. She had truly been in love and thought he had been as well.

But she was more concerned for her sister than for any man so shallow he'd let something like that influence his life. How could she risk her sister's feelings again? Besides, Mac had never given her an indication of any interest beyond caring for Tommy.

Except the kiss at the beginning of the New Year.

And dinner last night.

This wasn't a date. It was a job interview.

"Tell me what he can and can't do so I don't panic if we come on our own," she said, keeping her gaze and attention firmly on Tommy McAlheny. There was no return to day-dreaming about his father.

By the time Sam left it was after one. Upon returning to the McAlheny household, Mac has shown her where things were located in the kitchen. She and Tommy had explored his bedroom and Mac had explained some routines Tommy followed. A lunch of peanut butter and jelly sandwiches and milk had been shared and Sam had actually tucked the little boy in for his nap.

She turned into her own driveway satisfied she'd quelled any personal thoughts about Mac and could handle the task of watching his son until they had enough money to pay off the roof and get the back of the house repaired.

Charlene was in her quilting room, putting the finishing touches on the wall hanging she'd been working on. "I guess from how long you were gone that the job is yours?" she asked as soon as Sam entered.

"It is and Tommy is darling. I wish you could see him. He has blond curls and big blue eyes. He talks a mile a minute, but I miss some of the words. I hope this works out. The money is good and the job is so much better than working for Jordan Cleaning." She was not going to tell Charlene any of her mixed feelings about working for Mac. She was not even going to think about Mac for the next—three seconds. She sighed. She had to get over this obsession.

"What are you working on?" Sam turned the topic of conversation to her sister's work and soon they were discussing ways of getting it into the hands of boutique owners who might be interested in carrying some of her quilts.

"I could just go door-to-door," Sam mused as she fingered the pretty vest her sister had just made. "If I wear this, the owners are sure to be interested."

"Sounds too easy. There are women in my quilting guild who have tried that. Too many great quilts, too few outlets."

"But they are trying to sell bed quilts which don't compare with the art pieces or the clothing you've made. And you have your patterns. Have you tried a fabric shop to see if the owner would offer them?"

Charlene shook her head. "I'll think about it."

"How about the place that you buy all your material from?"

"Why would someone want my patterns?"

"Why would they not? The designs are fantastic. Think how many woman love to quilt but aren't creative enough to come up with special designs."

Sam wondered who she might talk with to find out more about marketing. She was a whiz at fund-raising. How much different would this be?

She wondered if Mac's marketing team would have any suggestions. Could she find a way to ask? After she'd proved herself taking care of Tommy, of course.

Monday evening promptly at six, Samantha knocked on the door at Mac's home. An older woman answered a moment later.

"You're Ms. Duncan?" she asked.

"Yes, call me Sam. Are you Mrs. Horton?"

The woman opened the door wider and stood aside so Sam could enter.

"I am. Glad to see you're prompt. I hope that continues. I have class to get to."

"I will always do my best," Sam said, a bit surprised by the less than friendly greeting.

"I'll be off. The boy's in the family room watching Mickey Mouse."

Sam took off her coat and hung it in the closet, setting her purse on the entry table. She took a deep breath and headed for the family room, glad Mac had given her a tour of the house on Saturday. Mrs. Horton didn't seem like she wanted to stay a moment longer than she had to.

"Hi, Tommy," Sam said.

He looked up and his expression lightened. He launched himself off the sofa and ran to Sam. "Hi." He lifted his arms and Sam reached down to scoop him up, hugging him. "How are you?" she asked, smiling at his sweet face.

"I watching Mickey Mouse," he said, turning to point to the television.

"So I see. Shall we watch it together?" she asked.

A moment later they were sitting on the sofa, Tommy in her lap, watching the Disney character.

"I'm off, then," Mrs. Horton said, coming into the kitchen. "There's a casserole in the oven, which will be ready by 6:30. I hope you'll clean up after you eat."

"Of course," Sam said. She would not get upset by the woman's austere attitude, but secretly wondered how she interacted with Tommy all day.

"Bye, Tommy," Mrs. Horton said.

"Bye," he said, waving, his attention on the television.

When the show ended, Sam switched off the television and went to prepare their meal. She set Tommy on the counter so he could help, making sure she was never more than a step away.

The little boy looked enchanted. She handed him a spoon and he held it carefully. Taking down two plates, she took the hot casserole from the oven, placing it on the counter across the stove from Tommy. There was crusty bread on the counter which she figured was also for dinner.

"I helping," Tommy said proudly.

"You are." She handed him the bread. "Hold that until I'm ready to cut it, okay?"

"'Kay," he said, solemnly holding the bread.

The back door opened and Mac walked in.

She looked up in surprise. "I didn't expect you home so early," she said.

"Daddy! I helping," Tommy said proudly, clutching the bread to his chest.

"So I see." Mac came into the kitchen and gave his son a kiss. He looked at Sam. "I thought I'd see how things went this first evening. It looks as if you have everything under control. Is there enough food for me, too?"

The casserole would feed a family of six. "Plenty. Do you need me to stay?" If he were home, he had no need of a sitter for Tommy.

"Please. I'll be working in the office part of the evening. Just wanted to make sure you found everything you needed. Mrs. Horton left at six, I take it."

Sam nodded, hoping that was the reason and not that he didn't trust her. She took down a third plate and carried it to the table. Taking the bread from Tommy, she lifted him to the floor. "Here," she said, handing him two forks to go with his spoon. "You set the table. Put these on the table and come back for napkins."

Tommy was clearly delighted to be put to work. Mac leaned against the counter and watched.

When they sat at the table, the settings left lots to be desired, but Tommy was clearly proud of his contribution.

"Good job," Mac complimented him.

Sam nodded again and began to serve the plates, giving Tommy a small portion.

"He won't eat all that," Mac said when she put the dish down on the table.

"Too much?"

"He's only three. He doesn't eat a lot."

"I'll remember that. She served his plate and then hers. Tommy squirmed and ate a few bites, talking to his father, telling him something fascinating, Sam thought. But once again when he began these long monologues, she didn't understand most of the words.

Mac began to laugh. Sam watched him, intrigued by the change. He should do that more often. His eyes crinkled in laughter and his whole face seemed younger. That enticing dimple appeared and she knew she was staring. He caught her gaze and shook his head.

"I don't understand half of what he says, but he's so earnest about it."

She smiled and looked at Tommy. For a second she thought of how they'd look to an outsider peering in. This was like a normal family. Father, mother, child. The kind of dinners she remembered when her parents had been alive and she and Charlene the much-loved children.

Feeling a pang at the loss of her parents, gone nine years, she shook off the feeling and rose to get Tommy some more milk. He might not eat much, but he loved milk.

Sam felt on edge as the meal progressed. Was she on probation? Every time she looked up, Mac was watching her. He'd look at Tommy or at his food when she caught his eye, but it made her nervous. If he hadn't thought she capable of watching his son, why hire her?

Once finished, Mac rose. "I'll be in the study if you need me. Have Tommy come see me before he goes to bed."

She breathed a sigh of relief when he left. She had Tommy help clear the table carrying things that couldn't break if he dropped them. Quickly cleaning the kitchen, she checked the time. Almost seven-thirty. She'd give Tommy a bath and read him a book before having him say good-night to his dad.

Leaving the door a bit open after she'd tucked Tommy into bed, she went quietly to the stairs. Mentally running through her checklist, she had done all she was supposed to. She waited a moment at the top of the stairs to make sure Tommy wasn't calling out, then went down. Mac waited near the bottom.

"In bed?"

"Went quietly. I always thought kids protested," she said, slowing as she descended the last couple of steps.

"He's always been good about going to bed. I wanted him to get used to your tucking him in. Normally if I'm home, I do it," he said. "He seems taken with you."

"I'm glad. He's so darling. It doesn't feel like work to watch him."

"He's not always so congenial. Sometimes he throws temper tantrums like any kid."

"And when that happens, do I just ignore them?"

"For the most part. Do what you feel is best."

It didn't sound as if he didn't trust her. She frowned. "So why did you come home early?"

Mac didn't answer for a moment. Then shrugged. "Just to make sure you didn't feel thrown in over your head your first night."

"Can you hear him in your study if he cries?" she asked.

"Yes, I have a baby monitor there. And another in the family room. So nights you're here after he goes to bed, you can hear him if he cries out. Though he rarely gets out of bed in the night."

"Okay. Well, I've cleaned the kitchen to Mrs. Horton's standards, I hope. Tommy's in bed, so I'll be off," she said, stepping away. She wished she could stay and talk, find out more about Mac and what he'd done all day. Share some of the surprising contributions that came in after last week's luncheon. But he made no move to detain her.

"I'll be home late tomorrow night," Mac said.

"I'll be here until you arrive," she replied, going for her coat.

"Drive carefully. It's getting colder, so there may be some ice on the road." He took a step closer and took her coat from her hands. Her gaze met his and Sam felt the butterflies again. She needed to develop some kind of immunity to the attraction that flared every time she was with him. She was hired to watch his son—nothing more.

Slowly she turned around and let him help her put the coat on. When she turned back, she met his eyes again. They were dark and mysterious and compelling. She could look at him forever, if she could only breathe at the same time.

Taking a quick breath, she broke off the eye contact. "Good night, Mac." She had to get out of here before she did something stupid.

He opened the door for her. The way he watched her made her conscious of how she must look after a long day at the office and then taking care of his son. No lipstick. And who knew how her hair looked?

"Good night, Sam."

What she wished for, she thought as she turned on her car engine a moment later, was a kiss, not a polite good-night.

How stupid was that? Mac didn't seem the type to play around with his staff. The kiss at New Year's had been magical, because of the setting, the nostalgia at the end of a year and the promise of a new one. And probably loneliness because he missed his wife.

"Well, that puts me in my place," she said as she carefully backed out of the driveway and headed for home. "Cinderella was a fairy tale. Not my life."

Mac stood in the doorway watching Sam drive away until the cold had him step back and shut the door. He listened for a moment, but heard nothing. Tommy was already asleep.

Returning to the study, he sat behind the desk and leaned back in the chair.

He'd done some checking on Samantha Duncan—from one of her biggest fans, Timothy Parsons at the Beale Foundation. He was full of praise for Samantha's work and the fact she'd overcome obstacles at a young age that would have defeated older women.

Mac learned more about the accident that had changed the direction of her life. And about her sister, Charlene, whom Timothy also held in high regard.

Taking the ticket had been a lark, Mac was sure. It sounded unlike the woman he was coming to know. He had thrown it away after all. Was it fate to put her into his path? he wondered. He'd enjoyed dinner tonight more than any dinner recently— except perhaps the one on New Year's Eve. Louise had always had dinner ready when he came home but she refused to eat with them. Tonight he had not given Sam the choice. He had some prior commitments the rest of the week, but he'd see what he could do to be home for dinner in the future.

Tommy seemed to like her.

Mac was pleased, since he knew Mrs. Horton and his son didn't hit it off as well. At least for a few hours a day, his son would have someone he really liked to be with. Mac had called the agencies again this morning, but there were no prospective live-in housekeepers on the horizon. He'd expanded his search with two more agencies. Surely someone was out there who would relate well with Tommy, and keep his house.

Not that he was in that much of a hurry now. It would mean he'd have to let Sam go. He was looking forward to some more dinners together before then.

By Friday, Sam felt she was in a comfortable routine. She left work to head for Mac's house. She and Mrs. Horton would never be best friends, but the woman was considerably more cordial now than on Monday. Tommy loved seeing her arrive and she was surprised at how much she relished his enthusiastic greetings.

And she took a few moments before leaving each evening to speak with Mac about what Tommy had said or done. He had not returned home before Tommy's bedtime after Monday. Still, he was always eager to hear about his son. He'd also ask how Sam was faring and listen as if truly interested.

Tonight she wondered if he was taking some lovely young woman out for dinner and dancing. The weather continued cold but clear. Tomorrow it was forecast to warm up a bit, at least above the freezing mark. Mac had asked her Wednesday night if she could watch Tommy on Saturday and she'd agreed. Maybe she'd take him to the zoo. She remembered loving to visit the zoo as a child. She'd have to get Mac's permission tonight. Wouldn't that be a nice surprise for Tommy if his dad agreed?

She had a hard time thinking of Mac as anyone's father. He seemed too sexy to be connected with children. She considered the Black and White Ball the perfect setting for Mac. Or as head of a large corporation. Yet he obviously adored his son and Tommy loved him equally.

She had never given much thought to marriage and a family. Since Chad had broken her heart, she'd been determined to get her degree and go after the job in the National Park Service she so wanted. She so longed to see the west, to live in a national park where land was as it had been for millennia. Some nights she could hardly stand her life the longing was so strong. She read books, had several travel videos of the western parks. She knew more than the average person on flora and fauna of the western region. Maybe once she had a job, she'd find just the right man. Maybe another park ranger.

One day she'd get her chance. But being patient was hard.

Not that she regretted providing a home for her sister. But if Charlene could find an outlet for her quilts and become totally self-sufficient, that would free up her sense of responsibility a bit. Once Sam had her degree, everything would change. Nothing would stop her from her goal.

Sam drove through Atlanta's evening traffic heading for Mac's home. She forced her thoughts to the job at hand and not the dreams that had languished for years. Anticipation rose. Even though he was probably escorting some other woman to dinner, she'd see Mac when he returned home. Those few moments at the end of each evening caused Sam to check her makeup, replenish lipstick and brush her hair as soon as Tommy went to bed each night.

It wasn't much, but for a few moments each day, she relished being in Mac's company.

CHAPTER FIVE

AFTER Tommy was in bed, Samantha brought out the book she'd been reading and settled in the large recliner in the family room. Glancing around, she relished the peace and quiet. Tommy had been more rambunctious this evening than normal and she was glad he was finally asleep.

Mrs. Horton kept the house immaculate and Sam was grateful for the serene room to relax in. This job sure beat working for Jordan's. She could feel guilty for taking Mac's money for the few hours she'd worked so far, but he'd made the offer and she really needed the supplemental income.

The book held her interest until fatigue won out. She'd worked long hours all week and the quietness of the house soon lulled her to sleep.

Mac pulled around Sam's car and into the garage. It was late. He hadn't meant to stay at the party so long, but Peter and Cindy were there. While Mac never liked Cindy all that much, he and Peter had been friends for years. For a little while it had almost been like old times—he talking with a friend while Chris had been elsewhere at a party talking with her friends. Only he knew the difference. They would not be going home together.

To his surprise, he'd enjoyed the evening.

Entering the family room, he saw immediately that his

babysitter had fallen asleep in the recliner. He closed the door quietly, hoping he hadn't wakened her. For a moment he studied Sam, her hair tousled and mussed. Her long, slightly curved lashes brushed the top of her cheeks. Her lips were devoid of lipstick, but still looked kissable.

He frowned and shrugged out of his coat, slinging it across the back of the sofa. He hadn't forgotten their kiss at the ball. She'd been receptive, but that was before he knew her or she him. Would she be equally receptive tonight? The past week he'd found it difficult not to rush home every night to see Sam. When he did arrive, she properly gave him a rundown of Tommy's activities and then quickly left.

He'd offered her the job because he'd gotten her fired and believed in righting wrongs. But now he wanted more than a mere employee. He wanted someone to talk to, someone who cared a bit for his son and his best interests. He wanted something beyond what he'd shared with his former house-keeper, Louise.

But would Sam ever want the same thing? She'd been so proper and distant this week. An employee-employer barrier? Or was she really not interested and that was her way of showing it?

There was only one way to find out. He crossed to the chair and brushed her hair away from her face. The gentle touch seemed to waken her. She blinked once and then looked up at him.

"Sorry, I think I fell asleep." Her voice was husky. She looked warm and content and alluring.

"No problem, as long as it was after Tommy did."

She nodded and stretched, pushing her breasts against her sweater.

Mac swallowed hard. He sat on the armrest, reining in on the impulse to pull her into his arms and snuggle together in the warm chair. "Busy day?"

"Busy week. I'll get my stuff and head out," she said. But

before she could rise, he stood and offered her his hand, pulling her to her feet.

"Thanks," she said.

She tugged on her hand, but he didn't release it. Looking up, she raised her eyebrows in silent question.

Slowly he rubbed his thumb across the back of her hand. "Thanks for watching my son. I'm glad you came into our lives."

Sam looked as if she didn't know what to say. After a couple of seconds, she smiled wryly. "Maybe it was meant. If you hadn't thrown away the ticket and if it hadn't fluttered out of the trash, we never would have met."

He didn't want to think their meeting was so chancy. He would have met her at the charity luncheon. But would he have? They'd sat at different tables. Normally when he went to such events, he left as soon as the program ended.

"Come to dinner tomorrow night," he said, giving into one impulse.

"I can't," she said. "I need to spend some time with my sister. I've been here every evening all week."

"Bring your sister." It wasn't his initial thought, but he'd be glad to include her if it meant Sam would be back.

She shook her head then looked thoughtful. "You and Tommy could come to our place," she offered slowly.

That surprised Mac. But he'd take what he could get. "Fine. What time?"

"Actually, since you wanted me to watch Tommy tomorrow, I was going to ask if I could take him to the zoo. They have a great petting zoo. I think he'd love that. Then I could bring him back to our place and you come over when you are finished or by six or so. Would that work?"

He nodded.

He still held her hand. She tugged again and he let her go. She was instantly all business—giving him a report on Tommy and then going to get her coat. He helped her put it on, turning her to face him, his hands on her shoulders.

"Thanks for taking such good care of my son this week," he said.

"It's a pleasure. He's so funny and sweet. He cuddles up like he's known me all his life. You have a great son."

He nodded, watching her lips as she spoke. When she stopped, he kissed her. He felt her start of surprise and then the giving as she returned the kiss. He gathered her close, unwittingly noticing she was smaller than Chris. Her mouth was warm and sweet and the taste of her sent waves of pleasure through him. All thought of Chris fled. This was Samantha of the pretty brown eyes and the taste of sunshine.

He wanted her in his bed.

But would they ever reach that stage?

Sam ended the kiss a moment later by turning her head slightly. She was breathing hard and her mouth was rosy and damp from their embrace.

"I need to go," she said, avoiding his eyes.

He turned her face and tilted it up until she met his gaze.

"Thank you again for all your help with Tommy." Should he apologize for kissing her? He didn't regret a second.

She stepped back. "It's my job, isn't it?" With that, she opened the door and hurried into the cold.

With a start of surprise, Mac realized he wanted it to be more than that.

"Stupid, stupid, stupid!" Sam chanted as she backed out of the driveway and began driving home. She needed to keep her distance. Was she sending some kind of vibes that she was fascinated by him? Was that the reason he kissed her? Of course she was totally fascinated, but she worked hard all week to keep that knowledge under wraps. She hardly spoke about her job or Mac to her sister. She kept her second job a secret at work. No one could accuse her of flirting. She didn't linger when he returned home each night, though she longed to settle in the comfy sofa and share a late-night beverage of coffee or hot chocolate and talk. She wanted to find out all she could about the man and what he thought about current issues. What were his future plans? Was he as much fun at the end of a hard day at work as he was when on a date?

But she'd been determined to keep her distance.

So why had he kissed her tonight?

She swerved the car slightly as she let herself delve into the memory of the kiss. It had been better than the one at New Year's. At the ball, at least, there had been some excuse. Tonight she was at a loss to know why. Yet she couldn't help the slight smile that touched her lips. Who cared why? Apart from the ball, she hadn't been kissed in a long time. And never like Mac kissed.

Oh, no. She'd invited him to her home. Now she was going to introduce him and Tommy to her sister, share a meal together in her home—which couldn't begin to compare with the lavish place in which he lived—and have to make small talk without revealing how his touch affected her. Or giving away her confusion to her sister.

Not that she wasn't content with her own home. How many women her age owned a house that had no mortgage? Most of the rooms were fine—it was the kitchen that needed work. And a little touch-up here and there from the water damage when their roof leaked.

She groaned. How in the world was she going to cook an impressive meal using camping burners and no oven? What had she been *thinking?*

She hadn't been, obviously. Still, she was excited to see him again. And tomorrow evening she wouldn't feel like Tommy's nanny, but a competent woman entertaining at her home.

What would Charlene say?

She had acted instinctively—not wanting to miss a chance to spend time with him but knowing she should spend time with her sister after being gone so much.

What a mess. Now she had to explain everything to Charlene, without giving away her mixed-up feelings. Then spend the day at the zoo with a three-year-old and still come up with some kind of meal to impress Mac.

Panic set in. Taking a deep breath, she tried to calm herself. She didn't have to impress him. She could cook spaghetti, that didn't need an oven—except for the garlic bread. Maybe she could use her neighbor's oven for that. Ruth had been generous in offering her kitchen whenever the Duncan women needed it. They'd taken her up on it a couple of times.

There, one problem solved.

Now if it were just as easy to explain to Charlene…

Timothy Parsons had been to dinner a couple of times. Now she was inviting her new boss. It sounded weak when she considered she didn't feel the same about having Mac over compared to Timothy.

And after only a week? The reasons for the invitation she dared not reveal. She wanted to see him again when she wasn't strictly Tommy's nanny. Was that a rational reason? Would Charlene see through it and suspect the truth? That Sam was fast getting a crush on her new boss?

And if she did, so what?

Sam could admit she admired Mac. But that's as far as she could go. She had her own plans for the future once she could swing things financially. And right now that did not include being tied down to Atlanta or the obligations Mac would bring to a relationship.

It was merely a friendly dinner for her boss. She needed to keep that thought firmly in mind.

Sam dressed warmly the next morning. The temperature hovered around freezing. She debated canceling the zoo visit, but really thought the little boy would love the exhibits. They'd visit the petting zoo and then stop for some hot chocolate to warm up before returning home. Even though it had been years since she'd been to the zoo, she remembered vividly the many outings her parents had taken Charlene and her on. They'd been such fun. She hoped to make it as fun for Tommy.

When she arrived at the McAlheny home, Mac met her at the door, dressed casually. Was this how he went to work on Saturdays? She let her gaze roam briefly from the wide shoulders down the long legs, and felt that nagging increase in her heart rate. She took a breath and stepped in, smiling widely, hoping he couldn't see how he affected her. Just because she was intrigued with the man didn't mean she had to show it to everyone—especially not him!

"It's freezing. Tommy needs to dress warmly," she said as she stepped inside. Trying to ignore the attraction she felt around Mac could prove a full-time effort in itself. She longed to reach out and touch his arm, just to connect. He had looked fabulous in his tux, dynamic in his business suit, but now he was so downright sexy that if he kissed her this morning, she'd be a goner.

She looked around for Tommy. The sooner they left, the better for her. Nothing like a shock of cold air to erase any lingering longings.

"He's dressed as warmly as I could get him. Cords, wool socks and he even has mittens that Louise knit for him," Mac said. The little boy came running into the foyer, his face alight. He ran up to Sam and hugged her legs.

"Are we going to the zoo now?" he asked, leaning back and lifting his arms for her to pick him up. He wasn't the lightest thing, but she relished the sturdy little body in her arms and happily picked him up for a hug.

"We sure are. I see you're dressed for cold weather. It's sunny, so I think we'll be okay. And after we see the animals, we'll stop for hot chocolate."

"Yeah! I love hot chocolate," he said, beaming. Then he squirmed to get down. "Let's go, Sam."

* * *

"Jacket and mittens first," Mac said. He patiently put the jacket on his wiggling son. Handing him the mittens, he watched to see if Tommy could manage on his own. With a glance at Sam, he said casually, "I thought I'd join you if you don't mind. My meeting today was canceled." No need to tell her he'd been the one to cancel it. Somehow compared with seeing his son enjoy a visit to the zoo, the meeting on production planning came in a very distant second.

She looked at him in surprise—that wasn't horror on her face, was it? If so, she recovered swiftly.

"Oh, well, then if you can take him, I needn't go." He definitely picked up on the disappointment in her voice.

"He's been counting on you," Mac said, knowing that would ensure her going. He felt he was getting to know Samantha Duncan and how her mind worked.

"Oh." She bit her bottom lip for a moment. He wanted to reach out and brush it with his thumb, feel the soft warmth against his fingertips. Feel her against him again like last night.

"Okay, then we'll all go," she said as if making up her mind.

He hid his amusement as he went to get his own jacket. Sam should never play poker; she didn't hide her feelings very well. She clearly didn't want him along, but wasn't willing to disappoint Tommy. It was easier to have two watch Tommy than just one as she'd find out once they were at the zoo. He planned to enjoy himself and he hoped she did, too.

Mac insisted on driving since the car seat was already in place in his car. Tommy talked nonstop about seeing monkeys and petting animals and drinking hot chocolate. At least that was the gist of his excited discourse. Mac was glad Tommy didn't feel the undercurrents swirling around in the car. It seemed as if Sam had gone tongue-tied on him. She gazed out the window, her hands clenched into fists. Every time he glanced her way he noted something new. Her profile was pretty. Nice nose, classic lines, soft hair pulled back so it wouldn't fly into her face with the breeze.

Everything about her was pretty and feminine—from her dark hair to the faint pink tinge on her cheek. Her skin looked soft as satin and he knew her lips were. Swallowing hard, Mac forced himself to focus on the road and driving in the light traffic rather than keep looking at his son's nanny.

He refused to think about the kisses they'd shared, that would likely have them ending up in a crash. He'd save up those memories for nights when he felt especially lonely in his bed.

The zoo was not crowded even though it was a Saturday. Probably because of the cold weather. The wind was light, but really carried a bite. They entered through the Flamingo Plaza, the birds not in evidence. He hoped they were bundled into someplace warm. Tropical animals wouldn't fare as well in today's cold spell. Only a few hundred yards from the parking lot and he already wanted out of the cold.

Sam reached up and undid her ponytail, allowing her hair to cover her ears and neck hoping for some warmth. She suspected this outing had been a mistake. It was freezing! She held Tommy's mittened hand and wished she'd brought gloves. How long before they could stop in one of the restaurants and get warm?

"Maybe we should stop for hot chocolate before venturing to the petting zoo," she said as she watched Mac zip his jacket closed.

"I don't think all our party would concur," he murmured.

Tommy was pulling Sam along as he charged ahead, his excited voice talking about animals and petting. His exhilaration was contagious and she felt her own spirits lift in response.

"Okay, we'll see the petting animals then go somewhere warm."

Once in the children's zoo, she let go Tommy's hand and watched him run a bit ahead.

"My hand is cold after holding his," she said, smiling as the little boy skipped and ran to see the giant tortoise. Before she could think, Mac took her hand in his warm one.

"Can't have you getting frostbite. You may need to drive home," he said, tucking both hands in his jacket pocket.

Cold fled. Warmth swept through. A moment later she could speak. "Why is that?"

"Because I may freeze to death before it's time to go. Your hand can keep me warm, too." He looked down at her and she was struck again by how gorgeous the man was. Holding hands meant she was right beside him, feeling the warmth from his body along hers. She wanted to lean closer, find a sheltered spot out of the cold and just gaze at him forever.

However, duty called and she dragged her gaze away to look for Tommy. He was talking to another little boy next to the giant tortoise. She wondered if the other child could understand him any better.

"I should have checked the long-range forecast before offering this treat," she said as they followed Tommy when he darted here and there to see everything. They reached the petting area and entered, finding it marginally warmer with all the small animals crowding around. It was also sheltered from the wind.

Tommy was in heaven. He solemnly followed the instructions of the zookeepers on duty and gently patted the rabbits and the goats. There was a donkey. A cow. And ducklings and baby chicks in a warming box.

Sam enjoyed the little boy's reaction to all the animals. His laughter rang out when one of the baby pygmy goats gently butted his side. But she was totally caught up in the feelings racing through her holding Mac's hand. She struggled against releasing all the cares of the world for a short time. She wanted him to pull her into his arms and kiss her until she forgot about the cold. If she were granted one wish, it would be for him to see her as more than his son's temporary part-time nanny.

Shocked at the thought, Sam pulled her hand free. "Let's buy some of this food for the animals. Tommy will love feeding them."

Tommy came rushing back when she called and Mac caught his son and lifted him high in the air before settling him against his chest. "Having fun?"

Tommy nodded and began to tell about petting the animals as if his father hadn't been watching him. He squirmed around to point out the different ones he'd patted.

Mac listened until he ran down.

"Want to feed them?" Sam asked. She held a small ice-cream cone full of the pellets. Mac put Tommy down and then stooped down beside him to hold his hand flat so the little goats could eat off his palm.

Tommy shrieked with laughter. "It tickles," he said.

Sam watched the two of them and was suddenly glad Mac had come with them. This reminded her of going with her parents and sister—a family outing. It was made more special for both her and Tommy because Mac was there.

"Ready for some hot chocolate?" He looked at Sam. "I am. Then we'll hit the highlights of the rest of the zoo and find a warm place to eat lunch. Snow is predicted for later this evening. If the temperatures stay so low, I wonder how the animals will cope."

"I'm sure the zoo has arrangements for the weather. But I bet some of them are surprised to find it colder than the African veldt," she replied.

The rest of the morning passed swiftly. Tommy laughed at the monkeys and then made faces at the wise-looking gorillas. He wanted to pet the elephant and threw a short-lived tantrum when Mac said he couldn't.

They decided to eat at one of the places opened in the

zoo, and then browse for a keepsake for Tommy—like a stuffed elephant.

The drive back was different. Tommy fell asleep almost before they left the parking lot. The silence was cozy rather than awkward. Sam felt pleasantly tired, but not at all sleepy. She had dinner to prepare when she returned home. She'd thought she would have Tommy underfoot all afternoon, but since his father was home, she wouldn't.

"You're still coming to dinner, aren't you?" she asked when Mac turned onto his street.

"Wouldn't miss it."

"I thought to make spaghetti if you like that. It's something we can cook on our camp stove, and I know Tommy likes it."

"Camp stove?"

"I told you that a large old oak fell through the back of our house during Hurricane George. It pretty much destroyed our kitchen. We've been cooking on a camp stove until we can afford repairs."

Mac frowned. He knew the hurricane had damaged her home; she'd said that was the reason for the second job. But he hadn't realized they were still impacted by it. "Hurricane George was months ago."

"I explained that before," she murmured.

"I thought you were paying off repairs, not waiting to get them."

"We had the roof repaired and that's what we're paying off. Next on our agenda is the kitchen. Maybe by spring, with the lavish salary you're paying me, we'll be able to get that repaired."

He said nothing, soon turning into the long driveway to his home.

"Come in and get warm before heading home," he suggested.

"Maybe for a minute. Need any help with Tommy?"

"I can manage. If he doesn't wake up when I take him out

of the car seat, I'll put him in bed to nap as long as he wants. Today was exciting for him and I think he might stay asleep for a long while."

He did just as Mac thought.

Sam waited in the foyer while Mac took Tommy up to bed, and then returned.

"Coffee?"

She nodded and followed him into the kitchen, where a moment later he realized there was no water coming from the faucet.

"Odd," he said, trying both the hot and cold. A trickle came from the hot, soon diminishing to a drip.

"Pipes frozen, I bet," she said. "It's cold enough."

"As long as they don't burst," he said, heading downstairs to the basement. The area was cooler than the rest of the house, but not as cold as outside. The pipes looked fine.

He joined Sam in the kitchen. "If they are frozen, it's outside somewhere."

"So I'll pass on the coffee."

"With Tommy sleeping upstairs, I can't run out to a coffee bar," he said, slowly, stepping closer, invading her space. Sam resisted her inclination to step back. Her heart pounded. She studied his dark eyes, wishing for things unknown. It had been a long time since she'd felt special feelings for a man. She had her heart set on moving west, but until then, she wouldn't mind a little companionship—more than her sister provided.

"I should be going home," she said a second later. Should, but didn't want to.

"Thanks for suggesting the zoo. Tommy had fun."

"I did, too."

"Me, too," he said, leaning over to brush his lips against hers. "We'll be at your place at six."

Sam nodded and left, proud of the way she walked and didn't run to her car.

* * *

By six o'clock Sam was a nervous wreck. The sauce was simmering on the camp stove burner. Water boiling for the spaghetti noodles. She'd told her sister she was inviting the McAlhenys and received a boatload of questions—starting with should Charlene admit she'd been the one to strongly encourage Sam to use the ticket.

"Should I thank him for giving you a job, or would that be awkward since he got you fired from the other one?" she asked.

"I'd made a big deal about getting fired, now I don't want flak about taking a job with the man. I still feel a bit funny about it. I know he offered because he felt guilty. He didn't deliberately get me fired. Just treat him like Timothy Parsons when I had him to dinner last summer."

"We had a working kitchen then," Charlene murmured, studying her sister. "As I expect Mr. McAlheny does. So why invite them here?"

"For a home-cooked meal," Sam said, ignoring the fact Mrs. Horton cooked for them every day.

"And he's coming here to dinner, with water-stained ceilings and a kitchen that's half gone? A dining room that looks like a sewing factory and dinner in the living room?" Charlene looked at Sam as if she'd lost her mind.

Sam shrugged. "Thank goodness Ruth next door let us use her oven. I'd hate to offer spaghetti without hot garlic bread."

"Hey, pancakes would have been fine," Charlene teased, mentioning a meal they'd eaten a lot of over the past few months. Apparently realizing her sister wasn't going to answer the other questions, she stopped pushing.

"Tommy would love that, I'm sure," Sam said.

"I can't wait to meet him. I hope the chair won't put him off. We've never been much around kids, even when we were little—except ourselves."

Sam shrugged. "That's what happens with small families."

"So go get married and give me lots of nieces and nephews," Charlene said.

Sam shrugged again. Did her sister have no expectations of marriage and kids herself? Would it be possible? They'd never discussed it. Sam felt a new sense of sadness at the thought of her sister never having a family of her own. Even if she couldn't give birth, adoption was an option.

Only, Charlene went out even less than Sam—and she hadn't had a date that Sam knew of since the accident almost ten years ago. Her older sister had been popular in high school and college. It wasn't fair. Some man was missing out on a wonderful, loving woman.

Maybe instead of selling her patterns and quilted goods, Sam should be brainstorming ideas for Charlene to meet eligible men.

But not tonight, she thought as the doorbell sounded.

Mac held Tommy as they entered. Sam introduced everyone. The little boy looked around at their house, his eyes opening wide when he spotted Charlene. He tilted his head slightly to take in the chair and the woman sitting in it.

"Does that move?" he asked.

"It sure does," Charlene said. "Want a ride?"

Tommy nodded and struggled to get down. Mac put him on his feet and peeled off his jacket before turning him loose.

Charlene leaned over and lifted Tommy to her lap. "Sit still and off we go," she said, turning the chair and heading for the dining room.

"Is that allowed?" Mac asked quietly when Sam reached for Tommy's jacket. She hung it up in the closet and then took Mac's.

"Why not? I think it would be very cool if I were a kid. It's only if you know she'll never get out of the chair that it becomes more sad than fun."

"It was nice of her to offer," he said. He handed her a bouquet of flowers.

"They're lovely. Thank you," she said, smelling the crisp cinnamon scent of carnations and touching the mums with gentle fingers. "I love fresh cut flowers," she said. How long had it been since anyone had given her flowers? She thought it might have been forever.

"Something smells delicious," Mac said.

"Good. I need to run next door to get the garlic bread and then we'll be ready to eat in a jiffy. What happened with your pipes?"

"I called a plumber, but he couldn't get out today. Said pipes are freezing all over the city, apparently this cold is so bad and long it's penetrating the soil."

"Yikes. We're lucky then, to still have running water."

"Sounds like you deserve a break after George. Can I see the kitchen?"

"Come on back."

When they passed through the dining room, Mac stopped to look at the projects underway: the finished quilts and clothing on one side and the large quilting frame set up for sewing. "I have a friend who would love this. Maybe she can come over sometime," he said, fingering one of the wall hangings Charlene had done. "She's into this kind of stuff."

"She'd be welcome. I love talking about quilting. Unfortunately my sister tolerates it only. She'd rather be out in the wilderness talking about mountain lions," Charlene said with a teasing look at Sam.

Mac raised an eyebrow and turned to look at Sam. "Mountain lions?"

"An old dream. Come on back." She felt a pang thinking about the wildlife talks she could have given over the years, if things had been different. But they weren't and most of the time she really didn't regret the lost opportunity. Like when she was asleep.

Mac followed her into the kitchen, leaving Tommy talking a mile a minute to Charlene as they headed back toward the living room in her wheelchair.

"Whoa, this is a mess. How have you two managed all these months?" he said when he saw the plywood-covered opening, the gaping space where a range had once stood.

The back of the room was boarded up with plywood. The destroyed stove and other debris had been removed. The room was drafty and cold. The tree had missed the sink, but it was still old with chipped enamel. Nothing like the modern open floor kitchen he had.

The camp stove she'd talked about sat on a makeshift table near the wall, a pot of spaghetti sauce bubbling merrily in one pot. Water boiling for the noodles threw steam up from the second pot.

"It wasn't very bad before it got so cold. The roof was of more importance. I told you about messing up with the insurance coverage. I rectified it immediately, but it wasn't retroactive. We almost have that roof repair paid off. Then we can see about getting in a contractor for bids on this work and start saving for that."

"I know a couple of guys who might give you a good deal," he said, walking around the perimeter assessing the damage.

"I'll be glad to have them. I know nothing about this kind of thing. We think now we'll wait until spring. It's cold enough in here with the plywood—can you imagine how cold it would be with no wall for a few days?"

"You two could stay at my place," he said.

She spun around and looked at him in surprise. "You don't know us well enough to make such an offer."

He looked back. "I just did. What does length of acquaintance have to do with it? I have known some people for decades who I would not want in my house."

"Thanks for the offer, but Charlene has special needs. This place is set up for her. We'll be fine." Sam turned back to add the spaghetti noodles to the boiling water. For a few seconds she could imagine staying at Mac's lavish home. She'd seen the bathrooms, Huge in comparison to their own. She had explored the house one evening after Tommy went to sleep, and could picture herself staying in the guest bedroom with the lovely old-fashioned bed and en suite bath.

But his house wasn't set up for a handicapped person so they would not be staying with Mac.

"I'll have the names and phone numbers for you on Monday," he said.

"Okay, thanks. Can you watch this? Just give it a stir in a minute, I'll be right back."

Sam dashed to the neighbors to get the bread as soon as she put the noodles in the boiling water. By the time she returned, dinner was ready.

She and Charlene had set up a table in the living room to eat—where it was warmer than at the table in the kitchen. The fire in the fireplace gave it a nice ambiance and Sam turned down the lighting so the well-worn look wasn't as evident.

Tommy loved the spaghetti. To Sam's delight, so did his father.

The evening went better than expected, with Charlene coming out of her shell and talking easily with Mac and Tommy. Mac didn't seem the least bit off put by Charlene's situation, which pleased Sam no end.

There was only ice cream for dessert, but Tommy relished every spoonful.

"Thank you for dinner," Mac said when they finished. "I had better get Tommy home before he falls asleep in the empty ice-cream bowl."

Charlene glanced at Sam. "Why don't you walk them out? I'll clear the table."

"We can help," Mac offered.

"No, thanks. I have my own method," she said easily.

Sam was surprised at how her sister had blossomed during the McAlhenys' visit. She wasn't falling for Mac, was she? For a moment Sam felt almost sick. What if her sister fell in love with him? He had been kind to her over dinner, but she didn't see any special interest in his eyes. Not like when he looked at her.

The thought caught her by surprise. She had no illusions about an affair with her boss. But the odd feelings she had if she imagined her sister with him caused her concern. She would do nothing to stand in Charlene's way of happiness.

"See us to the door, but not outside. It's even colder now than during the daylight," Mac said as he bundled Tommy up in his jacket and mittens. He donned his own jacket and glanced back at the dining room. Charlene was no longer there. He turned and looked at Sam.

"Thanks for having us to dinner," he said, leaning over and brushing his lips against hers.

Sam wanted the kiss to last longer. She was growing to expect them. Maybe they should part more often; it seemed to engender kisses now. She leaned down to hug Tommy. "Stay warm," she said, afraid to look at Mac lest he see something she didn't want to reveal in her expression.

In moments they were gone. The cold had blown in with the opened door and she was glad she wasn't going out in it tonight.

When she carried some of the remaining dishes from dinner into the kitchen, Charlene was humming as she wrapped the leftover food before placing in the refrigerator. She looked up at Sam.

"Wow, he's something else!"

"Who, Tommy?" Sam asked, avoiding her sister's searching gaze.

"No, silly, Mac. He's the one who danced divinely at the ball, right?"

Sam nodded, not wanting to get into what else he did divinely.

"That Tommy is as cute as can be. How old did you say he was?" Charlene asked.

"Three. I'm not sure when his next birthday is." Sam thought she should find out. If he celebrated his fourth birthday while she was still working for his father, she'd want to do something for him.

"If I were a walking woman, I'd go for him myself," Charlene said.

Sam turned and glared at her sister. "There's no reason for you not to become involved with anyone you want. Walking is not the only thing that defines a person."

"I know, I'm just saying most men don't want to be tied down with a cripple."

"There's more to you than that. You're funny, intelligent, talented, creative—"

"Whoa, sis. Thanks for the great endorsement, but let's face it. I'm never going to get married."

Sam felt her eyes fill with tears at Charlene's statement.

"That's not true, but you would have to go out a bit more," she said, blinking and turning away.

"So it's up to you to get married and give me lots of kids to play with."

Sam brushed her cheeks and began to run the hot water to wash the dishes.

"I'm not getting married—at least not for years. If I can swing it, I still want to work out west. Once the repairs are made, it'll only take another year to get my degree. Then, watch out."

Charlene put the rest of the food into the refrigerator and moved over to be near Sam.

"I'm holding you back. If it weren't for me, you would have fulfilled your dream years ago."

"You don't know that. Besides, everything happens for a reason. This way, I'll be more mature, more certain what I want, and have lots more experience dealing with people than I would have at twenty-one."

"Don't you want to get married?" Charlene asked.

"One day, maybe. I might meet a fellow ranger and we can be married at one of the parks."

"Oh. I thought you could fall for Mac and have an instant family for me to spoil."

"Too much baggage. I couldn't do all I need to do if a young child was involved. I'd have to spend time with him for years and that would set me back even more."

"Don't you like Tommy?"

"Of course, who wouldn't?" Sam felt like a Scrooge calling Tommy baggage. But she knew what would happen if she fell for a man who had a family to care for. She'd be tied down even longer. She wouldn't be able to walk away to pursue her dream.

Keep that thought firmly in mind, she told herself. No more wishing for kisses from Mac McAlheny. She needed to focus on her goal and not get sidetracked by a sexy guy who could kiss like no one else she'd ever known and who sent her heart into spins every time she thought about him.

"I know you've had your goal of a job out west since you were a teenager. If it hadn't been for the crash, you would have had years of service under your belt by now. But don't close your mind to other forms of happiness because you are too focused on your goal. National park rangers have families and friends. They own homes and take vacations and live normal lives."

"I know that. But they don't have a spouse two thousand miles away, which is how it would end up if I got involved with someone from Atlanta."

Charlene didn't say any more and in a few moments moved back to the dining room.

Sam finished the dishes trying to keep her mind a blank. She did not want to dwell on might-have-beens. Or could be. Life was as it was. She never would have met Mac if she hadn't used that ticket. Closing her eyes, she could see the expansive vistas of the western parks—soaring mountains snowcapped all year long, or distant horizons with a hundred-mile view. That's where she wanted to be. Learning all she could about the history and natural resources that made the places so special. Walking the land where Indians had once roamed and the cavalry had ridden.

She was not going to get sidetracked by falling for some man who had a darling little boy. A child who would not understand why a mommy lived so far away.

Not that Mac had given any indication of moving beyond the boss/nanny scenario they now had. Except, maybe, for the kisses.

CHAPTER SIX

SUNDAY evening Sam was about to take a quick shower before bed when the phone rang.

"Sam? It's Mac. The water pipes are worse than first thought. They burst near the water main at the street this morning. We have a real mess out front, as do several of the neighbors. And no water. An estimated three days before everything is restored. You and Mrs. Horton can't work here with no water, so I'm taking some time off from work and will get a hotel room for Tommy and me."

"Don't do that," she said. "You offered me a place to stay, let me return the offer. We have four bedrooms upstairs that aren't being used at all. I can't volunteer Charlene to watch Tommy, but I bet she won't mind if Mrs. Horton watches him here during the day and I'll be home evenings to take over."

"I can't impose like that."

"It's no imposition. I know Charlene would love the company. She was captivated by Tommy last night. And so far our water is flowing."

"Be careful what you say, you'll jinx it."

She laughed, suddenly feeling inexplicably happy. "Come on over. You can even have the first shower in the morning."

There was a pause, then Mac said, "Thank you, Sam. We will take you up on the offer."

* * *

Mac replaced the phone and remained at the study desk. He had other resources. He could even take Tommy to stay with Chris's parents or his own for a few days. They'd love to have their grandson visit. But both sets of grandparents lived in Savannah and he didn't want Tommy to be so far away.

He could have taken a few days off and found a motel for them both. Staying with strangers hadn't figured in his plans. Yet when she'd offered, he hadn't thought about it for long before accepting.

Now what? Was he getting into a relationship that would prove sticky to get out of?

Leaning back, he considered the ramifications. Which he should have done before. He was content with his life, with the casual dates and superficial relationships he'd had over the past couple of years.

Was that changing?

What message was he giving by staying with Sam and her sister? Especially when he had friends of long standing who would put him and Tommy up in a heartbeat. Why hadn't he called them?

It wasn't too late. But even as he had the thought, he reached for the phone to call Mrs. Horton and let her know about the change of venue for the next couple of days. He just hoped Tommy wouldn't be too much trouble and wear out their welcome before the pipes were repaired.

Monday morning Sam waited for Mac and Tommy to arrive before leaving for work. It continued to be cold and now snow was predicted. She'd talked to Charlene about Tommy's being watched at their home for a few days. She said little about his daytime caregiver and hoped her sister could get along with Mrs. Horton.

Of course, the nanny arrived first. She glanced around the

entryway and frowned at Sam. "Does Mr. McAlheny expect me to clean this place while I'm here?"

"Not at all," Sam said defensively. Maybe the home did not meet Mrs. Horton's impossible standards, but it was clean and tidy and more suitable, in Sam's opinion, to a young boy's exuberant activities than his own home.

Her sister glided into the foyer to meet Mrs. Horton. For a moment Sam worried the older woman would make some unkind remark, but she merely shook hands and began to take off her coat. Her eyes caught a glimpse into the dining room at the array of fabric spilled over the table and she stopped and stepped closer for a better look.

"Quilting?" she asked, her gaze roaming over the various projects hanging from the wall, or spread on adjacent tables.

"I quilt," Charlene said.

"As do I. Only not as good as this!" Mrs. Horton, still wearing her coat, walked into the room and began exclaiming over some of the art pieces Charlene had created. She stopped before one of a garden as if seen through a leaded glass window.

"This is breathtaking," she said, tilting her head and studying every stitch. "I wish I could do something this lovely. What a talent you have. I envy you."

Sam looked at her sister in surprise. Who would have thought dour Mrs. Horton could have such passion?

"I have a pattern," Charlene offered, wheeling over next to Mrs. Horton. "And I'd be glad to help you get started."

"I should love that," Mrs. Horton said, giving the first smile Sam had ever seen.

Sam heard voices outside and went to the door to open it before Mac could ring the bell.

"Mrs. Horton is already here," she said as she welcomed them into the foyer.

"She's always punctual," Mac said.

"Where's Charlene?" Tommy asked. "I want another ride."

Samantha laughed at his excitement and reached down to unfasten his coat and help him out of it. "She's in the quilting room with Mrs. Horton. Wait until they finish talking, okay?"

"Okay." He ran into the room and Sam rose, putting Tommy's jacket over the knob to the closet. She looked at Mac.

"How's the water situation?"

"Major repairs are now underway on the street. The agency was on the job before we left, digging up the asphalt, a dozen men standing around waiting to work when they can get to the pipes. In the meantime, there's slush bubbling up from the break."

"It's still freezing out and expected to grow colder," she said. "And I hear snow is coming. Did you bring suitcases?"

"They're in the car. I'll bring them in now."

Sam closed the door against the cold when Mac left, watching through the small glass panes near the top of the door. When he returned, two suitcases were all he brought.

"Where to?" he asked.

Sam led the way upstairs, already nervous about the sleeping arrangements. She'd cleaned her parents' room thoroughly after Mac's call and made up the bed with fresh linens. That would do for Mac. The room next to hers she'd prepared for Tommy. She showed him the rooms. His was opposite hers. With the doors open, they could look directly into each room.

"Nice."

"Ignore the water stain on the ceiling. Another gift from George," she said, looking at the room with nostalgia. Sam had rearranged the furniture, bought a new bed and repainted after her parents' death. They'd hoped their aunt Lila would come live with them, but she retired to Florida and had died less than two years after her sister. The room had never been used since Sam's remodeling.

Mac put one suitcase by the bed and studied the ceiling for a moment.

"You know, Samantha, I might be able to help you a bit, in exchange for letting us stay here. I know a bit about repair work."

"Like?"

"Like it looks as if it would only take a couple of sheets of drywall, and some new paint, to repair this problem. Unless something is damaged above in the attic."

"No. We had the house inspected after the hurricane, and got a list of all problems. The rafters are sound, the water didn't sit—it poured through."

"The main damage was to the kitchen," he said, turning and carrying Tommy's suitcase.

She showed him the smaller room next to hers and they headed back downstairs. She entered the living room beneath the master bedroom and gestured to the ceiling in the corner.

"That's stained as well. It's not as noticeable because it didn't get as wet."

"Easy fixes. What else?"

"Can you do kitchens?" she asked wistfully.

He shrugged. "We can look at it and decide the best strategy."

Her hopes soared. Then plunged. She didn't even have enough money saved to buy the supplies and she did not want to get into debt. "We'll discuss it later. I have to get to work now."

Checking on Tommy proved he was well taken care of by Mrs. Horton and Charlene. Sam was surprised by how different Mrs. Horton looked when she spoke with her sister and Tommy. Maybe she just didn't like her!

"Can I drop you at work?" Mac asked as they walked outside a few moments later. "The roads are slippery."

"Thanks, but I need the car later."

"I'll come straight back after work, to make sure Tommy doesn't make a nuisance of himself," Mac said.

"Okay, I'll see you for dinner, then." She left with a glow she hadn't felt in a long time. How foolish, just because she knew ahead of time she'd be eating with Mac and Tommy.

Sam could hardly concentrate on work. Twice in the morning she called home to see how things were going.

Both times her sister told her everything was fine. "Instead of only Alice watching him, he has two women. But I'm going to have to get new rubber for the wheels if we keep riding around like this."

Sam could tell from the tone of voice that Charlene was having a great time.

"Who's Alice?" she asked.

"Alice Horton, the woman who watches Tommy during the day." Charlene sounded as if she thought Sam had lost her marbles.

"Oh, I didn't know her first name."

"Mmm, did you ever ask?" Charlene said.

Sam didn't reply to that. "Well, I just wanted to make sure Tommy wasn't too much."

Hanging up, she debated calling Mac, but it was a trumped-up excuse at best, so she didn't. For some reason, thinking of them staying with her for a few days changed things. She felt more proprietary about Mac and Tommy.

She tried to focus on the project at hand, but thoughts of Mac kept interfering. She remembered how terrific he looked at the zoo. He was definitely high on the masculine chart, yet was gentle with his son. He wasn't afraid to show his love for Tommy.

What would it be like to have him turn those brown eyes on her with the same expression? She shivered slightly at the thought. She already knew what kissing him was like.

How would living with him be? Not that she was exactly *living* with him—he was just staying with her and her sister until his water pipes were repaired. But surely there'd be a few moments when Mac and she would be alone. Would she learn more about the man, or end up stealing kisses?

Sam rose, determined to get those fantasies out of her mind. She had work to do—here and at home. She was still Tommy's nanny in the evenings. Mac might come home tonight to make sure Tommy was all right at her place, but that wasn't going to be the norm.

Despite telling herself a dozen times during the day to forget about Mac, she left work promptly at five in a state of high anticipation. She could not wait to see him again!

Arriving home later than expected due to traffic delays because of weather, Sam was surprised to see Mrs. Horton still sitting on the sofa with Tommy, talking with Charlene. She looked up in surprise. "Is it time to go already?" she asked.

Sam blinked. Usually the woman met her at the door in her coat.

"It's a bit after six. I'm sorry to be late...the roads are treacherous," she said, taking off her coat and reaching down to give Tommy a hug when he struggled down from the sofa and ran over to her. He began telling her something about a truck but once again his enthusiasm ran away with his words and Sam was hard-pressed to understand much.

"I'll run up and change and then get dinner started," Sam said. She hoped she didn't show the disappointment that Mac hadn't returned yet. Maybe he had decided to work late after all. A dozen things could have come up to delay him.

"I need to be going," Alice Horton said. "I'll just make it to class as it is. But the time flew by."

"I look forward to tomorrow," Charlene replied. "Tommy and I will see you out."

Sam bid the woman goodbye and then ran lightly up the steps. She swiftly changed into warm pants and a thick sweater. Even with the heat from the camp stove, the kitchen was cold. She had just turned the knob on her door when Tommy knocked.

Opening it, she smiled down at him.

"Charlene said find me a sweater, I'm cold."

"Of course I will, sweetie, come on." They went into the guest room where Tommy was staying and Sam found a warm sweater for the little boy.

"Pictures," he said as they began walking toward the stairs. He darted into her room and gazed at the large posters she had all around. Arches National Park and Rocky Mountain, Glacier, Yosemite. All the ones she someday hoped to work in. She loved the vistas the posters displayed. It had been years since she put them up, but she never got tired of the views.

"Tommy?"

Mac stood in the doorway. He smiled as his son raced across the room and flung himself into his daddy's arms. Standing, Mac looked at Sam. "I hope he wasn't making a pest of himself."

"Not at all. He was just looking at the pictures." She gestured a bit self-consciously. How many grown women had posters all over their walls?

"They're pretty," he said, stepping in another couple of feet so he could see them all. Mac took his time studying each one. Then he turned his eyes to the bed Sam slept in. It was not the frilly feminine kind he might have pictured. The dark blue quilt hung to the floor. There were several pillows to snuggle against if she wanted to read in bed. The lighting was prefect for that.

He glanced at her and saw her still gazing at the posters.

"All national parks out west," he guessed. Most had names blazoned across the bottom.

She nodded. "One day I want to be a park ranger."

"One day?"

"That's what I'm working on my degree for. If I can get a good job, I can afford to take Charlene with me."

"You want to leave Atlanta?" he asked. The thought surprised him. It showed how little he knew about her.

Sam nodded. "I would have left years ago if not for my sister—not that it's her fault of course, but she needed me around. So instead of graduating from college when I might have done, I'm still slogging away. But one day…" She trailed off as she smiled at the pictures. They gave her heart a lift. She couldn't wait to see the actual scenery herself.

"I know you've mentioned this in passing," he said slowly. "But I didn't realize how solid a goal it was for you."

She looked at him. Was there something more in his tone? Did it matter to him if she left? For a moment she almost smiled. Maybe he'd miss her.

Suddenly Sam realized she'd miss him. She hardly knew him, but she already felt he was a part of her life. What would it be like when the pipes were repaired and he left? Once she had enough money for all the repairs and she would no longer need a second job?

She didn't want to think that far ahead. That would mean not seeing Mac and just the thought of that was disturbing. She stared at him, wondering if going west was the big deal she'd always made it. She was aware of every inch of the man, from his solidly planted feet to the top of his head, which just cleared under her door frame. He looked breathtaking in his dark suit and white shirt that looked as fresh holding Tommy right now as it had that morning.

For a moment the intimacy of being in her bedroom hit her. It was as if he belonged here. Which was an odd thought. No man had ever been in her room before.

They had never done more than exchange a few kisses. But for a moment she felt as if he'd come in here a thousand times.

"I need to get supper started," she said. Mac and Tommy blocked the door. The room seemed to grow smaller. Would he come help? Instantly the image of Mac and her working together sprang to the forefront.

"I came up to find Tommy." He eyed her clothing and added, "And change before supper."

"Plenty of time. See you downstairs."

It took Sam a few moments to get her equilibrium under control when she reached the kitchen. She had no reason to want him to help her. The space was limited and she'd manage better alone—especially if she felt that anticipation and awareness every moment he was around. How could she concentrate on ingredients if she was distracted?

But what a distraction.

She laughed softly at her silliness and set to getting things ready for a meal.

When she was almost finished, she went to the archway to the dining room. The place was empty but she heard voices from the living room. They'd placed the table there to eat the other evening and would be using it until the McAlhenys left. She and Charlene usually just ate in the kitchen. It was easier for her sister.

Walking through to the living room, Sam saw Mac sitting on the floor with Tommy playing cars. Charlene was nearby, watching them as she and Mac talked.

Sam was torn. Despite herself, a small spark of jealousy rose. Yet she was delighted her sister forgot her situation long enough to talk comfortably with such a sexy guy. Maybe—

Tommy spied her and jumped up, running to her. He never seemed to walk when he could run.

"Is dinner ready?" he asked, jumping up and down.

"Yes, we just need to set the table," she replied, glancing once more at Mac.

"I can help," Tommy said.

Mac rose effortlessly, all flowing male muscles and sexy good looks. His hair was a bit mussed. The look in his eyes make her heart race. She wished she could drag him away somewhere and kiss until neither one of them knew their names. But a quick glance at Charlene convinced her she better watch her step. Her sister was studying her with a speculative expression. No sense giving credence to that growing speculation.

"Okay, come on then," Sam said to Tommy.

He beamed a smile and nodded, already heading for the kitchen.

It took a bit longer than it otherwise would have with Tommy helping, but soon they were sitting down to pork chops and rice with two vegetables. Tommy protested, but his dad told him he liked them, so the little boy was soon eating.

Sam took a bite and caught Mac's eye. The food turned to sawdust in her mouth and she couldn't look away. The slow heat that built surprised her. For heaven's sake, she was at dinner with her sister and his son. But it felt as if it were just the two of them in the world.

Making an effort to break his gaze, she quickly finished the mouthful and took a long drink of water. If that happened again, she'd never get her dinner eaten. She deliberately kept her eyes off the man until she'd had enough food. If she went gaga every time she looked at him, the entire world would soon notice—especially Mac.

That sobering thought had her reviewing all the times they'd spent together. She hadn't acted like a total idiot, had she?

Mac watched Sam as they ate. She met his gaze only once the entire meal. Was she regretting inviting him and Tommy to stay with them? Maybe he should find other accommodations for the next few days. He didn't want her to feel awkward in her own house.

Or was it that? Did he imagine the faint pink tinge to her cheeks? Maybe there was a reciprocal feeling on her side. He'd watched the clock all day in anticipation of returning to the Duncans' home. Only to be met by Sam with the information she wanted to move away from Atlanta. That was his home. The place his business was thriving. The place where he'd buried his wife. It had a special hold on his life. Now Samantha was talking about leaving.

Chris. What would she think of all this?

For a moment the ache of loss hit him again. But oddly, it didn't feel as devastating as before. More like an old injury flaring up, but not the immediate intensity of the injury. Was he finally getting over her?

Panic touched. He'd loved Chris for years and he didn't want to get over her. He wanted to mourn her all his life. They should have had fifty or sixty years together.

Instead he was staying with a newly met woman, and feeling some of the same tug of awareness he'd once felt for his wife.

Mac frowned. Staying here had been a mistake. Yet one look at Tommy's face, with his sunny smile, bright eyes and way he hung on everything Sam or Charlene said made the stay worthwhile. Mac would do anything for his son. Chris had missed so much. He ached to think she'd never seen Tommy smile, heard his laughter. Helped him get dressed, or eat. She'd missed it all.

And Tommy had missed having a mother. Louise had been wonderful, but she'd left. Mrs. Horton was temporary, even Sam was temporary. He should provide better for his son.

But to get married just to give Tommy a mother? He couldn't do that. Not after knowing and loving Chris. He needed time to think. Or to find the perfect housekeeper who would stay until Tommy grew up.

He'd interviewed one woman last week, but found fault with her. Was he being too particular? No, he rejected that thought immediately. Not where his son was concerned.

Charlene said something and Mac looked at her. "I'm sorry, I was woolgathering, I guess. What was that?"

"I was just saying how much I enjoy Alice. She's an avid quilter, you know."

Quilter? "No, I didn't know." Truth be told, he knew little beyond her references and application. He was always in a rush to leave when she arrived, and now Sam was home when he got back each night.

"We had a lovely time today when Tommy was napping." Charlene turned to Sam. "She's going to try my garden window pattern."

The talk about quilts reminded him about Chris's friend who so loved quilts. He'd have to give her a call after dinner and see if she'd come look at Charlene's work. If it was as good as it seemed to him, maybe Monica could find an outlet for some pieces which would bring in some much-needed money to this family.

Which reminded him of another project.

"I asked one of the contractors I know to check out your kitchen this week and give me some directions for things I can do. I thought I'd get started on Saturday. But I need help."

How blatant was that? If Sam had any doubts he wanted to spend the day with her, that should settle them. Though he wasn't sure she'd find working on their kitchen fun. But it would at least give them a chance to talk while they worked.

She looked at him then and smiled. "You were serious about helping," she exclaimed.

He nodded. He always kept his word.

"Thank you."

She quickly explained to her sister who joined in offering to watch Tommy so he wouldn't get in the way while they worked.

Mac thanked her, wondering how a wheelchair-bound woman would watch a rambunctious little boy like Tommy. But at least he'd just be in the kitchen, not far away if she needed him.

When dinner ended, Charlene insisted on doing the dishes. When Sam agreed, but said she'd clear the table, Mac felt free to spend time with Tommy until bed. Then he'd call Monica.

* * *

Once he put his son to bed, he went to the small room Sam had pointed out as their home office. He pulled the door shut and looked up Monica's number.

"Mac, I haven't heard from you in ages. What's going on with you? How's Tommy?" she asked after greetings had been exchanged.

"Growing as fast as he can. I'm calling for a favor. I've recently met a woman who does quilts."

"Ah, is she important?"

"Not in that way. But I think the things she's done look great and wanted an expert opinion. Would you mind?"

"Things are a bit slow now with the Christmas rush over. I could squeeze in something for an old friend. As long as I get to see you and Tommy."

"Tommy for sure. I'll try to make it."

They chatted for a little longer and Mac gave her the address. He had barely hung up when Sam knocked on the door.

He crossed over and opened it. "I was on the phone. Come in, I want to talk to you."

He took her hand, and immediately felt a tingling awareness that caught him unaware. Shutting the door, he leaned against it and pulled her into his arms. "I really did want to discuss something with you, but it'll have to wait." Lowering his head, he kissed her.

For a moment he thought she wouldn't respond, but in only seconds, Sam pushed against him, encircling his neck with her arms and kissing him back for all she was worth. It was spectacular. Endless time floated by as he felt her body stretched against his, the sweetness of her mouth. Her tongue danced with his as they extended the kiss.

Finally they were both breathing hard. He rested his forehead on hers, gazing down into her warm brown eyes.

She smiled at him, dreamily. He felt desire sweep through him like lightning. He wanted her. He hadn't felt anything like this in years, maybe ever. It was as if his next breath depended on Sam being in his life.

"That's some discussion," she murmured.

"Oh, yeah, that." Slowly he released her, making sure she was steady before pushing away from the door and stepping away. He needed some space if he was going to be able to think.

He told her about Monica and her agreement to visit and see if Charlene's quilts were something she could sell.

"What do you mean?" Sam asked, suddenly wary.

"Monica has a fashionable boutique in the Galleria. She agreed to see if she could do anything with Charlene's work."

"You asked her without checking with us first?"

"If Monica says no, there's no harm done," he said easily. Why was Sam getting upset?

"Do you know how long it's been since Charlene was in that accident? Almost ten years. In all that time she has never tried to sell a quilt. I think her work is beautiful, exquisite. But what if not everyone agrees with me? Think how her self-esteem will be shattered if your friend waltzes in and declares them not worthy."

He leveled a gaze at her. "What if she comes in and thinks the pieces are as exquisite as you and I do? What if she can sell them and provide a source of income for Charlene?"

Sam stared at him, slowly allowing the idea to enter her mind. He could almost see the wheels turning.

"Talk about a booster," he continued. "If she sells one or two quilts, or those arty pieces she does so well, don't you think that'll go a long way to her own acceptance of being in the wheelchair? You can't think she can't do it, not with where you work and how you enable disabled people to find all kinds of jobs."

"Of course she can do it," Sam said fiercely. "I'm afraid of her being hurt."

"Being hurt is part of life. It's what we do when setbacks

happen that makes us grow. I don't think Monica would say one word to hurt your sister. I think she'd be as delighted with the pieces as you and I are."

"Why would you do this?" Sam asked, still studying him as if he were some new, exotic species.

"You're helping us out by putting us up while our pipes are repaired. It's not that big a deal."

"Oh, yes, it is," she said, coming over and reaching up to pull his head down for another kiss. Her palms on his cheeks were warm. Her lips moist and hot. He was drowning in sensation from her kiss. What would it be like to make love to Sam? To sweep her into his arms and carry her upstairs and close a bedroom door behind them?

Mac groaned with the image and pulled back. There was only so much a man could stand. There'd be no taking her into some bedroom while Tommy was sleeping nearby, or her sister was in the house. What was he thinking?

"Are you okay?" she asked when he broke their embrace.

Mac paced to the opposite end of the small room and nodded. It was obvious—he hadn't been thinking—only feeling. And wishing.

"When is Monica coming?" she asked, sitting on the edge of the large old desk.

"She's going to try tomorrow or the next day. I figured she'll pop in, check out the merchandise and then take any she can sell—even if she only takes one to make sure Charlene's feelings aren't hurt. She was a friend of my wife's. She's not going to hurt your sister, I'm sure of it. I'm hoping she can help."

Sam swung her legs slightly, banging them softly into the side of the desk. "So do we tell Charlene beforehand or not?"

"Your call—you know her better. I'd say I have a friend stopping by to see her quilts. Let it go from there."

"Okay. She and Alice Horton sure enjoyed talking quilts today. I've never seen your housekeeper so animated."

He tilted his head slightly, a puzzled frown marring his features. "Alice Horton animated? I thought that was mutually exclusive."

Sam giggled and then frowned at him. "Don't be mean. She's not warm and friendly, but I think she's a really nice woman."

"She has excellent references."

"Is that how you judge everyone, by their references?" she asked.

"No." He stepped closer. "You didn't have any, as I recall."

Her eyes danced in amusement as he drew near. Like a moth to flame—he couldn't resist. She was flirting with him, and he loved it.

"Shall I provide you with some now?" she asked, the look in her eyes making his heart skip a beat.

"Too late, I already spoke with your boss, Timothy Parsons. He raves about you."

Another step and he could reach out and touch her. But he held back, extending the anticipation. She looked him up and down. She was deliberately provoking him.

"It's too bad bosses don't come with references, then I could read up on you," she said.

When he reached for her she spun away, almost falling off the desk, laughter ringing out. "Maybe I don't have references on you, but I could see that coming a mile away," she teased, dancing out of reach.

With a mock growl, he cornered her and put a hand on the wall on either side of her head. "Now what?" he asked.

"Your call," she said, touching his chest, rubbing her fingers over the sweater he wore. When she looked up at him, he was lost.

The kiss went on forever—or was that merely wishful thinking on his part?

CHAPTER SEVEN

OKAY, she was in dangerous territory, Sam thought a moment later. The kiss had been wild and wanton, stopping just short of indecent when she pushed gently against him.

"I have a sister who could come in at any minute," she said. Sorry to put the brakes on things, Sam was nothing if not conscientious.

This man was her boss—kind of. At least while she was hired to watch his son.

"I think I'll go tell Charlene your friend Monica will be coming by." Sam couldn't meet Mac's eyes. She felt flustered and uncertain.

She couldn't have a crush on her new boss! The job was only temporary—until she had enough money to finish the repairs on the house. And nothing good ever came from wishing for the unattainable.

He let her escape without any protest and Sam ducked into the downstairs bathroom to splash cool water on her face and try to erase that just-kissed look. Her sister would spot it in a heartbeat. It would take a while for her eyes to lose the dazed expression, she thought. She wanted to hug herself with the delight but didn't want to intrigue Charlene too much.

Sam finally went to find Charlene and let her know about the expected visitor, then fled to bed. Sleep was hard to come, however. Reliving the kiss kept her in a high state of longing for more. Mac was the most dynamic man she knew and falling for him would be pure folly. He was still hung up on his wife. Hadn't he said Monica was a friend of his wife's? He obviously still thought of Chris as in the present.

Besides, she thought as she turned on her side, just able to see the rim of the Grand Canyon poster with the streetlights, she had her own future and it did not include becoming involved with a man and his child and staying in Atlanta. She had wide-open spaces to visit, ecosystems to learn about.

But when she fell asleep, it was with the thought of Mac McAlheny and his kisses.

Mac had already left the house the next morning before Sam went downstairs. She wasn't late, despite the lateness of the hour when she fell asleep. Taking a deep drink of hot coffee, she willed the caffeine to take effect and make her alert. She wondered if he felt awkward this morning and that's why he'd left early. She wasn't sure how she would have met him, so was glad for the reprieve.

"Want breakfast?" Charlene asked as she glided into the kitchen.

"No time. We're having a staff meeting at ten and I have a bunch of charts to finish up," Sam said. She welcomed the distraction at work. Maybe she could get through the day without thinking of Mac.

No such luck. He called at nine.

"Would you have dinner with me on Friday?" he asked.

"Dinner?" she repeated.

"Did I get you at a bad time?"

"No. Wouldn't we eat dinner at my house?"

"If the water pipes aren't repaired by then the City of Atlanta needs a new work crew. We'll be at our place and I thought a thank-you dinner would be in order."

"For me and Charlene?" Of course he would include her sister. They were both his hostesses at the house.

"If she'd like to come."

"She probably won't," Sam said. "She doesn't like going around in public if she can avoid it."

"Then just you and me."

"You don't need to do this," she said slowly, already anticipating a quiet dinner for two at some elegant restaurant where perhaps there'd be dancing?

"It's the least I can do to thank you for your hospitality. I was going to ask last night, but got—sidetracked."

She smiled, thinking about how they'd gotten sidetracked. "Very well, then, I accept."

"We can work out details tonight when I get home," he said.

"Okay." When she replaced the receiver, she wondered why he had to call this morning. He could have waited until this evening to ask her. Unless he didn't want to wait that long to hear her voice—like she was glad she hadn't had to wait that long to hear his.

The charts awaited, but Sam wished she didn't have to work this morning. She wished instead that she could have had a leisurely breakfast with Mac, with Tommy being miraculously watched by her sister and Alice and no one to interrupt.

When the fantasy grew out of control, she glanced around to make sure no one was around and then plunged back into the work that needed to be completed prior to the meeting. She could end up wasting the entire day thinking about her temporary houseguest.

There was a strange car in the driveway when Sam returned home that evening. She recognized Alice Horton's vehicle. Mac wasn't back yet. Who was visiting? One of Charlene's quilting guild members?

Entering the home a moment later, Sam heard voices in the dining room. She hung up her coat and then walked to the dining room, amazed at the sight in front of her. It looked as if Charlene had every item she'd ever made spread out on every available surface. Patterns were pinned to each one, except the two that were spread out over the old dining table. Alice and a woman Sam didn't know were studying the designs as Charlene explained them. Tommy was sitting beneath the table, quietly playing with some small trucks.

"Hello?" Sam said.

Tommy scrambled from under the table and ran to her. She picked him up and hugged him, smiling at the others.

"Oh my gosh, is it that late?" Charlene asked.

"Where did the time go?" Alice said, standing up and looking around as if just remembering where she was.

The sleek, sophisticated woman leaning on the table looked up and smiled at Sam.

"You must be Samantha," she said. "I'm Monica Shaw, Mac's friend. I owe him big-time. These are fantastic."

Sam glanced around. "The quilts."

"Of course the quilts. And the clothing and the artwork and best of all are the patterns. Your sister is sitting on a gold mine, and I plan to tap it for all it's worth."

Charlene's smile was the biggest Sam had ever seen. "She thinks they'll sell," she said shyly.

Alice laughed. "That's an understatement. Monica thinks they'll sell for big bucks and wants all Charlene can do—an exclusive. The details still have to be worked out."

"Fantastic!" Sam was thrilled by the news, and suddenly grateful for Mac's call to his friend. She knew her sister's work was good and now the entire city of Atlanta would know it, too.

Monica checked her watch. "I guess I need to get going. My store manager will think I died or something. But I'll be back in the morning, around nine?"

"Fine," Charlene said with a bemused air. "I'll be here."

"I need to get going, too," Alice said.

"Stay for dinner. There's so much to talk about," Charlene said.

"Oh. Well, I guess I could." Alice looked uncertain.

"There's nothing waiting for you at home. You said they cancelled the class due to the weather. Please stay."

Sam walked Monica to the door, thanking her for coming by.

"I should thank you and Mac. The work is amazing. I'm so excited. To have an exclusive line everyone will lust after is what shopkeepers dream about. Your sister is very talented."

She gave a wave and headed out, just as Mac turned into the driveway. Sam closed the door against the cold, wishing she could have kept it open to see how they greeted each other. Just as casual friends—or something more? After all, Monica had known Chris.

"Forget it, Sam, he's out of your league," she murmured.

Tommy jabbered something. Sam nuzzled him as she walked back to the dining room where Alice and Charlene were. "I want to hear all about it, but Mac just came home. Maybe you should just tell us both at once, so you don't have to repeat yourself," she said.

"I wouldn't mind repeating myself a dozen times, but I'll wait until dinner," Charlene said. "I'm thrilled with everything right now."

"I'll change quickly and fix something fast," Sam said.

Sam carried Tommy upstairs. "Come with me while I change and you can help me fix dinner."

The suggestion met with Tommy's complete approval.

Sam changed into warm slacks and another sweater and took Tommy's hand as they began to descend the stairs. He jumped from step to step. He loved the game.

Mac entered and looked up the stairs at them. He'd been talking that long with Monica? Not that Sam was timing him.

"You two look happy," he said as he watched Tommy jump again, demanding that Mac watch him.

"I am watching," his dad said as he took off his coat and tossed it over the railing.

When Tommy was a couple of steps from the bottom he

launched himself forward, pulling out of Sam's grip. Mac caught him and spun him around.

"Good grief, I thought he was going to fall," she said, leaning against the banister and watching them.

"He thinks he can fly. I hope I'm always there to catch him," Mac said, placing Tommy on the floor and watching as he ran into the dining room.

"I spoke with Monica," he said as Sam descended the last few steps. "It's good news, isn't it?"

"Thank you so much for calling her. It seems unreal she likes Charlene's quilts so much. My sister said she'd give us the entire story at dinner. Which I'm off to make right now."

"Need some help?" He looked at her mouth and Sam felt as if he'd caressed her. Instantly she felt the need to feel him against her again.

She looked away before she did something extraordinarily stupid.

"If you'd like." At least in the kitchen, she'd have something to keep her hands occupied and her mind busy.

He nodded. "I'll change and be right there," he said, taking the steps two at a time.

He hadn't touched her, but Sam felt as if he had. She watched until he was out of sight, then grinned off into space for a couple of moments before shaking her head and heading for the kitchen. She couldn't wait to hear Charlene's story.

"That was truly amazing. I'll never be able to thank you enough," Sam said to Mac a couple of hours later.

Sam had hunted Mac down and found him in their office after she'd washed the dishes and he'd gone to put Tommy to bed. She shut the door and beamed at him.

"I told you Monica would be a good choice," he said, rising from the desk chair and coming around to her. He brushed back her hair, placed his palm against her neck and brought her closer for a kiss.

"I could get to like meeting with you after dinner," he said huskily when she stepped in as naturally as if they'd been following this routine for years.

"Me, too," she whispered as she kissed him.

A few moments later, he gently released her and went to lean against the desk. "Where do you want to go to dinner on Friday?"

"You choose," she said, walking to the desk and fiddling with one of the pencils there.

"Dancing?"

"Yes, please," she said with a quick smile.

"Then we'll eat at a seafood restaurant I like and move to one of the clubs."

He reached out, as if unable to keep from touching her, capturing her hand in his, his thumb gently rubbing it. "I'm glad Monica liked Charlene's patterns. That's the most likely source of a continuing income."

"That was the most amazing part. The quilts will bring in a lot, but she thinks she can get the patterns published and have ongoing revenue for years. And Alice is going to be a big help. Who would have thought it?"

"Her references *were* great," he said again.

She laughed. "But not in quilting or in knowing someone in the textile industry who might jump-start the process."

"It's always who you know," Mac said. "Looks like your sister is poised for the big time."

Sam nodded, her smile wide. "I'm so happy for her. One of our New Year's resolutions was to try to sell some of her work. Wow, this is it in spades."

"What was another resolution?"

"Get the house repaired."

"Carson stopped by this morning, the contractor I told you about. He'll have some estimates before the end of the week. He seems to think it would be better if he handled the repairs. I don't know why he doubts my ability."

She laughed. "He probably thinks you are too high-tech. Charlene didn't tell me that he'd been by."

"He called me after he left. I guess her later news drove it out of her mind. He says it could be done in a week or so, once the appliances had been ordered and arrive. With Charlene's sales to Monica, you'll have the money to get started right away."

That had also been mentioned at dinner. It was the only downside that Sam could see. If they had money for repairs, she had no reason to continue as a nanny for Tommy. The thought came unbidden.

"What?" he asked, picking up on her change of expression.

"Nothing. Let's wait until everything is signed, sealed and delivered. You know the saying about a bird in the hand."

"Miracles take a little getting used to, is that it?" he asked, swinging their hands back and forth.

"Yes. Did Tommy go to bed all right?"

"He did. Sam, I also got a call from City Works today. The water pipe repairs will be complete tomorrow. Tommy and I can move back home then. I asked Mrs. Horton if she could watch him on Friday evening and she said yes."

"For my thank-you-for-your-hospitality dinner," she said, trying to keep her tone light. Things were spinning out of control. They were leaving. Soon she wouldn't need to have a second job where she saw Tommy or Mac every day.

Which meant she could get on with her schooling and get her degree sooner than expected.

Somehow, the thought didn't excite her as it usually did.

And, if the action plan Monica outlined for her sister came into being, Charlene would start earning money on a regular basis for patterns with extras here and there when one of her quilts sold. That, with her transcription job, would assure plenty of money for repairs.

Nothing would stand in the way of Sam's future.

So why wasn't she happier about the idea?

Charlene knocked on the door. Sam let go Mac's hand and went to answer it.

"Am I interrupting?" she asked.

"Not at all. Mac invited us to dinner on Friday. He told me they are going back home tomorrow and wanted to thank us for having them here."

Charlene looked beyond her sister and smiled at Mac. "Thanks, but I'll pass. Take Sam, though. She doesn't get out much."

Gee, thanks, sis. I need to have the man I'm crazy about think I'm some kind of stay-at-home loser! But Sam didn't voice the comment aloud. "We can go someplace you're comfortable with, Mac said."

"No, actually I came to ask if Tommy could stay here Friday night. Alice said you asked her to watch him and she and I wanted to get started on a new project I have in mind. We'd take good care of him and not begin work until he was in bed."

"Fine with me."

"You could pick him up Saturday morning—maybe come for a pancake breakfast or something," she said, glancing between Sam and Mac.

"Unless you have other plans for Saturday," Sam said, turning halfway around to look at Mac. "You don't have to come by. I could drop Tommy off."

"I'd like a big pancake breakfast," he said, puzzled at Sam's comment. "I'll spell Mrs. Horton by getting home early, letting her come over here and then I'll bring Tommy when I come to pick up Sam."

"Sounds like a plan. Alice just left. I still can't believe all Monica said."

"She's coming again tomorrow, right?" Sam asked.

"Yes, with some preliminary contracts. I'll have to hire an attorney to review them and guard my interests."

Sam smiled at her sister. Charlene might have led a quiet

life these past ten years, but she was smart and would do well in the business end, she predicted.

Mac stood. "I hope it works out extremely well for you."

"I need to do some things before bed," Sam said, using the interruption as an excuse to leave. The McAlhenys were leaving the next day. She'd not leave Mac in the lurch with child care, but if Charlene made as much from the sales as she said at dinner, Sam could soon resume the normal pattern of her life that had been disrupted by Hurricane George.

As she went up to her bedroom, she wondered how long it would take to forget about Mac and Tommy. A very long time—if ever.

The house seemed empty the next evening after Mac and Tommy had left. They'd eaten dinner one more time with the Duncan sisters and then headed for home.

"That Tommy is cute as can be," Charlene said as she sat watching Sam finish the dishes. Mac had offered to help, but she'd sent him off. She was glad for something to do.

"He is," she agreed, smiling as she remembered Tommy telling them something at dinner. He was so serious when explaining things. She just wished she understood him better.

"And his dad's not bad, either," Charlene said slyly.

Sam ignored that and refused to look at her sister. She was trying for a rise out of her and Sam wasn't going to snap at the bait.

"You don't have to work that second job anymore," Charlene said. "I'm so glad after all this time I can do something for you. In fact, if you want, with what Monica thinks I'll bring in this first year, you could quit your job at the Beale Foundation and go to school full-time. You'd have your degree in one more semester if you attend full-time."

Sam turned at that. "Trying to get rid of me?"

Charlene shrugged. "Trying to let you get on with your life—you put it on hold all these years for me and now it's time for you to live it the way you want."

"I've been happy these years, Charlene."

"But I know you want to work out west. Take the opportunity now."

"You need to bank that windfall in case Monica's estimates are a bit inflated," Sam said practically.

"I plan to bank some, but not all. I want to feel I can contribute. Let me do this, Sam."

More than her feelings for Mac were spinning out of control. Sam nodded and wiped down the counters, finished with kitchen chores for the night. "Thank you," she said with a smile.

Later, she commandeered the family computer to check out registration dates for the spring quarter. She had time, if she walked her papers through. Yet the excitement she'd expected to feel just wasn't there. Acting on impulse, she searched for Mac on the computer, and found several articles about his business. And one on the death of his wife. Chris had been a pretty blonde—probably where Tommy got his hair color. Sam stared at the picture of Chris and Mac together for a long time. They looked so in love. Would she ever have a man look at her like that?

She shut down the computer and went up to bed. Her future lay in a different direction than Mac McAlheny and his son and it was time she acted like it.

Friday Sam was ready before Mac arrived. Alice had come straight from the McAlhenys' home and shared a light dinner with Charlene. They were both still in the kitchen talking a mile a minute. Sam listened from the dining room, amused to find out how chatty Alice Horton was once she shed her gruff exterior. She and Charlene were fast becoming best friends. Who would have thought it?

Sam checked her appearance once more in the downstairs mirror when she heard Mac's car. The dress was warm enough for Atlanta's freezing winter nights, but festive enough for any place he chose. Feeling excited as a teenager, she tried deep breaths to calm her nerves.

He knocked and she threw open the door, smiling widely.

The thing about Sam, Mac thought, was he knew where he was with her. Her smile warmed him. Her excitement was refreshing and welcome. The women who he'd seen since Chris died were too self-centered for his own tastes. Too polished and sophisticated. He'd liked being seen with them and they had relished spending time in the limelight, but there was more to life than strutting around to be seen. Sam was genuine and he liked being with her.

He stepped inside, closed the door and wished he could draw her close for a kiss.

"Hi, Sam," Tommy said.

Mac loved his son, but right now, he'd rather he'd run to find Mrs. Horton rather than stay to greet Sam.

"I sleeped in my bed last night," he announced.

"I know you did. We missed you here, though."

"Want to come sleep over at my house?" Tommy asked.

Mac wished he dared second the request.

"Oh, I have my own bedroom right here in this house. Tonight you can sleep over again. Alice and Charlene are in the kitchen, making a special treat—cookies."

Mac scarcely had him out of his jacket before Tommy headed for the kitchen at a run.

"Are you ready? I'll tell Mrs. Horton we're leaving," he said, looking at her and feeling the warmth in his chest. Sam was pretty, but it was her personality that sparkled.

"I'm ready."

He brushed her cheek with the back of his fingers as he passed to go let Mrs. Horton know he was leaving Tommy in her care.

He couldn't wait until it was just he and Sam. She looked fantastic. He wanted her to have a good time tonight. The place he chose was close to the nightclub and once they ate, they'd go dancing. He couldn't wait to hold her in his arms again; it had been too long. And when they were part of an anonymous crowd, it wouldn't matter if he snuck in a kiss or two. No one would know but them.

The ladies in the kitchen had already put Tommy to work adding chocolate chips to the cookie mix. He knew his son was in good hands. Hurrying back to the entryway, he saw Sam standing where he'd left her. Mac smiled as he reached her and swept back her hair from her face and leaned over to kiss her. Her lips were warm and welcoming. His were cool from the freezing outdoor temperature, but she warmed them in a heartbeat.

He could have stood all night kissing Sam, but he wanted more from their evening.

"Ready?" he asked again.

"I sure am," she replied with a wide smile.

The restaurant was crowded. It was Friday night and the spot was popular in Atlanta. The wait was short, however, due to their reservations and soon they were seated at a table for two. The background noise faded as he gazed at her while she studied the menu. She frowned in concentration then glanced up to see his gaze on her.

"What?" she asked.

"Nothing."

"You already know what you want?" she asked.

"I do."

Her.

The thought came unbidden and floored him for a moment. Then he let it settle in. He wanted her—in all the ways a man wanted a woman. Yes, he wanted to take her to bed. But he also wanted to wake up with her. Share meals together. Make plans for the future and do all the mundane chores around the house together.

He was falling in love with Samantha Duncan!

CHAPTER EIGHT

MAC quickly dropped his gaze to the open menu. He knew what he wanted for dinner, but the thought that just crossed his mind had him needing a moment to himself.

He had loved his wife. He mourned her passing every day. How could he be falling in love with someone else? And with someone so different? There were few similarities between Samantha Duncan and Chris. How could he even begin to find another love when Chris had only been dead three years?

The intellectual side of his mind knew life went on. It also knew Chris would have wanted him to be happy. As he would have wished that for her all her life.

But to think of starting life anew with another woman was unthinkable.

Unless it was with Sam.

He looked at her. Her dark hair fell on either side of her face, soft and glossy in the subdued light. He knew how silky it felt. His fingers itched to feel that soft texture again. Faint color highlighted her cheeks. When she looked up, her choco-late-brown eyes held a question. Mac felt like an idiot.

"I think I'll have the scampi," she said, giving him a gentle smile. It kick-started his heart beating out of control.

"Sounds good. I'm having the surf and turf."

"Such a guy thing," she said, wrinkling her nose at him.

He wanted to reach across the table and kiss her. Taking a

deep breath, he deliberately leaned back in his chair and glanced around. Time enough later for that, he hoped.

"Do you come here often?" she asked, closing her menu.

"I've been here once or twice before. Always business meetings. I like the food."

"Do you have many business dinners?" she asked.

He shrugged. "Not often—if I can help it. But if we have out-of-town customers, wives are included and it makes it a better situation all around."

She nodded.

After the waiter had taken their order for dinner, Sam leaned over a bit and said in a conspiratorial voice, "I don't like business dinners."

"Why's that?"

"I find it hard to make small talk with people I don't know. When we have business lunches, it's usually with prospective donors. But dinners have spouses who have no interest in the donation process. Though sometimes they are interested in the services the Beale Foundation provides."

"Our business dinners are to woo customers in placing megaorders with our company. Chris used to love them. I find them a necessary task, but would just as soon have pizza at home with Tommy."

She smiled brightly, but falsely.

Way to go, idiot, he chided himself. Bring Chris up. Was he using her as a defense? Sam had done nothing to make him think she wanted anything beyond what they had—a casual friendship. Granted, she'd been receptive to his kisses, but she hadn't followed up on any of them with suggestions like the women he'd dated over the past couple of years.

In fact, when he thought about it—she had usually spoken of her great dream to move out west and work in a national park. Did that mean she wouldn't be interested in seeing what might develop between them?

It was too early. He still felt floored by the idea of falling in love again. Tonight was to thank her for her hospitality—and give her a respite from watching Tommy. He needed more time to think things through.

There had to be more than physical attraction, though Sam held that for him in spades. But how much did he know about her?

"Next weekend Tommy and I are going to see his grandparents in Savannah. Would you like to ride along?" Mac asked.

Okay, that was changing the subject. "Your parents?" she asked in surprise.

"Mine and Chris's. What, did you think I didn't have parents?"

"I guess I didn't really think about it. Ours died so long ago it seems strange to us to find people with parents and sometimes grandparents living."

"Both my parents are alive and well and so are Chris's. I take Tommy to visit every few months—especially at this age. He's prone to forget people if he doesn't see them frequently."

"I better not," she said slowly. She'd love to see where Mac grew up. To meet his parents. But she'd feel awkward—especially around Chris's parents. Would they see her as a candidate for their daughter's place in Tommy's life? She dropped her gaze. She was sure Mac had no intentions along those lines. They were just—friends.

"Come with us and I'll give you a tour of Savannah while Tommy is with Jerry and Becca. Those are Chris's parents and I let him stay there alone part of the weekend so they can spoil him all they want."

"Must be fun for him."

"He enjoys the visits. Come with us, Sam," he urged.

She longed to go. Would it hurt? "If Charlene is comfortable with me being gone."

"Your sister's really taking off with this quilting thing, isn't she?" he asked.

"She's in heaven! She loves every aspect. I can't believe how much she's blossomed in the past few days. The accident really changed her from the older sister I remember and now it's as if she's coming back."

"Tell me about her when you were young."

Sam smiled and readily complied. In the telling, she related how happy their family had been, how full of hope and promise. The tragedy of the automobile accident had changed everything—and none of it for the better. But she never complained. He never detected a note of self-pity. She met life head-on and adjusted as the path twisted and turned.

"So now, if she gets some income, maybe it'll be more than enough to support her along with the transcription income she earns."

"And that's a good thing?" Mac knew it was, but wanted Sam's take on it. He was fascinated by the way she thought.

"Yes, for Charlene. It'll mean she's back in charge of her life and won't feel dependent on her younger sister. And, once the repairs are completed and paid for, I can get back to my original plans."

"Ah, the great scheme of moving west."

She smiled and nodded. "I can't wait!"

Mac felt as if he'd been kicked. He didn't want her to move west, or anywhere. Unless it was into his home.

"There are national parks in the east as well," he said easily.

"Sure. But I've lived here all my life. The west is so different. Wide-open spaces, different wildlife, mountains. So much to see, to learn. It's been my dream since I was fifteen."

"We have the Appalachians."

"Foothills compared to the Rockies or the Sierras. I want to see it all, be a part of it. Spread my wings and fly."

He nodded, hoping he gave nothing away. Her passion for her goal wasn't what he wanted to hear. He couldn't move his business or his home. He had a son to raise. He wanted him near his grandparents. Mac wanted Sam to be a part of his life, not try to find a way to fit into the future she looked for so hungrily. Was that selfish of him?

When their food was served, Mac deliberately changed the subject, hoping to find common ground. They discussed movies they liked. No common ground there. She liked chick flicks and he preferred action-adventure epics. When they discussed books, he wasn't surprised to hear that she avidly read everything she could about the American west—history, geology, Native American cultures. His favorites were mysteries where he could try to figure out the ending before it was revealed.

Food was one area they had in common, both liking seafood, Italian and rich desserts.

They talked through dinner, through dessert and beyond. It was late when he realized the restaurant was practically empty and he and Sam had been talking for hours. It had only seemed like minutes.

She glanced around at his look. "Gracious, are we almost the last? What time is it?"

"Close to eleven."

"I've had such fun," she said, smiling at him.

Mac caught his breath at the feelings that cascaded through him at the sight of her smile. Her delight with the evening was clearly evident. He could go on forever.

"Ready to leave? We can still go dancing."

"Maybe not. If you wouldn't mind, I'd like to call it an evening. You could come in when we get home and have a nightcap or something."

Disappointed he wouldn't get to hold her, dance with her as they had on New Year's Eve, he nonetheless welcomed the invitation.

But they were not alone when they entered the house. Charlene and Alice were together in the dining room, with papers spread all over and different quilts folded nearby.

"We got Tommy to bed at eight. He went right to sleep," Alice reported.

"We're hard at it now, so if you two won't mind, we won't join you. It's late and we want to wrap up soon," Charlene said.

"No, we were just going to have something to drink," Sam said, bemused by this side of her sister.

She and Mac entered the kitchen.

"What'll it be?" she asked.

"Hot chocolate. It's too late for coffee if I want to sleep tonight."

"Want to stay over? Seems a shame to wake Tommy now. He's fine here."

"I'll go home and come back in the morning to get him."

"For pancake breakfast," she said, already gathering the ingredients for the hot beverage.

Mac leaned against the counter, out of her way. He could watch her all day and night and still wish he had more time. Odd, he'd never noticeably felt that way about Chris. Of course, he'd known her most of his life. He'd loved her for years. But there was something special about Samantha Duncan that captivated him in ways he hadn't known before.

Conscious of the two women in the adjacent room, Mac kept their meeting brief. He finished his cup of hot chocolate as soon as it was cool enough to drink.

"I'll be by in the morning around nine," he said, brushing her lips with his and then leaving.

Sam stared after him, hearing him bid Alice and Charlene good-night. She had expected something more. But how awkward would a full-blown kiss have been with her sister ten steps away. Or worse, if she'd come into the kitchen for something.

Sighing gently, she ran water in the cups and began to plan for tomorrow's breakfast. She'd see him again in a few short hours. Remembering all they'd talked about during the evening, she went up to bed in a happy frame of mind.

* * *

Sam was wakened in the morning when Tommy knocked on her door. Entering when bidden, he ran to her bed.

"Time for pancakes," he said, smiling at her.

What a great way to wake up. She smiled back, delighted in his innocent excitement.

"It just about is. How about I get dressed, get you dressed and we'll go make the batter?" she asked. He loved helping.

"'Kay."

In less than twenty minutes the two of them were in the kitchen pulling out bowls, mixing utensils and ingredients.

She didn't let him near the hot stove, but had him happily standing on a stool stirring the batter—thankfully only spilling a little. A small price to pay for his obvious happiness. She watched him, her heart swelling with love. He was a precious child. It was fun to see life through the eyes of a child. It made everything seem wondrous and new again.

She was turning sausages in the skillet when she heard the knock on the front door.

"I bet that's your daddy," she said to Tommy. Lifting him down, she turned off the stove and followed at a slower pace when he ran to the front door. The heavy knob was too much for him, so she knew he couldn't open the door before she got there.

Checking, she saw it was Mac and swung the door open.

He smiled at her and reached down to take his son up in his arms. "Hey, sport. How are you doing?"

"We making pancakes," Tommy said proudly, struggling to get down. He ran back to the kitchen.

"Making pancakes or a mess?"

"Some of each. Come on back, I have sausages on the stove and don't want him in there alone." She hurried back, feeling flustered and excited at the same time. She was glad she'd taken time to dress first thing and apply a tiny bit of makeup. The slim jeans and sweater fit perfectly and she hoped he noticed.

"What can I do?" Mac asked when he followed her into the kitchen.

"Set the table?" she suggested, keeping an eye on Tommy.

In a few moments, Charlene came in.

"Coffee," she said dramatically. "I may fall asleep right now if I don't get some soon."

Sam laughed. She felt bubbling with happiness. Pouring her sister a cup, she handed it over. "Don't want you falling asleep now, you might tumble to the floor. How late were you up?"

"Far too late." Charlene sipped the coffee. "Ah, ambrosia."

Mac had poured himself a cup and refilled hers. It was so domestic. As if they were choreographed.

"It was after one when Alice left. Then I was so keyed up, I couldn't get to sleep right away," Charlene said after taking another swallow of coffee.

"You should have slept in later," Sam said.

"Can't. Monica is coming over this morning and taking me to her shop. She wants my help displaying the quilts she's selling. And to see where she would let us offer classes. Alice is meeting me there."

"Cool. Maybe I'll tag along," Sam said.

"If you like. Otherwise, wait until we have it all set up and come in as a customer and give us your honest opinion."

"I'd like to see it, too," Mac said. "Maybe Sam and I can both come later. After lunch? Does that give you enough time to set up the display?"

"Perfect," Charlene said.

Sam sped up the breakfast, making Charlene the first pancakes, then some for Tommy. Sitting around the table, she was conscious of Mac sitting only a few inches away. His and hers were finished at the same time and she enjoyed the meal more than any she'd had recently. Unless it was the one from last night. Or the Black and White Ball. Okay, so any meal with Mac had been special!

* * *

When Charlene left, Mac offered to help with the dishes.

"No need. I can get them done quickly."

"Then I'm calling Carson. He said he'd have estimated cost for the repair work here. Maybe we can get you started on that."

"It would be wonderful, but you must have other plans for Saturday."

"Not this weekend. I told Charlene I'd bring you by after lunch. You're stuck with me until then."

She smiled; being stuck with him was not how she viewed it.

The trip to Monica's shop turned out to be fun. The storefront was larger than Sam expected—huge glass windows displaying completed quilts, crocheted sweaters and baby sets and knitted afghans. Plus displays of patterns, cross-stitch and skeins of brightly colored yarn.

The inside was also spacious, but with a warm and cozy feel. They wandered through—just like a customer might. Mac carried Tommy, lest he dash around and get into mischief. He walked beside Sam.

"Hello," one of the salesclerks greeted them. She smiled at Tommy. "Your son is adorable."

Sam blinked. Did the young woman think Tommy was hers? She opened her mouth to tell her he wasn't, but closed it and merely smiled. She couldn't blame her for mistaking the image they must give. Strangers would think they were a family. For a moment she felt a pang. Would she one day find a man who would love her, want to share her life? Someone she'd love?

It would have to be when she was established as a park ranger. She wouldn't find someone like that in Atlanta. That would tie her down when she felt the future was just opening up.

Except for Mac, something inside whispered. He would never tie her down.

But that would never work. Her dreams lay elsewhere. And he was still connected to his wife even though she was long dead.

Feeling a bit let down with the thought, she looked for Charlene. She saw Alice first.

After complimenting them on the display, hearing about the classes offered and watching as two women who were listening immediately signed up, Sam was content when Mac asked if she were ready to leave. This was Charlene's world now. And Sam was happy to see how well her sister interacted. She'd love teaching quilting and she was already happier than Sam had ever seen her.

"Yes," Sam said.

"Let's take Tommy to the park. There's enough snow still for him to try making a snowman," Mac said.

"I'd like that."

She had other things she could do, but Sam relished every moment she could spend with Mac. And soon enough there'd be no reason.

When Sam arrived at Mac's home on Monday after work, Alice waited, giving her a brief rundown on Tommy's day and then headed out for the class she taught. Sam had hardly begun dinner when Mac entered.

"I didn't expect you so early," she said.

"I wanted to have one of your home-cooked meals," he said.

The kitchen seemed instantly cozier, she thought. Tommy played with toys in the area farthest away from the cooking. He greeted his dad, then returned to the make-believe world he'd created.

It seemed natural for Sam to ask how Mac's day had been. He then asked about hers and the evening took on an even more surreal feeling. She remembered her mother and father talking together in the evenings, sharing the parts of their lives that were spent away from each other. Enjoying just being together.

As she did with Mac.

For the short time she had left.

Soon she wouldn't have to work for the extra money. But she didn't want to think about that yet.

Each evening during the week Mac arrived home earlier than expected. Whenever Sam suggested leaving, he'd always ask her to stay until Tommy was in bed. A ritual developed with them reading to Tommy and then both tucking him in beneath the covers. Mac would then offer her a cup of tea or something so she stayed even later. Each night ended in a kiss. Sometimes Sam wanted to leave earlier just to get her kiss earlier. But she reveled in every moment together.

Thursday he surprised her again. "I asked Mrs. Horton to watch Tommy tomorrow. Same deal as last week. She and Charlene are meeting in the evening, so he was invited to your home again."

"With pancakes for breakfast Saturday?" she asked.

He nodded. "Or we can eat somewhere on the road to Savannah."

"Let's eat at home. Then if anything gets spilled, we can clean him up before we leave."

"I like the way you think."

"Do your parents know I'm coming?" Suddenly Sam wondered if this was a wise move. They wouldn't read anything into their relationship, would they? It wasn't as if he were taking her home to meet the parents, so to speak. Merely to show her Savannah while Tommy was with his maternal grandparents.

"I mentioned I was bringing you. Is that a problem?"

"No, they probably want to know Tommy's caregiver," she said, trying to be practical.

"I think of you as more than that," Mac said quietly.

"Tomorrow night we'll eat a quick bite and then definitely go dancing."

Sam liked the way he said that, as if he would not take no for an answer. As if she'd give one. Dancing with him at the Black and White Ball had been thrilling. She couldn't wait to repeat the experience.

She wore a new dress to dinner. One that had a flaring skirt that would allow her to dance slow, fast and in between. The rich burgundy color made her look her best.

Mac took her to an Italian restaurant.

"You remembered how much I love Italian," she said. Their conversation last week had encompassed all kinds of information exchanges.

"We're not going to talk all night this time," he said as he followed her to the table.

"Because we'd miss the dancing," she said with a laugh. Feeling almost giddy as she sat opposite him, she pulled out the menu and glanced through it. Taking a deep breath, she loved the aromas that filled her senses. She peeked at him and found his gaze on her.

"I'll have the ravioli," she said.

He signaled the waiter and gave their order.

Sam was brimming with news. She beamed at him. "I may have just the nanny for you. Someone who can live in. That way you wouldn't have to juggle schedules between Mrs. Horton and me, but have someone there all the time. She came into the office earlier this week looking for a live-in position. We've done a reference check and everything is perfect. She's very capable, energetic and loves children. She worked for several years in a preschool in Augusta and moved to Atlanta after her husband died to be near their only daughter who's going to Georgia State."

"Someone from the Foundation?" he asked. Mac knew there would be changes with Charlene now contributing to the family income. But he didn't expect Sam to talk about leaving so soon.

"Yes. She's almost deaf, can only hear a few sounds. But in watching children, she doesn't turn her back."

"I don't think so. I need someone who can deal with a rambunctious three-year-old. Too much could go wrong with someone who can't hear." He appreciated her offer. But he wanted Sam in their lives. For as long as she'd stay.

"She has a service dog—he's her ears." Sam leaned forward. "Donations are great, the Foundation needs every penny we get, but even more, we need people to be willing to hire qualified employees who may have a slight disadvantage. I would never recommend anyone who would cause a risk to another—especially to a child. Would you at least interview her?"

"Let me think about it," he said. He didn't like the way this conversation was going.

"I think it would easier for Tommy when I stop watching him to move into a permanent nanny. And I think Mrs. Horton might find a new direction if she continues to work with Charlene on this quilting business."

"I said I'd think about it."

Sam nodded, sitting back, her expression resigned. Mac felt a twinge of guilt. He couldn't consider someone else watching Tommy when he wanted Sam there full-time.

Sam felt let down. She doubted he'd even give Kristin a chance. She knew the situation could end up a perfect solution for all concerned. What little boy wouldn't love to be around a dog, one so well trained as Buddy. And Kristin loved to cook and bake. She'd brought enough batches of cookies and treats into the office that Sam could give a testimonial. And her own daughter was proof of how well she watched children. Kristin had hated to give up her position at the day care center in Augusta, but wanted to be closer to her daughter.

But the age-old concern about disabilities always rose.

Mac reached out and caught her hand in his, squeezing slightly. "I meant it, I'll give it some serious consideration. Maybe you can arrange an interview. I'm not making any promises, but I will interview her, see what she can do. I want harmony in my household, someone for Tommy to like."

She was afraid to hope, but she'd take what she could get. "I'll see what I can arrange."

"But if I think it would in any way endanger my child, no, I won't consider it."

"Neither would I," she said, wondering if her real goal was to find Kristin a position, or find a reason to continue contact with Mac. Her hand tingled from his grip, and her attention was on Mac, not the possibility of finding a perfect match for one of their registrants. She hoped it was because she wanted the best for the older woman. But it wouldn't hurt to have an ongoing connection with the man opposite her after her stint as child care provider was over.

The waiter arrived with their salad. Sam hated to have Mac release her hand. She wished they could have held hands throughout dinner.

She had it bad. And instead of saying something scintillating and enthralling, she had to talk about his hiring someone else to watch Tommy.

She resolved right then that the rest of the night was going to be for them, no talk about Charlene or Tommy and especially not Chris.

They discussed what time they would leave in the morning, what to see first in the historic city on the Georgia coast. Sam told him of a documentary film she'd seen recently and they discussed likes and dislikes of documentary filmmakers.

When they finished eating, Mac called for the check and they were soon on their way. In less than ten minutes they entered the nightclub and immediately felt the rhythm of the music. They were shown to a table near the dance floor, drink orders taken, and as soon as the waitress left, Mac rose and asked Sam to dance.

The pace was fast and fun. She moved with the beat and was delighted to note what a good dancer Mac was. This evening would prove fun on all fronts.

They danced the next one as well, stopping to take a quick break when Mac saw their beverages on the minuscule table.

"I love dancing," Sam said, draining her sparkling water. She was warm from all the exercise, but having a terrific time.

"We'll have to do it often," he replied, his eyes on her.

A slow song started and Mac rose again. "This is why I came," he murmured, pulling her out onto the floor and folding her into his embrace. She snuggled up against him. She was glad he wanted to dance so close. Her forehead rested against his jaw. Partway through the song, he turned his head to give her a kiss. She looked up and he lowered his face to kiss her on the lips.

Smiling against his mouth, she returned the kiss. Tonight was as magical as the Black and White Ball had been. Only better. She wasn't worried about someone finding out how she came. Tonight, she'd been invited.

The evening continued in a like manner until closing time. They danced almost every dance. Sam especially loved the slow ones. Conversation was difficult, but she didn't mind. Mac held her as if she were precious and important to him.

Finally the last call for drinks was given.

"Oh, I didn't realize it was so late," she said, looking at Mac's watch. It was well after midnight.

"Ready to leave?" he asked.

"No, I'm having too much fun, but all good things come to an end," she said, picking up her purse. "Let me make a quick stop and I'll be ready to leave."

"Not ducking out like last time," he said.

She looked puzzled then laughed. "No. I'll be right back."

The drive home through the darkened streets almost put Sam to sleep. She was pleasantly tired. She hated to end their night together, but Mac was a father who had to be up early in the morning. And she had planned to be up early, too. Tommy would be in to see to that.

Mac walked Sam to the door reluctant to say good-night. But it was late and he needed some time to come to terms with his feelings for her. It felt wrong to leave her at the door. He wanted her to belong with him. To share his life. Help him raise Tommy, and maybe have a few children of their own. Some sweet little girl with her mother's big brown eyes, and her delightful laugh. Or another son or two.

When he entered his home a short time later, he looked at it as he imagined she must see it. He'd bought the house after Chris died. They'd struggled so hard to get the business established, forgoing all but the basics until it took off. By the time it had, she hadn't been there to enjoy the fruits of their labor.

Did Sam know that? Did she like the way the house was decorated or wish to change things? His mother had decorated it. He wouldn't care if Sam changed everything except Tommy's room, if she'd agree to marry him.

Marriage!

He went through to the living room and sat on the sofa, the lights off. Leaning against the cushions, he let his mind wander in the dark. He realized he really did want to marry her. He never thought he would go that route again. The agony of losing Chris had been almost unbearable. If he hadn't had Tommy to care for, he wasn't sure he would have made it. Could he open himself up to the possibility of such terrible loss again?

What choice did he have? Risk everything to savor every moment spent together, or part now and feel as if he was losing an arm or a leg—or having a large part of his heart ripped out.

Even knowing the devastating pain that could be waiting, he'd choose to spend whatever time they had together. With any luck, they'd have another fifty or sixty years together. He couldn't risk not spending those years with Sam. How bleak life would be if she wasn't a part of it.

He'd ask her tomorrow to marry him. They could shop for a ring together in Savannah, and then he could introduce her to his parents as his future wife. Tommy already loved her. They would, too, in short order. Just as he did.

Already impatient for the morning, Mac rose and went to bed. He'd probably not sleep, but the sooner the night hours passed, the sooner he could ask Sam to be his wife.

Sam wished she could have slept in late on Saturday, but she only lingered in bed a short time after she heard Tommy. Rising, she went to peep in his room, but the bed was empty. She heard Charlene's voice, so knew Tommy would be fine while she took a quick shower to wake up.

She'd had such a marvelous time last evening. Remembering their dancing as she showered, she couldn't keep the silly smile from her face. It had been so special. And she had all weekend with Mac. She could hardly wait. She'd only been to Savannah once. It was a charming city and she'd get an insider's view with Mac giving her the tour.

When she entered the kitchen after dressing, Charlene already had bacon frying and Tommy was mixing the pancake batter like last week, spilling a bit over the edge of the bowl every couple of swirls of the spoon. He was having a grand time and it was obvious Charlene was, too.

"Good morning," Sam said, heading for the coffeepot. This weekend it was she who needed a huge jolt of caffeine.

"Hi. Did you have fun last night? I tried to wait up, but by eleven-thirty I was too tired."

"I didn't get home until way after two. Good thing you didn't wait up."

"I making pancakes," Tommy said proudly.

"So you are," Sam said, walking over to give him a quick kiss on his cheek. "Looks good." She glanced at her sister. "Thanks for watching him while I dressed."

"He's no trouble. We had fun last night. Alice and I popped popcorn and then we all watched a Disney movie. He was out like a light before it ended."

"Then you and Alice talked more about your quilts?"

"Yes. We are excited about our classes—they start next weekend. And we'll have one on Wednesday nights. With her background in teaching adult education, she's given me lots of great ideas. I can't believe all this. Sometimes I think I'm dreaming."

"So Alice would participate?" Sam asked.

Charlene nodded. "With the Saturday classes. Maybe Wednesdays, too, after next semester when her teaching assignment is up."

"Or if you have daytime classes, I think I have a replacement for her with Mac. If he likes Kristin, Alice and I could both be out of a job. Kristin would live in. I hated to take Alice's job away, but Mac really wanted a live-in housekeeper cum nanny."

"She knew the job was temporary. She'll be as excited about this as I am," Charlene said.

Sam sipped her coffee, delighting in the change in her sister. Nothing was mentioned about feeling awkward going out in public in the wheelchair. Not that she should feel that way, but for years, she'd scarcely left the house. It was only recently she'd started making friends in her quilting guild. Now this. Sam was amazed. And gave full credit to Mac for bringing Monica into the mix and making it happen.

When the doorbell sounded, Sam's heart skipped a beat. She put down the cup.

"I'll get it," she said, trying to sound normal. But her heart rate soared as she hurried to the door.

Mac grinned when he saw her. He stepped inside, closed the door and pulled her into his arms for a long kiss. His face was cold, but that thought lasted only a second before the deep feelings she experienced each time he kissed her took over.

When they broke, she was breathing hard. She had missed him since seeing him a few hours earlier.

"Sleep well?" he asked, taking off his jacket.

He was wearing a dark sweater and dark pants. He looked enticing, dangerous and oh so sexy.

"Slept well, if not long. You?"

"No, I missed you."

She blinked. "Really?"

He glanced into the dining room.

"Are Charlene and Tommy around?" he asked.

"They're in the kitchen. Tommy's helping with the pancakes. You don't want to stand too close—the batter is being spread liberally all around."

"That's my kid."

Mac reached for Sam's hand.

"Come on, we have coffee all ready," Sam said.

"Wait a minute," he said. "I have something to ask you. I know we haven't known each other for long. But it feels longer. You know what I mean?"

She nodded. She felt that way each time she saw him.

"And we get along together. Tommy is crazy about you, and you've been wonderful with him."

She smiled, pleased Tommy liked her so much and that she was able to take care of a child when she had no experience doing so before.

"Samantha Duncan, would you marry me?" he asked in a rush.

CHAPTER NINE

Sam stared at him. Had she heard him correctly? He wanted to *marry* her?

For a moment her mind was paralyzed. She couldn't think, couldn't speak. Blood pounded through her, making a roaring in her ears. He had not asked her…*he had not!*

Then she shook her head and pulled her hand free, stepping back two steps, feeling the shock through every inch. She had never expected this. What had he said? That Tommy was crazy about her. That she and Mac were good together?

"I can't marry you." Her dream of living in the west flashed into mind. She clutched it desperately. She'd been planning to go west for almost half her life. Suddenly Chad's face appeared in her mind. He'd let her down so badly. Could she trust in Mac? She wanted marriage—someday. But after she'd done what she wanted with her life. Not put it on hold again like she'd had to do when Charlene needed her.

Panic made her blurt out, "I'm leaving Atlanta. For the first time since my parents died, I don't have to be responsible for Charlene. I can't get burdened with a child, someone who would need care for years to come. I'll be an old lady by the time I get to finally do what I want. That's not fair to ask me. I can't marry you. I can't!"

Instantly she wished she could recall the words. Make them sound different. Tommy was a delightful child but he was young and needed parents to raise him for the next decade and beyond. She felt her heart race. This wasn't what she had expected when she opened the door. For a moment she felt resentful that Mac had changed everything.

Mac's expression closed. He stared at her impassively. He could have been a stranger.

"I apologize if I threw you into a panic. I misread the situation," he said stiffly.

Sam felt as if she were standing in quicksand. Everything was shifting. "I thought you wouldn't ever marry again. You said that once. I haven't led you on, have I? I mean, I like being with you and with Tommy. But I can't get married before I have a chance to do what I've wanted to do most of my life. Don't you see? When would I have time for me? I can't marry anyone!"

"I understand." His voice was cool, his expression still closed.

She was in full panic mode. Yet she noticed his change— as if the lights had gone out of his eyes. It was frightening to see him so reserved and controlled. But he'd shocked her. She hadn't expected a proposal from him.

"I told you about wanting to be a ranger," she explained, trying to sound reasonable. She felt as if she'd explode. Her skin felt too tight to contain her. Her heart pounded. How could he ask her? He knew she had plans, goals that finally looked as if they were within reach. He wanted to change everything. How could he ask her to choose?

"You did," he acknowledged.

"Didn't you believe me?" she asked, wondering what she could have done differently. She hadn't meant to lead him on. These last few weeks had been delightful but they hadn't altered her life's goals. She loved spending time with Mac, but she had never thought it would lead to this!

"I do believe you. I thought—never mind what I thought. Let's forget I ever said anything," he said.

"Oh, Mac, I won't ever forget. Thank you. I…if things…

I don't know." She turned and ran up the stairs. Already regretting her words about Tommy being a burden, she couldn't tell him he'd ruined everything. Why couldn't they have just continued as friends? He meant more to her than anyone she'd ever known. But she was wary of commitment—thanks in large part to Chad. But the past couldn't be changed and the future she'd always dreamed about was finally in sight. Mac wanted her to give up her dream and stay in Atlanta.

Entering her room, she closed the door quietly and paced for a moment, her energy levels off the charts. Her nerves were shot. How could he? Going to the window, Sam stared out not seeing a thing. *Friends,* that's what she wanted. How could he have misconstrued that?

Closing her eyes, she could almost feel his arms come around her. Feel how alive she felt when she was in them. Opening them again, she glanced around at the posters that filled her wall. Mesa Verde, Grand Canyon, Arches. She wanted so much to be part of that. She couldn't tie herself down to Atlanta for the rest of her life.

Yet she felt as if a part of her had just died.

What now? Did they continue with her watching Tommy until he decided if Kristin would suit? It wouldn't be fair to him if he loved her. To have her around every night.

But wait—he hadn't said anything about love.

She frowned, replaying his words in her mind. There had been nothing about undying passion for her. About finding her so irresistible he couldn't live without her. About loving her as much as he'd loved Chris.

Suddenly she realized what had happened. She'd recommended Kristin for the live-in position last night and somewhere along the line Mac had decided Sam would make a better live-in nanny. If they were married, she'd be home most evenings and they'd only need a daytime housekeeper. Much easier to find a daily when Alice Horton left.

Leaning her forehead against the cold windowpane, she let

the sadness wash through her as the panic gradually faded. If she wanted to stay in Atlanta, never getting to try the ranger job, she could not ask for a better man to make a life with. Mac was caring for his son. Had suffered a terrible blow yet managed to move on and make a good home for Tommy. He was wildly successful in business and seemed to have lots of friends.

A life with him would be easy and fun.

But not without love. She couldn't imagine marrying anyone who didn't adore her. There were too many ups and downs in life to go through it with someone who only wanted her to watch his son.

Tommy is crazy about you.

"Oh, Mac, why couldn't *you* be crazy about me?" she said softly.

Sam didn't know how long she gazed out the window, the churning emotions and jumbled thoughts making time fly; or stand still. How would she ever face him again? Her heart ached. These last few weeks had been wonderful, exciting, different. But he'd changed everything with his proposal. And she wasn't sure she could work for him anymore.

She had to introduce him to Kristin immediately and hope they clicked. If so, she'd be able to make plans for her final classes at college. Move forward toward her goal.

Her intercom sounded. They'd installed it right after the accident in case Charlene ever needed her in the night.

"Sam, can I talk to you?" her sister asked.

She didn't want to talk to anyone. She didn't want to move. His words echoed over and over in her mind. And her rationale strengthened with every heartbeat.

"Mac and Tommy are gone. Please come down," Charlene said.

She crossed to the speaker and pressed the button. She had never refused when her sister needed her.

"I'll be right there."

"What's going on?" Charlene asked when Sam reached the stairs. "Mac came into the kitchen and said he had to take Tommy home. Before he even had his pancakes. That didn't sit too well with Master Tommy, I can tell you. What happened?"

"He asked me to marry him," Sam said slowly as she descended the stairs.

"He did?" Charlene's face lit up. "How wonderful! I didn't know how to bring up future plans when you've done so much for me and all. But Alice and I have been talking about her moving in. She wasn't sure if you'd approve, but if you're getting married, that'll work out fine. You won't have to worry about me. Alice said she'd help whenever I need it. And she and I are going to be so involved with the…" Charlene trailed off, studying Sam's expression. "What?"

"I turned him down," Sam said, sinking down on the third step.

Charlene looked puzzled. She rolled her chair to the foot of the steps.

"Why ever in the world did you do that? Don't you love him?"

Sam went still. She *liked* Mac, a great deal. She enjoyed being with him. Despite his wealth, he wasn't arrogant or overbearing, but fun to be with. His kisses were like magic, making her feel special and cherished. She rubbed her chest where her heart ached inside it. Did she more than like him?

Stopping the directions of those thoughts, she avoided her sister's gaze. She was not going to fall in love with Mac. She was *not!*

"The timing for marriage isn't right. I want to be a park ranger."

"Is the one mutually exclusive of the other?" Charlene asked.

"It is if he only wants to marry me to get a nanny for Tommy."

Charlene looked surprised at that. "That was his reason for proposing?"

Sam nodded. She met Charlene's gaze. "I'm glad you'll have someone to watch out for you. I'm going to see about applying for a final full-time semester at college like you suggested." The decision was easy when everything fell into place. Charlene would have enough help to stay in the house with Sam gone. And with her job and the extra income from quilting, she'd have more than enough money to support herself.

Kristin would make the perfect nanny for Tommy.

And Sam would have the job she'd always dreamed about.

Somehow she expected to feel happier about everything.

"That surprises me," Charlene said. "It sounded so romantic, meeting at the ball, him tracking you down. Almost like Cinderella."

"Which makes you the mean stepsister," Sam said, not willing to see anything good about the situation. Romance was overrated. She'd discovered that ten years ago. "Besides, by tracking me down, he got me fired from my job."

"And gave you a better one with more pay."

Sam nodded. There was little to fault with Mac. And a lot to admire.

"I'll miss Tommy," Charlene said wistfully. "He's so cute. But I guess that's the way of things." She turned and rolled her chair into the dining room.

Sam sat in gloomy silence for a couple of minutes. She'd miss Tommy, too. He was an enchanting child. She'd miss his father even more. Feeling as old as the mountains she planned to explore, she rose and went to their study to use the computer. She'd check out class schedules, and maybe look at job opportunities at some of the parks she wanted to see.

Mac drove home only halfway listening to Tommy's chatter. He felt numb. After Chris died, he'd never expected to find another woman he would want to spend his life with. Irony struck. For the past couple of years he'd been considered a prime marriage candidate. Now the one woman he wanted didn't want him. Wouldn't his ex-girlfriends love to hear that?

He glanced in the rearview mirror at his son. Tommy was quietly babbling to the little car he held in his hand. For a moment, Mac's heart clutched. Sam had called him a burden. How could anyone think this precious child was not worth the effort to raise him? He'd been fooled. He'd thought the attention Sam gave his son was genuine. He didn't realize it was just part of her job. That she was friendly with everyone and he was no exception.

He had said he'd interview the woman she was recommending, but now he wasn't sure. Maybe it would be better to sever all ties with Sam immediately. Seeing her, knowing she didn't care for him, would only hurt.

Not as much as losing Chris had, but pretty close. At least Sam was alive and soon to be happy doing what she wanted. He wanted to be glad for that. But he could only see the gaping hole her leaving would make in his life.

"Pancakes?" Tommy asked when they reached home. Mac hadn't waited to see if Sam would come back downstairs. There was nothing else to say. He'd bid Charlene goodbye and brought Tommy home. Now it was up to him to fix pancakes. How he wished his own disappointment could be resolved so easily.

Once they finished eating, Mac put Tommy in his car seat and began the drive to Savannah. He'd thought Sam would be with him. He'd even mentioned to his mother that he'd be bringing someone home with him. He had hoped this last week that it would be as his fiancée. Instead she wasn't even accompanying them. The weekend loomed long and lonely.

Monday morning Sam contacted Kristin about interviewing with Mac. The woman was delighted for the opportunity. Sam made arrangements for her to be at Mac's office at ten and then called Mac's secretary to confirm the time. He had obviously told her about the interview as she was expecting Sam's call.

"Will you be accompanying Ms. Wilson?" she asked.

"No, Kristin can manage on her own. It will give them a chance to speak candidly and help Mac see how competent she is." She longed to see him. She'd been miserable all weekend. At a loose end since the trip to Savannah hadn't materialized for her, she tried to fill the hours with information on the western parks. But their final conversation echoed in her mind, distracting her. She was very ashamed of the way she'd turned down his offer. It had been due to shock, but that was no excuse.

Even if he didn't love her, he had offered to marry her. She should have been kinder in her refusal.

"And will you be at the house when Mrs. Horton leaves tonight?" the secretary asked.

Obviously Mac had told her the entire story.

"Of course. Until he hires a replacement." She would keep up her commitments no matter what. But she knew it would never be the same. If he arrived home before Tommy's bedtime, she'd have to leave instantly. No more friendly meals. No evenings spent together talking over everything under the sun.

No good-night kisses.

She hung up the phone and tried to capture some of the enthusiasm for her future job. The anticipation she expected when it was finally within reach was dampened by the memory of Mac's face when she'd crudely refused his offer of marriage. She needed to apologize for that. She should have been more gracious. But he'd caught her by surprise.

When Sam arrived at Mac's at six, she saw an unknown car in the driveway. It wasn't Mac's or Alice Horton's. Hurrying in from the cold, she opened the back door and saw Kristin at the stove and her service dog, Buddy, lying nearby, watching Tommy. The little boy had several trucks scattered around and was playing some game with them.

Alice sat at the table. She nodded at Sam when she entered. Kristin Wilson turned and gave her a bright smile. "I may have the job," she said in her monotonal voice. She smiled at Tommy and looked back at the stew she was preparing.

"Mr. McAlheny brought Mrs. Wilson over this morning to see how she got along with Tommy. I've been helping and, for the most part, observing. I think they'll get along fine. That dog nudges her anytime there's any sound—like Tommy asking something. She's already taught him the sign for milk and cookies."

"Great." Sam's heart sank. It looked as if her connection with Mac and Tommy was ending even earlier than she thought.

"I can wait until tomorrow to give Mr. McAlheny my report. Or you can tell him when he gets here. Mrs. Wilson should get to know Tommy's bedtime routine as well."

"I'll stay until Mac gets home," Sam said, shedding her coat and laying it across the back of one of the chairs.

Once Alice had left, Sam crossed over to Kristin.

"How are things?" she asked, facing the other woman so she could see her lips.

"I think fine. The little boy is well mannered. I expect there will be times when he has a hissy fit, but I can manage. Buddy will warn me about any sounds. And I can hear a high-pitched scream. I heard enough of the children at the day care center."

"Something smells wonderful," Sam said, peering at the pot on the stove.

"A stew. It's simmered all afternoon."

Kristin Wilson could talk in a monotone. She didn't hear her own voice, but had perfected the ability to communicate in a hearing world.

"This is a beautiful home," she said, watching Tommy. "It would be a wonderful job if I get it. And not far from the college. Mr. McAlheny even said my daughter, Sarah, could stay over when she wanted. I can't thank you enough for recommending me."

"I'm happy it's going to work out." Sam was happy for Kristin. It was her own selfish self that wanted to hold back the inevitable.

Tommy came over and looked at the two women. He then went and leaned against Kristin's leg. "I'm hungry."

"Dinner ready soon. Want to wash your hands?"

He nodded. Kristin picked him up and took him to the powder room in the hall. Sam watched, feeling another pang. Just last Friday Tommy would have run to her. Now he was already switching his allegiance.

Isn't that what she wanted? She would feel terrible if he had separation anxiety when she left. He'd been very attached to Louise and still missed her.

That obviously wouldn't be a problem with her departure.

Sam heard Mac's car. Her heart sped up. Kristin and Tommy were still down the hall. She'd greet him alone.

Jumping to her feet, she considered running out the front door when he came in the back, but that was a chicken way to act. She'd done nothing wrong—except in the way she'd refused his offer of marriage. She owed him an apology for that.

He opened the door and stopped a moment when he saw her. Coming inside, he closed the door, his gaze moving around the kitchen. "I see Mrs. Horton's car is gone. But Kristin's is still here."

"Yes. Alice said she does well with Tommy. And apparently Tommy loves her dog. I knew he would."

"Where are they?" he asked as he took off his jacket and put it across the chair next to the one where Sam had laid hers.

"Washing up for dinner."

"Something does smell wonderful," he commented.

"Alice said she'd give you her full report in the morning,

but I could tell you she thinks Kristin will be perfect. Tommy already goes to her."

He inclined his head in a half nod. "I was impressed when we met this morning. I called all her references this afternoon and haven't heard a single negative word about her or her work."

"Great. I thought she'd work or I wouldn't have recommended her. She's terrific with children and loves working with them."

Mac reached into his suit coat inner pocket and withdrew an envelope. "In anticipation of a good report, I drew up a final check. I'll be sure to be home early until Kristin gets settled in. We won't need you to come by anymore." He handed her the envelope.

Sam blinked. She knew she wasn't needed, but it felt like a blow to hear him say not to come again. She gave a valiant smile. "I know Tommy will be in good hands."

"I hope he won't be a burden to Kristin."

"Mac, I'm so sorry. It was thoughtless and wrong of me to say that. He's adorable and I'll really miss him." She wanted to say more, but the words wouldn't come.

Mac didn't say anything. He studied the stove, avoiding Sam's eyes. She put on her coat. "I'll keep in touch with Kristin so I'll know how things go."

"If you like. Thank you for the services you provided. It helped in the transition period."

She put on her coat, buttoning it slowly. "Was your trip to Savannah fun?"

He glanced at her and shrugged. She heard Kristin talking to Tommy as they entered the kitchen. Buddy leaned against his mistress's leg and Kristin looked up, smiling when she saw Mac.

"There's your daddy. Run give him a hug," she said, putting Tommy down.

Sam watched the familiar scene. Mac scooped up his son

and hugged him gently. Settling him on his arm, he told Tommy to tell Sam goodbye.

"Bye-bye," Tommy said, smiling.

Sam whispered goodbye and left, tears stinging in her eyes. She really had no reason to ever see the McAlhenys again.

Two weeks later Sam entered her home to silence. She knew Charlene and Alice had their first evening quilting class, working on one of the patterns Charlene had designed. Monica had told them twenty-three women signed up for the six-week class.

She ran upstairs to change and then entered the kitchen to see how much work had been done that day. Because of a cancellation, Mac's carpenter friend had been able to start renovations to their kitchen ahead of the original schedule. The roof repair had been paid off and with Charlene's recent check from the sale of two quilts, they had enough to start on the kitchen.

The back wall had been framed and insulation installed. She could feel the difference in temperature already. There was still plenty to do, but at least the elements would stay at bay.

The mail had been placed on the counter in the kitchen. Sam glanced through it, her eye stopping on one with a National Park Service logo. She opened it and read through, not understanding at first. She'd been accepted for a volunteer project at Mesa Verde National Park starting in March and lasting for six weeks. She stared at the letter. She hadn't signed up for volunteer work. She had sent out inquiries about job openings. Was this a way to get her foot into the door?

But starting in March? That was less than a month away. She couldn't just leave her job for six weeks.

Or—maybe she could. There was vacation time accrued and leave of absence possibilities. She clutched the letter to her heart. At last, she was going to start doing what she wanted all her life! She spun around. There was no one to share this with. Charlene wouldn't be home for hours.

Spotting the phone, Sam crossed without thinking and dialed Mac's home number.

"Hello?"

Just hearing his voice after two weeks was wonderful. "Mac, it's Sam. I'm going to Mesa Verde!" she said excitedly. "I've been selected for a volunteer's position. I don't know how exactly, but it starts in three weeks and lasts for six. I'm going west!"

"I'm happy for you, Sam. I know how much you have wanted this. What will you be doing?"

"It says working on repairing and marking trails in time for the busy summer season. The park provides a place for me to stay and meals. I can't believe it. I applied for jobs, but haven't heard about any of those. But this is an honest-to-goodness official letter. It details when I should arrive, how I'll get there from the airport, everything."

"Who knows, maybe there will be a job opening while you're there and you can segue over and continue," he suggested, his tone polite.

"I thought I'd need my college degree first."

"Maybe not. I'm sure there are jobs to be had without one. Once hired, you can work your way up."

"I'm so excited. I wanted someone to share it with. I'll send you a postcard from Colorado."

"Tommy would love that," Mac said.

The bubble burst. Of course Mac wouldn't want to hear from her. She was lucky he was as cordial as he was on the phone. She hadn't any illusions she had hurt him with her refusal, especially since Kristin was working out so well. For a moment she wished he'd protest her leaving. Say something to show he cared for her beyond child care for Tommy.

Sam had spoken to Kristin only a few days ago. She loved the position and had already had her daughter over.

Mac had his future secured, so he had no reason to continue a friendship with her. His friends traveled in circles much more exalted than her own. He'd have no trouble finding women companions. If she had any doubts, the fact he hadn't phoned or dropped by proved it to her.

She'd missed him more than she'd anticipated. Every day she hoped one of the phone calls at work was Mac calling and talking about his day, or about Tommy. Or even a call in the evening. None came.

"I'll send him one every week. I've got to go. Bye." She could scarcely talk with the strain of tears in her throat. She was getting what she wanted, so why did she feel like crying?

Mac heard the connection end and slowly hung up. Hearing her voice was bittersweet. He was happy she liked the volunteer position. With Charlene's help, he'd applied in Sam's name. It wasn't the ultimate job she hoped for, but it was a chance for her to realize her dreams earlier than waiting until she received her degree. He'd arranged for help at the Beale Foundation in her absence and sweetened the deal with a hefty donation. Her boss was sorry for her to go, but wouldn't stand in her way. As she'd find out when asking for time off.

Mac closed his eyes, seeing her face so clearly. She probably sparkled with happiness at the news. He could picture her dark eyes lighting up in delight. He'd already heard the exhilaration in her tone. She was probably already calling for airline reservations and thinking of which clothes to take, and dancing around the kitchen in excitement.

He wished he was going with her.

No, he wished she was staying and marrying him. Wished she'd put him ahead of her teenage dreams.

But she'd made her choice abundantly clear. That wasn't in the cards. He'd get used to it someday—he hoped.

In the meantime, he wanted her to be happy. It wasn't her fault she didn't love him. He still wished her the very best life had to offer, and if this was her life's dream, why not get it? Except for Chris's death, he'd gotten most of what he set out to do. And he hoped he had another forty years or so of growing his company and meeting the challenges ahead. Watching Tommy become a man. For a very short time he'd thought there could be more children, if he married Sam.

Knowing her had opened his mind to the possibility of finding another woman someday whom he'd fall in love with. Maybe.

He rose and went to find Tommy. Who was he kidding? He had been lucky enough to find two women in his life he cared enough about to want share his life with. He wouldn't find a third. And right now he didn't want to. He could picture Sam in every room, making changes, bringing life to a rather somber home. And to a man who had thought life was over except for his son.

The past two weeks had seemed empty. Alice had stayed until Kristin was fully ready to take over. He'd talked to Charlene twice. Did Sam know that? But he hadn't heard Sam's voice or seen her once. He missed her. How would he last another forty years without her?

"Mac? It's Charlene again."

"Anything wrong?" he asked. He hadn't talked to Sam's sister in the weeks since she told him about the volunteer job.

"Not exactly. Sam's leaving in the morning. Her flight leaves at nine. I can't make the airport. I'm doing so much better about getting out in public and all, but I'm not up to that."

"Your classes are doing well. Mrs. Horton came by the other day to see Tommy and told Kristin how well things are going. I'm glad for you, Charlene."

"Thanks. It's not as easy as others think it ought to be. But I can't go to the airport. And I want someone to see Sam off. You know, I think she won't be coming home. Once there, she's sure to find a job that will pay enough to live on. I know she'll be back for visits, but I just have a feeling she won't ever be living here again. Unless— Never mind. Can you take her, please?"

"Me? She doesn't want to see me," he protested. Yet even as he said it, he thought of seeing her again. One last time before she left Atlanta. How could he refuse?

"Forget I said that. Whether she does or doesn't, I'll take her. What time should I pick her up?" he asked.

"Oh, that would be perfect. She was getting a cab, so she didn't have to park her car at the airport. She needs to be there early. So I'd say around seven."

"I'll be there by seven."

"Thanks, Mac. You know, I'm sorry it didn't work out between the two of you. I thought she— Never mind. Thanks for taking her. I know it won't be easy. But I didn't know who else to ask."

So the next morning he'd pick up Sam, take her to the flight that would whisk her west—where her heart lay. He'd say a final goodbye to the only other woman he'd ever want to marry and return home hoping to find the strength to go it alone.

He'd never been able to say farewell to Chris. She'd gone so fast.

At least Sam was healthy and happy. She'd be free for the first time since her parents' death. Not burdened with her sister or that old house. And not a young boy who had years to go before being grown.

Sam carried her bags to the front door, wishing Charlene had not arranged for Mac to take her to the airport. A cab would have been fine.

Her sister glided into the entryway. "He won't be here for another few moments. Why don't you at least have some toast."

"Can't eat a thing." She was nervous. Not about going to Colorado, but about seeing Mac again. She'd thought about him endlessly since that last night at his place. Wished a dozen times or more to pick up the phone to call him, hear his voice. She missed little Tommy, too, nearly as much as she missed Mac. When she'd called to share the news about her new opportunity, she'd felt as if she'd been wrapped in home hearing him speak.

Wiping her palms against her slacks, she looked out the side glass by the door. No car yet.

Winter was starting to fade. In a few weeks, the azaleas would be in full bloom, flowering trees would burst into color. She'd be back in time to catch some of the late spring-time blossoms. What were western mountain springs like?

She saw the car turn into the driveway.

"He's here." She could hardly wait to see him again.

"I'm not sure I'm ready for you to leave," Charlene said suddenly.

Sam turned, startled. "What?"

"Forget I said that. Alice will be here tonight and moving the rest of her things in by the end of the week. It's just—"

"I know," Sam said, giving her sister a hug. It had been the two of them against the world ever since their parents died. Now she was leaving. Life as they knew it was changing again.

"But you'll be just fine." Sam truly believed that. Charlene had blossomed beyond her wildest dreams these last weeks. Sam wouldn't have left if she hadn't known her sister would manage perfectly well with her gone.

"I know it. And you, too. You'll finally get what you've always wanted," Charlene said, but her eyes filled with tears and her smile was wobbly.

"I guess," Sam said, feeling her own throat tighten with emotion.

"Isn't it what you've always wanted?" her sister asked sharply.

The knock on the door saved her from answering. She opened it and saw Mac. He looked tired and thinner than she remembered, but he was still the most gorgeous man she'd ever seen.

"Hi." She wanted to throw herself into his arms. Have him pull her close and kiss her like he had before.

"Ready to go?" he asked.

"Yes. I have these two bags." She drew on her jacket and gave Charlene another kiss. "I'll call from Denver."

"I'm happy for you, Sam," Charlene said. "Do what makes your heart sing."

Mac stowed her bags in the trunk and held the passenger door open for her. She slipped in, fastening her seat belt before he could get behind the wheel.

"I appreciate your giving me a ride. If you drop me at Departures, you shouldn't even be late for work," she said brightly. She hoped he wouldn't hear the nervousness in her voice. There was so much she wanted to say. That apology still needed to be voiced. Could she do it before she left?

"I plan to go as far as security will allow," he said. "We can wait there until your flight is called."

"You don't have to," she said, hoping he would. Now that the moment was here, she was scared. What if working in the national parks didn't prove to be the most wonderful job in the world? What if she couldn't do it? What if—

"Tommy sent you this," he said, handing her a wrapped package. By the way the paper was bunched up at one end and barely touching at the other, she suspected Tommy had been the one to wrap it. She tore off the paper. A small truck sat in her palm.

"It's his favorite. He wanted you to have it on your trip."

"Thank him for me," she said, clutching it tightly. Her throat was tight again. She blinked her eyes and stared straight ahead. She should have gone by the house when Mac was at work to see Tommy before she left.

Mac handed her a card with his name, home address and private phone number written on it.

"For those postcards you're sending."

She smiled and nodded, feeling his warmth still on the card. "I already have it, but I'll keep this, too," she said, slipping it into her pocket.

Traffic was heavy and conversation was light. He parked in short-term parking and carried one bag while Sam insisted on carrying the other. Once the luggage was checked, he offered to buy her a cup of coffee.

"No, thanks. I'm sure I'll get some on the flight." She wouldn't be able to drink a thing with him. Her nerves stretched tighter. They walked to the security area. The line was short.

"You don't need to stay," she said, glancing at the line and then back at Mac. "I'll go on through and head for the gate." She rolled and unrolled her ticket folder. "Thank you for bringing me," she said.

"No problem. Enjoy yourself."

She glanced at him briefly, then gazed ahead, gearing up her courage. "Mac, I wanted to apologize for my rude response to your proposal of marriage. Not that it excuses anything, but you caught me by surprise and I just blurted out words without thinking."

"Sam."

She looked up at him.

"Have the best life you can. Grab hold and wring it for everything it's worth. Your dream is coming true. That's a gift not everyone gets."

Mac kissed her, drawing her close against him, holding her as if she were precious and fragile. Then he broke the kiss and smiled at her. "Bon voyage, Madam Ranger."

"Goodbye." She turned and headed through security, resisting the urge to turn to see him one last time as she walked away. It was the hardest thing Samantha had ever done.

CHAPTER TEN

DEAR Mac. It's more spectacular than I imagined. I can
see forever when I'm on top of a mountain. The air is
so clean and clear. There are areas where I don't see
trees for acres and acres of windswept land. And then
thick lodgepole pines grow so close together I can't
imagine walking through them.

She stared at the words. Stupid. She bunched up the
postcard and tossed it into the trash. The third ruined one
tonight. Leaning back in her bunk, Sam gazed at the
wooden ceiling. The bunkhouse where the volunteers were
housed was rustic. Built of the lodgepole pines she was
trying to describe, it gave the western ambiance she'd so
yearned for.

How to convey all she was feeling in a postcard?

And why should Mac care? She'd said no. End of relationship.

Rolling on her side, she blinked back tears. She did so not
want it to be the end. She had achieved her heart's desire and
it wasn't proving to be what she thought it would be. Instead
of throwing herself into her tasks each day, she kept wondering what Mac was doing—if he was attending some charity
event where he'd meet someone new. Fall for another woman
who would not hesitate a moment to accept his proposal and

then share his home and help raise Tommy. Maybe even have more children.

A pang of remorse hit her—again. Why had she said no so quickly? Maybe she should have asked for time to decide.

Kristin was managing fine, just as Sam had predicted. Sam had spoken to her a few times using the TDD service of the phone company after Kristin started working for Mac. Everything sounded like it was a good match. Sam had called once from the main lodge after she'd arrived in Mesa Verde. Mac had not been home, so she had called back to have a short chat with Kristin.

When she asked after Mac and Tommy, Kristin merely said they were doing fine.

Sam missed them both with an ache that constantly surprised her. More even than she missed her own sister.

She'd called Charlene a couple of times as well, but it was hard to talk for long. With no cell service in the mountains the volunteers had to use the pay phone at the lodge. Standing by the outside phone, in the cold, wasn't conducive to lengthy conversations. Charlene remained enthusiastic about the quilting classes. She'd told Sam about an offer from a pattern publisher for one of her patterns. She bubbled with joy. Sam felt a moment of envy.

When Charlene asked how she liked Colorado, she was honest in saying it was beautiful. But she didn't tell Charlene how lonely she was. Her friends weren't here. Everyone participating in the volunteer program had jobs and homes and friends scattered around the U.S. She was the only one who had declared an interest in doing this full-time. To most, it was a change, a special vacation this year. Something different. They'd be returning to their normal lives when the six weeks ended.

She didn't know what she'd be doing next.

She missed hearing about Mac, seeing him. She sat up and picked another postcard, wishing she could just talk to him for a few minutes. Well, why not? Tossing the postcard on the bed, she hopped off her bunk and bundled up. She'd try again. It was after eight in Georgia, so Tommy would be in bed. It was Mac's voice she yearned to hear, surely he'd be home by now.

It was still light as she walked from the sleeping quarters to the main lodge. No one was using the pay phone so she stepped up and began feeding it change. The phone rang four times before clicking to an answering machine. She debated leaving a message. But what would she say?

Hanging up, she called Charlene.

"Hi, what's up?" she said when her sister answered.

"Not much, still working with Monica and loving it. How about you?"

"We did a lot of work on one of the trails today. It's hard physical labor, but really satisfying and the views are spectacular. I can't get over how different this part of the country is."

"I bet. One day I'll have to get out there and see for myself."

They chatted for a few minutes then Sam asked, "Have you heard anything from Mac?"

"No, should I have?"

Sam sighed softly. "No, no reason. I just wondered. I tried calling him earlier, but it rang to the answering machine."

"Did you want to tell him something?"

"No, um, I just was going to tell him about Mesa Verde. Glad your classes are going so well. I've got to run."

"Thanks for calling, Sam."

Sam hung up and gazed around her. She did enjoy being here. But she also began to realize it was a perfect vacation. Just like the others in the group. She wanted to return home when the six weeks was over. She wanted to see Mac and Tommy and maybe even attend one of Charlene's classes to see how she handled it.

She thought about the people she worked with at the Beale Foundation, hoping some of the men and women she placed were doing as well as Kristin was. Wondering if Timothy had found more sponsors for their grant program.

Mostly, she thought, as she slowly walked back to the bunkhouse, she wanted to see Mac McAlheny. To hear how his day had gone. To visit the zoo or someplace else with him and Tommy. To hold hands. Kiss. Share meals. Share a bed.

She blinked. Gazing over the beautiful landscape, Sam realized she loved Mac. She probably had from the first moment he'd rescued her from the drunk at the Black and White Ball.

She hugged herself and stared across the land. "I love Mac," she said aloud, astonished. The wind carried the sound away. The breeze swept through her, chilling her in the colder evening air. "He never said he loved me, but that doesn't change anything. I love him." For a moment she wished he'd appear and ask her to marry him again. Or that she could change the past and realize sooner that dreams sometimes aren't meant to come true. That life changes and new dreams replace old ones. The reality was she loved Mac and wanted to spend the rest of her life with him. In Atlanta, vacationing in the west, doing everything together. With Tommy and maybe if they were lucky, with several more children to fill up the house and have it ring with laughter—and love.

"He never said he loved me," Sam said once again to the sky as if to convince herself.

An old axiom her mother often said sprang to mind. Actions speak louder than words.

He had asked her to marry him. Was it for more reasons than simply because he needed a nanny for Tommy? Had she misread the entire situation?

She felt slightly sick at the thought. She couldn't have.

Yet the man had a ton of money. He could hire three nannies if he wanted. But she was the one he'd asked to marry him.

She turned and went back to the phone, fumbling the money in her haste to get the call through. She had to talk to him. See if there was more than she'd thought. See if she could get a second chance.

She placed the second call to Mac's home. When the answering machine clicked on, she rushed into speech.

"Mac, it's Sam. Sorry you aren't home. I really wanted to talk with you. I'll be away from a phone most of tomorrow working, but will try you again about this time tomorrow evening. I hope you'll be home." She held on another few seconds, but couldn't find the words to say what she felt. "So, maybe I'll talk to you then." Slowly she hung up and slowly walked to one of the overlooks and gazed off into the growing twilight. It would be dark soon. The stars would be magnificent in the night sky without the ambient light of cities. The pinpoints of light ranged from faint to bright. She would never tire of looking at the night sky here. Or the endless scenery. Or feeling the dry breeze caress her skin—even if it was cold. In summer it would be a pleasant relief from the heat. She did like this vast space. She had felt she was contributing as she worked on the trails.

But was it enough to build a life on? Her friends were in Atlanta. Her only family was there. And the man and boy she loved were there. How could she have thought she could jettison all that and build a life so far away?

Finally, growing cold, she returned to the bunkhouse.

The next day it rained. The volunteers met in one of the conference rooms at the lodge and the rangers gave more information on the history of the park, what was known of the ancients who had built the cave dwellings. Pictures of the ruins were displayed and artifacts explained. It was fascinating, but Sam couldn't focus fully on the presentation. Glancing at her watch again, she was dismayed to find it was only five minutes later than the last time she'd looked. She was impatiently waiting for when she could phone Mac again.

How long would the day stretch out?

At lunch, as she listened to the conversation swirl around her, she considered calling now, while he was still at work. Only, she didn't want to talk to him there. She wanted time enough and privacy. She had to wait. But patience was proving hard to come by.

She wasn't sure what she was going to say, but if there was any chance she could renew their relationship, she wanted it. Mostly she wanted to hear his voice.

One of the women who worked in the office came in the lunchroom and headed for Sam's table.

"You have a visitor," she said, resting her hand on Sam's shoulder.

Sam looked up in surprise. "I do?"

"Waiting by the fireplace in the main room. Lucky you," she said with a friendly smile. She waved at the others and left.

Sam excused herself from the table and headed out. No sooner had she stepped into the main room than she wondered if her eyes were playing tricks.

"Mac?" She wanted to fly across the room right into his arms. But she drew a deep breath and walked across the space slowly. He watched her as she approached. He wore dark cords and the jacket he'd worn to the zoo. Her heart began to race.

"What are you doing here?" she asked.

"I was in the neighborhood and thought I'd stop by."

"I'm glad you did," she said, drinking in the sight of him. Her fingers still longed to trace that dimple, to thread through his hair. Her eyes could drink him in all day. Whatever he was doing here was fine with her.

"Come sit down by the fire," she said, leading the way to an empty sofa before the cavernous fireplace that contained a couple of logs burning merrily. She sat on the edge of the leather furniture. He shed his jacket and sat beside her.

"Are you liking it?" he asked.

She nodded. She should say something. She felt like an idiot.

"It was hard to tell from all those postcards you've sent," he said.

"I know, I should have sent more than that one to Tommy, but I was having trouble writing what I wanted to say." She wondered what he'd think of all the crumpled ones in her wastebasket right now.

"Too busy every minute?"

"Too uncertain what to say," she replied.

He started to say something, then shook his head. "So tell me about your day. Obviously you're not working in the rain."

"We might have if a project had been important enough. But we're restoring some of the trails and today was too wet to work effectively. So we've spent the morning in a classroom setting learning more about the park. Most days, when the weather's good, we're out early, working all day until time for dinner."

She went on to describe their tasks and how she was learning so much. She tried to infuse her voice with enthusiasm but trailed off after a minute.

"I can't believe you're here!" *Tell him now!* her inner voice urged. But she couldn't find the right way to open the subject.

"I won't be staying long. I just wanted to see you since I was close. See how you were doing."

"I'm fine. I still can't believe I was offered the position, but I've met a lot of people from all around the country. We all work well together."

"It paid off, then," he said.

"What did?"

"Getting you the job."

"What?" She stared at him. "I don't understand."

He shrugged. "I thought Charlene would have explained.

She helped me fill out the application because she knew all the personal information. That's why you were chosen. I thought once here, it'd be easier to get a permanent job than applying from Atlanta. They'd know you, what you can do."

She felt her heart drop. He hadn't wasted any time after her refusal getting her out of Atlanta. He didn't love her. He had moved on. And had practically sent her away.

"Oh. I didn't know." It hurt. She'd been bubbling with possibilities since she'd realized how much she loved him. Now it was as if he had shut the door on a future together when he told her that.

This changed everything. Had she been given a second chance? Was there a possibility he might still want to marry her? It was so important, she had to do it just right. But what if she had misread every indication? What should she say? Just blurt out, *I've changed my mind—I love you and want to marry you?* What if he'd changed his in the meantime? She bit her lower lip.

"Where's Tommy?" Great, bring up the excuse she'd used to refuse his proposal. Pangs of guilt flooded through her. "I miss him," she said. How could she ever have thought he might be a burden? He was a precious child bringing joy and delight to everyone who met him. She'd thought about their evenings together when lying lonely on her bunk at nights.

"Staying with my parents for a few days. I pick him up tomorrow night. He's doing well with Kristin. She's teaching him sign language."

She nodded. "I called your house last night, but there was no answer." Tension rose. How could she broach the subject? Time was ticking away. Would he stay long enough for her to say what was in her heart? It might have been easier on the phone. But she wouldn't trade these moments together for anything. She wished she dared reach out to touch him. Wished she knew the future, knew if he'd be open to building a relationship with her.

"I wasn't home, obviously. Kristin had the evenings to herself with us both gone. Maybe she went out with her daughter."

Sam nodded again, gazing at the fire. She cleared her throat. Maybe something would come out if she'd just start speaking. If she could think with the blood pounding through her. Her throat was dry. Words evaporated before she could voice them.

He stood. "I'll give Charlene an update when I get home. She'll want to know you're looking good and love this."

Sam stood and reached out to hold his arm. "You just got here. You can't leave." Time was running out, and she felt as dumb as dirt. Rubbing one palm against her jeans, she tried to come up with the words that would keep him here.

"I wanted to see you. Make sure you were happy. I've a long drive back to Colorado Springs," he said, taking her hand in one of his, brushing the back with his thumb.

"Thanks for coming, Mac. It's good to see you," she said, tightening her grip, wishing she never had to let him go. Instead, when he released her a moment later, she let her arm fall to her side. She remained standing near the sofa, watching him cross the vast lodge lobby. Watching as he walked away. She blinked back sudden tears.

He'd dropped by because he was in the neighborhood. Not because he'd come especially to see her.

Only—Mesa Verde wasn't in any neighborhood. It was a destination in itself. And it was more than a five-hour drive back to Colorado Springs. No one came that far just to say hi.

"Wait," she called, suddenly thinking of something. Not much, but it would hold him here another few moments. Would something brilliant come to mind by then?

He turned and waited while she hurried over.

"Can you pick me up at the airport when I get back home?" she asked.

He looked surprised. "You're coming back?"

"Why wouldn't I? I live in Atlanta."

"Only until you get a job here. Charlene said she didn't expect you back."

"She did? Huh. I didn't know that. Anyway, I don't have a job here and don't expect an offer for one."

"Oh, sweetheart, I'm sorry. Something will turn up, just wait."

The word *sweetheart* about melted her heart. The look of compassion in his eyes touched her.

"It's not quite like I thought it would be," she said slowly. Hoping she was doing this right. Please, let it come out right.

"Why is that?"

"I love it here. It's beautiful. I'm making a difference in the trail. All summer people from all over the world will be coming to walk on the trail I'm helping to repair."

"And you want to be here to see that," he said.

She shook her head slowly. "I want to be where the people I love are."

Mac didn't say anything and her heart dropped. He had never said he loved her. She had never told him she loved him. But these weeks apart had shown her as nothing else could how much she missed him. How much she'd yearned to hear his voice, to know he was safe and happy. To be part of his life.

"I want to be where you are, Mac," she said in a rush.

He dropped his jacket and reached for her, pulling her into his arms and kissing her like he had before. Those wonderful kisses that rocked her world. Sam couldn't say a word, so she just held on and kissed him back.

Endless minutes later he pulled back a scant inch. "I never thought I'd hear you say that, Sam. If you don't want marriage, we can be friends, do things together, though I love you so much it'll be hell on earth if you don't say you'll marry me. I thought I could do this when you said no.

Send you on your way and be glad you were happy. But these last weeks have been horrible. As bad as when Chris died. I never thought I'd fall in love again, or so completely that my life isn't my own anymore. But I have. With you. Oh, my love, say you'll share my life until we are both ancient and beyond."

"You love me? You never said."

"I didn't?" he asked.

She shook her head. "I love you, too. Only I was too stupid or too blind to realize it until I got here. I thought I ruined everything. Coming here is exactly like I thought it would be. But I'm not like I thought I'd be. I can't stop thinking about you. Wishing I was with you. To cook dinner together or take Tommy to the park or tuck him in bed together. To talk about everything under the sun. I want to be with you."

"Will you marry me?"

Before she could respond, he put a finger across her lips. "Think about what you want to say. I can't take another rejection like last time."

She threw back her head and laughed, then hugged him tightly. She couldn't even imagine what had gone through her mind that fateful morning. How could she have been so blind to her true feelings?

"I might have answered differently if you'd started that proposal with an I love you. Oh, Mac, I so love you! I would be very honored to be your wife. I'm sorry for that refusal. How dumb can one woman be? But I had this dream for so long, I didn't realize when it changed. Learning about these temporary volunteer positions is great. When I get the urge, I'll volunteer. The rest of the time, I want to be with you. Raise Tommy. Have a half dozen kids of our own. Watch Charlene take off. But mostly—always—to be with you."

"That can be arranged," he said before he kissed her again. A kiss that warmed her to her toes, and assured her their future would always be bright together.

Not Just the Nanny

CHRISTIE RIDGWAY

Native Californian **Christie Ridgway** started reading and writing romances in middle school. It wasn't until she was the wife of her college sweetheart and the mother of two small sons that she submitted her work for publication. Many contemporary romances later, she is the happiest when telling her stories, despite the splash of kids in the pool, the mass of cups and plates in the kitchen and the many commitments she makes in the world beyond her desk.

Besides loving the men in her life and her dream-come-true job, she continues her long-time love affair with reading and is never without a stack of books. You can find out more about Christie at her website, www.christieridgway.com.

For all those who've given
their heart to a child not their own

Chapter One

The woman on the sofa beside Kayla James suddenly sat up straight and looked at her with round eyes. "I've got it. I've finally figured out why you've been turning down men and declining invitations. You… you've broken the cardinal rule of nannies!"

Kayla ignored the flush racing over her face and focused on the bowl of pretzels sitting on the coffee table. "I don't know what you're talking about."

"Oh, yes, you do," Betsy Sherbourne said. Her long, dark hair was pulled back in a ponytail and she looked barely old enough to be a mother's helper, let alone a full-fledged fellow nanny. She wiggled, bouncing the ruby-colored cushions. "You know exactly what I'm talking about."

Kayla pulled the edges of her oversized flannel shirt together. There was a chill in the air tonight. "You're jumping to conclusions because I didn't feel like being the fourth in your blind double date last weekend."

"The fact is, you haven't gone anywhere in months," Betsy replied. "Your social life is limited to these weeknight, girls-only get-togethers we have with our friends from the nanny service."

Kayla latched on to the new topic like a lifeline. "Did I tell you that the others can't come tonight? Everybody had a conflict except Gwen, who should be here any minute," she said, naming the woman who owned and ran the We ♥ Our Nanny service which had placed both Kayla and Betsy with their current families.

"Yes, you told me," Betsy said. "And I won't let you change the subject."

"Look," Kayla responded, feeling a little desperate. "You know I'm busy with my job and school."

"Half of that's not an excuse you can use anymore."

Kayla sighed. Her friend was right. A couple months back she'd finally been awarded her college degree at the advanced age of almost twenty-seven.

Since then, her friends had bombarded her with suggestions about how to fill her newfound free time. "I should have never let you guys throw me that graduation party," she grumbled.

"Yeah, and other than those brief hours when we whooped it up, when was the last time you took some time out for yourself?"

"Today. I went shopping. I bought bras." Kayla rummaged in the knitting basket beside her, withdrawing the almost-finished mitten she was working on. "What do you think?" she asked in a bright voice, still determined to distract her friend. "Is this large enough for Lee? He's big for eight."

"Bras?" Sounding skeptical, Betsy ignored the mention of Lee, one of the two children Kayla looked after. "What color bras?"

"What does color have to do with anything?"

There was pity in the other woman's gaze. "Kayla, swear to me you have more than white cotton in your lingerie drawer."

She felt her cheeks go hot again. "Do we really have to—"

"Okay." Betsy relented. "Just tell me about these bras, then."

"The bras. They…" Kayla sighed again. "Okay, fine. They were for Jane."

"Jane! Jane's first bras?"

Kayla nodded, hope kindling that this would be the topic to derail the original discussion, even though it was a risk to bring up the kids again, as the second cardinal rule of nannies was to never get too attached to the children. "Can you believe it? All her friends have them now. Time has sure flown."

"Yes." Betsy reached for a pretzel and eyed Kayla again. "And you've given Mick and his kids almost six undivided years of yours now."

Uh-oh. She was losing the battle once more. "I've not *given* it to them," Kayla said, aware she sounded defensive. "I've been *employed* by Mick to take care of his daughter and son." It had been ideal. As a fire-fighter, after his wife died in a car accident, Mick had needed an overnight, in-house adult when he was on a twenty-four-hour shift. His schedule, however, had enough off-duty time in it that Kayla could pursue her degree part-time. But now that she'd graduated, and now that the kids were getting older, eleven and eight, the people in her circle were starting to squawk about Kayla making some adjustments.

Heavy footsteps sounded on the stairs. "La-La," a voice called from above. Mick's voice, using the name that toddler Lee had used for Kayla when she'd first come to live with them.

Jumping to her feet, she strode to the bottom of the staircase, her expression determinedly blank in case her nosy friend was watching her too closely. "You rang, boss?" she asked, focusing on his descending shoes since no one would show inconvenient emotion staring at shoelaces. His feet stopped moving at the bottom of the steps. She detected his just-out-of-the-shower scent now, and she put the back of her fingers to her nose in order not to inhale it too deeply. The soap-on-a-rope and companion aftershave had been her Christmas present to him and she should have thought twice before purchasing a fragrance that appealed to her so much.

"Hey, there, Betsy," he called over Kayla's head. "I'll be out of the way of you ladies in a minute." His voice lowered. "Can I talk to you in the kitchen?"

She glanced up. She shouldn't have.

When had it happened? When exactly had the widower she'd first met, the man with five o'clock shadow and weary eyes, gone from gaunt to gorgeous? The straight, dark hair hadn't changed, but he smiled now. There was warm humor more often than not in his deep brown eyes. She supposed he still had his demons—she knew he did, because on occasion she'd catch him sitting in the darkened living room staring off into space. But he'd found a way to manage his grief and be a good dad to his kids.

A good man.

One who looked at her, who treated her, just as

if Kayla was the fifteen-year-old girl next door who occasionally babysat when both she and Mick had to be out.

She followed him across the hardwood floor, trying not to ogle the way his jeans fit his lean hips or how his shoulders filled out the simple sport shirt. She'd ironed it for him as part of her job, of course, just as she'd helped Jane pick it out as his Christmas gift, knowing the soft chamois color would look wonderful with his olive skin.

In the kitchen, he swung around, nearly catching her too-interested examination. He was only thirty-four years old, but she figured he'd have a heart attack if he knew in which direction the nanny had been staring. With a flick of her lashes, she redirected her eyes to the calendar posted on the double-wide refrigerator that was nestled between oak cabinets and red-and-white-tiled countertops. Mick turned his head to follow her gaze.

"Okay," he said. "We're good, right? You've got your nanny service friends here tonight. Jane is working on her poetry project, but she's only two doors down and will walk herself home, after she calls so you can watch her from the front porch."

"Yep." They went through this routine every day. She didn't know if it was a result of Mick losing his wife in such a sudden way, if it was because he was a man trained for disasters, or just because he adored his children. All made perfect sense to her. "And Jared's mom will drive Lee home after Scouts."

"Bases covered, then." His mouth turned up in a rueful grin that she let herself enjoy from the corner of her eye. "So I really don't have any excuse not to meet the guys for pizza and a cold one or two."

"None that I can think of." She smiled, despite wondering if that "cold one with the guys" included a couple of hot women. He'd dated on occasion—well, he'd gone along with varying degrees of good grace when someone fixed him up—but she thought she'd detected in him a change there, too. A new tension that everything female in her suspected had to do with his growing need for opposite-gender adult companionship.

Something he surely didn't consider her in the running for.

He reached out and tugged on the ends of her blond hair in a manner that made that perfectly clear. Jane got the same treatment from him often enough.

"Why the sad eyes, La-La?"

She pinned on a second smile. "Just one of those days."

"Tell me about it." Mick shoved his hands in his pockets. "They're growing up, Kayla, and I can't tell you what a blow it was when Jane spilled about your shopping trip. All at once I felt about a hundred."

"Nonsense. You're only a few years older than I."

He shook his head. "Yeah, but today my little girl went to the mall where she bought…bought…" One hand slipped out of his pocket to make a vague gesture. "You know."

Amused by his inability to articulate, Kayla leaned nearer. "Bras, Mick," she whispered, a laugh in her voice. Her gaze lifted. "It's not a dirty word."

Their eyes met. *Oh,* she thought, as something sparked to life in his. Suddenly, more than humor seemed to warm them. With a soundless crack, heat flashed down her neck and the oxygen in the room turned desert-dry. She wanted to put out a hand to steady herself, but she was afraid whatever she touched would emit a jolting shock.

Bras? she thought. Dirty? Did one of those two words made it feel so…so naughty to be this close to him?

Mick blinked, severing the connection, then he turned away to grab a glass from the cupboard by the sink. With a steady hand, he filled it with water and took a long drink in a gesture so casual she figured she must have imagined that moment of…of… whatever.

Wishful thinking on her part?

Kayla cleared her throat and folded her arms over her chest, the shirt fluttering at her hips. Maybe if she wore something other than jeans and flannel around him, he might notice her. But he'd had years to do that—summers when she'd been in shorts and tank tops, vacations by a pool when she'd worn a swimsuit that wasn't *Sports Illustrated*–ready but that didn't cover her like a tent, either. He'd never appeared the slightest bit intrigued by any of it. When she'd recently cut twelve inches from her long hair he hadn't noticed for two weeks, and then only when someone else mentioned it.

Upon inspection of the new do, he'd appeared appalled by the change. She'd felt stupid, like that time he'd caught her about to bestow a good-night kiss on a date on the doorstep. The fact that she'd been glad of the interruption, and that afterward she'd daydreamed in her bed of Mick pulling her away from the other man and into his own arms instead, hadn't been good signs.

That event had occurred six months ago, and since then she hadn't dated anyone—or shown any interest in dating anyone—which had prompted Betsy's earlier conversation.

"Well," Mick said, pulling open the dishwasher

to rack his glass, "I guess I'll head out now. Have fun."

"You, too."

He strode toward the door that led to the garage, then hesitated. "Kayla," he said.

Her heart jumped. "Yes?"

"In case I've never said it…"

She held her breath.

"You're great. You've always been great." He swung around. Reached out. "Such a pal to me," he added, patting her shoulder.

Her skin jittered, his light touch zinging all the way through the heavy plaid fabric of her shirt.

No. Make that *his* shirt. She'd been attached to it like a new fiancée to her engagement ring since the last time she'd removed it from the dryer.

"Yeah." He patted her again. "Such a pal to me."

And as he walked away, the appreciative words slid down her throat like a medicinal dose of disappointment to land like lead at the bottom of her belly. Who knew that "such a pal to me" could cause such gloom?

But somehow it did, because…

Oh, boy. Oh, no. Oh, it was useless to deny the truth any longer.

Betsy was right, it seemed. Kayla *had* shattered

the number-one item on the no-no list. Because the cardinal rule of nannies was simple.

Never fall in love with the daddy.

It wasn't until the barmaid set the cold beer in front of Mick that he actually registered his surroundings. He looked around the place that should have been as familiar to him as the back of his hand. He'd been coming to O'Hurley's with his buddies Will, Austin and Owen for years.

"When the hell did they paint the walls?" he groused, scanning the cream-colored surface. "What was wrong with dingy gray?" Then he craned his neck to inspect the rest of the interior. "And new TVs? Were the other ones broken?"

Austin stared at him, his dark eyes perplexed. "Dude. Flat-screens. Each of 'em as big as the back end of my grandma's Buick. You'd rather watch the game on something smaller?"

Mick lifted his beer for a swallow. "I'd prefer things to stay just as they were," he mumbled.

Owen's brows rose. "Good God, Mick. You sound like a grumpy old man. Next you'll be yelling at kids to get off your lawn."

He felt like a grumpy old man. That was the problem. The store department he always averted his eyes from was now the new playground for his preteen daughter. His son was out of T-ball already. His nanny was a college graduate.

"The kids in my house are almost too old to play on the grass," he said. "Lee and Jane and Kayla are growing up before my eyes. I'm almost afraid to blink."

"Mick…" His friend and fellow firefighter Will Dailey wasn't blinking. He was staring, just like Austin had a few moments before. "Kayla's not a kid. You know that, right?"

"She's a student," he shot back. "That makes her a kid. Sort of." It sounded stupid even to his ears, but he could only afford to think of the nanny in those terms.

"I thought you told us she graduated. From college. And she's got to be in her mid-twenties."

Mick waved a hand. "Still a girl."

Austin grinned. "Looks like a woman to me. As a matter of fact—"

"She's off-limits," Mick ordered.

The other guys were staring again, so Mick jerked up his chin and focused on the television. "How about those Cowboys?"

"How about those cheerleaders?" Austin countered.

Which was exactly why Mick had warned the

other man off. He was all about the superficial stuff, flashy boots, short skirts, and big…pom poms.

"You can't keep them all under wraps forever," Will said quietly from his seat in the booth beside Mick. "Believe me. I raised my five younger brothers and sisters and among the many things I learned, besides how to stretch a dollar until it squeals for mercy, was that they grow up and then itch to get out on their own."

Mick groaned. "I don't want to think about that." It didn't take a genius to figure out why. After losing his wife, Ellen, and the future he'd envisioned for them had been snatched away so cruelly, he couldn't imagine how hard it would be for him to loosen his hold on his kids.

Will laughed a little. "Nature has a way of making that easier. It's called 'the teenage years.'"

"Yeah, I suppose." Mick took another swallow of his beer. "Though I've already explained to Jane there will be no dating until she's thirty-one."

Will laughed again. "Good luck with that. But maybe all this would be a little easier if you considered finding a love interest yourself."

"Not going to happen." He couldn't imagine it. Although life with Ellen had been good—despite the fact that they'd been so young he could hardly recognized the kid groom he'd been in the man he was now—he had no plans to add a permanent woman to his life. He barely managed his current situation. Single dad, fire captain and somehow a romantic relationship, too? Wasn't going to happen.

He couldn't take on the additional responsibility… he didn't *want* the responsibility, even for the tempting trade-off of regular companionship in his bed.

Not to mention the difficulty of finding someone the rest of his household would get along with, too. "What kind of woman would Jane and Lee like? And Kayla? Who would she approve of?"

"Mick, Kayla's the nanny. And she's not going to be with you forever anyway, right?"

Wrong.

No, no, not wrong. Kayla gone was just something else he couldn't picture in his head.

He had another image in there instead, one that had been impossible to banish, for the last six months. She'd been out for the evening and he'd just gotten Lee back to sleep after the third request for water when he'd heard a muffled thump coming from the porch. Without thinking, he'd yanked open the front door, only to find…to find…

It replayed in his mind. A young man, sporting a sandy crew cut, his hands cupped around Kayla's face, his mouth descending toward her upturned lips. The moment had stretched out, it seemed, forever.

Mick had time to notice the bright glint of Kayla's shiny blond hair in the lamplight, the dark sweep of her lashes against her cheek and then the stunning blue of her eyes as they lifted and she caught him witnessing her good-night moment.

They'd flared wide and her cheeks had flushed pink as she hastily stepped back from her date and away from the almost-kiss. "I…um…uh…" she'd said, her gaze fixed on Mick's.

Instead of smoothing the moment over and re-treating, Mick, bad Mick, had merely held the door open so she could slip inside. He supposed he'd been frowning, because it was the proper expression for a man feeling decidedly hot under the collar.

Like an overprotective father might feel.

Or a jealous—no!

But damn, ever since that night he hadn't been able to see her as "just" the nanny. Although she'd never been that, not with the way she'd taken to his children and they'd taken her into their hearts. But he hadn't seen her as a woman, a kissable, desirable, damn beautiful woman until that awkward instant on the porch.

And he hadn't been able to stop thinking about it for one day since, even though he didn't believe she'd seen that young man again, or any other in the six months that had passed.

She's not going to be with you forever anyway, right? Now it was Will's question on replay in his head. But damn it, she was with his family now, and he had a sudden compunction to return to his house, just to assure himself that she *was* still there and that everything else was also still the same.

Mick got to his feet and fished some bills from his pocket. Austin looked up. "Where you going?"

"I want to be home when Lee gets back from Scouts. I need to watch my daughter walk down the sidewalk." *I have to see that Kayla isn't kissing some man.*

He'd forgotten about her nanny friends, though. When he spotted their cars outside his house, he let himself into the kitchen through the back door and decided to make do with leftovers for dinner. The kids had already eaten and he'd run from the bar before the pizza they'd ordered with their beer had arrived.

Even with his head in the refrigerator, Mick could hear Kayla's voice rise. "All right, fine. You win."

Bemused by her beleaguered tone, he straightened. He strolled toward the doorway that led to the dining room and from there the living room, wondering if she needed him to distract her friends. It sounded as if they were on his pretty Kayla's case about something.

No. Not his Kayla. Remember that. Not. His. Kayla.

She spoke again. "I said I'll do it."

"You agree?" It was her friend Betsy's voice.

"That's what I said," she answered, sounding testy.

Poor girl. He took another step closer to the living room. He could picture Kayla's flushed cheeks, her silky blond hair mussed by frustrated fingers. Her eyes, surrounded by her long, dark brown lashes, would stand out like blue jewels as she gazed on her friends.

"You'll go on the date?"

Mick froze.

"I've got to do something," he heard his nanny mutter. "So, yes."

If there was more conversation from the living room, Mick didn't hear it, not when he was contemplating just why her need to "do something" had turned into a need to date. Not when he was wondering exactly how many front-porch kisses that would mean.

Not when he was considering if he could manage to interrupt every single one of them.

His footsteps retreated back toward the refrigerator as resignation settled over him. Kayla. Back to dating? Damn. And double damn.

Despite his best hopes, it appeared as if he was going to be forced into doing some kissing himself. As in kissing his status quo goodbye.

Chapter Two

Kayla's bedroom and bath were located down a short hallway off the kitchen, while the rest of the household slept upstairs. And they were still at it the morning after her nanny group get-together, which gave her time to stew alone while the coffee brewed. Both she and Mick liked theirs medium strong, but hot, hot, hot. After an internet search, last Christmas he'd located a new maker that he'd wrapped and placed under the tree. It had been tagged to both of them, from "Santa Starbucks."

Funny man.

But not the man she should be thinking about at the moment. A normal, non-rule-breaking nanny should be contemplating the double date she'd agreed to let Betsy set up—the other woman had an address book full of eligibles, apparently. Lord knew that Mick—the widower who wouldn't see her as a woman—wasn't one of those. She sighed.

Then sighed again, because darn it, she was thinking about him again when the only sensible thing to do was forget all about the man—or at least find a way to dispatch these inconvenient feelings she had for him.

Determined to put Mick from her head, she pulled a coffee mug from the cupboard and then directed her gaze to the window over the sink. It looked out onto the backyard patio, the sprawling oak beside it, and then the rectangular expanse of grass. Two sections of fencing had been removed to facilitate the neighbors' pool building. Like every morning for the last week, a good-looking man tramped around the area, taking notes on a yellow pad.

Pool contractor. A definitely good-looking one in that way of men who worked outdoors. His hair was breeze-tousled, the ends lightened by the sun. His face and forearms were tanned and the rest of him looked fit and strong.

As she watched, he turned and caught her eye through the window then gestured for her to come outside. Her heartbeat ticked up a little as she stepped through the sliding door that led to the back. They'd had a few conversations and she'd found him pleasant. Friendly. Betsy would place him squarely in the eligible category. "Hey, Pete," she called. "Everything okay?"

"I just wanted to let you know we'll have the fence back up on Monday." He paused to give her a smile. "How are you this morning?"

"Good." She smiled back. "Fine."

"And the kids?"

"Terrific." It struck her that a woman who didn't have a thing for the firefighter who signed her paychecks would be clearing something up for Eligible Pete about right now. So… "You know, um, Jane and Lee, they're not *my* kids."

"Oh, I got that," he assured her. "You're too young to be their mother."

She frowned at that. Technically, not true. "Well—"

"I was raised by a stepmom myself. Love the woman to pieces, even more for taking on the ragtag rowdies that were me and my little brothers."

They had something in common, she thought. "I have stepparents myself."

"A split in your family, too?"

"When I was ten. Both parents married other people, had more kids." Leaving her the lonely-only issue of their short-term union. Now her mother and father had big rambunctious families with their new spouses.

"That must make it crazy on Christmas and Thanksgiving for you."

She forced a laugh. "Sure." More often than not, though, each parent assumed the other had set Kayla a place at their table—which left her with no place at all.

"Yeah," Pete spoke again. "All that blended family business must mean you and Mick have a lot to juggle." His gaze shifted over her shoulder.

Kayla turned to see what had snagged the pool contractor's attention. Who. Mick. Coffee in hand, he was eyeing them out the window. Even from here she could detect the comb lines in his just-shampooed hair. The man liked his showers.

And just like that, her memory kicked in and she swore she could smell the scent of his damp skin. Her hands tightened on her mug as a little shiver tracked down her spine. She really shouldn't have gifted him with that delicious aftershave.

"How long have you two been together?"

"Six years," Kayla murmured absently, her mind still far away. When Mick returned home from work, he almost always made a stop in the laundry room on the first floor where he stripped off his boots, socks and shirt. If she could get away with it undetected, she'd watch him walk through the kitchen and then up the stairs bare-chested, the muscles in his back shifting with every footstep. There were a lot of those muscles—all along his spine and across his shoulders, although she particularly liked the ones that moved so subtly at the small of his back, right above the taut rise of his—

Pete's question suddenly sank in. *How long have you two been together?*

She whipped back to face the contractor. "Oh. Oh, no. Mick and I... We're not together."

"You don't live together?" Pete asked, his expression perplexed.

"Well, yes, obviously we live together, but we don't, um, *live together.* I'm just the nanny to his children. To Jane and Lee."

"Oh." Pete's confusion seemed to intensify. "He didn't mention that."

Kayla frowned. "You were talking about me to Mick?"

Pete gave her a wry smile. "Just trying to get the lay of the land, if you know what I mean."

He'd been asking about her? If Betsy was here, she'd be thrilled by the news. Kayla realized she only felt embarrassed. "I suppose I do."

"And Mick gave me the impression that the, uh, land was, already, uh…uh…"

She glanced at the house, then looked at Pete again. "Already, uh…uh…what?"

"I probably misunderstood," Pete answered quickly. "I asked for your cell phone number and he got this weird expression on his face."

She frowned. "What kind of weird expression?"

Pete hesitated. "The kind that made clear your evenings weren't free."

A burn shot up her neck. More embarrassment. Maybe irritation. Likely an uncomfortable combination of the two. Mick was warning men off from her—even though he didn't seem to notice she was even a girl?

Such a pal to me.

"It must have been a misunderstanding," Pete started. "Though I…"

Kayla didn't hear the rest of what he had to say, as she was already stalking back to the house. What right did Mick have to interfere? she fumed, her temper kindling. He'd already invaded her nightly dreams. Wasn't that enough for him?

She flung back the sliding door and stomped into the kitchen. The man she worked for looked up from the utensil drawer he was rummaging through. "Was that guy bugging you?" he demanded.

"No!" She frowned, even as she noticed he looked handsomer and fitter and stronger than the pool contractor she'd left outside. His jeans and faded sweatshirt were nothing special, so the eye was drawn to the masculine angles of his face. He was all guy, from his midnight-black bristly lashes to the scuffed toes of his running shoes. And all-out attractive, she thought, then shoved it from her mind as she remembered she was mad at him. "Bugging me is—"

"Kayla," wailed Jane from the doorway. "What will I do? I can't go to school like this."

Kayla whirled toward the preteen, saw the distress on her face and then the outstretched fingernails with their messily applied raspberry-colored polish. "Oh, Jane," she said, hurrying toward her. "Don't worry. We can clean them off in a jiffy."

"No." Tragedy laced the single word and was written all over the eleven-year-old's face. *"Every* girl is coming to school with their nails painted today."

Kayla glanced at Mick and took in his baffled expression. "Jane," he said. "It's no big deal. Let Kayla help you take all that junk off and—"

"I have an even better idea," Kayla said, widening her eyes at her employer to signal that he was an uninformed male moment away from a true crisis. "In my bathroom is this great little tool shaped like a marking pen that erases polish gone awry. Your nails will look perfect in five minutes."

It was more like ten, but when Jane returned to the kitchen with Kayla, she was all smiles. "Look, Daddy," she said, fanning her fingers for her father's eyes. "See how pretty they look."

Mick obediently bent for an inspection. Jane didn't appear to notice, but Kayla saw the dismay that washed over his face. Then he looked over his daughter's head to meet her eyes and she knew what he was thinking.

First bras. Painted fingernails. What was next? Jane was moving from little girl to young woman one morning at a time and he could do nothing to stop the transition. Even though she was still mad at him, Kayla moved toward father and daughter, and brushed Jane's hair behind her shoulder.

"Remember those spa sleepovers we used to throw, Janie?" she asked. "Your friends would come over and I'd paint all your nails with glitter polish and put avocado masks on your faces." She glanced at Mick, projecting the message that the same little girl who ran around in Disney princess pajamas and bunny slippers was still inside this growing child with her long, coltish legs and slender fingers.

"We should do that again," Jane said, turning to Kayla with eagerness.

"It would be fun," she agreed.

"And not just fingernail polish and facial masks," Jane insisted. "We'll also try—" her voice lowered with reverence "—makeup."

Kayla glanced at Mick again, catching his wince. *Makeup,* he mouthed over his daughter's head. *Makeup!*

She smiled at him, both amused and sympathetic. "Don't let it get you down, big guy."

He smiled back, his gaze wry and warm and so intimate that it was as if they were touching palm to palm. The sensation traveled up her arm to her chest where it wrapped around her heart. And she could read his mind again. He was thinking—

"Let's do it soon," Jane said, her voice breaking that bond between her father and Kayla. "Say we can do it tonight. It's Friday."

Kayla started. *Tonight!* She remembered what she'd already agreed to do this weekend. "Maybe the next one? I have a date, Jane." A double date with Betsy and the two eligibles. A social event she hoped would get her mind and heart off Mick, she thought with a frown.

Something that so far she hadn't managed for more than two minutes at a time.

* * *

Mick didn't consider himself an expert on females, not by any means. Take his daughter, for example. Her moods swayed with the breeze and made no sense to him at all. But Kayla…sometimes they'd share a glance or a smile and he swore he could see straight through her.

And right now she didn't seem too happy about that date she'd set up last night.

Strange how that seemed to put him, on the other hand, in a sudden good mood. "What's the matter, La-La?" he asked as he passed her on the way to the refrigerator. Like him, she was dressed casually in jeans, running shoes and a sweatshirt that read Mary Poppins Rocks. "Is it—"

He was interrupted by the arrival of his son, Lee, in the kitchen, looking half-awake in his San Francisco 49ers flannel pajamas and with his dark hair sticking straight up in the back, his brown eyes at half-mast. With zombie footsteps, he walked over to Kayla and simply leaned into her, as if he was no longer able to stand on his own.

She held him against her, her palm smoothing the boy's porcupine hair. "Morning, sleepy."

"Morning, La-La," Lee murmured.

Mick couldn't help but smile, his mood notching higher. His daughter might be racing toward lipstick and a driver's license, but at eight, Lee looked the same as he had at two. He still loved trucks and dinosaurs; and give him some sort of ball and he would amuse himself endlessly. So blissfully uncomplicated. So unlike—

"Daddy," his daughter said. "You messed up *again*."

Mick made a mental eye roll. "Yeah, how's that? Is my handwriting not good enough where I signed off on your homework? Or have we forgotten something at the store you need for school? It's my volunteer day, so I can bring it when—"

"No. You forgot to mark Kayla's birthday on the calendar. I remember the date and it's the Sunday after this one."

"Kayla's birthday?" He didn't know it off the top of his head, but every year when they got a new calendar he paged through the old one in order to mark down important events. It was something he recalled his mom doing, and as a single parent, he'd taken on the habit for himself. "I can't believe I missed that."

"It doesn't matter," the nanny said, as she pulled out a chair for Lee at the kitchen table.

"Birthdays matter," Jane countered.

"Not so much when you're turning twenty-seven."

Mick frowned at that. Twenty-seven. Last night, Austin had mentioned she was a woman, and of course Mick had been noticing she was a woman for six months now, but still…twenty-seven. She wasn't any kid. At twenty-seven he'd already been married and a father two times over.

"We have to have cake and presents," Lee said as he dug into the bowl of cold cereal Kayla had poured for him. "And balloons, and…"

Mick half listened to his son ramble on about his favorite birthday elements. He didn't think Kayla would want pony rides or an inflatable party jumper shaped like a pirate ship. Instead, he pictured her across a small table. A white cloth, wineglasses, gleaming knives and forks. A date scene. Definitely a date scene, because the menu he was envisioning with that table didn't include any kind of kid entrées.

"We'll go out," he said, cutting through Lee's Cheerios-muffled voice.

Kayla frowned at him. "I can get my own dates."

That's right. Although she didn't seem too excited about the one she'd set up with Betsy the night before. "I didn't mean—" he started.

"I'm sure I'll be doing something with my family anyway," she said, turning away. With quick steps, she crossed to the refrigerator and started removing the standard basics that comprised his kids' lunches.

He bent to retrieve the white-but-whole-wheat loaf from the bread drawer. For a few minutes their morning was like it always was when he wasn't at the station. The kids chattered, he and Kayla responded, even as they moved about the kitchen like a couple of contestants in that celebrity dancing show that Janie loved. In sync. He slapped the bread on the board, she spread the mayo, he squeezed the mustard. Turkey, a very thin slice of tomato (Janie was very particular about that), a crisp piece of iceberg.

When had they turned into a team?

No. He was merely being a father. She was just doing her job.

But that thought was so…unworthy, that he couldn't stop himself from saying, "If you're busy on your birthday, we can choose another day."

"The Thunderbird Diner," Jane put in. "Me and Lee love the fries there."

"I want onion rings," Lee corrected. "I had them when I went there with Jared and his parents."

Mick tried to ignore the small wrench of disappointment he felt at their words. Of course the kids would want to be included. Of course that was the appropriate way to celebrate their nanny's special day.

But he couldn't stop himself from seeing it in a

completely different manner. He could suffer through a tie. And she'd smell great, as a matter of fact like she smelled right now, a scent that was mostly flowery but with the slightest of spicy notes that said feminine with staying power. So Kayla.

He'd put his fingertips at the small of her back as they walked into the restaurant. The little twitch she made at his touch would mean that her breath had caught…and then his breath would catch, too. Once they were seated, their server would ask if it was a particular occasion like an anniversary or a birthday. Kayla would look at him, her heart in her eyes, because she would dislike any widespread attention. So he'd smile and just say it was always an occasion when he was out with a beautiful woman.

Then Kayla would—

"Daddy," his daughter whispered, breaking the bubble of his fantasy.

He shook himself and stared down at her. "What?"

Jane's face was so familiar…and yet so different. The cheekbones were sharper against her skin, her eyes seemed wider than ever before and her neck longer, somewhere between gangly and elegant. When she opened her mouth, that gap between her front teeth told him that he needed to make that orthodontist appointment he'd been putting off. A now-familiar sensation constricted his chest and he reached out to slide his hand down her hair.

"Daddy," she said again, under the conversation that Kayla and Lee were conducting about the merits of French fries versus onion rings. "We need to get Kayla the perfect gift."

He could see it. Other years it had been scarves and stationery and coffeemakers, but he knew her better now. He could see himself in that certain department he always made sure to keep his gaze averted from and there he would find something… not slinky, nothing so cheesy. Kayla's blond beauty would look best in a flowing garment, fragile layers that would only briefly cling to her curves and then float away.

Oh. Oh, man. It wasn't that he knew her better now; it was that he wanted to *know* her better now.

He shifted away from his daughter to pack the lunch items into Lee's lunchbox and Jane's brown sack—the last teen heartthrob lunchbox had been tossed away in a fit of preteen "maturity." Kayla joined him at the counter, completing her part of the morning ritual. Their hands both closed over the same sandwich bag of apple slices.

She raised her gaze to his.

It was his turn to twitch. Damn! How had this happened? He'd been no more aware of her than he'd been of the…the teakettle on the stove. But then he'd caught her almost kissing that bristle-haired Lothario and everything had changed.

He'd developed this weird overprotective thing. That was all. He'd realized that she was a woman, not just the nanny, and he'd felt responsible for her because she was a member of his household.

Yeah.

Her brows came together. "What's wrong?"

He'd claimed he could see inside of her, but clearly that went both ways—she knew he was unsettled. All because he saw her as a woman now, and because, damn it, he didn't want to see her as a woman! He had enough on his plate without taking on this…this…

"I'm fine," he said, turning so that he was no longer meeting her gaze. She was so pretty. And, face it, sexy.

The acknowledgment of that slid over him like a hot hand, stiffening his muscles, putting every cell of his body on hyperalert. She stood at his left side, just a few inches away, and his skin prickled, his pulse pounding against his flesh like a drumbeat.

His mind flashed on lingerie, intimate dinners, candlelight. He pivoted toward her. "Kayla…"

How could he ever have viewed her as a child or a girl or anything less than a full-grown, fully attractive woman? How could anyone miss that shiny golden hair and the vivid blue of her beautiful eyes? As he looked down at her he saw a rush of goose bumps scurry down her throat toward her breasts.

His mouth dried. He saw her tongue dart out to wet her top lip and in another mind-flash he wondered if she was wet somewhere else. Kayla. Wet for him. His body twitched again.

"Kayla," he repeated. Perhaps it was time to come clean. Perhaps it was time to tell her he was thinking of private meals, sheer fabrics, hot skin. He glanced up and could see on her face a combination of confusion and trepidation.

Still, he opened his mouth to tell her everything on his mind, but then that look on her face arrested him. Think, Hanson! *Confusion. Trepidation.*

Both were warnings that he should be cautious, too. What had he been thinking the other night as he sat beside Will? That he couldn't take on the responsibility of making another person happy.

Without a mother, Jane and Lee had to be his priority. Under the weight of making yet another relationship work he might crack, and then where would his beloved children be?

Kayla put her hand on his arm. He jolted back, but then steadied so he wouldn't look like such a wuss.

Still, he felt her fingertips as if they branded him. His groin grew heavy. Just at that!

"Mick. What's wrong?"

"I..." He felt an explanation stick in his throat. He couldn't seem to mouth an excuse, and yet he couldn't seem to make a claim, either. His claim on her.

Her fingers caressed his forearm. "You can tell me."

And he thought again that maybe he should. Maybe he'd tell her that she wasn't just an employee in his eyes. That somehow she'd found her way under his skin and that perhaps they deserved a special night to explore what might be.

A trilling sound broke the bond between them. She took her hand off his arm to dig for her phone in her pocket. Her brows came together as she glanced at the screen and then she held the phone to her ear.

He moved away to give her a bit of privacy for her call. As soon as it was over, though, he *would* come clean, he decided. Caution be damned.

Seconds later she afforded him—and Jane and Lee—a lopsided smile. "Confirmation of my double date with Betsy tonight," she said. "It should be fun."

Her date with a stranger. It made Mick's skin itch. Even though she wouldn't be alone with the guy, this other man was likely someone unencumbered by children, memories and a reluctance to take on a relationship. Mick inhaled a breath. "Good for you," he said.

And tried to mean it.

Chapter Three

One Friday each month, Jane and Lee's school, Oak Knoll Elementary, devoted the morning to track-and-field sports. There were the usual sprints, longer distance runs and broad jump, as well as other non-Olympic-type events such as a bean bag toss and Mick's brainchild, the Impossible Football Catch.

Parents guided the children from the event positions that were set up and run by yet other volunteers. Mick usually enjoyed these Friday mornings—he made sure he attended all that his work schedule allowed—but today he found himself squeezing the football and staring off into space instead of anticipating the next classroom of kids to come by his station.

His partner that morning was Patty Bright. He'd known the short redhead with the splash of cinnamon freckles across her face for years. Her husband, Eric, too, since their daughter and Mick's had attended preschool together. Patty and his wife, Ellen, had been good friends, and the couple often invited him and the kids to social occasions at their house. Kayla, too.

Across the field his eye caught on the nanny as she moved to the twenty-five-yard dash with Lee and his classmates. School volunteer was not part of her nanny job description, but she'd started putting in hours as a requirement for a childhood development course she was taking in college. She'd continued the gig on a regular basis. She bent down to retie Lee's shoelaces, and Mick's fingers tightened on the football as his gaze focused on her round, first-class curves.

"Quite a sight, huh?" Patty said.

Mick gave a guilty jump and shifted his gaze to the other woman's face. "What?"

"I was just commenting on how tall Lee has grown in the past few months."

Grunting in acknowledgment, Mick pulled the brim of his ball cap a little lower on his head. *Geez,*

Hanson, he admonished himself. *You have no busi-ness checking out the nanny during school hours.*

He had no business checking out the nanny *any* time. So what that her silky blond hair rippled in the breeze and the little chill in the air turned the tip of her nose pink and reddened her luscious mouth? She was off-limits to him, and he was determined to see her as a competent caregiver, not some sexy—

Realizing he was staring at her again, he wrenched his gaze away and scuffed his shoe in the dirt. He wouldn't let her distract him again. "So, Patty, Lee looks like he's growing to you? I was just thinking this morning that he was still my dinosaur-lovin', veggie-hatin', grubby little boy."

Patty smiled. "When I look at him I see that little guy, but I also see a lot of Ellen, too."

Ellen. Mick jerked his head toward his son and inspected him from cowlick to rubber soles. Ellen. Yeah, he could see it now, too, the same straight, dark hair, the wide grin, the masculine version of his wife's adorable snub nose. His chest constricted, a little squeeze to remind him of how short their time here could be.

A hand touched his arm. "I'm sorry, Mick. I didn't mean to bring up bad memories."

"Don't worry about it." He found a smile. "Memo-ries of Ellen aren't bad at all. We had a good life together." Remembering that he was all alone to raise the fruits of that good life—Jane and Lee—was what would get to him at times. How could he make sure he did the right thing by them? Could he stand up to the responsibility of ensuring their health and happiness?

"About that 'veggie-hatin'' of Lee's," Patty put in, apparently eager to move on to another subject. "They have cookbooks devoted to recipes that show you how to hide them in things that kids will eat."

"I've heard of it," he said. Maybe that was a present he could give Kayla for her birthday. Sort of like the vacuum cleaner his dad had gifted his mom one year. She'd locked him out of their bedroom for a week following the incident, and that might not be a bad thing in this case, either.

Not that he was anywhere near Kayla's bed.

But he'd thought of her there during the last six months. Her room was a floor away from his and he had no way of hearing her moving around inside it. Despite that, he'd imagined her in that room with the pale blue walls and white trim. Her bed linens were white too, the comforter lacy, and he'd pictured her tossing and turning between her sheets, just like he so often did, while replaying a smile she'd shot him over Janie's head or the accidental bump of her elbow against his ribs as they prepared a meal.

Something as simple as that smile or touch would arouse him in the privacy of his bed. There. He'd admitted it. For six months, thoughts of Kayla had been amping up his sexual meter. Sure, he'd reexperienced the natural urge for sex once the worst of his shock and grief over Ellen's death had passed. But this feeling was different. It had an edge to it that got harder and harder—oh, jeez, that word worked—the more he smelled Kayla's skin and the more he watched her move.

Once again, he remembered that night he'd witnessed her kiss on the porch. Damn him! And damn her, too, because the moment she'd brushed past him to go inside, her shoulder glancing his chest, a soft strand of her hair grazing the back of his hand, everything inside of him had shifted. Altered.

But he was working to put that "everything" back to rights, wasn't he? She was the nanny, he was the daddy and that was all there was to it.

"Mick…" There was a new hesitance in Patty's voice.

He turned to her. "What?"

The woman bit her lip. "Well…"

Frowning, Mick tucked the football under his arm. "What's the matter?"

"It's about Kayla. Well, about you and Kayla."

Mick froze, hoping like hell she hadn't guessed

his secret. He kept his voice nonchalant. "What do you mean? There's no 'me and Kayla.'"

It was Patty's turn to frown. "Well, of course there is. She's your nanny."

"And I've never thought of her in any other way." Mick voiced the quick lie. Although he didn't think Patty expected he'd never have another woman in his life, he didn't want her speculating on this crazy little…interest he had in the woman caring for his children. He was putting it from his head, wasn't he?

The puzzled expression on Patty's face made Mick puzzled in turn. He cleared his throat. "I'm sorry, Pat, but what exactly are you getting at?"

She sighed. "You know it's an unspoken rule of parenthood that you don't poach on other couple's babysitters."

"Sure." When Ellen had been alive, they'd learned that lesson right away when they'd asked the family down the street for the names of some reliable sitters. Not everyone was willing to share, and you had to approach the subject with as much delicacy as prying open an oyster for the pearl inside.

"So I wouldn't just go to Kayla myself, not without checking with you first," Patty assured him.

Frowning, he studied his friend's freckled face. "What the heck are you dancing around?"

She took a quick breath, and then the words tumbled out. "Eric has been offered the chance to work in the London office this summer. Well, starting late spring actually. And I think we're going to move—all of us. Danielle and Jason, too."

Danielle and Jason, Patty and Eric's kids who were the same age as Jane and Lee. "Sounds like a great opportunity," Mick said.

"Even greater if sometimes Eric and I could take a few weekend jaunts around Europe, just the two of us," Patty added. "Though there'll be other times it would be all five."

"Five?" His brow furrowed, then he got it. "You… you would like to take my nanny with you for three months?"

Patty bit her lip again. "It could last up to a year if we like it," she confessed.

Mick didn't know what to say. This was poaching of the first order! Taking his K—his nanny—away from his kids. Out of the country!

His expression must have looked thunderous, because Patty grimaced. "I know, I know. But I just had to ask, Mick. My kids love Kayla and I would feel completely comfortable leaving them in her hands when Eric and I could get away to Edinburgh or Paris. And it would be an opportunity for Kayla, too.

She told me that she traveled in Europe one summer. It sounded like a fabulous time for her."

Better than the years she'd spent hanging around a grumpy old widower, he supposed.

"I was thinking she'd go with us to Hawaii this summer," he muttered. It wasn't the British Museum or the Louvre, but at their young age, Jane and Lee wouldn't really appreciate a trip like that.

Patty nodded. "My kids would rather we were going to learn to surf as well, but this is an opportunity that might not come our way again. The company will pay for a lot of it and I've never been anywhere east of Dallas, Texas."

He scuffed at the dirt with the toes of his running shoes, unsure what to say. Sure, it would be a great opportunity for everyone…everyone but him and Jane and Lee. "The kids wouldn't want to lose Kayla," he said, focusing on them.

"And you'd miss her, too, I know," Patty added.

He didn't dare look up. "So…"

"So I was also thinking that your kids are getting older, Mick. Before they get too attached to their nanny, I thought you might be considering making a…a change."

Change! There was that poisoned word again. Change was what had messed up his ordered life.

The change in how he saw Kayla made him edgy. Frustrated. Damn needy.

But maybe Patty had something there. To get back to sanity, perhaps another change *was* required. He closed his eyes for a moment, depressed by the damn thought, then he looked over at his friend. "Could you give me a little time? To broach the idea with the kids and with Kayla? But by next week…by next week I'll tell her about your offer, okay?"

Patty smiled. "Okay." Her expression turned hopeful. "Or sooner?"

"Sure." He ignored his tight chest and the urge to glance around and assure himself that Kayla was still, for now at least, in the vicinity. "Or sooner."

Mick had half promised sooner, and even considered telling Kayla that very day, but obstacles kept getting in the way. She took off on errands in the afternoon. Then Jane and Lee were home, and he didn't want to discuss the subject with them in the room.

As he and Kayla made dinner, the kids got their weekend homework out of the way at the kitchen table. It was like it always had been, the kids fairly diligent, he and the nanny supplying help when necessary. As usual, they bickered with good nature over the best way to remember the spelling of the words on Lee's test.

The only difference this evening was that he could hardly stop staring at Kayla's mouth or finding some excuse to brush against her. His skin felt shrink-wrapped to his bones and inside he burned like a three-alarm fire.

He had it bad, and depressing thought or no, Patty had provided a prescription for relief.

"Kayla," he said, keeping his voice low. "I'd appreciate it if we could have a talk after dinner. Just, uh, just the two of us."

She glanced up at him, her face coloring. "Just the two of us?"

He shifted, embarrassed at how intimate he'd made it sound. "I mean, I want to talk about the kids."

"Oh. Right. The kids." Her head bobbed up and down. "But…Mick, I'm sorry, I have to get ready now for my date. I won't be here for dinner…or after."

"Ah. Yeah. Sure. Some other time." He felt like an idiot, because he was holding plates in his hands, ready to set the table for four. He'd forgotten about Kayla and her date.

She hurried out of the kitchen while he just stood there, his mind replaying her words. *I won't be here for dinner…or after.* She'd be with some other man for dinner…and after.

It couldn't be jealousy, he told himself, but God, the taste of something bitter and green stuck to his tongue. He served up the plates for himself and the kids, hoping that the chicken and rice would dissipate the god-awful taste.

The food smelled good enough.

The scent of it lingered in the kitchen as they ate and even as he cleaned up the dishes. But then a new note entered the atmosphere, one that drew him around immediately.

Kayla's perfume. And oh, God, there she was, in a silky short black dress, her hair gleaming against her shoulders. Her lashes were darker than usual, her mouth a soft and tender pink, and she was holding toward him a necklace of delicate links and a pearl pendant. "I hate to ask, but could you help me with this? I can't get it latched."

He took it from her, feeling as if the tendons in his joints had tightened to short steel cords. Without a word, he signaled for her to turn around, and she did, then held her fall of hair off her neck.

Her beautiful neck, the skin looking so sweet and delectable. Tempting. In a flash of lust, he saw himself putting his mouth against the thin flesh at its side and pressing against it a hot, sucking kiss.

Good God, he groaned silently. Yeah, he had it bad. Really bad.

So bad that as he breathed in her scent and felt the heat of her just inches from his hard, tense body, his clamoring need had him wondering if there wasn't another prescription altogether he should be considering for his sexual relief.

Already nervous about the evening's date, Kayla nearly jumped out of her skin when Mick's fingers brushed her neck. A wash of goose bumps paraded from her nape southward and she hoped he wouldn't notice the reaction. This was silly, right? She was determined to overcome these teenagerish, twitchy nerves.

But his warmth at her back didn't make it any less difficult. It was just too easy to imagine leaning against his chest, turning her head to take a kiss....

"Kayla?"

She made that turn she'd been picturing, she even found herself staring at his mouth. Heat washed over her as another band of goose bumps marched down her skin.

"Kayla, I..." He hesitated, his palm coming up to cradle her jaw.

The goose bumps took another lap. "You can say anything," she whispered to him, not even sure what she meant by the words. "Anything."

"What's it like going out on a date?"

At Jane's loud question, she and Mick jolted back from each other, his callused hand trailing for just a moment along her skin.

The young girl surveyed Kayla, then sighed. "You look so pretty."

"Thank you," Kayla said, managing a smile.

"So what's it like going out on a date?" Jane asked again.

Mick stepped forward. "Remember our agreement, little girl. Not until you're thirty-one."

His daughter didn't even pretend to believe him. "Daddy, you're silly. I'm talking to Kayla. I want to know what happens on a date."

"Uh…" Kayla shot Mick a glance.

He lifted his hands. "Don't look at me. The last date I had was so long ago I think I was still in the fire academy."

She frowned at him. "I seem to remember a certain someone meeting a certain someone else at a coffeehouse a few months back." Though she'd kicked herself for it, she'd been relieved when he'd freely admitted there'd been zero chemistry between himself and the lady.

He shrugged it off.

"So…?" Jane prompted.

Kayla pushed her hair over her shoulders. "It's like…like sitting next to someone new in the school lunchroom. You get a chance to listen to them talk, hear what's important to them—"

"I always look at what they eat," Jane put in. "The ones with the good mothers cut their sandwiches in triangles."

Kayla's heart squeezed. While Jane didn't have a mother in her life any longer, Kayla did cut her sandwich into triangles…it was what she'd wished her mother had done when she was little. She smiled at Jane. "Like that, but remember I cut Lee's in half."

The girl rolled her eyes. "He thinks it makes him macho."

"Hey," Mick said. "I thought we weren't supposed to judge a book by its cover. Now we're deciding on the quality of people's parentage by the contents of their lunchbox and the shape of their PB and Js?"

His daughter ignored him again. "What do you talk about, though? I think I'd like to go to a movie on a first date so that it would do all the talking for us."

"When you're older the talking part gets a little easier," Kayla said. "You can ask a guy about his work, his family, if he has any pets. Some men like to talk about their car."

"Stay away from that kind," Mick said, grimacing. "Deadly dull. Only thing duller is if he wants to expound on his fantasy football team."

"Oh," Kayla groaned, closing her eyes for a moment. "Why do I feel like this is going to be a disaster?"

"We could come up with a signal," Mick offered. "You know, you call home to check on things and I'll claim we need you back immediately."

She groaned again. "You really think it's going to be that bad?"

His expression softened. "No. I'm sorry. I shouldn't be bringing up worst-case scenarios." He reached out a hand to brush the hair away from her forehead.

At the touch, she couldn't stop the little jerk of her body. He froze, his fingers still wrapped by strands of her hair, his eyes narrowing. His thumb drew a short stroke at her hairline and then another.

A shiver jittered across her scalp and then down her spine. She didn't even try to hide it from him. Mick let out a breath. "Kayla," he said softly.

The tenderness in his voice and the sudden raw tension in the air between them made Kayla's belly tighten. Desperate to break the invisible cord, she jerked her head around, looking for his daughter.

"Jane…" she said, her voice too breathless.

"Didn't you hear Lee's bellow?" Mick asked. "Their favorite TV show came on. She scampered out."

Meaning they had relative privacy in the kitchen,

and he was warm and strong and touching her still…
Another shiver jittered over her.

"Are you okay?" His fingers trailed over her hair
and then his arm dropped.

She shook her head, looking away from him. It
didn't help. He hadn't moved, meaning she could still
feel his body heat and the weight of his gaze. Both
scrambled her thinking and made her heart pound
too fast.

"Kayla." He curled his forefinger under her chin,
lifting her head so their eyes met. "What is it?"

She swallowed, then shrugged a shoulder in a nonchalant gesture. "I'm nervous, that's all."

His head cocked. "Of me?"

"No!" Of course it wasn't him. She made *herself*
nervous, anxious to ensure she didn't give away her
unwanted, unwarranted desire for this attractive,
sexy, *ineligible* man. "You know, it's that first date
thing."

He was still holding her chin, now pinched between his thumb and forefinger. "What specifically
is bothering you?"

She watched his mouth move as he said the words.
His lips looked soft, the slight edge of whiskers
around them only serving to outline their manly
shape. "It's…it's the kiss," she heard herself blurt.
"Maybe I've forgotten how."

Heat washed up her cheeks. Great. She really wasn't thinking about kissing some man she'd never met, of course. It was Mick who was making her say silly, senseless things. It was thinking of him, his mouth, his tongue, his taste that was rattling her brain and tripping up her pulse. With a little shuffle of her feet, she tried moving out of his grasp.

His grip tightened, just those two fingers making her immobile, keeping her captured as he bent close. "Then let me remind you," he whispered, his breath warm against her face, "of exactly how two pairs of lips are supposed to meet."

Chapter Four

Kayla let herself into the quiet house at the end of her date. It was barely eleven, but the family was obviously already upstairs for the night. It was past the kids' bedtime.

She clicked off the lamp left burning for her in the living room and crossed toward the kitchen. On the threshold, she hesitated.

Don't think about what happened in there, she instructed herself. *Put it straight from your mind.*

Her heels tip-tapped on the wooden floorboards. Just a few hours ago she'd been standing right beside the sink, her skin heating up beneath the cool chain Mick had just fastened around her neck and then—

Don't think about it!

In her bedroom, she quickly slipped off her dress. Her cell phone rang as she pulled her sleeveless, thigh-length nightshirt over her head. The fire alarm–styled ring tone signaled that her boss had dialed her number. She froze, instincts warring. On the one hand, a purely feminine impulse urged she ignore the call. On the other, the nanny in her itched to answer. Was something wrong with Jane or Lee? Had the evening included a domestic disaster she should know about?

Yet another thought galvanized her: *If you don't pick up, he might come downstairs. Right into this room!*

Her leap for the phone was worthy of the elementary school's track-and-field Friday. "Hello?" The sudden broad jump had made her breathless.

"Kayla." Mick sounded concerned. "Are you okay? Is something wrong?"

She swallowed, trying to calm her galloping heart with the palm of her free hand. His deep voice, however familiar, had flustered her. "I'm good. Fine. Is there something wrong with *you?*"

There was a long pause. He muttered something she didn't catch. "Mick?"

"No. Nothing's wrong," he said. "I wanted to warn you…"

Had the kids seen something? Asked him about the— *Don't think about that!*

He started again. "Now, don't be mad—"

"I'm not mad," she said. "Why would I be mad? I mean, what's there to be mad about?"

The silence on the other end of the line was puzzled. "Uh, I haven't gotten to the part you might be mad about yet."

"Oh." He wasn't talking about the...thing she shouldn't think about in the kitchen. She'd thought he thought she might be mad about that thing. Her hand massaged her forehead. "What *are* you talking about?"

"I wanted to warn you...and apologize. The kids and I built a metropolis in Lee's room and I didn't make them pick it up before bed."

"Oh." He'd been so unimpressed with the thing she didn't want to think about in the kitchen that he'd spent the evening—unlike her—not worrying about it, and instead building one of the extensive wooden blocks-and-LEGO worlds that used up acres of floor space and a ton of primary-colored toys. "That sounds like fun."

"But now we're all just one misplaced footstep away from agony. So, fair warning."

"Ah." Yes, more than once the bottom of her bare

soles had found the sharp edge of a plastic brick.
Agony described it well. "I understand."

"The kids and I'll take care of the cleanup in the
morning."

"Okay. Thanks." Good. Really good. With that
little exchange it was as if the thing in the kitchen
had not happened at all and they were back to their
stable boss-employee relationship. Discussing toys,
kids and cleanup. See, nothing had changed.

"Was your evening, uh, enjoyable?" Mick asked
now.

She swallowed. "Sure. Betsy and I and our dates
had dinner, then we saw a movie," she said, adding
the name of the latest action-adventure blockbuster.

"Did you like it? I saw a trailer for it and the plot
sounds kind of far-fetched."

It had a plot? She didn't remember the sequence
of events or even the faces of the actors in the movie.
Her mind had been on another reel altogether, and
it had kept playing and replaying in her head, a loop
of—

"Kayla?"

"It was pretty spectacular," she admitted.

"There were explosions?" Mick asked.

"I thought the top of my head might come off."

"Wow. That intense, huh?"

"Intense doesn't—" She stopped herself. He was

discussing the movie, she suddenly realized, while she...she was not. "I think you'll have to see it for yourself."

"I just might do that."

An awkward pause ensued. Kayla shivered a little, and pulled back the covers so she could get under the sheets and comforter. "Anything else to report?"

"Like what?"

She could wrap this up, she supposed. Say good-night. But as she settled back against the pillows, she found herself reluctant to end the call. Maybe because it took her mind off places it shouldn't be wandering, she told herself. "I never asked you how your part of track-and-field day went. Impossible Football Catch another success? It's always popular."

"Because I dish out Life Savers candies on the sly. Don't tell."

"Mick Hanson!" She pretended to scold. "You know as well as I do there's a rule against providing sugary treats during the school day."

His voice lowered until it was almost like a whisper in her ear. "What'll I have to give you to keep my secret?"

Her secret made itself known then, as a rash of goose bumps broke out over her skin. He didn't have to do that thing she didn't want to think about. He didn't have to touch her in any way at all. The

forbidden attraction she had for him made itself
known anyway. "I…I…" She felt tongue-tied and
awkward and worried he'd suspect everything she
was trying to hide from just the squeaky tone in her
voice.

He saved her by clearing his. "So," he said, dropping the subject of secrets. "Back to your date. Are
you planning on seeing this gentleman again?"

She couldn't even picture what the "gentleman"
looked like. His appearance had made that little of
an impression due to the fact that ninety percent of
her brain had been occupied with different visuals
altogether. Guilt gave her a little pinch. "He's very
nice."

Mick winced. "Ouch."

"What?" Guilt pinched her again because she
knew she'd barely given the nice guy the time of
day. "He represents a national window supplier and
he's successful, hardworking—"

"Transparent," Mick put in.

It took her a moment to catch on. "Hah. Window,
glass, transparent, I get the joke."

He laughed, low. "No flies on you, sweetheart."

At the endearment, her blood turned to honey in
her veins. The word itself moved, slow and sweet,
through her. Although goose bumps rose again on
her flesh, she had to kick off the covers. "Mick…"

"Hmm?"

But she didn't have anything to add. She'd only wanted his name on her tongue as her physical response to him overtook her once again. It wasn't good, she knew that. But being good had gone out the window just a few hours ago, when—

"Did my, uh, little reminder come in handy tonight?" Mick asked, his voice very, very soft.

And then it happened. What she'd been trying to prevent since she'd walked back into the house. The memory of Mick's little "reminder" burst in her head like a time-lapse photo of a blooming flower.

Both of his hands had moved to cup her face. The palms were a little work-roughened, and warmer, even, than the heat climbing up her neck and into her cheeks.

She'd flinched a little at the contact and he'd murmured to her, in the same tone she figured he'd use for a treed kitten. "Shh. Stay still now."

Her fingers had fisted at her sides instead of reaching out and hanging on to him like they'd wanted to. She'd watched his face descend until she was afraid this pre-moment kiss was just a dream. Then she'd closed them and felt her heart pounding harder against her breastbone. *Mick,* she'd thought to herself. *Mick is a breath away from kissing me.*

Of course he'd been gentle. At first.

At first it had been with sweet affection. Instead of relaxing, though, she'd tensed more at that tender touch, half-afraid that it was the sum total of the lesson he had for her—and half-afraid it wasn't. When he'd increased the pressure by just the smallest amount, she'd parted her mouth. The tip of his tongue had met the silky underside of her bottom lip. Icy heat had washed over her skin and she'd grabbed his waist before her knees failed her.

He'd moved into her hold. Into her mouth.

Their tongues had tangled. She'd smelled his soap, felt his heat radiating toward her, tasted him.

Wanted more.

Wanted him.

Her nipples had contracted in an almost-painful rush as her mouth widened to take his deeper thrust. His hands had moved, one sliding around to the back of her head, the other sliding over her shoulder and down her spine. She'd felt his palm bump over the strap of her bra and her breasts had swelled, aching for him to touch her there, too.

"Kayla," he'd said against her lips. She'd felt his hold loosen, his kiss gentle. As reluctant as she'd been to let him go, she'd forced her hands to drop away from him.

"Kayla," he said again now.

"Yeah, Mick?" she managed.

"I don't regret it," he admitted, obviously reading her mind.

She did. She'd been right not to want to think about what had happened between them in the kitchen. Because when she did, she was very afraid no other man, no other kiss, would ever measure up.

The following Saturday, Mick woke to the light bounce of his mattress and a click from the television situated in the walnut-finished armoire across from the bed. Soon it was emitting zany, cartoon noises. Then came another, weightier bounce followed by the meow of a cat. He opened his eyes just as the animal settled on the small of his back.

His gaze landed on his children, their eyes glued to the TV set. Lee was in the middle, his hair in its characteristic cowlick of surprise. His daughter, à propos of who she was at eleven, clutched a gossip-and-fashion magazine aimed at preteen girls, although her attention was captured by the television screen.

Mick sighed as the cat started purring against his spine and Lee's kneecap dug a friendly hole in his rib cage. Not only didn't he have metaphorical room for a woman in his life, there was literally zero space for her in his bed. Really, it was as simple as that.

"Dad," Lee said, his eyeballs tracking the movement on the TV.

"Yeah?"

"You think La-La will make me my favorite Saturday breakfast this morning?"

And there you go. The opposite of simple. Not just because of that, uh, lesson in the kitchen the week before, but because of that still-unspoken European offer on the table. Both had rolled through his mind, oh, about a thousand times in the last eight days. He'd still not mentioned Patty's proposition to the nanny, though.

"I can make your favorite breakfast, pal," he told Lee. "We shouldn't rely on Kayla for everything, you know. What, um, *is* your favorite Saturday breakfast?"

"I decided last weekend when you had to work," his son said, over Jane's mock retching noises. "Open-faced grilled cheese."

"That's not so bad."

"With pickle relish on top."

Mick felt a little like retching himself and he stirred, disturbing the cat so that it leaped off the bed with a disgruntled *"lurp."* "I can do that. *We* can do that, the three of us together."

After he dressed in workout gear, they paraded down to the kitchen to prepare breakfast then, and over the relish fumes Mick thought it was perhaps time to bring up the subject of the nanny and her future with their family. He didn't want to go into much detail—he'd save that until he heard Kayla's own reaction to the offer—but it made sense to remind his children that she wasn't a permanent fixture in the household.

"You know, guys," he began. "Kayla—"

"Kayla what?" Her voice asked.

He started, jerking around to see her stepping through the doorway that led to the short hall and her private quarters, dressed in her long flannel robe and slippers. "I...I..." Something had to be said, yes? Though he realized he was just staring at her, remembering the scent of her perfume, the smooth skin of her nape as his fingertips brushed it when he latched the necklace, the soft press of her lips as she kissed him back.

She'd kissed him back. God, hadn't that felt great?

The hem of her robe fluttered around her ankles as she made for the coffee. He dropped his eyes to stare at her bare ankles instead of her mouth, but he'd already noted the tired look in her eyes. Maybe she'd been experiencing fitful nights of sleep, too.

"You look tired," Jane commented, turning in her chair. "Were you dreaming about your date from last week? You never said how handsome he was. And what about sexy?"

"Sexy!" Mick frowned at his daughter. "That's not appropriate kind of talk." Then he slid his gaze toward the nanny, trying to assess her unspoken response for himself.

Yeah, how sexy was he?

Kayla's cheeks were pink. "Your father's right, Jane. You shouldn't ask other people about—"

"But is he The One?"

"And not that, either," Kayla scolded. She poured herself a cup of coffee and then topped off Mick's. "Lee conned you into grilled cheese and relish?"

"I've decided I could market this concoction as a diet aid. The smell of it at 8:00 a.m. has put me right off my own breakfast."

Her gaze lingered on his chest, then cut away. "I think you're right. I'll shower before I eat anything. You have it handled in here?"

"Of course." It hit him, then, that she was standing exactly where she'd been last week when she'd complained about forgetting how to kiss.

As if she remembered as well, her gaze lifted to his. Their eyes locked like their lips had done. There was something besides the scent of coffee and pickle relish in the air. The atmosphere crackled with a tension that edged down Mick's back like the sensuous scratch of a woman's fingernails.

"I should go…." Kayla murmured.

"Don't," he heard himself say. He didn't want her to go. Not away from the kitchen. Not away from him.

Then Lee bounced between the two of them, breaking the bubble that had seemed to enclose the pair of adults. Mick moved back to give his son more space and remembered again.

He didn't have room in his life for anyone. Even for Kayla.

She disappeared in the direction of her room, closing the hall door behind her. Mick let out a long breath of air and turned back to the breakfast prep. "We've got to get a move on. Two basketball games this morning." Both his children played in the local rec league and he coached the teams himself.

"Daddy," Jane said, "can I go home with Kayla between the time mine ends and Lee's begins? I'll be b-o-o-o-red with nothing to do but sit in the bleachers."

"I don't know that she'll be coming to basketball today," he replied.

Lee turned to stare at Mick as if he'd spilled there was no Santa Claus. "But La-La comes to watch everything I do."

Oh, boy. Due to his firefighter's schedule, their nanny didn't have the regular eight-to-five, Monday-through-Friday gig that she might have with another family. It meant she did chauffeur the kids to—and attend—events that would normally be a parent's responsibility.

"Lee, I'm off today. That means Kayla can do whatever she wants. Maybe she'd rather go shopping or read a book or see a movie."

His son merely blinked. "La-La comes to watch everything I do," he repeated.

Like a mother, Mick thought, feeling his belly clench. He reached out and wrapped his big hand around Lee's neck to draw him in for a hug. "I know, pal, and you've been lucky in that. But we have to respect her days off."

"Remember how she came back early from that girls' weekend she went on to see my ballet recital?" Jane pointed out.

"She *likes* to watch me play, Dad." Lee pulled away and headed toward the door leading to the nanny's room. "We can ask her—"

"No." Mick lunged for his son and caught him by the flannel pajama sleeve. "If you ask her, you'll put her on the spot."

Lee shot a glance at his sister. "Like when Jane asked her if her date was 'The One'?"

"Yeah. Like that." Although Mick couldn't help but remember that Kayla hadn't answered the question. "We should—"

"It was a stupid question," Lee proclaimed. "There's no The One for La-La. Not yet."

Jane brought over her empty cereal bowl to rinse in the sink. "How come? Are you still planning to marry her yourself when you grow up?" she teased.

Lee shoved his sister in the arm. "Shut up about that. I was just a baby when I said it."

"You said it like last week."

"Did not."

"Did, too."

"Did not."

"Wait, wait, wait." Mick laid a hand on the shoulder of each kid. "That's enough."

He had one of those parental headaches starting to throb at the base of his brain—yet another reason he couldn't bring a female into his life. How could you subject your children's Saturday morning bickering on another adult and look yourself in the eye? "You kids go up and make your beds and then get ready for basketball."

Lee's lower lip stuck out. "I only meant that La-La can't leave us until after I sign with the San Francisco Giants," he said. "You know, when I go pro."

The throb of Mick's headache kicked into higher gear. "Lee. Son."

"What?"

"Look. You need to understand…" He hesitated.

"Understand what?" Lee demanded.

"You see…" Mick couldn't get the words out.

Rolling her eyes, Jane jumped into the conversation. "He doesn't know how to tell you you'll never play professional baseball, brat-face."

"Jane." Mick shook his head. "Don't." Then he sighed. "Let's go sit down."

His feet were slow following the children to the kitchen table. How hadn't he seen this coming? He'd never thought about explaining to his kids that Kayla wasn't a permanent fixture in their family. At first he'd been too busy grieving, then too involved with keeping up, then…just so damn grateful that he'd probably taken it as much for granted as the eight- and eleven-year-old who expected her to make every basketball game and every ballet recital.

Damn! Some days single fatherhood especially sucked.

And he still didn't feel he should get into specifics about Patty and Eric Bright's Europe proposal until he found the right time and place to discuss it with Kayla. He'd run into a burning building with more eagerness than he felt at diving into this discussion with his kids.

Their expressions were apprehensive, he saw, as they settled around the table. Damn, he thought again. "Look, guys, there isn't anything to be worried about."

Except that the woman who's looked after you as long as you likely can remember may be leaving us for another family.

"Remember, we've talked about this kind of stuff before. Uh, life goes on. Winter, spring, summer, fall."

Lee nodded, ticking off on his fingers. "Basketball, baseball, swimming, soccer."

Mick grimaced. Leave it to his son to think of everything in terms of sports. "Well, that's right. We move on season to season. It would get pretty, uh, boring if we stuck with just basketball year-round."

Their expressions turned puzzled. "We play *H-O-R-S-E* even in the summer," Jane reminded him.

He tried again. "You know what I mean. Nothing lasts forever. You grow out of your favorite shoes. You stop obsessing over those little furry gizmos and take up yo-yos instead. You think you won't like your new teacher as much as the old one, but the new one turns out to be perfectly nice, as well."

Lee blinked. "I'm getting a new teacher?"

"No, brat-face," Jane said, comprehension appearing to dawn. "He's trying to tell you he ran over your bicycle."

His son gasped. "Dad!"

"I did not run over your bicycle, Lee." He shot a look at his daughter. "Not helping."

She flounced in her seat. "I don't understand what you're saying. I thought it was the bike."

"It's not the bike. It's not about toys or...teachers. Not exactly. I'm just trying to make sure you kids know that things change." And God, he hated that word, but pretending it didn't exist hadn't worked at all.

"Change how?" Jane asked, wary now.

He waved a hand. "Specifics aren't necessary. Not at the moment. But sometimes people find out that they've outgrown their current situation, like the shoes, you know? So you have to get a different pair and they're good, maybe even better than the old pair, which were getting a little ragged anyway."

"My last pair had that broken shoelace, remember?" Lee said. "La-La replaced it with a bright green one and they were as good as before. I didn't need any new ones until right before Christmas."

Mick stifled his sigh. He wasn't making himself

clear to his son. "But you eventually needed a new pair, didn't you?"

"Yes." Lee brightened. "Do you mean you think we should get Kayla new slippers for her birthday tomorrow? I saw you looking at the ones she was wearing earlier."

When he was avoiding looking at her mouth, he thought, focusing on the tabletop. "What I mean is that maybe we should be thinking about getting a new *Kayla*, kids."

A sound caught his attention. His head shot up, just in time to see their current Kayla disappear toward her bedroom. Oh, God. Had she heard him? And if she had…

Sighing, Mick dropped his head into his hand. Upon waking, he'd called his situation simple. What a crock, huh? It didn't take a genius to realize his circumstances were a thousand times more complicated than a too-small bed and a too-burdened heart.

Chapter Five

Following the morning basketball games, Kayla had a date for lunch with her friends from the nanny agency. Wearing a clingy knit dress in powder-blue and her black boots, she pushed open the glass doors of the large restaurant anchoring one corner of the mall. Her gaze immediately found the small cluster of women in the waiting area, each wearing a smile and carrying a brightly colored gift bag.

"Happy Birthday!" they chorused together.

She smiled at them, then was immediately swept along with the group as they followed the hostess to their table. Betsy linked arms with her. "Excuse me for saying so," she murmured, "but your celebration face seems a little sad around the edges."

"Of course not," Kayla started, then sighed. "Okay, maybe so. I guess it's the birthday blues." Or what she'd thought she'd overheard Mick say that morning. *We should be thinking about getting a new Kayla.* Had she misheard, or had he really expressed the sentiment?

Betsy directed Kayla to sit at the head of the table the hostess indicated. "I declare this a blues-free zone. We have presents! We're going to order desserts after lunch!"

Kayla relaxed against the back of her chair. "I'm being silly. Twenty-seven tomorrow isn't so bad."

"If you like, over lunch we can be seventeen instead," the irrepressible Betsy said.

"Good idea," agreed Jamie, another of the nannies. She had boy-short hair and took care of an "oops" infant whose closest sibling attended high school. "We'll talk about nothing but clothes, boys and sex."

"Shh!" Gwen, the head of the nanny agency, glanced around them even as she laughed. "We have a reputation to uphold, ladies."

Betsy leaned across the table. "Gwen. I'll have you know that nannies can have—" she paused and lowered her voice "—*S-E-X,* too."

Gwen raised an eyebrow. "I thought we'd all been unanimous in recently lamenting the deplorable state of our love lives."

Betsy grimaced. "Point taken. We'll leave it that nannies *want S-E-X,* too."

Their server arrived, derailing the discussion for the ordering of beverages and then their meals. As it was a birthday celebration, the friends agreed they should supplement their main course salads with an order of potato skins.

Jamie sighed as she swallowed a bite of the decadent appetizer. "Speaking of love lives, how did your double date go, girls?" Her gaze moved between Betsy and Kayla as they each remained silent. "That good, huh?"

"No sparks," Betsy admitted. Her glance cut over. "Kayla, you feel the heat?"

Not with the blind date. With Mick, before, during and after. She shook her head. "Mine called a couple of times since, but I've made excuses."

Betsy frowned, then brightened. "I may have another prospect. This very great-looking man moved into the house next door. He was a little put-out when my twin charges found their way into his backyard, but…did I mention he's great-looking?"

Given that Betsy was nanny to a pair of adorable but demonic four-year-olds, Kayla couldn't exactly fault the next-door neighbor's irritation, but she wasn't ready for another setup. "Why aren't you interested in him for yourself?"

Her friend was already shaking her head. "He grills meat. Every night, great hunks of meat."

Betsy was vegan—at least that was this month's claim. "I appreciate the thought, but I've decided to try finding my own men from now on," Kayla said.

So they spent the rest of the meal scoping likely prospects while eating lunch and giggling as if they were, indeed, seventeen again. The presents added to the festive atmosphere, and Kayla loved the matching scarf and gloves, the perfume, the books and candy she received from her friends. A dose of chocolate in the form of a triple-threat dessert only bubbled her mood higher.

It didn't crash until they were leaving the restaurant. "What's up for tomorrow?" Gwen asked. "Will the birthday girl be visiting with her parents?"

Kayla didn't let her smile fall, though. "Something like that." Nothing like that.

"And tonight?" Betsy queried. "Any plans?"

"I'm having dinner with an old friend from high school." Karen lived in Tucson now, but she had business in northern California. "It should be fun."

Betsy leaned in close. "Funner would be a man and *S-E-X*."

Kayla figured that possibility was as likely as contact with her parents on the actual day she turned another year older. But she kept her expression set on bright as she waved her friends goodbye and turned into the mall. Maybe she'd buy something new to wear.

She found herself on the children's floor at the department store, however, instead of at her favorite boutique. Lee needed new socks, she told herself. Lee always needed new socks. Turning down an aisle, she bumped into a familiar figure inspecting a rack of small shirts.

Betsy gasped in surprise, then looked sheepish. "You, too?"

"I'm after socks," Kayla said, then sighed. "Is there something wrong with us?"

"That we're spending a free Saturday shopping for our charges instead of for ourselves?"

"I just wonder what it says about me that I'd rather look at kids' clothing than a new pair of jeans."

Betsy ran her hands over her hips. "If you're me, it's because you've promised yourself to drop five pounds before buying another pair of pants."

Kayla didn't think that was why Betsy was really perusing blue clothes in size 4T. "A lot of people like their work, but I'm pretty sure it's not hip for women our age to be as into kids as we are."

The other woman toyed with a small button-down printed with a wild pattern of red biplanes. "When did you first start watching little ones?"

Kayla thought back. "I was twelve. The couple three doors down had an infant and an active social life. I was their go-to sitter until I started college. I took care of Lisa from when she was three months old. The first time I sat for both her and her little brother Curtis, he was only twelve days old. I was with them two to three times a week, even if only so their mom could meet a friend for a game of tennis or a cup of coffee."

"And you liked it."

She had. By then, her mother and father were both already remarried, each heavily involved in their new lives, and she'd showered on the kids she'd babysat the attention that she'd wanted for herself. The kids had given back to her as much as she'd given them, she'd realized early on. They were thrilled when she came to the house and sad when she went home.

Betsy nodded. "I was the neighborhood sitter, too. I've always wanted my own children."

"You don't worry that Duncan and Cal aren't filling up that place in your heart?"

"No." She grinned. "And if I were honest, there come some days when I thank God those little imps aren't mine 24/7. But then, Jana, their mother, admits they could try the patience of several saints."

Kayla knew her friend was devoted to the twins, but wondered if it was different for herself, the live-in nanny for motherless children. They didn't have a feminine presence besides herself who peeked in on them at night, no other woman pressed her palm to their foreheads checking for fever, not another female voice was in the house to calm their fears. Perhaps it was Mick's job that made her own different from Betsy's, too. With his twenty-four-hour shifts, there were times when she had all the responsibilities of a parent.

We should be thinking about getting a new Kayla.

What had that meant? She should have stopped in her tracks and demanded the answer. Instead, she'd let it stew into a bad-tempered brew that was now ruining her Saturday.

"You know, my oldest sister doesn't want kids, and I think that's fine," Betsy continued. "My cousin can't have any and she's made peace with that, too. Their feelings are legitimate and so are ours. There's nothing wrong with loving children."

But there was something wrong with Kayla's day and she was determined, she decided, to address it. "I've got to be going," she told her friend. No more letting it fester. She would confront Mick and find out just what was going on at the house on Surrey Street.

Minutes later she was pulling into the driveway. Gazing on the cream-and-green split level, she took a moment to gather her thoughts then strode to the front door. She reached for the knob just as Mick yanked it open. Her balance off, she swayed until he caught her by the shoulder.

Their eyes met.

The mood she'd brought back with her from the mall receded. His hand felt heavy, masculine, where it grasped her shoulder and heat zinged down her arm. He had gone without shaving that morning and the dark edge of whiskers only drew her attention to the shape of lips. Only helped her recall their tenderness on hers. Her mouth tingled now and she remembered that sizzling moment when his tongue touched hers and her heart had stopped.

His fingers gentled on her shoulder, the contact turning to a caress. She watched his chest expand on a breath. She, on the other hand, couldn't draw air into her lungs.

"Hey…" His voice was husky.

She remembered it speaking other words. *We should be thinking about getting a new Kayla.*

The memory galvanized her again. She jerked

away from him, and his arm dropped to his side. Narrowing her eyes, she focused on her goal. She had to get this out so she could clear the air and banish her blues. "Look," she said. "Pity parties are not my style, so—"

"So come along with me," he said, smiling.

It was the smile that undid her. "What?" But he had a hold of her again.

"We heard you drive up. The kids have been waiting all afternoon," he said, drawing her toward the dining room.

"Surprise!" yelled Jane and Lee.

Helium balloons bounced on the ends of ribbons attached to the backs of chairs. Presents sat on the long table, surrounding a cake with her name on it. The kids wore silly party hats and Lee started honking one of those loud party blowers. Kayla looked at Mick, then at the kids, then back to Mick again.

He shrugged. "We got a little excited and couldn't wait until tomorrow for your birthday."

Lee and Jane ran over. "You don't mind?" the girl asked.

Lee hugged Kayla so tight that her lungs felt like toothpaste in the tube. She was afraid they might be squeezed from her mouth, so she kept it shut and shook her head, blinking against the sting in her eyes. Her palms—those surfaces that had felt for fevers so many times—smoothed Lee's cowlick and the warm crown of Jane's head.

Stewing was done. Her mood hovered somewhere above those multicolored balloons. *There's nothing wrong with loving children,* Betsy had said.

There might be nothing wrong, but there might be something dangerous about loving two specific children who didn't really belong to her. Yet with them this close to her swelling heart, she didn't care.

The second hard-and-fast rule of nannydom had been broken eons ago, she realized, probably on some not particularly eventful night when she'd tiptoed in to turn off a light or tuck a stuffed animal beside a small, slumbering body.

She thought of Mick's children as hers, and no questions or clearing of air were going to change that.

Mick had been waiting all day to explain the comment he suspected the nanny had overheard that morning.

But watching her *ooh*ing and *aah*ing over her birthday gifts, he knew that replacing her would be impossible, just as it was impossible to look away from her now. The blue dress she wore accented her eyes and molded her slender body. High-heeled black boots made her legs go on forever.

Still, it wasn't his choice as to whether she would remain with them as the family nanny. He'd already stalled for more than a week without telling her about Patty's offer. And didn't he just feel low as a worm about that?

"Dad," Jane said, interrupting his thoughts. "Can we cut the cake now?"

"Sure, but you and Lee go hunt down the paper plates and the plastic forks, will you? A party shouldn't include doing dishes, not for any of us."

The kids scampered off, leaving him alone with Kayla in the dining room. She smiled at him. "I particularly like the loaded iPod. After I ruined mine in that unfortunate pool incident, I haven't replaced it because I couldn't bear the idea of having to take the time to re-create my playlists. Thanks for doing that, Mick."

"I'm ancient compared to you," he warned. "I know what you like to listen to, but I snuck some stuff on there you might consider oldies."

"Why do you keep bringing up our age difference?"

So I don't have to bring up the European proposal. So I can remember yet another reason why I shouldn't kiss you again. Sighing, he pulled out a chair to join her at the table. The sugary smell of the frosting made his belly hurt—or at least he thought it was that.

"Kayla—"

"We found 'em!" Lee bounded back in the room, paper plates and plastic forks in hand. "Me wants cake."

His gaze and Kayla's met across the table and they both grinned. That was Lee's signature party line. "He'll be saying 'me wants cake' on his wedding day," Mick told her.

God. The thought of Lee marrying sobered him. The boy was already eight and if these first years were any indication, the next eight and the eight after that would pass in the blink of an eye. His daughter would marry, too—despite his avowed moratorium on her dating. So where would that leave Mick? Who would be at his side to watch his children move on with their lives?

A profound loneliness leaked like dark ink into his heart, making it throb instead of beat. He glanced toward the living room and found the close-up photograph of his wife, Ellen, on the mantel. It was terrible to admit, but he could hardly conjure up the sound of her voice anymore. He didn't remember her scent. But at times like this he missed her presence with an ache sharp enough to cut.

"Mick."

He blinked, his gaze shifting to Kayla. At the other end of the table, the kids were forking down birthday cake like they hadn't been fed breakfast, lunch or dinner in a lifetime. Kayla pushed toward him his own serving on a paper plate decorated with more birthday balloons.

"I had a bit of the blues today myself," she said softly. "Is it catching?"

"Of course not, it's—"

"I know that look," she continued. "Where do you go, then?"

He realized she *would* know that look. Just as she knew when Jane required jollying or Lee needed to be headed off before turning into a whirling boy dervish, Kayla could read his moods.

Shaking his head, he frowned at her. "Who recognizes and tends to your bad moments?"

She waved a hand. Smiled. "Me? I don't have bad moments."

"You just said you did. Everybody does."

Jane piped up, making it clear she was getting to that age where she was acutely tuned to adult conversation. "Kayla talks to her nanny friends."

"You should be able to talk to us, too," Mick said. "Me."

"Or me," Jane added again. "You know, when you want to talk about boys and stuff."

Lee made a sour-lemon face. "Don't talk to me about boys. That makes me want to barf."

"But *I'd* like to hear it," Jane said. "I want to hear all about you finding The One."

Kayla laughed. "I don't know about this The One, Jane."

Mick's daughter turned to him. "Tell her, Daddy. Tell her The One is out there waiting." Then she didn't give him a chance. "My dad told us he saw my mom at a friend's wedding—she was a bridesmaid—and he said to himself, 'Well, hah. There she is.'"

"But she didn't like him right away," Lee put in, drawn into the story despite his professed repulsion to all things romantic. "She told him he was stuck-up and she didn't date good-looking guys."

Jane frowned. "Why did Mom say that? Why didn't she want to date cute boys?"

Mick shrugged.

"Because cute boys often know they're cute," Kayla said. "If they're courteous and cute, okay, but overconfident and cute...you have to be careful."

"I better say please and thank-you a lot, then," Mick said.

"Is that what made Mom change her mind about you?" Lee asked. "You remembered the golden rule and junk?"

Mick nodded. "And I remembered to wash my

hands when I was supposed to." Part of parenting was sneaking in a practical lesson at every opportunity.

Lee rolled his eyes.

Part of parenting was realizing your attempts to sneak in a practical lesson at every opportunity was extremely obvious, even to an eight-year-old.

"So Mom gave Dad a second chance to impress her," Jane said. "Maybe you need to give somebody a second chance, too, Kayla. You told me that man you went out with last week didn't wow you. Maybe *wow* doesn't happen on a first date."

Now it was Kayla's turn to shrug. "Or *wow* might be overrated. What about *hmm* or *maybe* or—"

"It should be *wow*," Mick said, firm on that.

She glanced over at him.

Mick's gaze tangled with hers. He was aware of the kids dashing off, likely fueled on sugary icing for the next week, but still he didn't say anything.

She broke the silence first. "So it was like that with you and your wife? Wow?"

"Yeah."

"Just like that," she persisted. "One look and wham. Bam. Wow."

"Yeah. But I was also in a place and time to be whammed, bammed and wowed," he said. "Not to mention I've always been a sucker for weddings."

Her expression was doubtful…or disappointed, he wasn't sure.

"I don't think *wow* has to hit like a frying pan, though," he added. "Maybe one day you wake up and look at someone you've known for a while and realize that the *wow* is right there in the room with you both."

And as he looked at her, he knew it was true now. *Wow* was as real as the balloons and the remainder of the birthday cake that read THDAY KAYLA. But for God's sake, he couldn't let *wow* lead him around this time! It might be zinging from wall to wall and floor to ceiling, but he was an older man, a widower, a father with two kids who couldn't just follow where *wow* led.

He had responsibilities; she had the world ahead to explore.

But he couldn't just blurt out the Europe offer to her now, either. Not with wrapping paper all around and balloons in the air. Not while she was putting in her earbuds and smiling at him like a hero for piecing together a playlist for her.

Goddamn, she was so sweet.

So hot.

And he wasn't ready to open the door for her to go away quite yet.

Chapter Six

Though it was technically her day off, Kayla pitched in with the cake cleanup and then the organization of the kids' evening events. Both had sleepover invitations that night and she would see them off before meeting her old friend for dinner. She handed the sleeping bags to Mick after fetching them from the hall closet.

"You have plans tonight, right?" he asked. "More birthday celebrating?"

"Sure."

"Your family?"

"Sure," she said again, though she didn't know why she bothered to lie about it. Still, it made her feel better, somehow, for Mick to think she was connected to something bigger, something like he had with his kids. She didn't want to feel like the unwanted, forgotten appendage to her mother's and father's new tribes, let alone have someone else—Mick—see her that way.

Jane showed up in the doorway to her room. "Help me find something to wear and then help me with my hair...pleaaase," she said, in that new dramatic manner she had, as if world peace and global hunger both dangled in the balance. "If you flat iron mine, I'll do yours."

Mick frowned. "Doesn't that flat-iron thing take a while? Kayla probably wants to relax before her big family deal tonight."

The big family deal that wasn't. Kayla could use a distraction from that fact. "Choosing clothes and playing with hair...there's nothing more relaxing than those two pastimes."

It didn't take long to pick out an outfit for Jane's sleepover. Mick was adamant that an eleven-year-old should dress like a girl and—as he'd said for Kayla's ears only—not like a sex-starved single woman. Because Kayla figured she *was* a sex-starved single woman, she had little trouble directing Jane to appropriate choices during shopping trips. Tonight they selected from the girl's closet a pair of lace-edged leggings and a two-piece tunic. A long, racer-back striped tee was layered over a white, peasant-styled blouse. With the addition of black flats, she looked appropriate *and* stylish.

They left the hall door leading to the bathroom open as they waited for the flat iron to heat. Jane's hair was as dark as her father's and thicker than Kayla's. The straightening process wasn't a quick one, but the shiny result was enough to make the effort worthwhile. Once they'd achieved the girl's straight, silky fall, Kayla switched places with her.

As Jane worked on a section of Kayla's hair, Lee wandered in to sit on the edge of the tub. "I like your hair the normal way, La-La. The wavy way, like a lasagna noodle."

Jane rolled her eyes. "Just what a woman wants to hear—being compared to something you serve with pasta sauce and cheese. You'll never get a girlfriend, Lee."

"Fine with me." He shrugged. "I don't want a girlfriend, not ever."

His sister shook her head. "You say that now. But what about when you're older? When you're in your twenties, do you want to be all alone?"

"La-La's in her twenties. She's all alone."

"Gee, thanks for that little reminder, buddy," Kayla said, grimacing. "But I should point out, Jane, that a person doesn't necessarily need a girlfriend or a boyfriend—a love interest, let's just say—in order to live a happy and complete life."

"Yeah, Jane," Lee chimed in. "Look at Dad. He doesn't have somebody and he's happy."

Jane pursed her lips and met Kayla's eyes. "Do you think that's so?" she asked softly. "Do you think he's happy?"

"I..." Kayla hesitated, unsure what to say. While it would be easy to tell Mick's daughter to put that question to the man herself, Jane was smart enough to know he'd answer in the affirmative no matter what the state of his true feelings. As the nanny, the caretaker of the children, wasn't it up to her to also float the possibility that Mick might find companionship one day? That it was a normal, healthy urge to want to share your life with another person?

"I think your father has you two special somebodies to love who keep his life very full," she finally replied, chickening out.

"My friend Drea's dad went on vacation to some beachy place and came home married to a woman she'd never met before—and that her dad had never met before his vacation, either! That would be so weird."

"Love can make people impulsive sometimes," Kayla said.

"What's *impulsive?*" Lee asked.

"When a person does something quickly and without a lot of thinking about it first."

"That doesn't sound like Dad," Lee announced, with an air of decided satisfaction.

It doesn't sound like me either, Kayla thought, though she wasn't certain she felt as content as Lee at the idea. Twenty-seven years old tomorrow, and she couldn't think of one time when she hadn't considered long and hard before doing anything more complicated than changing brands of toothpaste.

That Drea's dad had gone off on a vacation and come home with someone to love…well, right now that impetuous act sounded more romantic than wrong. She sighed to herself, wondering if that was what she needed—a change of scenery.

Or at least a drink with a little umbrella in it.

When she was out with Karen tonight, Kayla would order one with a silly-sounding name and see if her luck changed. She smiled at the thought and pleasant anticipation of the evening ahead blossomed.

"Still," Jane said, moving to work on the other side of Kayla's hair, "you never know. Dad could marry someone else, Lee."

The boy frowned. "Why would he want to do that?"

"To have a wife again. To get you a mother who will spank you when you're bad."

"Jane!" Kayla glared up at the girl. "Don't talk like that to your brother."

A glint appeared in the girl's eye. "Maybe she won't spank you, Lee. Maybe your new mother will only make you go to bed without dinner or video games."

"She'd be your mother, too—and maybe she'd say you're ugly and you smell like a pickle burp."

A pickle burp? Kayla just managed to hang on to her straight face. "*I'm* going to punish both of you with no TV tomorrow if you keep this up. Let's try to be nice to each other, huh?"

There was a common moment of semisullen silence, then Lee began thumping the heels of his rubber-soled shoes against the tub's porcelain. "I don't like talking about a new mother," he confessed. "I barely remember my real mother."

"Oh, Lee." Kayla's heart squeezed. He'd been only two when she'd died, so of course his memories had to be very dim, indeed.

"She used to have me pick out my barrettes before she brushed my hair in the morning," Jane said. "It didn't matter if they went with what I was wearing or even if they matched."

Kayla surreptitiously rubbed her knuckles over the

center of her chest. Jane had never mentioned that before, and she was sure that when she took over the little girl's care she'd likely done the barrette selection herself. "I wish I'd known," she said, touching the girl's hand. "I would have let you do the choosing, too."

Jane shook her head, her unfettered hair swirling around her shoulders. "It's all right. It wouldn't have been the same anyway."

No. And Kayla had never tried to mother them at the beginning. Aware that there wasn't a person who could step in and take on that role when they were still bewildered by their loss, she'd treated them more like an older sister would. Later, as time went on, she'd recognized her maternal feelings toward the kids, but had realized she couldn't expect them to ever feel toward her the reciprocal daughter-and-son sentiments.

"I really only remember her yellow sweatshirt," Lee suddenly said. "It was soft and the color of the sun, and I can picture her leaning over me at night to turn off the light and then tuck me in. Then I felt just as warm and happy as that sunny shirt."

Kayla froze. Oh. Oh, God. She knew that sweatshirt. Just as she knew the woman wearing it hadn't been Lee's mom. When she'd first started working for the family she'd worn her good-luck, high school sweatshirt over her T-shirt and jeans nearly every day. One of the school colors was egg yolk–yellow, and she remembered how much the little boy had loved it—even asked about it after she'd lost the thing during some park outing or another.

Meaning the memory Lee had of his mother was a memory of Kayla instead, which of course she could never say.

And she couldn't cry about it in front of him, either.

"Hair done?" she said, her voice tight but bright as she stood.

"I guess," Jane answered, moving back. "Though—"

"Though nothing. It's perfect." Kayla barely glanced at her reflection in the mirror. "I've got to get going so I'm ready for my evening out."

By breathing deeply, she made it to her room without emotion overcoming her. There, she sat on the edge of the bed, taking more steady breaths to keep herself from toppling onto the mattress and succumbing to sadness.

It hit her anyway, though, and it was then she remembered Mick's words she'd heard earlier that day.

We should be thinking about getting a new Kayla.

Now she thought she understood what he'd been getting at. He realized that she was too close to the kids. They weren't her children; she wasn't their mother, and forgetting that could end in heartache, especially for her.

The solution? As Mick had said, the family was going to need a new nanny. She would have to move on, to another family or another kind of situation. Soon.

Leaping to her feet, she decided to leave early for her dinner. She was still in her dress and boots from her lunch date so there was no need to change. It would be better to get out of the house ASAP and at least start pretending to have a good time. She grabbed her cell phone from the bedside table. It was in her hand as she rushed toward the front door. Mick was just stepping over its threshold.

"Dropped them off," he said, smiling at her. "On your way out to your birthday celebration?"

"Yeah." Her gaze shifted to her phone as it buzzed in her hand. An incoming text message. It only took a moment to read the short line.

To realize…

Mick put his hand on her arm. "Kayla? What's wrong?"

To her dismay, she burst into tears. Already in emotional overload thanks to Lee's memory of the sweatshirt and her awareness that she couldn't stay the family's nanny forever, the text message sent her straight over the edge.

Mick's grasp on her tightened. "Kayla?" he said again.

"There's not going to be a birthday celebration," she confessed. "I'm all dressed up with no place to go."

It was just like Mick had imagined a week before. A date scene. Small table covered in white cloth. Gleaming cutlery. A bottle of wine and two glasses.

Kayla's birthday dinner.

When she'd blurted out that she was all dressed up with no place to go, what other option had there been? Well, there'd been another option, that of him comforting Kayla in the now-childless house, and that had seemed like a terrible idea. Hell, terri*fying*.

So he'd handed her a handkerchief, quickly changed into slacks and a sports shirt, then hustled her out, driving them both to a spot where men took women who were dressed in pretty clothes and whose blond hair fell in a shining, touch-me waterfall. Sure, it was a date scene, but at least thirty inches of table-top separated them.

She was still just the nanny, he told himself.

Sad and in need of a friend, but just the nanny all the same.

He clinked the rim of his wineglass against hers as the waiter settled the bottle onto the table and then turned away. "What should we toast to?"

"Me not making such a fool of myself ever again."

Her waterworks had been brief, but their aftereffect had lasted long enough for him to get her to his car and to the restaurant with minimum protest. She sighed, obviously doubting the wisdom of it now. "I don't know why I let you take me here. I'm sorry, Mick."

"There's nothing to be sorry about." He sipped at the wine. "You comfort and care for my family every day. I don't mind offering a little of that back."

"You probably had plans for yourself tonight." The only evidence left of her emotional outbreak was the flush on her cheeks and clearly embarrassment had overcome her sadness.

"The only plan I had was kicking back in front of the TV. Fifteen minutes of that in a house without the kids and I would have been so bored I wouldn't know what to do with myself."

"Then maybe you would have popped up from the couch and done…I don't know. Something."

"Yeah, because I'm so impulsive like that."

She grimaced. "Funny, the kids and I were talking about impulsiveness today. I got to thinking about how less-than-spontaneous I am. Have you ever thought you could use a little recklessness in your life?"

"You, Miss Twentysomething, can be reckless," he said, pointing in her direction. "Me? Father of two? I'm better off being a stick in the mud."

Shaking her head, she smiled at him. The candlelight flickered, casting shadows under her cheekbones and bringing a sparkle to her big blue eyes. His gaze dropped to her mouth, her throat, and farther to her—no, that way lay danger. He forced himself to look back up.

"Mick…" she started.

"Mick…what?" He smiled too, now, pretending his attention hadn't wandered. "Mick, you're exactly right, you're one step away from the retirement home?"

"No." She laughed. "More like, Mick, you're an attractive, sexy guy who should—"

The waiter arrived with their meals and she stopped talking as he served their plates. Mick promised himself he would leave the rest of her sentence well enough alone. It seemed like a stupid idea to insist she finish her thought. *Mick, you're an attractive, sexy guy who should…*

Stop thinking sexy thoughts about the attractive nanny a mere thirty inches away.

The attractive, sexy nanny who would go home with him tonight to an empty house.

He tried drowning that small fact in a large swallow of wine. Then he applied himself to his food, letting silence fall between them until he could think of something besides dark rooms and satiny skin. *You're here for a reason,* he reminded himself. *Remember that friendly comfort you wanted to offer Kayla?*

"So what's going on?" he asked, putting that parental timbre into his voice he used when he was trying to shake down the kids for information on the source of a sibling squabble or what weekend homework was yet unfinished. "What upset you earlier? It was more than the canceled dinner."

She glanced up at him, then back to her food. "It's nothing."

"Kayla." He waited until she looked up again. "We're buddies, right? Let me help."

"Buddies." Her smile was rueful. "No. We're boss and employee."

"Not only that," he insisted. He didn't want to get more specific, he shouldn't get more specific, but he also couldn't let her get away without asking about those tears. "Face it. We're almost fam—"

"Don't say the word," she put in quickly. "Don't say family."

He raised an eyebrow. "Is this about yours and your birthday celebration that isn't?"

She sighed, then looked away, her fingers toying with the stem of her wineglass. "The truth is, I was supposed to be meeting an old friend. There was no birthday celebration planned with my parents and half siblings. They usually forget."

"About the date?"

"About me."

He attempted to keep up. "I'm aware your parents are divorced…"

"And when I was about Jane's age, each remarried and went on to have more children with their respective new spouse. I have seven half siblings. I'm the only one who is the product of my mother's and father's relationship."

"How does that explain forgetting your birthday?" He was a father. He had kids. How could you forget the date a child came into your life?

She shrugged. "Think about it. I'm the inconvenient one. The one that doesn't completely belong with either tribe."

Mick stared. "For God's sake, Kayla. That's not a reason to forget about you."

"It's no big deal. I understand it—I understood it

years ago. I remember when my dad was looking for a new job. It was right after I graduated from high school and he wanted to show me what a résumé looked like. The last line read, 'Married, with four children,' and there it was. He has four kids with his second wife. I wasn't one that counted."

Mick felt… Mick didn't want to feel. Maybe if he was just some guy, he could have adopted her casual attitude. But he was a father, and the idea of ever pretending, ignoring—what would you call it?—one of his children made his belly ache. And more…so much more, he hated the idea that Kayla had been hurt, no matter how she tried to dismiss it. Appetite gone, he pushed his plate away and saw that she'd already abandoned hers.

"Are you ready to head home, honey?" he asked, aware of the intimacy of the question and the tenderness in his voice, yet not regretting either.

"Yes," she said. "I'm ready."

His arm naturally went around her waist as they walked toward the exit once the bill was paid. In the foyer, he was surprised to find his friend and fellow firefighter Will Dailey. The other man stood beside his wife, obviously waiting to be led to a table. Mick's feet slowed as Will's gaze landed on the proprietary hand he had on the nanny.

Just the nanny, he reminded himself, letting his arm slide away.

Kayla knew Will and his wife, Emily. The station was another kind of family and she'd met those two at summer barbecues and at potluck dinners the station hosted for those working the holiday shifts. They exchanged a round of pleasantries, and Kayla expressed delight in the news that the other couple was expecting a baby. It was news to Mick, too. He clapped his buddy on the back and kissed Emily on the cheek.

It was Mick's wife, Ellen, who had wanted children early in their marriage. He hadn't objected, though honestly, he hadn't felt as compelled as his wife to start diapering so soon. Now, though, he couldn't imagine life without Jane and Lee. Not only because they were his remaining link to Ellen, but because… they were who they were. Because they made his life richer and brighter.

He grinned at Will. "You get to do Disneyland again," he said. "You don't know how much you've missed the magic of Mickey until you go back with your own little ones." That's what they did, he thought. Kids brought special magic into an adult's life.

A woman could do that, too, Mick realized, as he drove Kayla home. He breathed in her scent and the danger he'd felt at the beginning of the evening at the idea of being alone with her dissipated. It was pleasure he felt at her warm presence beside him. There was no denying the appreciation he had of her beauty, the loveliness he found in her silky hair, blue eyes, tender mouth.

The darkness closed around them, intimate and private, as they walked into the house. They came through the back door and into the kitchen, their feet pausing at that exact spot on the hardwood floor where he'd instructed her on how to kiss.

Her gaze turned up to his. A new tension rose, swirling as thick as the darkness and the unfamiliar quiet. He knew Kayla sensed it, too, because her voice turned breathless. "Well," she said, low and husky. "Well."

"Well," he whispered back, smiling a little. "Well."

Why had he been concerned about this closeness with her? he wondered. It seemed as unsurprising as it was easy now, a simple extension of all the ways they teamed together as a unit to keep their intertwined lives running smoothly. He almost laughed at himself at the thought, because did he really think it was so simple as breakfast, lunch, bed? But it *was* simple in that it didn't require anything but breathing for him to want her as he hadn't remembered wanting anyone before.

He'd been close to Kayla tonight, closer than he'd been to a woman in years and elevating that intimacy to another level seemed natural now, not problematic.

Maybe one day you wake up and look at someone you've known for a while and realize that the wow *is right there in the room with you both.*

Right now, something was in the room with them for sure. Desire. Need. Sex.

She was so damn irresistible, with her shiny blond hair, her sweet scent, her lovely eyes that he'd been staring into all night long. "God, Kayla."

"Mick…" Her gaze heated and he saw the same yearning on her face.

He cupped her head in his big hands. She made a sound low in her throat, and then there was no more thinking or considering or even second-guessing. Her mouth, so soft and luscious-looking, was impossible to turn away from. He found himself taking it, taking her into his arms, feeling her female shape against his body, tasting the warm, wet flavor of her mouth. God. God.

The quiet tightened around them. Their kiss deepened and she melted along his hard frame. The surrender of it galvanized him. Desire speared through him, a flame that burned and fired his need. His hands tightening on her, he backed her toward her room.

Her bed.

Once beside it, he had to be sure. "Kayla?"

"Yes," she said, answering his unspoken question. "I told you I need a little recklessness in my life."

Chapter Seven

A woman could want a warm body in her bed on her birthday, right? That it was technically the night before her birthday didn't matter. That it was technically Mick Hanson, not just some warm body, didn't matter, either.

Who was she kidding? That it was Mick Hanson only made it the best present ever.

She ignored any twinges of concern that this would change things forever between them. It didn't need to. And anyway, who could predict forever? Nothing was predictable except that at this moment she couldn't move away from Mick.

His mouth trailed across her cheek and down her

neck, inciting goose bumps and then chasing them with his tongue. Her pulse thrummed and her body shivered against his. "Cold?" he whispered.

She shook her head and ran her hands up his chest. His muscles, those hard muscles that she'd been watching for years as he walked half-naked up the stairway to his shower, hardened against her palm. She crowded closer, unable to help herself from pushing her belly against the stone strength of his sex. He groaned, his hips pushing back against hers. "Kayla, sweetheart. I want to take this slowly."

"No," she murmured, drawing his mouth back to hers. "Now. More." As sure that she couldn't predict forever, she also couldn't predict past the single instants ahead—the next kiss and then the next touch. If they lingered, she was afraid something would interrupt—conscience, kids, a call from the fire station.

The fragility of this moment, like a bath bubble floating in the air, only made her heart pump faster. Her mouth opened under his and her hands drew along the cotton of his shirt to his buttons. They clumsily unfastened them.

I ironed this shirt, she realized. She'd hung the pants he'd take off to take her. The thought made her fingers fumble. What was so familiar—his clothes, his body, his voice—would all take on a different kind of familiarity once they took this step.

The turn of her mind must have telegraphed to him. He lifted his head, his gaze trained on her face, his mouth curved in a half smile. With his thumb, he traced the wet surface of her bottom lip. "I want you," he said. "But only if—"

"I want you, too," she interrupted, determined again. She made a second awkward attack on his buttons.

He chuckled, a soft, sexy sound, then pushed her fingers away. "I'll do that."

"Okay." She reached for the zipper at the back of her dress.

His hand captured hers. "I'll do that, too."

In fact, he did it first. His mouth came back to the side of her neck as his fingers latched on to the tab of her zipper. The rasp of it sliding down sounded loud in the dark. Air touched her spine as the sides of her dress parted, and it felt like a succession of cool kisses. More of them tickled across her shoulders as Mick pushed the fabric over them and it dropped to the ground.

He shifted back to stare at her body.

Cool turned hot as she saw his gaze move over her white lacy bra and matching panties. With her high-heeled black boots, she supposed she didn't look much like a nanny at the moment. "Mick…" she whispered, shaking.

His callused palm cupped her cheek. "You're so beautiful," he said, then let that raspy skin move down her neck, across her throat and around to her fabric-covered breast. He rested his hand there a moment, and she felt her nipple tighten against the slight pressure as her heart pounded in insistence.

"Mick…" she said again, a longing note in her voice.

His fingers slid beneath her bra, the tips just brushing the aching center. She swayed toward him, anxious, needy, so ready for more. *"Mick."*

He took his touch away. She swallowed her moan because he reached around to unlatch her bra. It fell to the ground, the white startling against the shiny leather of her black boots. His gaze followed hers to the sight, then moved upward slowly, past her calves, her trembling knees, her thighs. His hand joined in, caressing her flank, then catching on the elastic edge at the top of her panties.

Just that, and melting heat flooded between her legs. She felt her flesh soften and swell. He stared at his long fingers as they toyed there, rubbing the lace, then sliding beneath to the tender skin covering her hipbone.

Kayla couldn't breathe. She couldn't think beyond *hurry. Hurry, hurry.*

But Mick was still in slow motion, and apparently mesmerized by his own hand or the feel of her flesh beneath it or both. Then he stepped close again. His cloth-covered chest brushed against her tightened nipples as he took her mouth in another possessive kiss. Both hands slid beneath her panties to grasp the globes of her bottom. She pressed herself against his erection, giving in to the kiss, giving everything she had to him.

Her panties skimmed down her thighs. At his urging, she found herself stepping out of them. Then he broke the kiss and moved away once more, and she realized she was naked—except for her knee-high black boots.

She wasn't the nanny anymore.

And she figured that's exactly what Mick wanted.

Even though she was as turned on as she'd been a moment before, she felt herself relax. Okay. Okay. From the avid look on his face, this wasn't something she had to rush through before the Cinderella spell was broken and they found themselves fully clothed and washing dishes or sweeping floors.

On a slow turn, she reached for the covers on the bed to draw them back. She could feel Mick's gaze on her backside, and she let herself picture what he did—her pale skin gleaming in the light filtering from the hall, her black boots with their darker, naughtier shine. The image paralyzed her for a moment, and then Mick was behind her, the crispness of his clothes brushing her shoulder blades and her bottom. His hand caressed her hip.

"I'll never look at boots the same way again," he said.

She titled her head to rest against his shoulder. He hadn't said he'd never look at her the same way again, but that wasn't the point. The point was, it was Kayla's birthday and he was her gift of the night.

His palms covered her breasts. With a gentle touch, he molded them, exploring their weight. When his thumbs brushed her nipples, she whimpered.

He kissed his way down her neck and his fingers plucked at those ruched tips, each little pinch tighter than the one before. She pushed back with her hips, loving the scrape of cloth against her, but wanting him naked even more. Her hands moved behind her and she yanked the tails of his shirt from his waistband.

"Get naked," she whispered, deciding a girl in black boots could give an order or two.

He laughed again, his breath warm against her throat. "If you get on the bed."

She did so, eagerly. He shed his shirt first. It fell on top of her discarded clothes and the mere symbolism of it goosed her with a little sexual thrill. His eyes narrowed at the shiver that ran through her. She thought his breathing moved in and out a little faster.

Then his hands shifted to the fastening of his pants. It took only a moment for him to shuck the rest of his clothing, and she was glad for it, because she couldn't find air in the time it took for him to get completely naked. Her heart shut down in anticipation. She'd seen him from the waist up. She'd seen him from the knees down. But now she had it all, including his long, muscled thighs and the matching erection already in its fully aroused state.

He set a condom on the bedside table—had it been in his wallet? His pocket?—then he crawled onto the bed, and her heartbeat restarted. Operating on instinct, she parted her thighs and he fastened his gaze on her slick center as he moved closer. "Kayla," he said, and two of his fingers reached out to skate over the swollen flesh. "You're so beautiful all over."

She was burning, that was sure. As he played with her drenched tissues, she sank deeper into the pillows. Her thighs opened wider, giving him more access. A finger slid inside and she gasped, her hips bowing. Mick glanced up. "I promise I won't hurt you. Just open up for me, baby."

He eased a second finger inside and the fit was tight. Deliciously tight. She writhed against them and then writhed some more as his thumb nudged the bud at the top of her sex. "Mick." Her head thrashed on the pillows and she reached out to palm his shoulder. "Please."

"Yes," he murmured. "I'll please you." And then he moved over her, taking a nipple in his mouth as his fingers continued to fondle her sex.

Her fists gripped the sheets. He plumped the other breast with his free hand and she went wild at the different caresses: the wet suction of his mouth, the tender touch on her breast, the insistent impalement of his thrusting hand and that arousing, knowing thumb.

When his mouth switched to her other nipple, when his fingers thrust and his thumb pressed one time, a second, she pushed into those maddening touches…and came.

Maybe he was maddened, too, because just as her quakes turned into shivers he slid his hand away and impaled her with something else instead. But he was going slow again, entering her in increments of inches, taking his time to fully seat himself. When he was inside her all the way, he groaned, and came down on her mouth in a hot kiss, his tongue thrusting.

She wrapped her legs around him, the leather of her boots sliding against his hips. It was another image she'd take with her forever and she held it in her mind as their bodies rocked into sweet, sweet oblivion.

When it was over, he rolled to the pillow beside her, and then rolled her against his side. She put her head on his shoulder and listened to the thudding beat of his heart. His hand made soothing passes along her upper arm as her gaze found the bedside clock. Midnight.

Happy birthday, she mouthed to herself. *Yes, indeed, you gave yourself quite the present.*

And she didn't regret a moment of it, even as things he'd said and promises she'd made to herself came back to her.

He'd said: *I'll please you.*

She'd thought: *Having sex wouldn't change things between them.*

He'd said: *I'll never hurt you.*

Ah, well. Of the three, she suspected only the first would stand the test of time.

In the morning, Kayla awoke to an empty bed and the sound of dishes clattering in the kitchen. Maybe it had been a dream, she thought for a moment, but then she spied her boots, left right where Mick had tossed them last night after they'd made love and before he'd pulled the covers around them.

Her skin heated at the memories and she wondered exactly how to handle this morning-after business. Without hiding, she decided, getting up and heading for the shower. She was twenty-seven and old enough, woman enough, not to slink around like she was ashamed or embarrassed. Checking herself in the mirror, she didn't blush at the fact that the pink shirt she wore with jeans was one button lower than usual, that she'd double-coated her mascara or that her mouth was still so red from his kisses that she didn't need lipstick.

Her head was high as she walked into the kitchen.

But her heart sank. Because there he was, like a hundred times before and yet it was like no other time before. His back was to her as he worked at the stove while wearing another pair of worn jeans and a ratty T-shirt that she should have consigned to the rag bag ages ago.

I could just rip it off him right now, she thought. Smooth over this morning-after business by smoothing her hands up the muscles of his back, only to smooth them down the front of his chest to the fastening of his pants.

Perhaps she made some sort of sound at that, because he glanced over his shoulder. Smiled.

"Sleepyhead." He said it fondly, as if she was Jane or Lee. "Happy birthday." Then he pushed a mug of hot coffee in her hand and pulled out a chair for her at the kitchen table.

Unsure what else to do, she sat, then couldn't help her own smile when he served her a breakfast plate: bacon, wheat toast, a pile of sunny scrambled eggs topped by a pink birthday candle.

Who wouldn't be in love with that? With him.

She was in love with Mick. She'd admitted that to herself over a week ago. Even though she didn't believe he reciprocated those feelings, that didn't mean they couldn't explore this new territory of their relationship, right? She'd gone into it as a one-night stand and she'd been afraid it would alter what they already had together…but was that such a bad thing? Couldn't they have an affair with the hope that it might lead to more?

She was old enough, woman enough, to express that plainly, right?

He was staring at her. "Well?"

Oh, God. Was she supposed to blurt it out right

now, right here, over scrambled eggs and strawberry jam? "Um…what?"

"Well, aren't you going to make a wish?"

"Oh." She relaxed against the back of the chair. "Sure." Closing her eyes, she tried formulating words that would express her greatest hope and her greatest fear.

Don't let what I say ruin anything.

The wish wasn't perfectly precise, but she blew out the birthday candle anyway.

Mick took the seat across from hers, and just as if it was any other day, he handed her the front section of the newspaper and picked up the sports page for himself. The only thing missing was the kids squabbling over who got the prize in the cereal box. Now it was her turn to stare. Did he really expect it to go like this?

After a moment, he glanced up. A wry smile flashed over his face. "Sorry. Am I doing it wrong? I'm not well-practiced in mornings-after."

"That makes both of us." She tried out her own little smile.

He folded up his section of newspaper. "Maybe we can muddle along together."

"We've managed to do that for the last six years, I guess." Surely they could muddle their way into an affair and then…

"Yeah." But his expression closed and he glanced away from her. "Kayla…"

Her belly hopped at the note of regret in his voice. She swallowed, though, determined to not let this chance pass by. "Let's be honest with each other, Mick."

"All right. I think that's a good idea."

"I know last night I said I wanted to be reckless, but it…" She was losing her nerve. "It didn't feel reckless with you."

He reached across the table for her hand. "I'll take that as a compliment. You mean a lot to me, Kayla."

It wasn't exactly a declaration on the scale of what she wanted to say to him, but still she steeled herself to put her heart on the line. "And Mick—"

"That's why I feel so guilty."

She stilled. "Guilty?"

"Guilty," he confirmed. "I've known something for more than a week, after a talk I had with Patty Bright. She, uh, told me something about you."

Heat washed up Kayla's throat. Patty Bright was a nice woman who had been close to Mick's wife. Had she detected Kayla's feelings for her friend's husband? It was one thing for her to tell him herself, but what if the two of them had been talking about the lovesick nanny? Maybe even laughing about the lovesick nanny.

Her stomach churned. "I don't know what she could know about me," she said. "We're only casual acquaintances."

Mick grimaced. "She knows you better than you might think."

So Patty had told Mick that Kayla had feelings for him and now he felt guilty because last night he'd come to her bed out of...what? Pity? At the thought, Kayla rocketed to her feet. "I think you've got the situation entirely wrong." To hell with honesty. And she didn't need to sit here and be humiliated. "I have to...get going. Do something. Visit my family."

He raised an eyebrow at the blatant lie. "What's got you running, honey?"

"I don't like Patty discussing me." Kayla's voice was as hot as her face.

"Only because she didn't want to poach without giving me a heads-up first."

"Huh?" Wait. "What?"

Mick sighed. "Sit down?"

Confused, she returned to her seat. "I don't understand what's going on."

"Because I've been holding back on you." He took a breath, blew it out. "Here goes. Patty wants you to go to work for her family."

That cleared up nothing. "I have a job. Here."

"But the Bright family has an opportunity to spend several months in Europe. They thought you might see it as an opportunity for yourself, as well."

Kayla blinked. Europe? With another family? Leave Mick and Jane and Lee?

We should be thinking about getting a new Kayla.

Now she thought she understood what he'd meant by that. And why he'd been floating the thought by the kids. If she went to work for the Brights, then the Hanson family would need her replacement.

But no one could replace Mick and the kids in *her* life!

"Is that what you want?" Even though her heart was going at a jackhammer pace, her voice sounded steady to her own ears. "For me to leave you?"

He closed his eyes for a moment, opened them. "What I want, Kayla, is…" His palm swiped across his face. "Look—"

"Honesty, remember?" Her heartbeat pounded so loud in her ears now she didn't know if she would hear his answer. "You promised to tell the truth."

He glanced away, then it was he who rose to his feet in an abrupt movement. "I want what I've always wanted. To raise happy and successful kids. Not to have that responsibility make me crack."

With jerky movements, he yanked open the dishwasher and loaded his plate and mug, then slammed the door shut. "Which means I want to keep all the damn balls I already have in the air."

He snatched the newspaper—unread, not that she planned on mentioning it—off the table and threw it into the recycle bin by the back door. "And not add yet another to the mess I'm already juggling." A drawer was shoved shut with the flat of his big hand. "I don't want to risk screwing everything up."

Then the frying pan landed with a clatter in the sink. "What I want, Kayla, is no more changes!" The faucet gushed on. "Is that so hellishly demanding of me?"

Kayla gasped. She'd never seen his temper flare like this before. Mick had a long fuse and he'd always managed to smother the spark before an explosion. But now he appeared a breath away from an authentic, man-size detonation.

With his back to her, he grasped the edges of the countertop. Those muscled shoulders she always so admired were tense beneath the thin cotton. "I'm sorry," he said after a moment. She heard him take in a long, audible breath, then blow it back out. "Really sorry. I don't know what's wrong with me."

She knew. Last night they'd upset the order. They'd

initiated an alteration that he didn't desire. Mick wanted a nanny, not a lover.

Meaning he definitely didn't want her in the same way that she wanted him—and he definitely didn't want to want her that way. There would be no affair with the possibility of something else altogether.

So she stood again. "I understand," she said. "I understand perfectly."

Mick spun around. "You can't. You don't. Because I don't even—" He broke off at the sound of the front door opening and children's footsteps clattering against the floorboards. Jane and Lee's father groaned. "Look—"

"I get the message," she told him, as the children's voices drew nearer. Whether he wanted her to leave his employment for Europe was unclear. But she knew perfectly well now that he didn't want their previous platonic relationship modified in the slightest way. "And I'm happy to reassure you. What's between you and me hasn't changed," she said. "And I'm quite okay with that."

It might not be honesty, but her birthday wish had come true—*Don't let what I say ruin anything*—if Mick's relieved expression told the truth that she hadn't.

Chapter Eight

Surely every parent had moments when they silently groaned at the untimely arrival of their beloved children. When assembling a tricycle, say, on Christmas Eve or when downing a spoonful of chocolate chip cookie dough straight from the tube. But this time Mick wasn't wielding a wrench or guiltily ingesting a concoction of uncooked eggs, flour and sugar. He was midway into discussing some serious subjects with the nanny.

With Kayla, whom he'd made love to the night before.

He glanced over at her as the kids came rushing into the kitchen and the closed expression on her face and her stiff posture told him everything he needed to know. He hadn't handled the morning-after thing well, not since he'd slid a breakfast plate under her pretty nose.

Damn him!

Last night had been... God, last night he'd been in bed with a naked woman wearing black leather boots! He hadn't even fantasized something so good since a million years ago before marriage and kids, and that it was Kayla's soft flesh and Kayla's sexy footwear only made it sweeter...and hotter.

The kids were chattering to them both about something and he pretended to listen as he cleaned up the pans. He'd fumbled presenting her the Europe opportunity, too. He could have mentioned it in a neutral manner, but the idea of her leaving them had singed the edges of his brain. So he'd ranted about change, stomped around like a two-year-old and generally made an ass of himself.

An ass she'd probably be happy to leave behind in the States when she went off to Europe with Poaching Patty and family.

Mick realized he was strangling a handful of cutlery, so he forced his fingers to relax and dropped them into the dishwasher. Okay, he had to calm down. He had to calm down and then talk to the nanny like a rational being and express to her that he was completely fine with her decision to leave them, if it came to that. And then he'd agree with her last statement to him. Sure, they'd been intimate last night, but that didn't mean anyone had to change their life over it.

He didn't *want* to change his life over it.

So he'd be sure the nanny understood that he understood that the joining of their bodies the night before hadn't created a snarl in their domestic lives that couldn't be loosened.

With that decision made, he interrupted Jane's blow-by-blow description of the movie she'd watched with her girlfriends the night before. "Kids, go up to your rooms and put your sleepover stuff away. Leave the sleeping bags beside the hall closet and I'll stow them on the shelf later."

"Daddy—"

"Now, Janie." He gave her the "or else" eye, which put a puzzled look on her face, mainly, he supposed, because he wasn't big on "or else" parenting. But she left the kitchen anyway, her little brother trailing behind her.

As soon as they were gone, he turned back to Kayla. "Listen…"

She was already on her way to her room. He leaped to catch her, managing to snag her arm. They both stilled. It was the first time he'd touched her since leaving her bed. At dawn, he'd come awake, and from the pillow beside hers, he'd stared at Kayla, taking in the tumbled hair, the mouth still swollen from his kisses, the feathery delicacy of her eyelashes. He'd looked at people sleeping before—had watched his kids' snoozing away a hundred times—but watching Kayla sleep had sent him straight into panic.

Because he'd wanted to wake her up and he'd wanted to watch over her sleep—in equal measure. He'd wanted her like a man wants a woman and wanted to protect her...like a man wants to protect a woman, too.

"Kayla." Looking down, he realized they were standing in that magic place again, the one that had been the site of their first kiss and then for their next one that had led them straight to her bed. "This spot has got to be like that phantom tollbooth or that oddly numbered railway platform."

She didn't laugh. The seriousness of her expression told him he'd really, *really* blown it before. But with her so close, he couldn't seem to think of the best way to make up for it. And then he realized she was trembling at his touch, and his chest started to ache again. "Kayla," he murmured, leaning down to kiss her.

"Dad!" At Lee's shout, Kayla jerked away from

him. Her arm slid through his grasp like water, leaving his hand open…and too empty.

"Dad." Lee's sneakers slid on the hardwood floor as he came to a stop. "Where's Goblin? We can't find her anywhere."

Mick stifled his sigh. "Are you calling for her? You know that sends her deeper into hiding." The perverse creature seemed to enjoy being elusive. "Remember, we have to trick her. If you go about your business, sure enough she'll show up."

"Why are girls like that?" Lee demanded.

Jane, stepping into the kitchen, scowled at her little brother. "Maybe because boys are so stupid. Always shouting and rough."

Mick winced, thinking of his clumsiness this morning. No wonder Kayla had tried to escape to her bedroom before he could clear things up with her. "Uh, let's not use the word *stupid,* okay, people?"

His daughter's face took on that teenish stubborn cast that made him dread the future. "But, Dad—"

"Jane, why don't you check the linen closet in your bathroom?" Kayla put in. "You know how Goblin loves to knock over the stacks of towels in there. Lee, you look under your bed."

The kids filed out of the room, distracted from an incipient argument. What would they do without Kayla? Mick wondered. Surely he'd need the nanny as teen hormones continued to rise. Only she could help him manage creatures he feared might start behaving like werewolves under a perpetual full moon.

But he wasn't supposed to be thinking of a future with Kayla in it, he reminded himself, as he heard the kids' footsteps on the stairs. He was supposed to be making it clear she'd was free of him and his family if that's the way she wanted it.

Turning to her, he started the discussion that had been interrupted before. "You need—"

She clutched his arm. "Mick," she whispered. "Did you bring in the cat last night?"

His eyes widened. Crap. *Crap.* Goblin had adopted them at approximately age one and she'd clearly been accustomed to being outdoors at least part of the day. They managed to get her in each night—though he didn't want to think about how often he'd had to wander around the yard to lure her from the darkness with a piece of cheese or salami. Yeah, she was a deli kind of cat. But last night…

"Last night I wasn't thinking of much besides…"

"I know." She bit her lip even as her grip tightened on his arm. "We should have remembered, though. Think of all those gruesome coyote stories we've heard."

He saw her shudder. "It's going to be okay. We'll fan out, find her safe and sound somewhere."

Although she nodded, her face looked miserable. The ache in his chest sharpened. "Honey," he said, tucking her hair behind her ear. The strand was silky and her skin so soft beneath his fingertips. It was bad of him, he knew it, but he bent and left a swift, hard kiss on her mouth. "We'll handle it."

"Okay." She nodded again. "Okay. We always handle what comes, don't we?"

"Yeah, but—" Then the kids were there again.

"No Goblin," they said together, both small faces worried.

Mick slapped his hands together. "Let's go track her down, then. Backyard, front yard. After that, we'll hit the sidewalk if she hasn't shown up."

She didn't show up.

Thirty minutes passed and they had to conclude that the cat either wasn't nearby or she wasn't coming out of hiding even for turkey bologna or a slice of Monterey Jack. "Damn it," he murmured to Kayla. "Really, does she have to be this difficult?"

"Are you talking about me, Daddy?" Jane demanded, popping up at his elbow.

He was not going to survive to see her at seventeen, he thought, pressing his fingers to his throbbing temple. And then Lee was tugging on the hem of his shirt. "Promise me, Dad," his son said, with tears in his eyes. "Promise me we'll get Goblin back."

A hammer went to work on Mick's other temple. It was a parent's nightmare, being asked to make promises he knew he couldn't guarantee. "Sure, son," he said, pulling the little kid close. And then Jane did one of her child-teen turnarounds and threw herself against him, too.

Kayla stood nearby, looking just as glum as the kids. Without a second thought, he scooped her into the family embrace. He didn't feel guilty about it, not for a second, even though he realized a group hug wasn't the best way to untangle the new knot of intimacy they'd recklessly created the night before.

After the upheaval of the past week—the unsatisfactory aftermath of the night with Mick, the unsettling news of the European nanny job, the continued and upsetting absence of Goblin the cat—it became clear to Kayla that she needed to find ways to loosen her ties to the Hanson family. When Joe Tully, her recent blind date, had called yet again, she'd stopped making excuses and agreed to go out with him again.

Maybe she'd been wrong about her feelings for Mick.

And maybe *wow* could arrive on the second date.

She drove to the restaurant under her own steam, unwilling to introduce Joe to the Hanson family. Tonight was supposed to be about distancing herself from them, and she tried envisioning each block was a mile as she drove to a local seafood-and-steak place that she'd suggested. As she walked inside, she smoothed her soft, printed skirt and checked that the thin cardigan she wore with it was buttoned securely to the throat.

Her date stood up and kissed her cheek when she found him in the bar. Joe was not yet thirty and he wore a pair of flat-front khaki pants and a knit shirt that displayed an impressive breadth of shoulder and well-developed biceps. His medium brown hair was clipped short, he had friendly green eyes, and he smelled like an insert in a men's magazine.

"I'm glad we could finally get together again," he said, as they took their seats and the waitress settled them with drinks on small square napkins. "I thought we might not have a chance before I had to go out of town again."

"My calendar has its own limitations," she said. "I work around a firefighter's schedule, meaning there are stretches when I'm responsible for the kids twenty-four hours a day."

"But you said it was a good position for you while

you were going to college. Now that you have your degree are you going to use it?"

She'd thought she might. Teaching or counseling at the elementary level held a definite appeal, although each would require more schooling. "I haven't been considering much beyond my next homework assignment and the family's next load of laundry for so many years that it's hard to wrap my mind around the future."

"You could do anything," Joe said. "Think about it, you're young, healthy, single. Though I sometimes complain about all the travel I do for my job, most of the time I really enjoy it. Highly recommend seeing as much as you can of wherever you can afford to go."

Like Europe. At twenty, she'd taken off for the summer and bummed around several western European countries. Everyone she'd told about it before or since assumed it was the adventure of a lifetime—and she had taken pleasure in seeing sights that she'd only read about before. But she'd also experienced a heavy sense of loneliness as she wandered down the streets of London and the lanes of Provence. Adventures— at least for her, she realized—needed a partner and she hadn't been able to shake the notion that if she'd disappeared in the middle of Covent Garden that no one would have noticed...or cared.

Upon coming home, she'd almost immediately made herself indispensable to the Hansons. But sometimes she wondered who needed whom the most.

This night was supposed to take her away from them and those kinds of thoughts. So she pasted on a friendly smile and encouraged Joe to tell her his favorite travel destinations. He was waxing on about a trip to the Florida Keys when her chair was bumped by someone heading for a bar stool. "I'm sorry," the woman automatically said, but then she paused. "Kayla! Hey, good to see you."

Marcia Wells was a young mother she knew from Jane and Lee's elementary school and whose dimples dug deep when she smiled. Usually she was dressed in bright workout gear, but now she had on dark jeans and a pretty blouse with silk ruffles around the plunging neckline.

"You and Wayne are out on the town tonight?" Kayla guessed.

The other woman wiggled in a little jig, her high heels tapping on the floor. "Date night with my hubby. Moms like us don't get many of those—" She broke off, obviously realizing a moment late that Kayla wasn't anyone's mother. Her gaze jumped across the table to handsome Joe. "Um, it looks like you're having a good time, too."

Kayla made the obligatory introductions. "Marcia

and I served on the Faculty Follies PTA committee," she explained to Joe.

"We were in charge of the refreshments last year. This girl and I make a mean fruit punch," Marcia boasted, her dimples flickering again. Then her gaze caught on a figure entering the bar. "Here's Wayne now. You two have a good time!"

"Likewise," Kayla murmured to the woman's retreating back. Then she glanced at Joe, who was studying her with a new intensity, his green eyes narrowed. "Um? Do I have margarita salt on my nose?"

He shook his head. "Nah. I'm just catching on to what you do, is all. You're not just the nanny. You don't just babysit those kids."

She shrugged, for some reason embarrassed. "So I serve on a PTA committee or two."

"I don't even know what PTA stands for."

"You'll find out someday, I'm sure," she said.

Now it was his turn to shrug. "I'm in no hurry, believe me. My brother has kids and all he does is tell me about how much they cost and how they can't even walk down the street by themselves. He's trying to channel our dad who laid down the law and woe to he who broke a single one."

Kayla tried not to frown, but Joe's brother sounded, frankly, like a jerk. Mick had never complained about the expense of raising Jane and Lee. He was a protective father, that was true, but he gave them opportunities to walk down the street and venture on other independent experiences without heavy-handed supervision. And while her own father had been good with laying down the law those weekends she'd spent with him as a child, through them she'd come to realize there was more to being a parent than rule-making. He'd been absolutely clueless about her emotional landscape.

Mick got his kids, even though he was wary of what lay ahead as Jane and Lee approached their teen years. She was convinced he'd do a good job navigating troubled waters, with or without her.

Without her. Remember? Tonight was supposed to be about their life without her—or more correctly— her life without them. So she spread another smile across her face and asked Joe about his car.

He liked to talk about his car.

The meal was delicious, though she kept sneaking glances at her watch. *Was this any way to look for* wow? she admonished herself, even as she peeked at it again. But the whole evening felt more like *whatever,* she realized, as she ordered coffee to keep him company as he ate dessert.

It was not that there was anything wrong with Joe. Enjoying travel and a single's lifestyle or expressing an uncertainty about wanting children wasn't egregious. She knew all this. It was unreasonable of her to think a man unwilling to commit to a kid didn't make good date material. But…

You get to do Disneyland all over again.

She remembered Mick saying that to his friends Will and Emily when they'd shared the news they were pregnant. Kayla understood the sentiment. Through the kids she enjoyed…well, to be honest, maybe she enjoyed the childhood she hadn't experienced.

Joe wasn't obligated to feel or appreciate the same, but at twenty-seven, should she spend her free hours with someone who didn't share her interests or focus?

Her watch didn't have the answer, but she took another glance at it anyway, frowning to see how slowly the minutes ticked by. Maybe something was wrong with it. With a vague feeling of unease tickling the nape of her neck, she excused herself.

On the way to the ladies' room, she dug into her purse for her cell phone and powered it on. Four missed calls from Mick. Her breath hitched, then she thumbed the dial button.

He picked up. "Having fun?" The light question sounded forced.

Her breath hitched again. "What's wrong?"

"Nothing. I…um, had a little moment earlier, but it's all under control now."

"'A' little moment? You called four times within ten minutes, Mick."

"Yeah, well. About that. Three of those were Lee using my phone before I stopped him. The last one was me."

"What's wrong?" she asked, repeating herself.

"Nothing. Nothing that should interrupt your evening with…uh, Jonah? Jasper?"

"Joe."

"Well, nothing should interrupt your evening with Joe. So go back to—"

"He drives a sports utility hybrid," she said quickly.

Mick was silent a moment. "Ah."

"It gets fifty miles to the gallon and has headlamp washers."

"Um," Mick said. "Green and clean."

"He doesn't think he ever wants children."

"That's not a crime."

"I keep telling myself the same." Then she hesitated. "For dessert, he ordered apple pie with whipped cream, not ice cream."

Another silence came over the line. "Well, that *is* a felony in my book."

"Mine, too," she admitted. Her hand tightened on the phone. "Why'd you call, Mick?"

She could practically hear the gears in his head turning. It took a few moments, then he finally spoke. "Could you come home, Kayla? We have a little emotional emergency on our hands."

Joe accepted her sudden defection with good grace, though she hardly took the time to assess his reaction. While she was glad Mick made clear that no one's physical health was at stake, the words "emotional emergency" had her heart pumping double time anyway.

He was waiting for her on the front porch, his hands stuffed in the pockets of his scarred leather bomber jacket. The jeans he wore had a paint stain on the knee from the time he'd helped her refurbish an old bookcase she'd found for her room. His chin was stubbled with whiskers he hadn't bothered to shave on his day off.

She ran up the walkway, desperate to cross the distance. "What's going on?" she demanded.

They stood beneath the porch light. Six months ago, she recalled, he'd found her in this exact position with that other fix-up date Betsy had talked her into. Instead of retreating to the house, he'd stood sentry, waiting for her to say goodbye and go inside. She'd felt…something vibrating off him then. Awareness? Maybe a little jealousy?

There was a mix of both in his gaze now. "Kayla. I shouldn't have—"

"Mick." She took two handfuls of leather and gave his jacket a little shake. "I'm here now."

"Yeah, but I shouldn't have imposed. I realized that the second after I hung up. You didn't answer when I called back."

"Because you couldn't have kept me away." So much for distance.

One hand emerged from his pocket and he brushed his thumb against her bottom lip. She shivered, and only barely stopped herself from tasting him with her tongue. "I'm having that same problem myself," he murmured.

Then his hand dropped as he sighed. "Are you prepared for a memorial service, honey?"

Chapter Nine

Mick had a secret. As a firefighter he'd walked into many gruesome, tragic scenes. He'd seen people's worlds shattered due to loss of property or loss of limb or life. He remained stoic and focused when on the job. It was only afterward that he'd have nightmares. For a few weeks following a particularly disturbing situation he'd endlessly dream of singed teddy bears or small, single sneakers in the middle of a highway.

He suspected many of his colleagues suffered similar symptoms and didn't talk about them—but the nightmares weren't his secret.

What Mick never let anyone know was how one

of those terrible events could make him around his kids. Watching them suffer an emotional blow while he was still undergoing the aftereffects of a stressful shift at work could bring him to his knees. He figured he'd be father toast if they ever figured it out. Dad having a bad day? Put on a sad face and he'd promise you the world to make it all better.

Two nights before they'd responded to a motor vehicle collision. A family in a compact, a guy in a construction rig. Two kids had been hurt, their mother killed. Mick didn't think he'd be sleeping well for the next month.

So when he'd caught a tear-stained Lee calling Kayla while she was on her date, Mick had found himself pretty desperate for another adult. Someone who would help him deal with what his kids had been planning since dinner. But now, faced with Kayla's concerned expression and taking in her date wear of skirt and sweater, he just felt guilty.

"You should go back to him," he said. "Finish your evening."

She crossed her arms over her chest. "Certainly not. What is this about a memorial service?"

Images flashed through his mind. The mangled car of two nights ago morphed into the car that Ellen had been driving the night she died. He remembered the bewildered expressions on his children's faces during their mother's funeral and then Lee's heartfelt distress tonight when Goblin was again a no-show for dinner.

"They want to hold a service for the cat," he explained. "A goodbye to Goblin."

"Oh, Mick."

"Yeah." He sighed. "Lee said he couldn't sleep without doing something. It was all Jane's idea." And Papa the Pamperer couldn't deny them a thing when he was under the influence of those black, sleepless nights. "You don't need to be invol—"

She was already walking through the front door. "Lee?"

The little boy rushed from the kitchen and into her arms. "La-La," he said, burying his face against her. "She didn't come home for dinner again. We don't think Goblin is *ever* coming home."

Mick felt his chest tighten. He thought his son was right and it was killing him. Kayla ran her hand over Lee's hair and looked over to meet Mick's gaze. The tears in her eyes only made him feel more like a louse. "I'm sorry," he mouthed. She deserved her evening out and he'd drawn her back to this.

"What do you and Jane have planned?" she asked Lee, her voice soft, her hand gentle on his head.

The boy's arms tightened on the nanny's middle. "We'll go outside with candles and stuff and talk about what a good cat she was. About how much we loved her."

Jane emerged from the kitchen. "Daddy, can you turn the speakers on outside so we can play Goblin's favorite song?"

"Sure." He would sing it himself—and he couldn't carry a tune in a paper bag—if he had to. "Uh, what *is* her favorite song?"

"That old one from the Christmas CD. 'Baby It's Cold Outside.'"

Dean Martin. And Deano's voice had Mick almost crying as they trooped into the chilly winter air, all of them bundled in coats. Kayla had helped Jane with the final preparations. On the round patio table sat a fat pillar candle. Its flicker added to the soft lighting from the landscape fixtures. The burly oak in the backyard stretched over them, its leafless eeriness adding to the somber mood.

"So how do we proceed, Jane?" Kayla asked, her voice hushed.

His daughter, who'd been businesslike during the organization of the ceremony, now hesitated. She shoved her hands in the pockets of her faux-fur-edged jacket. Then she looked over at Mick. "Daddy?"

Oh, God. He remembered the first night she'd sneaked into his room after Ellen was gone. He'd been trying to read in bed, when he'd really just been staring at the black squiggles on the white page. Looking up, he'd spotted a tiny, white-gowned ghost in the doorway. His heart had jolted, then his daughter's voice had called his name, breaking in just the way that it did now.

"Daddy, I miss her."

Then, like now, he opened his arms for his daughter. "Come here, baby."

She burrowed against him and Mick closed his eyes for a moment, wishing, as he had then, too, that he could absorb all her pain. Across the table, Kayla took Lee's hand in hers. "Shall we start?" she asked the boy, as Dean warbled about going away.

Mick's son nodded. "Goblin had beautiful yellow eyes and the fluffiest black fur."

"Remember when she first showed up?" Kayla prompted.

"She was thin and didn't have a lot of hair."

"That's right. And we went around and asked all the neighbors if she belonged to them and one called her, 'That ugly little thing.'"

"Her fur grew and turned shiny once we started feeding her," Jane put in.

"Maybe we fed her a little too much," Mick added. "But she'd yowl once her bowl of dry food was down by half. When we'd gone through that first bag of crunchy stuff the vet said we'd better put her on the low-calorie version."

"Probably because she was still supplementing with lizards," Kayla groused.

That surprised a laugh out of Lee. "La-La, you're such a big chicken. You sent me into the pantry with a broom to chase out the last one she trapped in there."

Kayla sniffed. "Because I was dealing with the twitching tail the reptile dropped to get away from her."

"You called Dad at work," Jane said, pointing at the nanny. "And said there was nothing in the nanny rule book about handling scaly stumps. You put a box over it and he had to throw it away once he got home after his shift was over."

"I was only making your father feel useful," Kayla said, straightfaced. "And Goblin enjoyed playing watch-cat on the box all afternoon."

There was a long moment of silence. "Goblin watch-catted me at night," Lee said. "I'd wake up and not feel scared or alone because she'd be on the pillow next to mine."

How often did his son need company in the dark? Mick wondered, regret swamping over him again. With his job, he wasn't always there to reassure his little boy.

Kayla gathered him close. "Yes, but you know you only have to call out and your dad will come, or if he's not home, you know I am. You're always safe, Lee."

"I know."

The grip on Mick's heart eased a little. "Always safe, buddy."

His son looked to his sister. "Now, Jane?"

She nodded. "Okay."

The boy detached himself from the nanny and headed to the house. He was back in a moment, balancing a paper plate in his hand. His movements solemn, he set it on the patio table. "Goblin's favorite treats," he said.

Mick's eyebrows rose. The cheese and salami were no surprise. But there was also a pile of taco-flavored corn chips, a tablespoon of ice cream and three pitless black olives.

The cat must have spent its days at the Hanson house suffering from serious indigestion.

"Thank you for your time with us," Lee said, looking into the darkness and taking Kayla's hand. "You were a nice cat."

"A pretty cat." Jane took her brother's hand and then Mick's.

"Who started scraggly," he added.

The candlelight flickered over Kayla's face. "But

who turned out to be as beautiful on the outside as she was on the inside."

Mick reached for her hand to complete the circle. It felt so small and fragile in his hold, hardly bigger than Jane's. That's how this moment felt to him, he thought—fragile, small, but important in a way he couldn't explain. Because their connection to the nanny felt so temporary now?

Jane sighed. "She needed a family."

"She needed us," Lee corrected.

"She did," Kayla agreed softly, her fingers tightening on Mick's.

He was going to lose it, he thought. He was going to lose it in front of his kids and all because it was hitting him from a thousand different directions that everything he held so dear was so transitory. The cat left their lives, the kids became independent, the nanny moved on to somewhere else.

Someone else.

He closed his eyes.

"What's the matter, Daddy?" Jane said.

"Moment of silence," he quickly put in. "Let's all close our eyes for a moment of silence."

He counted off the seconds in his head, giving himself a full sixty in which to get a grip. At forty-five, his daughter shrieked. He started, then stared.

Goblin. The damn cat was on the tabletop, lapping delicately at the melting ice cream.

Everyone else came alive, too. While they petted the missing feline, she continued eating, unperturbed. Then Jane hugged Kayla. Lee hugged him. Mick was left looking at the nanny.

And as if it was the most natural thing in the world, they went into each other's arms. "I'm glad you were here," he said, against her soft, fragrant hair. "I thought this was going to be a disaster."

"As usual," she murmured, "we muddled through."

"And found our way to triumph," he finished.

How much better, he realized, each of those could be with this woman in his arms.

The night of Goblin's reappearance strengthened the bonds between everyone in the Hanson household, Kayla thought, as she dusted the living room furniture early one morning before the kids left for school and before Mick returned home from his twenty-four-hour shift at the fire station. Jane and Lee were doting on the cat; Kayla and Mick were smiling at each other again. Not in the old way— there was still that simmering sexual tension beneath the surface—but she thought they were both more accustomed to the feeling now. Neither had broached the subject about what they should do about it. She figured they both accepted it wasn't going to up and evaporate.

For her part, when Joe Tully had called again, she'd made it clear there wouldn't be another date. However, she had agreed to a lunch with the Bright parents after finally speaking to Patty about the nanny position. While she'd been polite but also up-front about not being seriously interested in the offer, they'd insisted on taking her out for a meal to discuss it. She'd decided not to mention it to Mick, who hadn't brought up the idea of her leaving the family since her birthday.

Hope was blossoming again that she'd have everything she'd ever wanted. Even though she felt Mick struggling to keep his distance, that magnetlike tension between them made her believe he couldn't hold out for long.

Against her hip, her cell phone vibrated, and she dug it out of her jeans pocket. She glanced at the screen. The man himself.

"Good morning," she said.

"It's morning anyway," he answered, his voice weary. "Everything okay there?"

"Yeah." Was he aware that he always called home at the end of a particularly grueling shift? "Tough one for you?"

"Hearing your voice helps. Talk to me so I stay awake on the drive home. Do you need anything at the grocery store? I can stop on the way."

"We've got what we need, but thanks for asking. Well, unless you can find in one of the aisles the spelling worksheet Lee thinks he left in his desk at school yesterday."

"The one I suppose is due today but he's yet to finish."

"You're so smart," Kayla said, laughing. She ran the dust cloth over the surface of an end table.

"My son, on the other hand…"

"Has already figured out a work-around. He'll beg Ms. Witt to let him stay in at recess to finish up and he's counting on his charm and good looks to win her over."

Now it was Mick's turn to laugh. "Uh-oh. Should I claim he gets that confidence from dear old dad or not? Fact is, it sounds like you had a hand in that suggestion, La-La."

It was a childish nickname, *Lee's* nickname for her, but when Mick used it now, his low voice rasping in her ear, warmth flooded Kayla. Since she'd started the job, they'd talked on the phone often, but these days the calls held a new intimacy. If he'd been in the room he would see the flush on her face and perhaps sense the other physical effects he had on her. Even miles away with only his voice touching her, she felt her skin ripple with sensitivity and her nipples tighten.

"Cat got your tongue?" he murmured.

The warmth turned to heat and she shivered. The tongue in question was stuck to the roof of her mouth. "Mick…" she managed to get out.

"You said my name just like that the night in your bed," he said, his voice even raspier now. "When you begged me to take you over."

Oh. Her body softened for him and between her thighs a pulse started to throb. "Bad man," she protested.

"After a night like tonight, that's what I ache for, honey. To be your bad man."

"No fair," she whispered. "You're in a car by yourself, while I'm here at home—"

"Just steps away from that bed where we were naked together. Don't believe I haven't been thinking of it. I remember the exact scent of the skin along your collarbone. I know the taste of the slope of your breast. I can close my eyes and feel the way your body clasped my fingers when I slid them inside you."

"Don't close your eyes now," she said, her laugh shaky as hot waves of desire crashed over her. "I don't want you getting in an accident."

"Me neither. I want to be all in one piece once the

kids get off to school this morning and we're home alone together."

Lust nearly swamped her this time. "Mick," she groaned. Had the dam between them finally broken? He'd been so careful about keeping his distance and now he seemed ready for that closeness she needed.

"I don't know about you," he said, "But I can't deny myself any longer. I want to be in your arms again if you'll have me."

Giddy with pleasure, she reached out blindly, hoping to clutch the mantel to steady her now-shaky knees. Her fingers brushed one of the photos propped there and it fell, hitting the brick hearth with a loud crash. Kayla gasped, then stared down at the broken glass and mangled frame in dismay.

"What happened?" Mick asked, his voice sharp. "Are you all right?"

"I…I knocked over a photograph. It broke."

She could hear the relief in his voice. "That's okay, then. No harm done."

Kayla shook her head back and forth, her stomach queasy. "It's the picture of Ellen that was sitting on the mantel, Mick. I'm so sorry. I'm so very, very sorry."

He was quiet a moment. "Honey…"

"I would never do anything intentionally to…to…

damage it. Honest, Mick. I know you love her. I know how much you must miss her every single day."

He was silent again. "Kayla—"

"I can't believe I was so careless as to break it. The frame's probably irreparable and the glass is just slivers, but the photograph itself is fine." She knew she was babbling but she couldn't seem to stop. "I'll take it to the framer's and I'm sure they can take care of it in no time. No time at all…" Embarrassed, she forced herself to wind down.

"I'm sorry," she finally said again.

"Me, too," Mick said. "You realize you're over-reacting."

"No! Yes. Well…" She blew out a breath of air. "I feel really bad."

"Likewise." Mick blew out a matching audible breath. "I should have talked to you about Ellen before."

"She was your wife. You love her and you always will. I get all that." Kayla went to the utility closet to grab the hand broom and dustpan.

"I don't think you do, honey, and that's my fault."

Tucking the phone between her ear and shoulder, she cleaned up the mess and then carefully laid the photo on the coffee table. "You're not to blame for anything, Mick."

"Listen. This…thing between us has nothing to do with Ellen. She's been gone a very long time and maybe if I hadn't had the kids…but I did, thank God, and because of them I managed to drag myself through the dark times and into brighter days. The days are very bright now, Kayla."

She sank to the couch, her gaze on Ellen's smiling face. "That's good to hear, Mick."

"So you're probably wondering why I…" He released another breath. "It's not grief or fear of loss keeping me from another woman…from you. From your bed."

Her hands twined in her lap. "So what is it? After that night you didn't seem ready to, uh, repeat the event. Until this morning. Until now."

"Oh," he groaned. "If you only knew how ready I've been to repeat the event. Again and again and again. A guy can only hold off for so long."

"Then why…"

"Baby, I don't want to hurt you." She heard the worry in his voice. "And I don't know if I think…"

"You're thinking too hard, then," she said, concerned that he was ready to renege. Mick was slipping into protector mode and she didn't want him to be her hero, but her lover.

What came after that? Was there a future for them? She wanted that, but unless he allowed himself to get close to her again they both wouldn't know if it could really work. "You let me worry about myself. I've been on my own for a long time and I'm pretty good at it."

"Kayla—"

"The nights have been lonely for me, too, Mick. Come home. Come home and let's be company for each other."

"Oh, baby." There was a new lightness to his voice. "You're sure?"

"So sure, Mick. So sure."

He clicked off, saying he needed all his concentration now and she put her phone back in her pocket, her smile as wide as piano keys. Yes! Then she hopped up, wondering if she had time to do a once-over in her room and bathroom before he arrived and the kids left for school. Her gaze caught on the photo and she paused.

Thank you, Ellen, for sharing them with me. I won't let any of them down.

Especially when it was so close, she thought, to the four of them merging into something new and stronger than before. "I'm loving them for you," she whispered.

Footsteps on the staircase had her turning around. Her mouth gaped. Jane wore a micro-mini skirt in black. The hot-pink tights beneath it were the only thing keeping her from indecent exposure. But the top she wore with it—vaguely corset style that laced up the middle—looked like something worn by a desperate woman on a street corner.

The black of the ugly platform shoes on her feet was matched by the liner that ringed her eyes. Blue eyeshadow and hot-pink sticky lip gloss completed the ensemble.

"Is this a, uh, costume?" Kayla asked, vaguely gesturing at the girl's clothes.

"No." Jane didn't do an eye roll, but it seemed like a close thing. "I borrowed some things from Maribeth."

"Ah." Maribeth had been shaving her legs since fourth grade and wearing makeup since fifth. Mick and Kayla had agreed that sleepovers at Maribeth's weren't a good idea for Jane, although they'd welcomed the other girl to their house more than once. Her bag was always packed with celebrity magazines and lots of hair products.

When Jane reached the bottom of the stairs, Kayla saw that she was wearing every bracelet she owned on her right wrist. On her left she'd twisted a white bandana printed with tiny black hearts.

"Cute scarf," she said, nodding at it. She decided the multi-bracelets look wasn't a problem either, not in the grand scheme of things. "But you're going to have to wear a different top—how about that white long-sleeved T-shirt of yours—and Jane, you know you can't wear makeup to school."

The girl stiffened, her expression shocked. "What?"

Kayla wondered if she'd really expected to get away with breaking the house rules. Recalling the angst of preteenhood, she softened her voice. "Janie—"

"Jane."

"Jane. You know that I can't let you wear makeup."

"All the girls are wearing it today." The girl's voice was hostile. "We made a pact."

"I'm sorry, but—"

"You're not sorry! You're just being mean."

Kayla gazed on her young charge, remembering that just last night they were snuggled on the couch talking to each other in the funny voice they consigned to Goblin.

Humans, you are beneath me.

You are so lucky I decided to stay and rule your world.

The one with a queen complex right now was Jane. "Sweetheart—"

"I'm not listening to you." The girl brushed past.

Kayla grabbed for her arm. "Jane, you must go

upstairs and change your shirt and clean off that makeup."

At her touch, Jane yanked away. "I won't. I won't ever listen to you!"

"Come on—"

"You can't tell me what to do!" the girl shouted. "You're not my mother!"

The words pierced Kayla's chest. "Jane—"

"You'll never be my mother!"

"Jane."

"Go away," the girl said, bursting into tears. "Go away and stay there!" Then she stomped past Kayla and ran back up the stairs.

She stared after the preteen, until a new noise caught her attention. Before she turned she knew who stood there, she knew who'd witnessed the entire ugly debacle.

You're not my mother. You'll never be my mother! Jane had said. *Go away and stay there!*

And the girl's father, the head of the three-person unit that she longed to make into a foursome, the man she wanted to be beside forever, hadn't said a word.

Chapter Ten

Mick acknowledged he'd screwed up big-time as he returned home after driving the kids to school. When he'd walked in on his daughter's mini explosion, he'd not taken charge as he should have. Fatigue from the previous night, surprise at her astonishing outfit and a certain fuzziness brought on by a recent phone call that had fogged his windows were the culprits, he decided.

And now that blame for his inaction had been assigned, a solution must be identified.

He must contrive some way to make it up to the nanny.

The house was quiet when he let himself back

inside. Not one noise gave away where he'd find Kayla. Stymied, Mick stood in the living room, and his gaze caught on the photo of his wife on the coffee table.

He moved closer to it, staring into her dark eyes. He saw Lee in the shape of her face and Jane in the deep bow of her upper lip. *I'm putting them first,* he assured Ellen. *And I won't let the teen years get the best of me.*

The mistake he'd made this morning was in being unprepared for the outburst. It felt like another load of bricks on his shoulders, but he realized he'd have to be prepared to handle Jane's growing pains on a moment's notice if he was going to keep the rest of the household happy at the same time. He couldn't let his daughter hurt Kayla's feelings again.

He was pretty sure *he'd* hurt Kayla's feelings. There had to be a way to handle that, too.

Without caffeine, though, his brain started to spin. So he made his way to the kitchen, where he found the nanny sitting at the kitchen table, studying the newspaper. In her usual jeans and blouse, Kayla appeared relaxed. Yet her mood was impossible to gauge as she looked up. "No mishaps on the drop-off?" she asked.

"None." He beelined for the coffeemaker and the

empty mug sitting there. "Let me apologize for my daughter."

Her mouth twisted. "You don't need to do that."

"I do. She's my responsibility and she was way out of line this morning."

"She washed off the makeup."

"Yeah." He sighed. And she'd changed her clothes. The only thing of Maribeth's she'd kept on was the clunky-heeled shoes. All the jewelry had stayed as well, but bracelets were no big deal in his book.

The coffee went down hot and strong. He felt marginally better as the caffeine hit the bottom of his belly. "I think she's channeling Goblin."

Kayla, to his surprise, burst out laughing. "I had the same thought."

His mood easing, he pulled out the chair beside hers. "I'm thinking all those princess flicks we took her to as a little kid were not a good idea."

"I'm not sure a moratorium on movies would stop the inevitable, Mick."

"Change," he muttered under his breath. "Yeah, I get that. And I get that I have to deal with it. I'll go completely gray by forty, but I'll manage."

Kayla's hand covered his on the table. "You don't have to do it alone, Mick."

He looked over at her. "It's my job."

"Mine, too," she said lightly. "And—"

"It's *not* yours," Mick protested. "I'm not shirking my duty, I swear."

"I didn't mean—"

"Plenty of single parents manage not to raise juvenile delinquents."

"I..." Kayla's hand slipped off his to wrap around her mug.

"Hey, don't look so glum," he said. "I'm not going to mess this up. I made myself a promise years ago that I'd be a lean, mean parenting machine and I'll be damned if I break my word to myself or let down my kids."

Kayla shoved back her chair and headed for the coffeemaker. She hesitated with her back turned to him, then she slowly spun around. "Mick, you're a great father. Single...or otherwise."

He shrugged off the compliment, aware the crucial years lay yet ahead. "We'll never know about the otherwise, huh?"

She went very still. "I...guess not."

Some note in her voice made him look at her more sharply. He still couldn't fathom her expression, but the sun started streaming through the kitchen window and it caught her hair, setting it to a golden blaze. The sight set fire to his blood, and his mind went back to that phone conversation they'd had before Jane's fateful tromp down the stairs.

The nights have been lonely for me, too, Mick. Come home. Come home and let's be company for each other.

He'd assumed the mood was spoiled, but he was thinking of her again, naked, that sunny hair wrapped in his fists, her sleek skin warming beneath his mouth. She was standing in that spot, he realized, that enchanted spot on the hardwood floor that she'd occupied the moment of their first kiss.

The noise of his chair legs scraping backward was loud, but not as loud as the sound of his heartbeat in his ears. His weariness drifted away as he walked toward her. She stood her ground, her blue eyes as wide as the sky in the window beyond her.

Should he say something—what?—because surely she read what he desired on his face. He wanted her and how she could make him laugh and smile and need like a man—and not just a father—lightened all of his burdens.

She didn't move as he approached. When he cupped her face in the palms of his hands, her lashes brushed her cheeks and her body swayed toward him. "On my way home from school, I promised myself I'd make up for my daughter's rudeness," he said.

Her soft laugh washed over him like more sunlight. "Is that what you call this, Mick?"

"No. I was planning on making you breakfast."

Her lashes lifted and his heart stuttered as their laserlike color hit him. "So it's scrambled eggs or sex?"

The teasing note in her voice lightened things even more. "Whatever you want," he said, then bent over to take her mouth, his tongue slipping inside to paint the slick surface just inside her lips, before surging forward to slide along hers.

Her body flowed against his. Smiling to himself, he put an inch of air between their mouths. "Bacon or more *besos?*" They'd learned that *beso* meant *kiss* in Spanish when they'd traveled with the kids to Baja, California, one year.

Her fingers clutched the cotton of his T-shirt. "I'm not sure you're playing fair."

"I'm just as happy to play dirty," he whispered. "Listen to this deal—orgasms now, omelets later. What do you say?"

She winced. "The alliteration is well…atrocious."

He laughed, feeling the last of his tension drain away. The sad things he'd seen on his shift, the worry he'd walked into when he'd caught Jane arguing with the nanny; they both evaporated as he caught Kayla closer against him. "But what do you say, honey?"

"I say…" She looped her arms around his neck.

"I say, take me to bed, Mick, and we'll concern ourselves with later…well, later."

It wasn't only fatigue and problems that dissipated in Kayla's room, though. Mick felt the years drop away, too. He was young again, the sensation of a woman next to him almost brand-new. His chest tightened as he unbuttoned her top and he saw her breasts swell over the cups of her bra. His thumb found the already-hard tips, and that was like a miracle, too.

"You're beautiful," he said. "You want me."

"Well, duh," she said, laughing at him, as she attacked the snap of his jeans.

They fought each other for supremacy then, each determined to get the other naked. He ended up picking her up and tossing her onto the mattress, then following her down to get the job done. But she shifted, straddling his hips so that their jeans were pressed together and her sweet breasts bounced into his range of vision.

He skated his palms up her sleek back and jackknifed forward to catch a nipple in his mouth. Sucking strongly, he felt her response through two layers of denim. She wriggled against him, her damp heat against his rigid erection. When he switched to lick the other nipple, she moaned and he yanked at her button and zipper, loosening her pants enough so he could run his hands beneath them and her panties. His hands cupped luscious curves as he pressed his hips upward, giving her the friction she needed.

"Mick." Her reedy voice had him moving again, switching spots with her so she was on the bottom and he loomed over her slender figure. With a sweep and tug, he had her naked. "Oh, God," she whispered as he bent low to take her mouth and his knee pressed into the juncture of her thighs.

"I want to make you feel good," he said, then slid his mouth along her cheek to her ear. "I want you to come in my hand and in my mouth and then I want to come inside you."

She shuddered. "We need to get your clothes off, then."

"My intentions are good, but my will is weak," he said. "I think I'll keep my pants on until we've completed step one and step two of my plan."

She protested, and even tried tugging at his hair, but firefighters could be single-minded when they had to be. While he loved her touch anywhere on him, he ignored it as he scooted down on the mattress. He ran his tongue around one areola, playing with the silky and wet folds between her legs.

She was swollen there, open for him already, and he took her with two fingers, then drew them out to paint them over the rigid nub at the top of her sex.

Kayla made sounds, sweet, sweet sounds, and he used them as his guidebook to her pleasure.

Indirect pressure and fast rhythm there, strong suction and the edges of his teeth here. Thank God he'd kept his pants on, but even then he was pressing hard against her lean flank, his own pleasure tightening, tightening.

She broke with a cry and he clamped down harder on his needs. *For Kayla, for Kayla, for Kayla,* he chanted in his head, and when her tremors calmed, he slid lower, pushing up and outward on her knees.

"Oh, my God," she said, her fingers clutching weakly at his hair. "I can't."

"Just try," he whispered, then blew air against that pink, glistening skin. She twitched, and then again as he breathed onto her pretty flesh a second time. When his tongue touched down her hand fell to the bed.

She tasted creamy-salty-sweet and he took her flavor into his mouth over and over and over, his tongue flat, his tongue flickering, his tongue telling her how lovely she was for sharing this with him in a soft rhythm and in a hard-driving pulse.

"Mick…" Her voice was breathless. "I can't…"

He knew how to coax. Kids on bicycles. Dogs from drainpipes. Frightened people from twisted metal. "Sure you can," he said. "I'm right here. I'll catch you. C'mon, Kayla."

And then she did come. And he held her quaking hips in his big hands and felt higher than he did when he'd climbed his first extension ladder as a rookie so many years before.

Her sated expression did nothing to diminish his desire. As he shucked the rest of his clothes, her half-drowsy eyes watched him like a cat content in the sun. But when he kissed her again, she went from drowsy kitten to wide-awake feline, rubbing against his naked skin, kissing his chest, his belly, his—

"Whoa, whoa, whoa," he said, lifting her away from there.

She pouted. "You're supposed to be making me feel good. That was making me feel good."

"And me too good," he murmured, flipping her yet again, then donned the condom he'd put on the bedside table. When she opened to him, her arms, her legs, he didn't hesitate again.

His body surged into hers.

He felt powerful. Wide-awake. And so damn young. Energy coursed through his veins and he was nothing like the overburdened father who feared the future any longer. He was a man on the brink of a new day—one he was looking forward to living.

Kayla's hips moved up, into his, and then she was

drawing his head down, taking him into a kiss that sizzled like a shooting star—and shot him right out of orbit.

They dozed. After the night he'd had, he was surprised he even roused when she moved.

"Where're you going?" he said, his voice slurred.

"I have a lunch date," she replied, but he heard it from far away. He didn't like the idea of her leaving, but sleep beckoned. Kayla wasn't really leaving him, he thought, as the tide took him back out. He'd fulfilled his plan and made her feel so good that surely she wouldn't ever go away.

"I'm so glad you could join us today. We've always enjoyed your company *so* much," Patty told Kayla with enthusiasm after they were seated at the café table. Then she cast a sidelong, guilty glance at her husband, Eric. "Okay, okay. I know I promised not to lay it on too thick."

Eric Bright, a lean man with short blond hair and wire-rimmed glasses, shook his head at his wife, though the corners of his mouth twitched. "Really, Kayla, thanks for coming. How's Mick?"

She thought of him now, as she'd been trying not to since she'd left the house. He'd been on his belly, his face buried in the pillow, the breadth of his shoulders and the long shallow valley of his spine exposed by the sheet bunched at his hips. A tingle rekindled inside her remembering everything that had led to his drowsy state. A flush rose up the back of her neck, so she took a swallow of her ice water to cool herself.

"Tired today," she managed to say. "I gather that last night they had to go out on more than one tough call."

Eric nodded. "And Lee and Jane?"

"Lee's good." Then she shrugged. "Jane's fine, too, but sixth grade…"

"Oh, don't I know." Patty rolled her eyes. "I was dreading fifteen, but eleven going on twelve has hit our family pretty hard. Danielle wanted to wear eyeliner to school today."

"Jane, too." It helped to hear that her charge wasn't the only girl with wild ideas this morning. "She wasn't too happy with me when I told her to change her clothes and wash her face."

"Wasn't too happy" was an understatement, of course. She'd been furious, and Kayla got upset just thinking about it. They'd butted heads from time to time, but the girl usually saved her moments of rebellion for her father—and now she had more sympathy than ever for what Mick's future might hold.

"I figure I'll get the cold shoulder until Dani needs

something at the mall or wants to have her friends over," Patty said.

Her husband groaned. "I must have been in the shower and missed this altercation entirely—for which I am eternally grateful."

Patty reached over to pat his cheek. "You'll pay when it's time to talk to our son about safe sex."

"He's only eight years old!" Eric protested.

"And when the time comes, you'll be repeating yourself until he's eighty-eight or married and out of the house, whichever comes first."

The waitress arrived to take their orders, then went away when they made clear they hadn't cracked their menus yet. The many-paged binder affair could take a whole hour to peruse, Kayla thought. She wondered if she'd make it back before Mick left her bed, and she didn't…

Don't think about that! she told herself. Nor did she want to think about that vague undercurrent of disquiet that had been running at the back of her mind since Mick had returned from taking the kids to school.

With a smile, she glanced up at the couple. "What are you two planning to have?"

Patty flipped a couple of laminated pages. "Eric, you're going to go for the eggplant parmigiana sandwich, right? Or maybe you feel like the patty melt?"

His eyes bugged out behind his glasses. "They have patty melts? You are the goddess of menu minders," he told his wife with sincere appreciation. "I didn't even see a patty melt or an eggplant parmigiana sandwich and I've been staring at this thing as long as you have."

Patty looked a little smug as she shot a glance at Kayla. "I always find exactly what he wants."

"It's a division-of-labor thing," Eric told Kayla. "She's on the lookout for my perfect lunch, I make sure she keeps her cell phone charged."

"Seems fair," she said. But it seemed more than that, it seemed sweet, and she enjoyed the thought of the couple looking out for each other in even those small ways.

"You and Mick probably have unspoken agreements like that, too," Eric said. "You make the coffee every morning, he regularly checks the oil in your car."

"It's not exactly the same," his wife pointed out. "Kayla's not Mick's wife, but his kids' nanny."

"Meaning Patty will check your oil *and* make the coffee every morning if you agree to go with us to Europe."

"Hey!" his wife frowned. "I thought you forbade me to arm twist. Kayla already said she was ninety-nine percent sure she was staying with the Hansons."

Ninety-nine percent? Kayla thought. Was it really wise of her to dismiss the offer so quickly? After that unpleasant scene with Jane that morning and then Mick's unsettling comments before they'd made love, she just wasn't so sure anymore.

Their orders were taken; their meals arrived. Kayla asked questions about their planned stay in Europe and listened intently, but studied the pair's interaction with equal care. They moved in a rhythm that she liked, that she recognized. She and Mick were similar in some ways, easily moving about the kitchen or packing the car for a trip, aware of each other's moves and depending upon each other's expertise.

Mick was a whiz at getting everything in the trunk. Kayla was the one to make sure everyone had a sweatshirt in case the day turned cold.

But Patty and Eric had more. Where she and Mick avoided physical contact, the other couple were easy with each other in that way, too. She brushed a crumb off his shirt. He fed her a seasoned French fry that came with his patty melt. What would it be like to have that with someone?

When Eric turned to the dessert menu, she excused herself for the ladies' room. She was surprised that

Patty didn't go with her—it was customary, in her experience, to make the trip with the other female in the party—but then she figured that the couple would take the few minutes to discuss her.

They'd outlined the duties of the nanny they were looking for. The possibilities for solo and family travel had been presented. A salary even mentioned. She imagined Patty turning to Eric now and asking, "Is there a chance that she'll leave Mick and Jane and Lee?"

Was there a chance? Kayla pondered the question for herself as she headed back toward the table. Before she'd come up with a solid answer, her cell phone buzzed in her purse. She pulled it free and looked at the screen. Her mother.

"Mom?" she asked. Her mother's calls were rare and even rarer was it to hear from her midday. She was a busy executive's assistant from eight-to-five who then went home to a bustling house filled with her husband and three active high schoolers. "Is something wrong?"

Karen Collins sounded relieved. "You took my call."

"Ye-es?" Kayla frowned. "And you're surprised because…?"

"I forgot your birthday." She hesitated. "Tell me your father didn't forget, too."

"I had a nice celebration luncheon with my girl-friends," Kayla said, skipping over the direct answer. "And then Mick and the kids surprised me with cake and balloons and really great presents."

Her mother groaned. "Oh, honey. I'm so sorry. Can you forgive me? Mitzi had a debate tournament that weekend and Doug Junior was doing something or other for Scouts. Not to mention that Annie had that 4-H—"

"I get the busy family thing, Mom, no problem," she said, ignoring a pang of sadness.

"It's a problem! Yes, I realize your friends stepped in and that your employer acknowledged your day, but you should have had something more. Your mom and your dad at least wishing you the best. And— dare I say it—a date."

"I had a date."

"You did?" Her mother sounded so eager.

Kayla swallowed her groan, wishing she hadn't mentioned it. "It was no big deal, but yes, I had a date."

"Tell me about him!"

She could see the table and Patty and Eric now. Her feet slowed. The couple were laughing together over something, their hands entwined. It was beautiful how they were so relaxed together, yet still so obviously attracted. They were a solid, comfortable unit that still gave off love sparks.

It was what she wanted. It was what she couldn't have with Mick.

"Kayla?" her mom prodded. "About your date?"

"It was nothing," she said slowly.

Or, to be more precise, it wasn't going to come to anything. For whatever reason, Mick had implied more than once that he didn't want a woman in his life on a permanent, intimate basis. She'd been trying to ignore that fact. Wishing it away.

But after her episode with Jane—*you'll never be my mother!*—and then his declaration this morning—*plenty of single parents manage not to raise juvenile delinquents*—she had to face the fact that Mick saw himself as a solo lean, mean parenting machine. In that case, he and the kids would never be hers in that real way she wanted.

She didn't think anything less was good enough for herself now, though. That was what had been running through her head since she'd left Mick in her bed. She'd told him during the early phone call not to worry about her—that she could take care of herself—and it was time to do just that.

She had to see the truth that Mick didn't want to commit, and after a lifetime of being forgotten or overlooked by family, she needed commitment. She wanted family.

And if she had to tear herself away from one to find her own…so be it.

With new determination in her step, she returned to join Patty and Eric.

Chapter Eleven

Kayla had been tossing and turning in her bed for a couple of hours when she heard her bedroom door pop open. Even horizontal, her stomach dipped. Mick?

She rolled her head on the pillow to see a slight figure outlined in the doorway. "Jane?" She lifted to an elbow. "What's wrong? Don't you feel well?"

The girl hesitated, then she ran toward the bed. "I want to make things right."

Relief washed through Kayla, making her almost giddy. "Me, too," she said, leaning to flip on the bed-side light. For two days, the members of the Hanson household had been tiptoeing around each other with exaggerated politeness. "Come here."

In her soft yellow pajamas, Jane climbed into the bed as Kayla scooted over so the girl could have the spot she'd warmed on the mattress. With the child tucked under the covers, Kayla dared to brush her dark hair from her forehead. "Is something going on at school?" she asked.

"I have that book project due next week," Jane said. "I don't know where to start."

Jane was notorious for putting off tasks she dreaded. Lee would tackle the assignment he most disliked—spelling—first, but his sister procrastinated until the deadline breathed down the back of her neck.

"Remember our strategy for that?"

"Break the project into smaller pieces," Jane said. "Focus on the first and not worry about the next until that one's finished."

"Right. So when you're ready tomorrow, we can sit down together and separate the whole into manageable chunks."

"I did finish reading the book," the girl said, brightening. Then her face fell. "Because Dad wouldn't let me watch television after dinner. He said maybe I was learning my rudeness from my favorite shows."

"I'm sure you can earn back the privilege," Kayla said.

"That's why I'm here."

Kayla's brows rose. "To get back your viewing quotient of *iCarly*?"

Both Jane's lashes and her voice lowered. "Not really. I don't like that I hurt your feelings."

Kayla blinked away the sting at the corners of her eyes. "Something tells me that I might have hurt yours, too."

Jane wiggled a little in place. "If only you would let me wear makeup. Just a little…"

She stopped as Kayla was already shaking her head. "It's your dad's rule," she reminded the girl.

"You could ignore it. Or you could tell him it was wrong."

"No, because I happen to agree with him. But the fact is, Jane, that even if I didn't agree you were too young for lip gloss and mascara, I'm the nanny and he's the father. Which means he gets to make the rules and I'm paid to help you follow them."

Something flashed in the girl's eyes. "He pays you to take care of us."

"True." Was that what was bothering her? "I do get a check for taking care of you." She tapped Jane's nose with a gentle fingertip. "But the caring *for* you and Lee comes from me, free of charge."

Tears welled in Jane's eyes. Kayla froze, then scooted closer to gather the girl close. "What is it?" This didn't feel like making things right. This felt like things going in the wrong direction. "Why are you crying?"

One fat drop spilled down Jane's cheek. "How could you care for us and plan to leave us at the same time?" she accused.

Kayla's face stiffened into a mask. She hadn't known how and when to broach the subject of the Brights' proposal and so had become as dedicated a procrastinator as Jane. How had the word got out? "What exactly are you talking about?"

"The other night…the night before I tried to go to school in Maribeth's clothes, Danielle said she overheard her parents. That they think you'll go to Europe with them and be their nanny."

"Oh. Well." That explained Jane's outburst, she thought, remembering the girl's impassioned *Go away and stay there!* that had occurred even before her lunch meeting with Patty and Eric Bright. "I hadn't talked to Danielle's parents about that."

"So it's not true?"

Kayla hesitated. She couldn't flat-out lie. "I hadn't talked to them about that yet," she amended. "Since then, they did speak to me about the possibility."

"So are you? Are you leaving us?"

Kayla sighed. "Oh, Jane." Where did this sit on the right-wrong spectrum? She hugged the child tighter to her, running her hand over her hair as she'd done a thousand times before. Her chest ached, brimming with maternal feelings that weren't hers to have.

The children weren't hers.

Their father wasn't hers.

"Don't you love us?" Jane asked, her voice sounding closer to five than eleven.

"Of course I love you," Kayla said. "How could I not love you?" But was assuring the child of that so wise?

Because it all felt so wrong now. She shouldn't have stayed for six years. Six years of wiping tears and spills, of packing lunches and suitcases, of wrapping owies and Christmas gifts…those six years had cemented the family into her heart.

But nothing cemented her to them in return.

"You'll go to college in seven years, Janie," she said, rubbing her cheek against the child's hair. "Lee in ten. How old will I be then?"

Jane sniffed. "Thirty-four when I go. Thirty-seven for Lee. Old!"

"Yeah. Old. Maybe too old for some of the things I want for myself." A husband. Children who belonged to her.

"I want you to stay with us forever," Janie declared, squeezing her tight.

"But *you* won't stay forever," Kayla pointed out. "College, remember? And then you'll have a job and an apartment and maybe a husband and your own kids after that."

Sighing, Jane tucked her head tighter to Kayla. "Sometimes I don't ever want to grow up."

"I know," she said, closing her eyes. "I know the feeling." But she'd been playing house for six years and it was past time for her to grow up, too.

The girl grew heavy against her. "Let's get you back to your bed," she whispered, then half led, half carried the child up to her room, her heart heavier than Jane's slender form.

As if she was still small, Kayla arranged a stuffed menagerie around the girl's drowsy body. Then she leaned down and kissed her on the brow. "Don't let the bed bugs bite."

Jane's hand crept out to clasp Kayla's wrist. "Do you have to go?"

She didn't mean right now. She meant away from them. Her free hand covered Jane's fingers as she searched inside herself for how to put things right. For what *was* right.

She thought of Ellen Hanson and the promise that she'd made to her just a few days before. She'd promised not to let her children down, and wasn't part of that being a role model for Ellen's offspring? A woman who hung on to hopes and didn't seek what she needed in life—love and family of her own—wasn't a good example for either Lee or Jane. To make things right—for all of them—it seemed clearer and clearer that she'd have to move on.

"I think I do, Jane," she whispered when she saw that the girl had fallen asleep. "I think I have to leave all of you."

She turned to the door, jumping when she saw a large shadow looming there. Her hand reached for her thudding heart. "Mick," she whispered. "What?"

He beckoned, and her nerves still jangling, she obeyed. In the hall, he reached around her to shut Jane's door, then, still silent, he pressed her against the wall and bent to take her mouth.

The kiss demanded her cooperation. She clutched at his naked shoulders—he was wearing only pajama bottoms—and opened her mouth to the thrust of his tongue. Her skin had cooled on her trek through the house in her oversized nightshirt, but now it was hot, burning, set on fire by Mick's mood.

It would be so easy to go under, so easy to surrender to skin and kisses and good sex, but none of that changed the fundamental conflict between them. She pushed him away.

"I want more," she said, her chest heaving.

"I'll give you all you want."

But she noticed he didn't move. She noticed his hands were at his side, his fingers curled into fists. Mick understood what she'd meant.

Running his hands through his hair, he turned away. "Do you really have to go?" he asked, in an echo of his daughter.

If she wanted to make things right, she really did.

Mick was in a foul mood the morning after his hallway encounter with Kayla. She was going to leave them, head off with Poaching Patty and her family to Europe to find adventure and everything he and the kids didn't have to offer her here.

She'd be visiting the Eiffel Tower while the only tower around the Hanson household was the tower of dirty towels that needed to be washed each week. Her day would be filled with exotic foods and handsome men instead of PB and J and an eight-year-old with a newfound ability to fart with his armpit.

Then there was Mick himself. A guy willing to share her bed, but who knew he didn't have the energy or the ability to make her happy as well as keep up with the rest of his life as fire captain and father.

No wonder she was leaving them.

But he was going to be gracious about it, he decided as he stopped at the elementary school close to the lunch period. Today the PTA was sponsoring a midday safety fair. He was on tap to provide a mouth-to-mouth resuscitation demonstration. Kayla would be there helping out. No doubt that traitor, Patty Bright, would be on hand, too.

Yet he wasn't going to let the impending change in his circumstances affect how he went about his day. No sour grapes or surly attitude on display.

"What are you looking at?" he barked at a little kid as he walked through the school gates with the life-size demonstration dummy.

The child's eyes rounded and he clutched his lunchbox to his chest. "What'd you do to the person?"

Mick realized he was carrying the mannequin with both his hands around its neck. He eased his strangling grip and softened his voice. "It's not a real person. We practice on it to save lives. Come see me after you eat your lunch and I'll show you."

The kid made a face. "My lunch is tuna fish. It tastes gross."

"You can breathe tuna fumes into Donald Dummy's face. That'll be fun."

The boy's interest kindled. "How about if I eat my carrots and cookies instead?"

A familiar voice piped up beside Mick. "Christopher Carter, I think you better eat everything in your box. Then you'll have enough energy for math after lunch."

Mick glanced over at Kayla. Her hair was pulled back in a golden ponytail and she wore jeans, a fuzzy white sweater and low-heeled suede boots. He wanted to take her home and snuggle with her on the couch.

He'd settle for taking her home and chaining her to the couch.

Instead, he cocked his head toward the little boy. "Pal of yours?"

Her gaze was on the youngster whom she waved to as he took off in the direction of the lunch benches. "I run a math recovery group that meets once a week. That guy's always claiming he's too tired to remember his times tables."

His eyebrows rose. "I didn't know about this."

"It's new. Once I got my degree in early elementary ed, I approached the principal about putting it to use. It's a mixed bag of kids who could use some extra help. I meet with them the last forty minutes before school ends on Wednesdays."

Just another thing she'd be leaving behind when she went on her search for adventure. "Where do I set up?" he asked, his voice abrupt.

She didn't comment on his brusque tone of voice. Maybe he was a better actor than he thought. Maybe he could really be gracious about all this.

He had a table in the auditorium. Beside him, the nutritionist for the school district set up a food pyramid. On his other side, the school nurse positioned little bottles of hand sanitizer to give away. The plan was for the event to be more casual than formal. The kids would be allowed to roam around the space and stop and ask about what interested them.

Not that he was trying to unfairly attract his share of the crowd, but he'd also brought turnout gear, including boots and a helmet, for the kids to try on if they wanted. Not to mention his other ace in the hole. He went back to sprucing that up when he heard a little voice behind him.

"It's Mrs. Thompson!"

Christopher Carter, with or without fish breath, had arrived on scene. He was staring at the dummy laid out on the table. "You made the dummy look like our principal."

A little firefighter's trick he'd picked up along the way. Nothing tickled kids more than to see a lifeless mannequin wearing a wig that resembled the hairstyle of their head administrator, along with a school T-shirt, a flowered skirt and the woman's ubiquitous

walkie-talkie in a fake rubber hand. He grinned at the
boy. "You want to learn how to save her life?"

"I don't know. She says no tag on the blacktop."

"No tag? That does sound a little harsh. Maybe
she'll have a change of heart if you give her mouth-
to-mouth."

The kid stared. "Eew. Gross."

Mick sighed. There was always this hurdle to overcome. "Maybe I should have dressed up the mannequin like somebody else."

Christopher Carter's smile turned sly. "Maybe.
Maybe like her." His gaze shifted to the auditorium
entrance, where Kayla was shepherding in a group
of little ones. Kindergarteners, he guessed, because
they had that special wide-eyed look and a couple of
them were holding hands unselfconsciously.

Mick cast a look at Oak Knoll Elementary's little
Lothario. "So you like Ms. James?"

The kid's expression said *duh*. "Don't you?"

His gaze went back to the blonde. "Yeah. Yeah, I
do."

She was leading a group of the teeny ones around,
pointing out the different displays. Hunkering down,
she helped a little girl unbutton her sweater and then
tied it around the kid's small waist. Mick had seen
her do things like that for kids—his kids—dozens
of times. But this time it made him catch his breath.

She wasn't just the nanny, or the hot sexy thing in black boots whom he'd taken to bed.

She was so much more: a gentle touch, a teasing laugh, a patient teacher, a kind friend. A woman who was walking out of his life.

He had to look away as she walked toward him now. "Captain Hanson," she said, a gaggle of kindergartners around her. "This is some of Room 2."

A five-year-old pointed toward the rubber figure. "Is it dead?"

"No." He didn't bother to explain it was dressed as the principal. Apparently his little joke was beyond the ken of kindergarten. "This is not real. It's a dummy—"

"Bad word," a gossamer-haired cherub said, frowning at him. "We don't call anybody a dummy. It's a Room 2 rule."

Mick's gaze met Kayla's. She shrugged, her amused gaze clearly letting him know he was on his own. Like he'd be, forever, after she left.

He glanced back at the little girl. "I'm sorry. It's a…like a doll. And we practice on it to save lives."

"So it is dead," the first kindergartener reiterated.

"I…" He gave up. "In a way, I guess you're right." Shaking his head a little, he moved over to the table and launched into his supersimple spiel about exchanging the breath of life. Whether the contingent from Room 2 got anything out of it, he didn't know. Not after he wound down and looked up, straight into Kayla's eyes.

Under his hand he felt the rubbery exterior of the dummy. It was just how he'd felt after Ellen's death. Lifeless. Emotionless. Stiff. But then time had passed and he'd heard his children laughing again and seen the sunshine in the hair of the pretty woman smiling at him over coffee every morning. Somewhere after grief and before Kayla going away he'd…

He'd fallen in love with her.

He'd fallen in love with her!

She gathered her charges around her now, a puzzled expression on her face, and herded them away while he just stood there, still as stupid as that dummy, because it had taken him so long to realize the truth.

How long had he been living with her and loving her? When had *wow* crept into the room with them? Not just the *wow* of sexual attraction, but the *wow* of…wow, she's it.

She's The One.

"Oh, that's just plain unfair," a new voice said.

Mick jerked out of his reverie to see freckled Patty Bright, her gaze on the turnout gear he'd brought. "What?"

"And an instant camera to take pictures of the kids wearing this stuff, too, ensuring yours will be the most popular station. I had no idea you were such a cheater, Mick."

He frowned at her. "It takes one to know one," he muttered.

Her gaze sharpened. "Excuse me?"

"Nothing." He recalled his promise to be gracious. But God, that was even more difficult now, knowing that Patty had lured away the woman he loved. Knowing he couldn't do anything about it because he had only those dirty towels, his testing daughter and his boy with the armpit farts to stack up against the call to adventure that came from the Brights. And because, bottom line, he still didn't believe that despite these feelings he had for Kayla, that he had the emotional vigor to take on the burden of her happiness on top of Jane and Lee's.

Not only must he put his children first, he couldn't, wouldn't, put Kayla last.

"Mick?" Patty came forward, concern on her face. "What's wrong?"

"Not a thing. You won." It was more growling than gracious, but hey.

"Won what?"

"The nanny, of course. My nanny." *My Kayla.*

"Mick," Patty said. "You're wrong. She turned our offer down."

He blinked. "She turned you down?" But last night she'd made it clear she was leaving. "Whose nanny is she going to be, then?"

"I don't know." Patty shrugged. "She said she thought it was time she made a change, but she didn't want to get so entwined again with someone else's family."

"What's she going to do, then?" he wondered aloud.

Patty shook her head. "I got the sense that she was considering leaving childcare altogether."

A thought that didn't put Mick in any better of a mood. If she wasn't seeking adventure in Europe, then why was she leaving them? Why couldn't she stay? Last night she'd told him she wanted "more" and he'd thought she'd meant the excitement of travel. The glamour of new possibilities on a new continent. But if it wasn't that…?

Screw gracious, he thought. Screw pretending he was in a better mood. He was going to get to the bottom of this.

Chapter Twelve

But Mick couldn't get the answers he wanted when he wanted them. He didn't catch sight of Kayla after his conversation with Patty at the safety fair. Then he had a meeting to get to and then he had to return to school for the kids. Once home, he remembered the nanny had her girls' night out scheduled with her crew from We ♥ Our Nanny. She'd already left for her friend Betsy's.

So he went through the father motions. Homework. A little basketball in the driveway with Lee. He started dinner and even went to work on creating a clean tower of towels by folding what he found in the dryer. Through it all he felt as if he carried a thousand-pound weight on his chest.

I might as well be a hundred and four. I feel that worn-out.

"Daddy, what's the matter?" his daughter asked him after dinner. They were in the family room. He was seated on the couch, but the kids were standing, eyeing him instead of the TV. Oh, yeah, he'd forbidden Jane to watch her shows for a few days.

He sighed. "You can turn it on, kids," he said, gesturing toward the screen. "Surely Zack and Cody or Phineas and Ferb are going about their zany business."

Neither child moved. Then Lee glanced at his sister. "Are you having a bad day, Dad?"

Mick tried to smile. "Yeah, buddy. I guess you could say so. But don't worry about it."

"I do worry about it." Lee launched himself forward, and snuggled in right next to Mick's side. "Tell me what to do. I can help."

Mick smiled again, this one more natural. He heard the echo of himself in his son's words. "Thanks, Lee. But I'm good."

"You're not good, Daddy." Jane found her place on the free cushion next to him. "Lee's right. We can do something for you."

He wrapped an arm around each of them, pulling them closer. "Just sit here with me a few minutes."

Closing his eyes, he let his head drop back and took in the warmth of his children pressing against him. As he blew out a long breath, he felt some of his tension ease. They were good, his kids. Holding them helped.

The ache in his heart was still sharp. It killed him to think he'd fallen in love with the nanny only to watch her walk away from him, but he'd survive. The kids would lighten the weight of it.

The kids would lighten the weight of it.

His eyes popped open. He looked down at his beautiful children and the way they'd rallied to him. The way they were cuddled up to him right now, adding their strength to his.

Oh. My. God. The kids would lighten the weight of everything. Meaning, Mick realized, that they weren't a burden on his emotional foundation, but a buttress to it. This was the magic he hadn't understood. It went way beyond Disneyland. Together, they were a team. And "together" meant he wasn't alone in ensuring the family's health and happiness. He should have known that. Seen that sooner.

He cleared his throat, new optimism filling his chest. He'd been a short-sighted dummy, but he'd been given the breath of life just in time. God, he hoped it wasn't too late. "Kids…about Kayla."

Jane looked up at him, her dark eyes solemn. "She thinks she has to leave us."

Lee shot upright. "What?"

Mick squeezed his son's shoulder. "I've got an idea about that." A hope about that. It gave him new energy and he pushed to his feet, a grin breaking over his face. "I think you two are going to approve." Forget a hundred and four. He was a young man with a plan to get his woman.

Although the night was cold, Kayla felt completely comfortable under a patio heater and beneath a soft old quilt on the tiny space behind her friend Betsy's little cottage. It was detached from her employer's house and adjacent to the neighbor's spacious back-yard. Kayla took a sip from her wineglass and noticed a male figure pass through the sliding glass doors at the rear of the big place next door.

"Is that him?" she whispered to Betsy.

The other woman nodded. "The crabby one. The smell of charred flesh is the giveaway."

"Ew," Gwen said. "Do you have to speak of grilled beef in that manner? There's nothing wrong with a man who likes to barbecue."

"There's something wrong with this one. I am definitely not fixing him up with anyone I know. He's taken to calling me Boopsie."

Gwen and Kayla glanced at each other. "The twins call you Boopsie."

"Exactly. So I don't know why you guys want to keep talking about him. Sure, he's handsome and everything. Not to mention that hard body of his. But he's disagreeable—hello? Crabby!—and I need a third four-year-old in my life like I need a hole in the head."

Kayla decided against pointing out no one said anything about Mr. Crabby getting *into* Betsy's life. Who was she to comment on someone else's business? She was in disentangle mode.

Gwen swiveled to gaze at Kayla again. "Your life hasn't been going smoothly either, I hear?"

"Huh?" Kayla frowned. "I don't know what you're talking about."

"Patty Bright came to me about her family's posting to Europe. She said she tried to persuade you to be their nanny."

Betsy gasped. "You're going to Europe? You're going to leave Mick and the kids?"

She didn't want to say that out loud. "No, I'm not going to Europe, Bets. That didn't seem to be the right step for me."

Gwen lifted an eyebrow at their hostess. "How about you, Betsy? Not that I encourage my nannies to play hopscotch with their positions, but it *is* a wonderful opportunity. Several months overseas, plenty of off-time for solo travel…"

Betsy looked down at her wine, then her glance stole across the fence to the house next door. "I'm not much of a solo girl. And my boys need their Boopsie."

"All three of them?" Gwen murmured, for Kayla's ears only.

Kayla hid her own sad smile. If she left town, she might miss the previously unscheduled but clearly upcoming adventures of Boopsie and Mr. Crabby. It wasn't a happy thought, but she'd come to realize that by filling her life with other people's families and other people's relationships that she was missing out on building her own.

It was just that Mick and the kids felt so much like her own!

"I'm leaving them," she said abruptly. "I'd appreciate it, Gwen, if you'd come up with some ideas for a new nanny for Jane and Lee."

Betsy stared at her with round eyes. Gwen took the news more calmly. "Is anything wrong? Is there something I should know about?"

"Nothing's wrong. Oh, I'm having a little trouble with Jane and lip gloss, but nothing unexpected. At heart she's such a warm and generous girl, and Lee is the same. The hardest thing about caring for him is keeping him in socks that don't have holes."

She felt her eyes begin to sting, so she focused her

gaze into the distance. "You'll find someone perfect for them, won't you?"

"What about Mick?" Gwen asked. "Is he difficult to work for?"

"The opposite." She waved a hand. "Easygoing. Pitches in wherever he's needed. Not demanding."

"But he's a problem for you," Gwen said.

Kayla shook her head. "No. No."

"All right," Gwen agreed, in her calm voice. "So then we should be looking for a new position for you. You don't want the Brights. You want to leave Mick and the kids."

She never wanted to leave Mick and the kids.

"I can't be a nanny again," she said, setting down her wine. "I'm no good at it."

Betsy scooted forward on her chair. "Don't say that, Kayla. You know you're fabulous at what you do. Best nanny ever!"

"No." Kayla was shaking her head again. "Worst nanny ever."

Gwen cleared her throat. "Kayla—"

"I broke the cardinal rules," she confessed, closing her eyes. "Betsy, you called it out weeks ago."

"Kayla—"

"I think of the kids as my own. And I've fallen in love with their daddy." She covered her face with her hands. "It's a disaster."

"Umm..."

"A disaster, I tell you," Kayla said.

Then, big, warm hands pulled hers away. She opened her eyes and there Mick was, his dark hair, his rangy build, the brown eyes that she'd seen grief-stricken, amused, hot with desire. Now there was tenderness in them and...?

She didn't know. Tugging against his hold, she tried to get away. "I made a mistake—"

"Nope. That would be me," Mick said, yanking her to her feet. "Now say goodbye to your friends."

He already had her halfway across Betsy's tiny patio. Wreathed in big smiles, they were both shooing her along. "He's a much better choice than Mr. Crabby," Betsy called out.

A disgruntled voice floated from the yard next door. "I heard that, Boopsie."

Once in the car, a mosquito whine started in Kayla's ears. It only got louder when Mick slid behind the steering wheel. "What—"

"Hold the questions until we get home," he said, shooting her a little smile. "Please?"

"But—"

"I made a promise to the kids that I'd get you back as fast as I can. If we start into this now...I don't know when we'll make it."

"Still—"

"I left them alone, Kayla. I know we're only five minutes away, but who knows what might happen. Jane could hide Lee's Pokémon game and he could say she smells like onions—"

"Pickle burps."

"Huh?"

"It's pickle burps." And then she shut her mouth and tried to tamp down her curiosity, her embarrassment and even that little sprout of hope that was struggling to surface inside her. Mick had witnessed her confession—*I'm in love with their daddy*—and he hadn't gone running for the hills, but that didn't mean...

She couldn't let herself believe it meant anything at all.

Then they were pulling into the driveway and then they were walking into the house. She heard the patter of footsteps on the floor and Mick's hand was at the small of her back leading her into the dining room. It was just like the day before her birthday: balloons, a cake, confetti strewn across the table.

"Surprise!" Jane and Lee yelled together.

She took in their excited faces. "Something's going on," she said. "Did I fall asleep and wake up a whole year later just in time for another birthday party?"

Lee bounced on his toes. "It's not your birthday, La-La. Dad realized it's your anniversary."

"*Our* anniversary," Jane corrected, grinning. "It's the anniversary of the date you first came to be our nanny."

She shifted her gaze to Mick. He shrugged. "What a coincidence."

What a crock, but she couldn't squelch the kids' excitement and there was something thrumming in the air when she looked at their father. Something newer than the sexual tension that she'd experienced before, but that was there still, too.

He gestured to the stairs with his thumb and nodded at Jane and Lee. "Scram."

They giggled and ran, then both ran back to Mick. Their hugs brought a new sting of tears to Kayla's eyes. He rubbed his big palm over both their heads. "My good luck charms," he said, then pushed them on their way.

Over her shoulder, Jane met Kayla's gaze. "Welcome home," she said.

Okay, the hope was really starting to flower now, but Mick was just staring at her, saying nothing. God, she didn't want to presume and then have this all wrong. Her eyes went back to the cake on the table. It read "Happy Birthday" in loopy letters of red frosting.

Putting her hands in her pockets, she pretended to

inspect it carefully. "They didn't have one that said Happy Anniversary?"

"To be honest, I didn't ask. This one seemed more appropriate." He came up behind her. She could feel his body's warmth just an inch from her back, but she forced herself to stand straight instead of leaning into him.

As if he read her mind, his big hands closed over her shoulders and pulled her into the cradle of his body. His head lowered. "I want this to be a birthday of sorts, Kayla. I want this to be the birthday of the real family I want to make with you."

Had he really said that? Or was it just her overactive imagination? But she could feel his heart thudding between her shoulder blades. He smelled of that scent she'd bought him for Christmas. The bright colors of the cake and balloons in front of her were impossible to overlook.

Okay, this must be real.

"Mick." Her voice sounded husky. Too full of emotion. She cleared her throat because she had to be certain about what he was asking of her. "You wouldn't say that…do this…because the kids, you, me, we have a routine that works—"

"No." His fingers tightened on her. "I respect you too much for that."

"Respect?" She closed her eyes. That sounded like

what she promised herself she wouldn't do—settle. "Respect isn't enough, Mick."

He spun her around. "Honey. What I'm trying to say is that I'm not asking you to be a chauffeur for the kids or a cook for the family or even the laundry lady. I want a lover. A wife. For me."

Yes. *Yes.* She flung herself against him and threw her arms around his neck. Their mouths found each other and the kiss was hot and possessive and certain.

Still, she pulled away, just far enough for air. "Are you absolutely certain? Because—"

"I love you, Kayla," he said, his forehead pressed against hers. "Don't you feel the *wow* in the room? You're The One. My One."

Kayla felt that silly telltale sting of tears again and she squeezed her eyes tight. He pressed his mouth to her cheek, her chin, her temple. "Am I too late?" he whispered.

She shook her head, and he drew her against him once more, enfolding her in his arms. "I worried I might be too late," he said.

"What took you so long?" she asked, her voice watery.

"I was all upside down in my thinking," he admitted. "I thought that if we were together, that it would make me responsible for your happiness—"

"*I'm* responsible for me, I told you that."

"Yeah, well, we first-responder types are notorious for believing the world won't turn unless we have control of the wheel." Then he loosened his hold so he could see her face. "But you've got a blind spot nearly as big as mine, honey, because we're better when we're willing to lean on each other when necessary. We're better together."

Together. She loved the sound of that. But…

"I started remembering all that we've shared over the years—from worrying about the kids' colds to panicking over the missing cat. It finally got through my thick head that our love would be a partnership, not a responsibility. That we—all of us—make each other stronger." He gave her a gentle shake. "So you're not on your own either, sweetheart."

"Together," she said, nodding.

"Right. We'll work together to make each other happy and our lives good. The kids are part of that, too." He smiled. "So…please, go ahead and give up being the nanny."

She swallowed. "And?"

"Take on the job as my wife and Jane and Lee's mother?"

Before her mouth could open, a train of sound came roaring down the stairs. Clattering footsteps, hoots and hollers, then the exuberant presence of two grinning children. Mick looked at them with a rueful smile. "Didn't I ask you guys to stay away until I gave the signal?"

Jane ignored her father's admonition. "Can I go with you to shop for rings?"

Kayla looked at the two children who so long ago had been taken into her heart. But did that go both ways? "You guys understand? You're on board with this?"

Eyes shining, Jane nodded.

Lee jumped up and down. "Hurry up and say yes, Kayla," he urged. "Me wants cake."

Her gaze met Mick's. "On his wedding day," they said together.

Then she drew Lee's dad down to kiss his mouth. "On *our* wedding day."

His eyes closed, his arms tightened. "Is that a yes?"

"It's a yes," she said, kissing him again, out of the corner of her eye, noting the curious cat was sitting on a chair, batting at a balloon. Then she pulled both kids into their circle of family. "And a yes," she added, kissing the top of Jane's head. She squeezed Lee as he wiggled closer. "And a yes."

Her tribe. Yes, indeed.

* * * * *

Discover more romance at

www.millsandboon.co.uk

- ❤ WIN great prizes in our exclusive competitions
- ❤ BUY new titles before they hit the shops
- ❤ BROWSE new books and REVIEW your favourites
- ❤ SAVE on new books with the Mills & Boon® Bookclub™
- ❤ DISCOVER new authors

PLUS, to chat about your favourite reads, get the latest news and find special offers:

- ⬛ Find us on facebook.com/millsandboon
- ➤ Follow us on twitter.com/millsandboonuk
- ❤ Sign up to our newsletter at millsandboon.co.uk

EB_SD

The World of Mills & Boon®

There's a Mills & Boon® series that's perfect for you. We publish ten series and, with new titles every month, you never have to wait long for your favourite to come along.

By Request

Relive the romance with the best of the best
12 stories every month

***Cherish*™**

Experience the ultimate rush of falling in love
12 new stories every month

***Desire*™**

Passionate and dramatic love stories
6 new stories every month

n o c t u r n e™

An exhilarating underworld of dark desires
Up to 3 new stories every month

M&B/WORLD4a